THE DEMON'S DISCOVERY

Octobre 23. 1811

Madame France

260

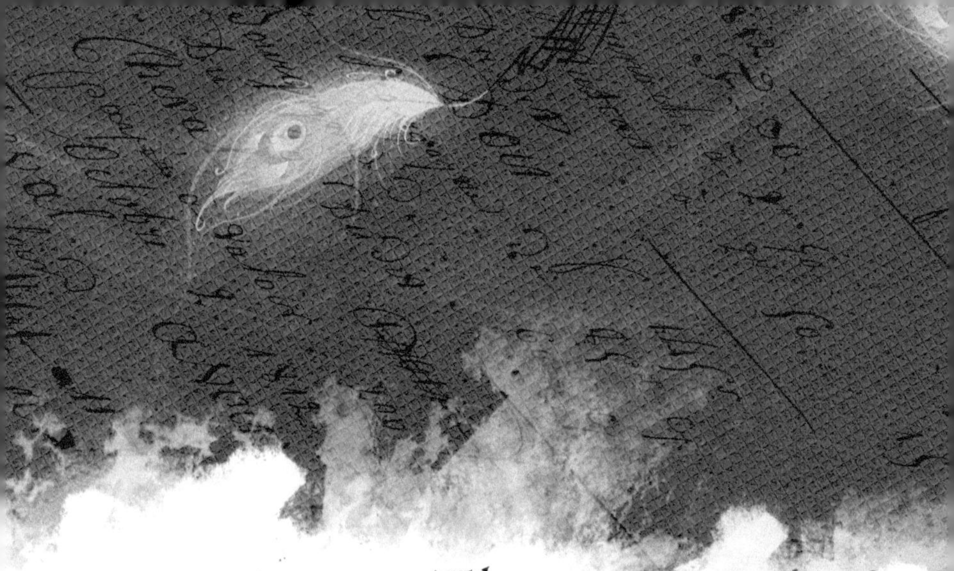

THE DEMON'S DISCOVERY

THE DEMON PRINCES
BOOK TWO

L. ALEXANDER

The Demon's Discovery
The Demon Princes Book Two

ISBN: 978-1-958933-05-3 (Ebook)
ISBN: 978-1-958933-08-4 (Paperback)
ISBN: 978-1-958933-09-1 (Paperback —Alternate Cover)

Cover Design: Jessica, Enchanting Covers
Interior Design: Stephanie Anderson, Alt 19 Creative
Edited by: Krista Dapkey

Alucard and his fellow white-haired, pointy-fanged brethren walked so Astarion could run.

I could not be more thankful for them all.

She looked

MY DEMONS

in the eye and smiled.

She fell for the very thing

I thought

SHE'D FEAR.
— VaZaki Nada

AUTHOR'S NOTE

This is not a dark romance, but there are some potentially triggering themes that come up throughout the book. You can find a list of tropes and content warnings below as well as on my website.

Please reach out to me directly for specifics if needed, I'm more than happy to give details, page numbers—whatever helps you best decide if your wellbeing and this story are compatible.

Tropes: fated mates, who hurt you, revenge, gargoyles, demons and fae, alchemy, pseudo-medieval European setting, praise, affection through caregiving, 'my wife', mist daddy, white-haired love interest

Content: explicit violence and brief gore, explicit sexual content (including 'eyes on me', 'use your words', 'I know', mild blood play, feeding while f*ing, etc.), mention of previous physical abuse, reference to Christian-based mythos for angels /demons

PROLOGUE
VASSAGO

October

"THE PIECE IS dreadfully important to my ... *our* family, you see," the duke explained, face solemn, as he reached for his goblet of wine after passing me a sketch of a necklace with an oval gem. The design, particularly the scrollwork around the setting, reminded me of my new sister-in-law's own heirloom. "Sadly, it's been missing for years. It would mean the world to have it safely back in our possession."

I didn't regret coming to Revalia, as it had reunited me with my brother and presented a new wealth of opportunities, but I was beginning to question my own judgment in accepting a proposition, sight unseen, from a duke who had ethics that were, at best, questionable. The lost relic they'd dangled as payment proved entirely too tempting, however, so now I had to see things through.

I pushed my wine out of reach as I looked around the den. Twice already, I'd automatically taken a sip only to be sorely disappointed by the bitter offering in my cup. Hanging on the wall were portraits of the duke, his wife, and a young child with yellow hair. There were several conspicuously empty spaces as well, as though decoration of the room had never quite been completed. Or perhaps the record of someone else had been removed.

"Well, I'll certainly give it my best effort. I've heard of similar-looking pieces in the area, so hopefully yours can be located."

"Yes, we've heard the same." Henrik nodded, a hopeful gleam in his beady black eyes.

The duke was clearly new to his money and title, all too proud to showcase his gems and finery without cause or decorum. One ring, perhaps the one with a square ruby and tiny diamond at one corner, would have sufficed. Instead, he wore different rings on six fingers and both thumbs, all obviously just for show.

I fought the urge to roll my eyes at his wife for similarly stacking her necklaces while I held a conversation with them both. "You previously mentioned two daughters, unless I'm mistaken?" They both stiffened and shared a glance that told me I'd asked a question which made everyone uncomfortable. "Forgive my nosiness, but I only see one in the portraits."

"We only have one daughter. The other girl is just an employee. A former ward," Lara was quick to say, tossing an accusatory glance at Henrik, as though this was a long-standing point of contention. "Henrik coddled her a bit too much when she was younger, but we've long since had that issue straightened out." Henrik patted her hand, mouth pinched tight.

"I see." My curiosity where this ward was concerned increased at least five thousand percent. The smug look on Lara's face told me she was beyond pleased with having won this disagreement between them. "Will I be meeting your daughters in the near future?" I reveled in the way Lara's eye twitched at my wording.

"They'll be at our country estate until summer," Henrik explained. "We've only returned ourselves to address several issues with the house and make preparations for our season here.

Hopefully, that can all be taken care of quickly. And we're so glad to meet with you, while we're in Revalia, of course!" Henrik gestured widely as if to flatter me with such attention. These people were suspiciously nervous and prone to wild mood swings. I couldn't help but wonder if there was something more potent than wine in their cups. "I'll be back frequently, in the interim."

"Mm. I'll need to interview all staff, as well," I said, pleased by the way Lara blinked in surprise.

"Oh? What for?" Henrik asked, nervously clearing his throat and shifting in his seat. "I assure you, none of them will know anything about the necklace. It's been missing ... well, I'm not sure exactly, but they would never have had any contact with it."

The more he fidgeted, the more positive I became that there was something to be investigated. "I've found it best to meet all members of a household—staff included—when any kind of item is being sought out. You'd be surprised the information I've gotten from seemingly unrelated conversations, the things I've found in unusual places. Many times, those responsible had no idea someone was looking for the item at all, nor that it held any value. Sentimental or otherwise." The couple shifted in their seats, humming thoughtful noises at my assertion. I lifted my eyes from where they'd drifted to the sketch to find Henrik staring at me. I stared back. "And my payment?"

His smile faltered, and he looked away. "You'll have access any time you come to this estate." He rose and walked over to a massive ornate desk. Henrik pressed a specific series of pressure points on the top and front with his back to us, allowing a hidden compartment to open. He drew out a heavy tome, and my heart began to race as he carried the book I'd sought for decades back to the table.

I forced my fingers to remain on the wood in front of me as he set it down between us. I took in the volume, noting that the green leather binding was in serious need of repair. Several pages were clearly no longer attached to the spine, spilling out at awkward angles along the edges. It seemed the ancient, hand-tooled metal latches were responsible for keeping everything together. I itched to lavish the priceless book with the attention it sorely deserved.

For the moment, I had to settle for being happy that the book, which I'd had and lost again for more years than I cared to admit, was quite literally within my reach. Which meant a potential cure for the curse the thief who'd stolen the book from me last had placed on me, was, as well.

"As I was saying, you're welcome to view it any time, but it's not to leave this room until you've delivered the necklace. After that, it's yours to do with as you please."

I cracked a grin, amused by the notion this man thought he had any kind of power over me. As if I couldn't simply take my book and leave if I so chose. But I would play along for now. At least until I grew bored of this assignment and their tiresome personalities.

It wouldn't take long.

He pushed the book toward me, inclining his head in invitation. "Please. I'd hate to see you leave today without at least looking at your prize."

I gently tapped the cover with my fingertip, debating the wisest course of action. "How generous," I soothed him, carefully unclasping the locks and inhaling the unique scent of old paper and ink as I opened the cover. A blast of images flashed into my mind—an incoherent assortment of memories trapped within the pages. I might never know which previous owners had left such a lasting impression, but I was grateful to them all.

"Several of my colleagues and I have looked through it, but it's written in at least one language none of us can decipher. Though perhaps you have a translator for such a thing?"

"Mm," I replied noncommittally.

The ancient script was perfectly legible to my eyes, and he had no idea the true value of the item he kept locked in his hidden drawer, though I appreciated his discretion and attempt at safety measures. I'd have to let Lilith know her grimoire had finally resurfaced; she'd no doubt be pleased to have an update on its whereabouts. I was thrilled to have it somewhere I could affirm its safety, in any case.

"It's quite a fascinating collection, I'm sure," I said, closing the cover. If I got started sifting through it, I was doomed to stay far longer than intended, and I didn't want to let on how much it was truly worth to me. How Henrik had managed to get his hands on it was another mystery entirely.

With regret, I pushed it back toward him and stood, straightening my vest. There would be plenty of time to explore the invaluable information scribed on the heavy parchment in a language that kept it hidden away from human eyes all too soon.

As he took it back to the desk, I noted how he touched the piece of furniture and where.

"I look forward to our next meeting, Mr. Feland," Henrik said as he escorted me toward the double doors of the den. "We appreciate you taking on this search."

I didn't want to give any kind of reply I'd later regret, so I simply tipped my head and walked down the long main hall toward the front door, plotting my next visit with the book I hoped held a way to cure me.

CHAPTER 1
GRETA

June

LIGHTNING FLASHED BRUTALLY through the gray sky, striking a tree close enough I could smell the heated ozone. Spatters of rain woke me from a brief nap, the peals of rolling thunder and fierce lightning that chased after them made my heart race.

I'd come out to the hedge maze to enjoy the last hour of the evening sun after helping with the dinner preparations. Yet another prospective job had fallen through thanks to a series of truly unfortunate events involving me breaking several wineglasses during my trial meeting, so clearing my head had been much needed. Unfortunately, I'd only gotten halfway through before exhaustion had forced me to sit ... and that had ended in an unexpected nap.

Something dark flashed along the edge of my vision, and I spun to find the cause. It wasn't unheard of for creatures of one nature or another to find their way into the hedge, but what I'd seen was too tall to be anything other than human.

"Hello?"

The only response was more thunder and the wind blowing through the tangled branches of the hedge in an eerie howl that was so much like laughter it made my skin crawl. Another bright flash of lightning lit up the sky, illuminating the whole center of the hedge maze. Deciding perhaps my imagination was running a little wild because of my badly timed nap, I tried to stand and fell instead, one leg still tingly from how I'd been lying.

My rear end hit the grass, and I managed to scrape my shoulder along the rough edge of the concrete bench as I went. I watched in awe as the wide trunk split in half, branches crashing to the ground as fire consumed the tree from the inside out. Bark hissed and popped while black-and-orange embers drifted down to the ground. As the rain became heavy, fat drops, I was shocked out of staring and scrambled to get to my feet, to clean up the failed experiment I'd left in progress on my worktable.

Thunder clapped loud enough to leave my ears ringing, and I jumped, the instinct to duck unavoidable. My hand bumped a vial of ammonium, sending a splash of it careening into another dish. Tiny splatters of acid hit my skin, making me hiss as they stung and burned. The combination also caused a plume of acrid smoke, which no amount of waving could disperse before it absorbed into my clothing and clung to my skin.

"Wonderful," I grumbled, using one of the old cast-off kitchen towels to wipe at my stinging hand before I mopped up the rest of the mess. I dipped the smoldering linen in the fountain just in case, then left it to hang off one of the stones.

All of my chemistry equipment went into a small strongbox which I then shoved under the worn table. It wasn't much, but it was functional, and nobody bothered my things out here. Inclement weather aside, it was a serviceable arrangement. Nothing like the old shed I'd taken over at the country house, but I made do.

My worktable was tucked into a far corner at the center of a hedge maze. Situated in the middle were several benches around a wide fountain that featured water cascading over several boulders and a statue of an angel, his broad sword raised to the sky and feathered wings fanned out wide as he climbed to the top. I loved lying on the bench in front of him, staring up into his ethereal face. I pretended he was protecting me, serving up justice on my behalf, and I talked to him as I worked through my experiments and tests. He alone knew all my darkest secrets, most paralyzing fears, and greatest hopes. I napped at his feet often, which is what I'd been doing when the rain arrived.

The maze was mine, perhaps the only thing in the Belettes' Revalia house that truly belonged to me. If I could, I'd stay out here all the time, much like I did in my shed. Besides, my employers were entertaining someone, and I had to keep myself out of the way and unseen.

I yawned and started to make my way out of the maze, hopeful the rain and the dense scent of night jasmine that crept along the walls would disguise the sour smoke still lingering on my clothes.

Once out of the hedges, I crossed through the open yard and past several vegetable patches to the back door of the kitchen. I pulled open the servant's door, getting a vague acknowledgement from the cooks who were banking down the oven fires and preparing to do the clean up as I slipped my shoes off and left them on the rug.

"Do you need any help?" I asked, absently rubbing at an ache in my left shoulder as I went to the sink. Soap and cool water removed the rest of the chemicals from my hands, soothing the burn.

"No, you've done enough for today, Greta. Go on and get changed." Caroline saw what I was doing and craned her neck. "Did you burn yourself? Again?" She tutted, pulling a tin out of the cabinet. "Let me see."

"Changed?" I asked as she smeared a heavy ointment over my hand.

She looked up at me, eyebrows drawn together. "You've gotten yourself good again, haven't you? Yes, changed." She put the tin back and scrubbed her hands on her apron. "Did Beatrice not tell you?"

"It's not that bad." My heart thumped behind my ribs. "No, I haven't seen Bea since this morning."

Caroline heaved a frustrated sigh, marching me toward the kitchen door. "She was to tell you Henrik requested your presence in his den. You're going to be late if you don't hurry, and you're half drowned."

"Henrik? What about?"

"I have no idea but take this." She shoved a chunk of bread stuffed with meat and cheese into the pocket of my skirt. "You'll need to eat. Saints know they won't have planned for your dinner."

The head cook shooed me with a flip of her dish towel. Caroline had been in this kitchen as long as I could remember and always offered me kindness. She was one of the best teachers I'd ever had, though I was still a dismal cook and only half-decent baker.

"Thank you."

Anxiety made me sweat as I walked quickly down the hall outside the warm kitchen. I had my head down, eyes on the worn planks of the wooden floor as I worked at the knot in my shoulder. I was so consumed with worry about what my employer wanted to discuss that I wasn't paying attention.

As the hall ended into the foyer, I accidentally caught the shoulder of a man as he stepped onto the rug ahead of me. I'd turned the corner sharply, expecting the path to the stairs to be empty. As we collided, his wineglass tipped, splashing me down the front.

"Oh! Pardon me," I apologized, the heat of a blush warming my cheeks.

"The fault is mine," he said graciously.

I blinked trying to clear my vision. The man was fuzzy around the edges almost, and several steps back from me, but I hadn't seen him take a single one.

"Honestly, you've done me a favor, that wine is atrocious. I was looking for a houseplant or something to dump it into, but I'm afraid you're wearing it instead." His hand appeared in my vision, holding a pristine white handkerchief. "Are you alright?" Warm fingers curled under my chin and lifted my face. I inhaled through my nose, panic surging through my veins. My skin tingled at his gentle touch.

"Fine, thank you." I met his golden eyes and tried to breathe through the blurred sensation I got in my head as he lowered the satiny fabric to my cheek and swiped away drops of wine.

"Here, I'll just …" His hand was extended as though he were going to attempt to wipe the stain from my shirt, but he stilled, pulling it back before touching me as the wetness mostly covered my chest. The cloth dangled there, the offer for me to take it open. "Perhaps you should instead?"

Face hot, I accepted it, blotting lightly at the damp fabric, but it was already too late. My shirt was cheap beige linen, and he had been drinking one of the dark-red wines Lara favored.

"Thanks anyway," I said, handing it back. "Sorry for staining your kerchief." I half-turned to go, but he was undeterred.

He waved a hand. "Keep it, with my compliments."

I twisted the square between my fingers, unsure how to proceed, as emotions furiously bounced around under my skin. Despite my many years of practice, I couldn't tear my eyes from his face and put them back to the floor where they belonged. He was looking right at me. My breath stalled in my throat, but it wasn't out of fear.

This man was *beautiful*.

Taller than me by several inches, he held himself with the poise and confidence of a noble. He had nearly white hair that flowed loose down to his mid back and a playful smirk on his lush mouth. His light-gold eyes traveled one end of me to the other in assessment. I flushed hotly all over.

"Are you alright? I'm afraid I may have ruined your shirt, but I'm much more concerned about your arm by the way you were holding it."

"Oh, no, really, I'm fine. My shoulder … that's not … Are you hurt?"

He chuckled at my question, but his eyes widened as he saw I was serious. "No, my lady. I'm quite well." His head tilted to the side, and he took all of me in once again. His hand rose to his chest, fingertips pressing into one of the gaps between buttons in his vest, the space over his heart. The intensity of his stare brought every last one of my nerves to attention. If I blushed any harder, I might burst into flames. "I'm sorry, have we met?" he asked quietly, voice tripping along my spine like a dark echo.

It might have been a come-on, but he truly didn't seem the type to proposition random women in empty hallways. I pressed my fingernails into my palm to quell the unusual sensation tingling under my skin. "Doubtful, my lord." Impossible, actually, but that felt overly dramatic to say out loud. My heart skipped a beat with the reality that I was in full view of and talking to a guest. The urgency to escape crushed down on me more by the second.

"Shall we remedy that?" He dipped into a formal bow, complete with hand flourish. "Vassago Feland, at your service."

"I'm Greta," I replied, looking around for a quick exit from this situation. "Pleased to meet you, Mr. Feland."

"The honor is most assuredly mine. Please, call me Vassago. I'm sorry again about my clumsiness." In one smooth gesture, he slid his fingers around mine and brought my knuckles to his mouth. My skin tingled everywhere his brushed mine, particularly his lips. My heart thudded so hard behind my ribs I worried I might pass out.

"Oh. I'm sure that was my fault," I repeated, thoughts harder and harder to organize the longer he touched me. "I—"

He frowned, turning my hand over. The shiny patches of pink skin caught the light in a particularly unflattering way. "Are you injured?"

I resisted the urge to tug my fingers back and forced a weak smile. "I work in the kitchen sometimes. Burns are unavoidable."

Those golden eyes raised from my hand to my face and my cheeks warmed. How I was certain he could see the lie was a mystery, but the way he scanned me told me he didn't believe my excuse.

He traced a days-old burn from the edge of an iron pan running across three of my knuckles. "This one perhaps came from cooking, but these"—he traced the small round marks from the acid—"are in quite an unusual pattern for a kitchen burn. And they're starting to blister." He tsked with his tongue, concern on his face. "How are you treating it?"

I swallowed, my throat impossibly dry. I'd informed him I was staff, and that was his response? At his lingering stare, I realized he was not going to let either my hand or his question go until he got a satisfactory answer.

"An ointment. It will be fine, I'm sure. I always heal, with time."

"Mm." He made a thoughtful noise as he released my fingers, and I clasped my hands together at my front so I wouldn't bury them in my pockets or tuck them behind my back. "Chemical burns can be quite nasty. That handkerchief is silk. When you apply the ointment again, wrap that over the top, it may help some. Don't worry yourself if it stains."

"Oh. Thank you." I twisted the cloth again, threading it through my first and second fingers.

"I trust you're being careful with your lovely eyes?"

I blinked at him, the polite scolding somehow endearing instead of insulting. It was nice to have someone concerned about me for a change.

"As much as I can be." Which was clearly not enough.

"That's good." His head tilted to the side again, thoughts scanning behind his entrancing golden gaze as he watched me.

I glanced around the hall, my concern not only for being seen with a guest but also for being late to meet with Henrik, as my tardiness increased with every passing moment. I was breaking nearly several of the rules set down for me in this house, but I was not about to offend this man. He lavished me with unhurried attention and his full dedicated interest. I honestly was completely unprepared to respond appropriately. Knowing what to do in theory and actually doing so in real life were very different things.

I felt incredibly rude for trying to escape when he was just being kind, but he also wasn't picking up on the urgency I felt to get away. I started to wonder if I was going to have to make a break for it in the middle of a sentence.

His head tilted almost imperceptibly to the side, and he smiled. "It's a pleasure to meet you, Greta. I'm sorry again for my clumsiness."

My heart skipped painfully as the tall wooden doors of Henrik's den began to open. "Yes, me too. If you'll excuse me, please?"

"Certainly. Apologies for detaining you." He accepted my hasty response while taking the blame yet again, eyes following mine.

I flew up the stairs, my bare feet scuffing along the rough red-and-beige-patterned rug Lara had insisted on installing the previous summer. I missed the feel of the smooth wooden steps under my toes. I went up two more flights to a hall of rooms that hadn't been disturbed aside from my dated, under-furnished suite in years. Lara never went beyond her own wing and the main floor unless she absolutely had to. It was mostly peaceful, though at times it was also lonely.

Stopping outside the door to my bedroom to catch my breath, my hand tightened on the knob as another revelation washed over me. I figured out why the beautiful man had seemed so familiar.

He looked like the angel in the fountain at the center of the maze.

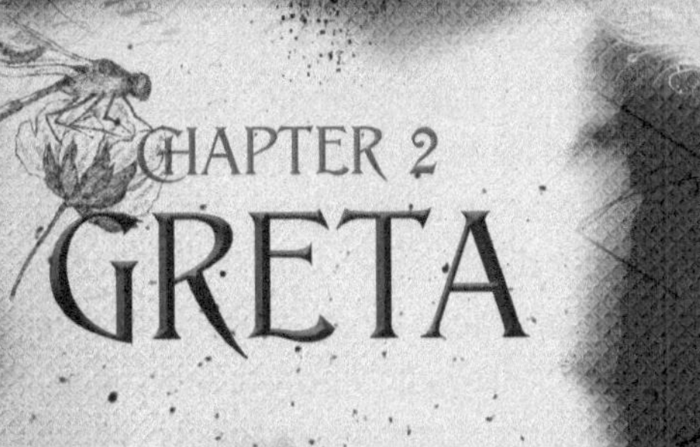

CHAPTER 2
GRETA

B Y THE TIME I'd pulled on a clean rough-linen dress and run back downstairs, a conversation was in full swing inside the den. By the sound of things, my employers had already drunk more than their fair share as they loudly discussed their daughter's many virtues.

I made my way toward the circle of furniture near the fireplace, hastily combing through my curls with my fingers. I slid onto the far end of a love seat, trying to remain as invisible as possible. Bea shifted closer to me once I was seated, took my hand, and squeezed it. It was our silent code, one we'd had since she was a toddler and I was still a child myself. The two quick squeezes she gave my fingers with hers were a greeting and comfort all in one.

I smiled at her, then my breath stalled in my chest. The beautiful man I'd run into in the hall was seated to the right of my employer. He'd been mostly hidden by the ostentatious wings on the ridiculous chair Henrik insisted on reserving for his most honored guests, but there was no mistaking him. Vassago's eyebrows lifted in recognition, and he inclined his head slightly in greeting, straightening in his seat.

"I'm sure there's an excellent reason for your tardiness, Greta." Henrik cocked his head, disappointment rolling off him in waves. Lara's scarlet-painted lips thinned to a straight line as she glared right through me.

"I apologize. Something … unexpected came up."

Lara's eyes narrowed. "I'm sure. Apologies, Mr. Feland, this one has the unbecoming tendency to lose track of time."

I sat straighter in my seat, shame heating my face.

"As I was saying, Beatrice is quite gifted at the piano, as well as botanical studies. Won't be long now until she's matched and off to make her own music as some blessed soul's wife," Henrik enthused.

"Yes, we'll certainly celebrate when that day comes!" Lara lifted her glass in a salute. "Actually, we were discussing it, and we wondered if you might be interested in—"

"What is it you enjoy doing, Greta?" the beautiful man interrupted, his eyes never having left mine. I'd always disliked my name, but it sounded less ugly, less harsh on his lips. I stiffened at the way my skin tingled in response.

"Oh, don't concern yourself with her, Mr. Feland," Lara tittered. "Despite my best efforts, she's never really conformed to ladylike ventures. Just today she managed to break no less than three wineglasses during a simple exercise for a friend of mine who'd considered taking her on as temporary staff. Disgraceful, really. Beatrice, on the other hand, excels in those areas. As I was saying, we wondered if you might care to—"

"I wouldn't."

"I beg your pardon?"

"I wouldn't care to."

"But I haven't told you what it is yet." Lara giggled nervously.

"And I didn't realize that things like music and botany were only meant for ladies to enjoy. Perhaps I should abandon my own talent with those things? I'm sure my brother will be absolutely crestfallen to hear he should no longer practice botany in particular, given his talent with growing rare plants to use in medicines and remedies." He raised an eyebrow, eyes sliding away from mine for a moment.

Lara turned a marvelous shade of bright pink under his judgmental gaze, clearly frustrated that he'd interrupted her as well as refused her outright. Henrik began to blabber about how that wasn't what she meant, but Vassago remained unimpressed. I was stunned but also appreciated someone taking both a stand for and an interest in me, especially to my employers.

"Mr. Feland," Henrik rushed to say, as though just realizing he'd never actually introduced me, "this is Greta."

Even though she wanted no part of it, Bea was always the center of attention. Henrik and Lara would always state some version of *Here's our perfect daughter, and here's ... this other thing, pay no attention to it* before parading Bea's beauty and skills. It had always been that way. It didn't matter how old I got, it was the same routine, and it was all beyond tiresome, especially since I'd graduated from being their ward to being their employee well before I came of age.

Vassago's eyebrows pulled together as he stared at Henrik. Finally, they smoothed out as he looked back at me. "Yes, we've met."

"You have?" Lara's tone lifted to a screech at the end of the word. She was no doubt horrified by the possibilities around how that had occurred.

"Indeed. I'm afraid it's my fault she was delayed in arriving. I was rather clumsy and spilled my wine all over her. So, I too, had an accident involving wineglasses. Seems it's going around. Apologies again, Greta. I'm sorry to have ruined your clothes. Are you sure you're not injured?"

Watching them both gape like fish was wildly entertaining. I tried to memorize every blink so I could revisit it later. "I'm fine, thank you for asking."

"I'm so glad to hear that." He turned his attention to Lara. "How odd that there are no portraits of her on the walls—you mentioned that she is now an employee, but was previously your ward? In fact, there are several bare spots—are you in the process of redecorating, duchess?"

Lara flushed red. "Erm, yes. Apologies for the disarray, I'm trying to update everything, and it's taking more time and effort than expected."

He squinted at her evasion of the question about portraits. There were none of me, not since the handful they'd had me sit for as a child had been systematically removed and, I could only assume, destroyed. Henrik had once treated me like a daughter, but Lara's will had won out on that. I'd never been anything more than a nuisance to her.

"Hmm." The thoughtful noise rumbled in his throat, almost an accusation. It made my skin tingle. "What were you saying, Greta? Your lovely sister enjoys the piano. Where do your passions lie?"

I glanced at my patrons who both stared me down intensely. "I practice the sciences," I said carefully, certain my cheeks were flushed with color under his gaze.

His eyebrow raised even higher, a gentle lift to the corner of his mouth. Based on our conversation in the hall, I was sure this was not new information. But his attention was so rapt, it was as if nothing but he and I existed for a moment. It was a potent, novel feeling. Nobody had looked at me in such a way since Bea was a baby, and I was performing what she believed to be magic tricks by making items disappear behind my back.

He slid forward in his seat and leaned toward me. I struggled to breathe, his focus on me was so intense. "Which specialties? My brother is headmaster at the Collegium d'Arcan. I've recently taken up residence there myself. We can always use more talented students. And staff, for that matter."

My heart skipped. Everyone in the city knew only a select group of gifted students were able to attend. But staff? Surely, I wasn't qualified. "I'm a chemist, mainly. I've studied that as well as alchemy." I caught the intense stare of Lara as I glanced away from his face for the briefest of moments. "But I'm afraid despite my intensive practice, I'm not very skilled at either."

"That remains to be seen. Passion is sometimes the most important virtue when it comes to learned skills. Perhaps you'd like to come see the campus?"

Bea squeezed my hand tightly twice again before letting it go. I'd forgotten she was there at all, let alone that she had a grip on my hand.

"Oh, I'm sure you wouldn't want to burden yourself with Greta, Mr. Feland," Lara blustered.

Vassago continued, ignoring her completely. "Monday? Say"—he tapped a fingertip thoughtfully on his chin—"after midday? I'll be happy to give you a tour, and I'm sure I could arrange some things for afternoon tea."

I glanced at Henrik, unable to avoid noticing that Vassago never looked away from me. He sought *my* interest, *my* consent, not that of my employer's. And it was not lost on me that Lara was addressing him formally, but he'd requested I call him by his first name. Something warm rushed through my veins. It felt bright, bubbly. Intensely dangerous.

At Henrik's slight nod, I agreed. "Yes, thank you. I'd enjoy that very much."

Vassago smiled, his teeth straight and white, though his canines were a bit longer and more pointed than normal. If I'd thought him beautiful before, he was impossibly gorgeous now, his sharply angled features softened by the joyous expression. "Wonderful. I'll send our carriage to retrieve you."

Henrik spoke up and accepted gracefully before I could stutter the denial that lingered on my tongue. "That's very generous of you, Mr. Feland. Perhaps Beatrice might also visit? You mentioned your brother has an affinity for botany, as well?"

Lara batted her eyes at him, but he wasn't looking at her. Bea, on the other hand, gave a polite smile but shrank into herself, clearly uninterested in inviting herself along.

"Perhaps another time." His tone was icy, shutting down any further discussion on the matter. There was also an odd play of the light, making his eyes momentarily appear red instead of the light gold I knew they were. "I very much look forward to your visit, Greta." He gave me what felt like a private smile, then a calm settled over him, his manner shifting to wholly businesslike. "To answer your earlier intentions fully, Duchess Belette, I have no interest in courting your daughter. She's lovely, and it sounds like she's well educated, but that's simply not going to happen. You've asked about my titles as well, and while I have many, I don't find them relevant to our business. I'd appreciate very much if you'd not mention either of those things again. Additionally, you may want to consider a different vintage of wine for serving to guests. The one you gave me before was far better suited to being spilled than consumed. Though I would still prefer the bitter flavor of it to the scent of your desperation." Lara blanched under his stare, the pale hue of her skin flushed red as her anger set in. Even Henrik shifted, uncomfortable with having displeased his guest but also torn about defending his wife's honor. "Shall we proceed with the interviews?"

"Interviews?" I asked, instantly braced for backlash at having spoken out of turn once I'd blurted the question.

"I'm trying to locate an item, an heirloom they"—he gestured to Henrik and Lara—"believe to be lost," Vassago explained. "I find it helpful to discuss things with every member of the household during my search. Those of you who arrived in the city only recently are the last on my list to speak with." He tilted his head, assessing me calmly. "Are you comfortable doing that here? Or would you prefer a more private setting?"

I swallowed, completely unprepared to answer that question but even less ready to find myself alone with him again. "Oh. No, here is fine." I held eye contact with him until he finally blinked and looked away. When I glanced over at Bea, she was staring back at me with her mouth slack and eyes wide.

"As you wish. Is there anything else before we begin?"

Henrik, clearly feeling as though Vassago had misunderstood, listed off the enormity of my failure as a chemist. He seemed determined to talk Vassago out of his invitation, despite already having allowed me to accept.

"All due respect, Henrik, none of that means anything. Chemistry can succeed or fail dependent upon the environment it's performed in. Perhaps she hasn't found the right tools or inspiration yet. In any event, d'Arcan welcomes her with open arms. I'm hopeful she'll find our facilities to her liking." He turned his eyes back to me, and I found I couldn't properly breathe for several seconds, not until he looked away again. When he did, it was to flash a smile at Henrik that felt unusually ... sharp.

Henrik tried several times to make a full sentence, finally changing the subject altogether.

Bea leaned into my side and asked softly, "What just happened?"

I let out a long, slow breath, heart still hammering against my ribs. Lara and Henrik were both focused on their guest, so I murmured back, "I have no idea."

"You're going to d'Arcan." Bea gripped my hand tightly in excitement.

It didn't matter that for the next hour Vassago asked a thousand and one questions of us both, most of which neither of us could answer. He wanted to know where we'd been on certain dates in the past, if we'd seen a necklace or other jewelry in suspicious places or with people they didn't appear to belong to, if anyone had ever talked about jewels. He drew a sketch out of his pocket, and asked if we'd ever seen the same color or type of gem as the ring he wore on his index and pinkie finger.

It didn't even matter that the longer the questions went on, the more my employers' hushed whispers and stares at me made my skin crawl.

No matter the consequences that waited for me on the other side of my visit, I was going to d'Arcan.

CHAPTER 3
VASSAGO

"**G**O AWAY, RYLAN," I implored my brother, walking away from him to further my point. "Collect your lovely bride, get in the carriage I know is downstairs ready to depart at a moment's notice, and simply go *away*."

We were up in the observatory of the collegium he'd founded, discussing class plans and other mundane administrative items. I'd known that being brought on as a teacher would require me to do such things but had vastly underestimated the sheer volume of mundanity.

Vastly.

How Rylan managed as headmaster with all the extra administrative minutiae was a mystery to me. Just the paperwork involved would drive me mad in short order.

"It's not that simple, Vago," he argued, glancing around at the stacks of star charts and his beloved telescopes.

"But it is, *Stolas*. Use your wings if you must, I don't care. Just get yourself out of Revalia for a little while. Take a rest. Enjoy some time with your wife that isn't overshadowed by some kind of impending doom."

He frowned at me, eyes squinted. Like the bossy big brother I was, I pulled out his old name when it was required, and he hated it.

"And what will you do in my absence?" He crossed his arms, pinning me with a stare.

"Exactly the same as I'd do with you here. Prepare lessons, do experiments. Eat Grace's food. Argue with Magnus." When he raised an eyebrow, I continued, "Do you trust me that little? Or perhaps believe me a child that requires constant entertainment? Should I be offended?" I teased. "I'll prepare a two-way mirror for you to install at the manor so that we can communicate somewhat easily if it will make you feel better."

Rylan sighed as he shook his head, chin sagging to his chest. I saw it then, the weight he carried around. This school was much more than his pet project, and he took it very seriously—and for good reason, of course. It served a sector of the community that nothing else did, and as an archmage of the realm of Cyntere, he was uniquely qualified and permitted to teach fledgling mages how to access and use their magic.

Besides the school, his life in general had been very eventful both in the several months leading up to my arrival and since then. Which, I thought, was all the more reason for him to take a break and go on a proper honeymoon.

His wife and fated mate, Calla, had been kidnapped by a witch who wanted to exploit her for her magic. Thankfully, we'd arrived in time to help free her, and she was progressing nicely when it came to her ability to control her immense earth magic. Needless to say, the early days of my visit had been quite tense.

There rarely seemed to be a truly quiet moment here, which in some ways left me longing for the monasteries I'd inhabited for decades at a time while training myself in discipline, the mystic arts and hunting down lost relics. In other ways, it reminded me of the constant activity of Hell, and who I'd been before coming earth-side. I was undecided on which I preferred.

"Of course not. I trust you. I know everything is in capable hands with you here. Grace wouldn't allow anything to happen on her watch, besides." His mouth twitched at the mention of his iron-willed cook. She ran her ship tight and loved the school at least as much as Rylan did.

"Too right. And that overgrown statue, Magnus, is around constantly, whether I like it or not. I'm surprised he isn't here right now, if I'm honest."

My brother smiled. "He'll be back later tonight, though likely in a foul mood. He had patrol today, and a meeting with the stone kin council. He hates day shifts almost as much as council meetings. Both in one day?" he grimaced and shook his head.

"Lovely," I said sarcastically. In truth, the gargoyle and I were friendly enough, but we thrived on a certain level of mutual dislike. "But there, see? The students are gone, Rylan. It's as quiet as it's going to get around here. I'll make you a mirror so you can check in. Go on your holiday, spend time with your mate. Everything will be fine in your absence, I promise."

"What about your other employer?" he asked, referring to Henrik. "Are you not worried your attention will be divided?"

I shook my head. "No. This jewelry he's trying to find is proving elusive. I don't see myself traveling beyond the city walls to seek it out for now. I have a couple new leads to follow, but they don't seem likely to bear any real information, just like the several I've chased over the last half a year." I exhaled my frustration. I'd been a fool to think it was an easy task I'd signed up for. At least I'd had the opportunity to sit with Lilith's book several times since first agreeing to seek out Henrik's gem, though I hadn't yet found the answers I had hoped its pages would provide. "He knows it will take however long it takes. They've allegedly been searching for nearly twenty years, so a couple more months isn't the end of the world." I cleared my throat, having the perfect opening to suggest my intended guest. "One of the members of his house is a chemist. Alchemist, perhaps, as well."

Rylan's head came up, as did one of his sooty eyebrows. "Oh?"

"I thought I could trial her skills here before the students come back. If I'm not mistaken, she's well into her twenties, possibly more. She could be either a student or a member of staff, depending on her aptitude." The fact that she'd been anxious to get away from our original conversation had only made me want to prolong it. Her interactions with her employers were odd to say the least, and I didn't care for it. Getting to the bottom of why I couldn't seem to ignore anything about her was also at the top of my to-do list.

My brother pinned me with a stare, thoughtful. "Have you spoken with her?"

"Yes, briefly."

"And she's interested?"

"Yes, I'd dare say enthusiastic about it, though her employers were cagey at best. She will hopefully be here Monday afternoon to tour the campus."

Rylan tilted his head to the side. He coughed out a laugh, crossing his arms over his chest. "Monday?"

"I figured if you disagreed, I could still convince you once she arrived. Unless you'd already left, in which case," I shrugged, raising my hands. "Forgiveness is sometimes easier to obtain than permission." I grinned as he narrowed his eyes at me. Getting a rise out of my brothers was something I never tired of.

Rylan started for the stairs, shaking his head. "And you wonder why I don't want to leave you alone?" he teased. "Fine. If she's well skilled, perhaps we'll add her to the faculty roster in the fall. If not, she's free to test for enrollment. She'll be under your supervision, of course?"

"Naturally."

"Very well. Perhaps some respite is in order ..." He tinkered with a few more objects before stuffing his hands in his pockets. Without another word, he strode toward the doorway.

"You're going to pack?" I shouted after him as he'd already vanished down the stairwell.

"Yes, I am. No need to gloat."

"Shall I make you a mirror then? So you can reach me, or I you, if there's urgency? All you'll have to do is speak a series of words to activate it, it's quite simple."

"I suppose. And I'll make you some extra tincture?" The words echoed back at me, growing further away all the time.

"Excellent idea." Rylan had been making me a specially formulated tincture for as long as I could remember to help me manage the bloodlust curse the book thief had left me with. Whether it truly helped or not was up for debate, especially as episodes had been slowly escalating in frequency and aggressiveness, but I took it religiously anyway. "Give Calla my love," I needled him. He grunted in response, which was an improvement over his normal growl.

Finding his fated mate had made my brother relentlessly possessive. My sister-in-law was lovely, and I was happy for my brother that he'd found his match, but she was certainly not someone I felt romantic about.

I gathered up the documents we'd been reviewing, a burn rising behind my ribs. I rubbed at my chest with the heel of my hand, trying to recall if I'd eaten anything suspicious as I made my way down the massive set of stairs.

Something fluttery invaded my chest the night I'd bumped into Greta and hadn't let go since. I was inclined to blame Lara's terrible wine. If I were human, mortal, or otherwise susceptible to illness, I might actually be concerned with the state of my heart. The only other explanation was some kind of magical interference, perhaps. My brother's gifts included being able to conduct and direct electrical current with his hands, so some kind of friction due to the magic between us was another—albeit less likely—option, as it had never been an issue between us before.

Once I'd made my way to the second floor, I turned down the hall and unlocked the door of my apartment. After dropping the paperwork on the low coffee table, I sank into the plush dark-gray sofa, grateful for the resourcefulness of my brother and his staff. While not luxurious, the faculty quarters I'd been provided afforded all the comforts I needed while living and teaching at the collegium.

I closed my eyes, and unbidden, the image of Greta and her flushed cheeks swirled in my mind. It was ridiculous how many times her face had presented itself to me since our brief conversations. Eyes open or closed, it didn't matter.

Her intelligent hazel eyes, incredible height, riot of short brown curls ... everything about her had arrested my thoughts in a way I'd long forgotten was possible. It was thrilling, but the novelty of it also terrified me. It wasn't like me to be so distracted by a woman, not even one such as her.

Frowning, I rubbed at my chest some more and got back to my feet. I decided distracting myself by setting up a two-way mirror and helping my brother pack was a far better option than sitting alone with my dangerous thoughts.

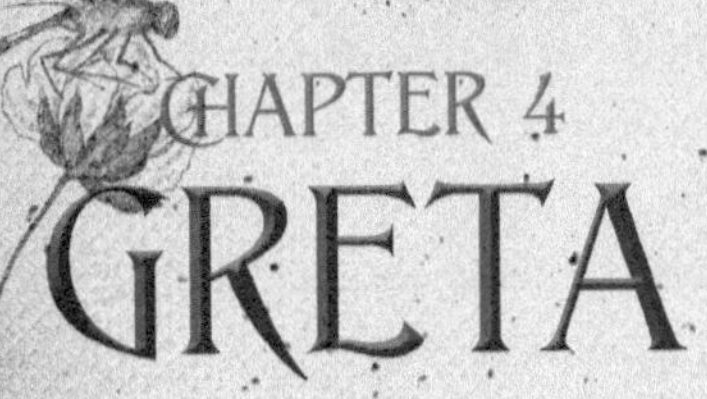

CHAPTER 4
GRETA

"Y OU MADE US look foolish," Henrik hissed, pounding his fist firmly against the tabletop.

My cup jumped, some of my tea sloshing over the rim as I stared at the collection of gouges and divots in the table, chagrinned but unrepentant.

"And you diverted all the attention from Bea to yourself. You have no idea how important Mr. Feland is! He has titles, likely wealth beyond imagining. He seemed interested in Bea and her talents before you interrupted with your late arrival. I swear, Greta. It's like you do these things on purpose," Lara ranted, frantically waving her fork as she spoke.

I stilled. They often twisted things around to suit their needs, even when it made little sense to me, but Vassago had been quite clear—he'd come to interview us about a necklace and had no desire in being a potential suitor. I was beyond confused by their description of his visit's intent. If he'd been there for Bea, I wouldn't have been invited into the den. "I thought—"

"I worry that you never think!" Lara pointed her finger at me, cutting herself off with a firm shake of her head. "After all we've done for you. All these years. I simply don't understand! Even your trial for Mariam was a complete disaster. I cannot continue to find such opportunities for you only to have you fail spectacularly at them, you know. That's seven now, *seven* potential other homes for you to gain work where you've botched the trial."

Misery made me sag. She didn't need to remind me about any of that. They'd gone so far as to allow me to do tests for other employers in their own home, and every single time, I messed it all up. The Goss brothers barely escaped me spilling their soup in their laps. I'd nearly fallen asleep at the feet of the old Cooke couple before he'd gotten through an incomprehensible series of interview questions. Each time was another crushing failure.

Lara huffed a breath. "By rights, we could have put you on the streets to fend for yourself years ago, if not for—" She stopped abruptly when Henrik cleared his throat. I looked between them, anxiety tingling along my skin at what they were leaving unsaid.

"We've always treated you uniquely to the other staff, and this is how you repay us?" Henrik asked, tone brutally quiet.

I clamped my lips shut and waited, all too familiar with the lecture I was receiving. Nothing much had changed since I was a child in that regard, either. Lara's claims were lofty at best. They'd kept me housed in a room with discarded furniture and little else in an abandoned wing of the manor. Even the walls and floor were bare and had been for decades. It was hot in the summer and cold in the winter, and if not for Bea and Caroline, luxuries like soap, towels, and bedding would have been virtually nonexistent. They fed me only as an afterthought, and I was provided cheap, often unviable chemistry supplies in lieu of any pay, despite working every single day of the week. The *special* treatment I got as an employee was anything but. In many ways, it was worse than if I were simply part of the hired staff.

"Lucky for you," Henrik continued, "Mr. Feland was a gracious guest and curious about your unusual interests. He would have been a perfect suitor for Beatrice, but your lateness was an unrecoverable distraction. As for the job with the Walkers ..." His lips pressed together, and he shook his head. Henrik's rage had been replaced with a heavy disappointment.

"You'll be docked for the cost of the glasses, of course," Lara snipped. "Needless to say, they won't be taking you on."

My stomach twisted, and threads of guilt I knew I shouldn't feel stole the joy I'd felt while under the unabashed scrutiny of Vassago's eye.

I put on my most contrite expression, found a gap in the conversation suitable to defend myself, and said, "I'm sorry for what happened. I didn't mean to be late. What Va—Mr. Feland said was the truth. We ran into one another in the hall and his wine spilled all over me, I had to go upstairs to change. If not for that, I might have been on time." I'd have needed to change my clothes regardless, but they would never have known that. Never mind that us running into each other had been a distraction all of its own. "I appreciate that you've kept me on all these years, especially after my failed attempts at finding employment elsewhere. I know what an imposition it has been to allow others into your home when the result could be them taking a member of your staff for themselves." Contrition, genuine or otherwise, was never ill-received.

"As you should. Giving grace to help who are clumsy and need constant rest is unusual at best. But we do. We have. And we allow you to follow your scientific pursuits, as well."

"I know," I capitulated, old guilt sinking its claws in again. "I am grateful, truly."

Henrik regarded me carefully for several long seconds, his nearly black eyes searching mine. I held my breath, willing him to believe me as Lara stabbed her spoon into the soft egg, exasperated with the whole thing.

I straightened my back, hands nervously folded together on the tabletop in front of me. They loved to accuse me of being lazy. Of misunderstanding things I said. Whatever suited the situation and made me the one at fault. If I'd learned nothing else, I knew when to keep my mouth shut. The whole truth mattered very little to them, particularly when it came to me.

Henrik stood, ambling over near the fireplace. "Your invitation to the Collegium d'Arcan was for Monday afternoon, correct?"

"Yes." Excitement fizzed in my chest.

"If nothing else, he'll be able to see firsthand your shortcomings, and then we can get back to business as usual around here." His eyes narrowed. In this case, best efforts equated to forced learning, but sure. "Your behavior will be exemplary?"

"Yes sir."

He stared at me for a long moment. "You're excused."

"There are several gowns on the settee in the foyer," Lara quickly added. "Take them to Beatrice," she ordered.

I pushed my chair back, nearly tipping it over in my enthusiasm to escape. "Yes ma'am. Pardon me," I muttered, rushing from the room. After collecting the massive pile of dresses Lara had mentioned, I carefully headed upstairs, turning down the first hall to find Bea.

How she'd gotten out of having breakfast with the family was a mystery, but I could only assume she was prepared for me to be in trouble and was sparing herself the discomfort of sitting through yet another meal where that was the main attraction.

"Bea? You in there?" I asked, rapping on her closed bedroom door.

"Of course I am," she called back, and I took that as my invitation. She smiled as I waddled inside. "I see you survived unscathed."

"Your mother was well prepared to blister me with her tongue, but I managed to get off light." I dumped the pile of dresses on her bed. "I blew the trial with Mariam, though, so it seems I'm not supposed to leave this manor."

"I'm sorry, Greta. I know you'd prefer to be self-sufficient. Perhaps something else will come through." She shook her head, golden curls bouncing as she did so.

I sat on the edge of her bed as she pulled the gowns from their heavy bags, sorting them into several piles on the floor. "What are all these for?"

"Mother is trying to find me something I can wear for the ball."

"Ball?" I asked, feeling even more out of my depth than usual. My shirt was obviously threadbare in contrast to the gowns' delicate satins and silks.

Bea sighed. "Yes. For my announcement."

"Oh." I scrunched up my nose, sharing her distaste for what was to come. "I thought they'd decided to put that off until winter?"

"Several of the more desirable suitors would prefer a summer event. Mother informed me this morning. It's why I had no appetite for breakfast." She grimaced again.

"I'm sorry, Bea."

She shrugged. "It's alright. I knew it was coming."

"You should have as much time as you need," I argued, knowing that it was only by luck and being found wholly deficient at most things that I'd made it to thirty without any such designs being put upon me. "Also, if Mr. Feland was supposed to be—"

Bea laughed outright. "He stated his feelings on that clearly enough. No matter how much Mother may have decided she wanted that, it was never going to happen." She grew serious. "It's alright, Greta. Truly. I'm not smart like you, but Father will ensure I find a good match."

My heart sank. She shouldn't have to marry off either, not unless she wanted to. "I won't let you be taken away by just anyone, Bea. And I'm sure Ellis will have plenty to say about who they consider for you." Mentioning his name brought a blush to her cheeks. The son of one of the local merchants, he was likely to end up in the suitor pool, and their long-standing friendship was no secret. I hoped if he was her happiness, they ended up paired. The alternative was too sad to imagine.

A smile returned to her pretty face. "I know. So, help me pick a dress, would you?"

I got to my feet and crossed to the pile of fabric on the floor. "What am I looking for?"

"I don't know, something ... special."

"They're all lovely, Bea. Do you want a certain color? Why didn't your mother call in someone to have a new gown made for you? Doesn't she always do that?"

"I'm not sure. She hesitated when I brought it up. I think ..." She stopped, lowering her voice even though we were alone. "I think perhaps money is short, so we're trading with her friends for gowns. I think that's maybe also why they're moving up my ball."

"I would never say anything, but I've noticed there are some silver pieces missing, tapestries, paintings ... Lara says it's because of her renovations, but ..."

Bea nodded solemnly.

We worked in silence for several minutes. I set aside a gown in a light blue that highlighted her eyes, and she chose one in green that she favored for how it looked with her skin.

"These are a start, I suppose," she sighed.

"When is it?"

"During Father's normal late-summer celebration."

"Is it even possible to put together something like this so quickly?"

"It's only for the announcement that I'm seeking suitors. I won't be married off after the cocktails are served." She laughed at me, far more serene about the situation than I was.

"You'll have to tell me all about it," I said, letting some of the lace slip through my fingers. I'd never had anything lovely like these gowns, only rough linen shirts or shifts, and wondered how the luxurious fabric would feel against my skin. I curbed my own emotions so as not to stress her further. "I never see much of the parties, aside from the trays of food going out and dirty dishes coming back. I'll help with your hair, if you'd like. Though there are others with much more talented hands than mine."

"I love when you do my hair." Bea smiled, but it was painfully brief. "Mother will no doubt have opinions on that, as well." Her words were so tart her mouth remained tight from them. Even she had grown weary of Lara's overbearing need to direct every aspect of her appearance. I think it was mostly luck—but perhaps the fact that Lara relied on me and other members of staff to act as nanny to Bea as a child—that she didn't end up spoiled and selfish. She knew how to say all the right things when her parents were around, but otherwise, she seemed bored with all the pomp and pretense required of her. It was one of the things I was most proud of.

We sat in the quiet for a moment, then Bea rose and dragged over a stool before retrieving her hairbrush from the bedside table.

"Please?" she asked, giving me the same pleading look she'd used since she was a baby to bend me to her will.

"Alright, sit down." I sighed, but honestly didn't mind at all. Brushing her ridiculously thick, glossy hair until it was smooth was my favorite of our long-standing traditions. Henrik and Lara had allowed us much more time together when she was younger, I suspected because I was a convenient babysitter, and they could bend my job description around Bea's needs. It had simply been nice to spend my days with a girl I considered my sister. I missed it.

Bea turned, and for a second, excitement lit up her face. "You're going to d'Arcan Monday, right?"

"Yes. I don't think Henrik would care to explain to Vassago why I didn't arrive as expected."

She raised an eyebrow. "First names already?" she teased. I blushed, unreasonably pleased that I was given permission to use his first name and my patrons were not. "Why do you look like you're still considering it?" She sat beside me on the bed.

"I'm going. I mean, I should ... right?"

"Absolutely, Greta! This is what you've been waiting for!" She turned and grasped my arm with both hands, eyes wide as she beamed. "What if this is it? The job you've been trying to find? Somewhere for you to go, something that provides a life away from this house?"

I hadn't dared hope too far that direction. "That's a lovely thought, Bea. Now turn around so I can finish, yes?"

She let out a little squeal but turned as I requested so I could move on to the next section. "Wait, didn't he say he was the arch-mage's brother? What if he was actually the archmage?"

I shook my head. "No, I don't think he'd lie about that. And wouldn't your father know? Besides, doesn't the archmage dress in black and have dark hair?"

"That's what I've heard," Bea confirmed.

"Right, so Mr. Feland is probably who he says. He reminds me ..." I let the thought taper off, picturing the angelic features.

"Reminds you?"

"I'm probably exaggerating, but he reminded me of the man in the fountain."

"Fountain? What are you talking about?" She laughed as though I were making a joke.

"In the center of the maze," I explained, knowing she'd proba-bly only been out there the handful of times I'd dragged her with me. "The angel in the fountain. He looks like that." I sped up my work and my words, embarrassed by the comparison despite the accuracy of it.

"Oh, so you thought he was handsome," she ribbed me, bumping my shoulder with hers before getting back to her feet.

"You saw him, too, he was ... beautiful, was he not?" Bea laughed openly then, enjoying my embarrassment. It wasn't often that

I was the one squirming like this. "Of course I thought he was handsome!" I argued. "I'm pretty sure everyone does."

I closed my eyes, summoning the memory of his silvery hair and sharp features. His bright honey eyes. I'd seen him plainly, but it felt like the image I conjured was too perfect. It was as though I were simply making up an impossible version of a man composed of equal parts the statue and my imagination.

"You could be his student," Bea mused. "Or his assistant or something. I think this is everything you've been waiting for and deserve, Greta. To hell with trading one job as a maid for one insufferable family for another." She leaned over to hug me, and I gratefully accepted the affection she provided. Resolve steeled deep within me about my visit to the prestigious school and the mysterious man who'd invited me there.

CHAPTER 5
GRETA

I CLIMBED OUT OF the carriage, breath caught in my throat as I paused to look up at the cathedral-like building in the cobbled courtyard. It seemed so untouchable from a distance, but up close, the tan and gray stone structure was welcoming.

Vassago straightened his vest as he walked over to greet me. "Welcome to d'Arcan," he said, bowing at the waist and giving a flourish of one arm.

I smiled in response, a flush in my cheeks. "Thank you. I'm honored to have been invited."

He extended his hand, and I accepted, his fingers warm in my palm. "Do you need anything before we begin?"

I glanced around, heart still thudding anxiously in my chest. "No, I'm fine, thank you. I appreciate you sending the carriage to retrieve me."

I paused as a raven of immense size boldly announced his arrival in the courtyard with several loud croaking sounds. He landed on the edge of the fence, tilting his head this way and that as he took us in.

"Hello," I said, leaning in the direction of the bird to get a closer look. "Aren't you pretty?"

The bird fluffed his feathers and lifted his chin, turning his head so he could focus on me with an intelligent eye. The raven blinked, pausing in his assessment as he danced along the top edge of the fencing. He turned his attention to Vassago, revealing that his other eye was scarred closed. He made a gurgling croak and then flew away again.

"Is he around often?" I asked, smiling broadly. The friendly raven had given me a thrill. I rarely saw birds that large at the manor, nor at the country house for that matter.

"I've never seen that bird before in my life," he replied, forehead wrinkled in confusion.

"Oh." I paused a beat, then laughed, surprised by his answer. "Well, he's rather comfortable here, I wonder if you'll start seeing him more now that he's introduced himself."

"Perhaps, though it seemed he was far more interested in you than me." He took several steps toward the building. "We're in for a bit of an adventure today. I have no set plans for a route," he admitted, fingertips gently tracing the inside of my palm. My pulse thudded in my ears at the intimate gesture.

"That's alright. I don't think there's a wrong way to see a place like this." He released my hand, and while it was only appropriate that he do so, I wished he hadn't.

We started with a grassy area stocked with hay bales and straw dummies hanging from poles where fight training was held. We continued past the stables, and he introduced me to a little girl called Sara who waved enthusiastically from atop a slow, gentle horse she called Clementine.

The massive tower drew my attention repeatedly. I shaded my eyes with one hand as I looked up at it. "I bet the night sky is a wonder from up there."

"Indeed. If you're up for climbing a hundred or so stairs, I'm happy to take you up. That's the observatory, of course."

I nodded, but the thought of climbing so many steps gave me pause. We stopped at some elaborate garden beds, complete with a small enclosure where several chickens pecked at the dirt off to one side.

"My brother planted several rare herbs here, as well as vegetables and flowers. There has been talk of expanding it so we can more readily feed the students and staff ourselves, but nobody has volunteered for that job yet." Vassago stopped to pluck a flower. I blushed furiously as he handed the lavender blossom to me. There was something else in his gaze, something my brain interpreted as borderline dangerous. The word hunger didn't feel quite right … but it also fit very well. When he smiled, I noticed again that his canine teeth were longer than they should be, and I nearly shivered.

"Thank you." I dipped my nose, surprised by the potent scent and happy to have a distraction as we made our way back to the main building. "It's quieter than I imagined," I said, my voice respectfully low as we stepped through the doors. The air was cool inside the vaulted structure, the feeling of the building solid, secure.

"No students," Vassago explained. "We're in our summer break, so they've all gone home until classes resume in the fall." He ushered me into the dining room, and I inhaled as I took in the high ceilings, broad wooden beams and unique animal carvings that decorated the heavy posts along the walls.

As though she'd been waiting for us, a woman appeared at the door of the kitchen with a tray of drinks.

"Welcome! Are you thirsty? Traveling always leaves me parched. I'm Grace." She reached out her hand for me to shake.

"Greta."

"Pleased to meet you. Vassago mentioned you're a chemist?"

"Yes, I practice the sciences. Though I'm not sure I've earned the proper titles—I've been learning about them since I was a child, but I'm certainly no expert."

Vassago raised an eyebrow at Grace, and she winked back at him. They clearly had an interesting conversation going without saying a single word, not to mention how casually she greeted him. I suddenly felt strange, like I might be witnessing a couple flirting with one another as I glanced between them.

"Well, I hope you enjoy your visit." Grace set the tray on the closest table and turned to Vassago again. "Might I borrow you for just a moment? I have a ... situation I need your assistance with."

Vassago blinked. "Oh. Yes, of course. If you'll excuse me?"

Grace gave what looked like a tense, private smile as she hurried off into the kitchen with Vassago right behind her.

I wandered slowly up the row of tables, admiring the detailed animal carvings. A hot blush crept into my cheeks as a series of muffled noises came from behind the closed door. My stomach twisted as I heard some kind of furniture thumping, then Grace's higher pitch squeal and a growl that could only have come from him. The noises made my ears burn and my hand rose to my mouth. I contemplated running for the door in mortification, but I hesitated too long. Cheeks hot, I could only watch in stunned silence as he emerged from the kitchen, disheveled and flushed.

"I'm so sorry for the interruption. Are you ready to continue?" Vassago asked, straightening his vest.

Emotions swirled within me as I struggled to form words. Had I just heard them ...? I couldn't even make myself complete the thought I was so stunned. Had I been so mistaken by the attention he'd paid to me at the manor? I knew my naivete was surely showing, but I felt like I'd wandered into a situation I had no preparation for.

"Greta" he asked, eyebrows drawn together. "Are you feeling alright?"

Embarrassment settled in, making me feel raw inside. I inhaled deeply, wishing I could fall into a hole somewhere. I couldn't understand how we'd gone from the lovely moment where he'd given me the flower to here.

My cheeks were intensely hot as he studied my face. His eyes seemed to change color moment to moment, which left me feeling further unstable. I already couldn't find the words I wanted to say, but his eyes glittering like rubies pushed me even more off balance, introducing some fear to go with the anxiety. I wanted to tell him that maybe I should go, because saints knew I felt like running away just then. That I appreciated his kindness, but clearly had misinterpreted several of his seemingly sweet gestures. How having lived at the manor exclusively had clearly stunted my understanding of relationships, and perhaps I needed a gentler introduction to the outside world.

His frown intensified, and he pressed the back of his hand to my forehead. "You really are quite flushed. Perhaps you should sit down for a moment."

He guided me to the nearest table, hands scorching through my clothing as he held tight to be sure I didn't fall. My mind twisted itself up in knots as he plucked the lavender flower from my clenched fingers and dropped it into the glass of water still sitting on the tray. The other, the one I'd already drunk from, he set securely between both of my hands.

"Sip slowly. Perhaps you became overheated outside?" he put the back of his hand on my cheeks as well, gauging my temperature. Concern etched into his handsome features as I carefully drank.

I fidgeted with my skirt, face blazing hot as he settled onto the wooden bench next to me. He smoothed his hair and adjusted his clothing, causing another wave of confused emotion to wash through me.

Grace burst through the kitchen door again, a sack held as far out in front of her as possible. Her hair was similarly mussed, her face pinched in disgust.

"I'm terribly sorry for interrupting your visit, Greta. Thank you very much for your help, Mr. Feland. That has been an issue for longer than I care to think about." She shook the bag as she went, something heavy shifting inside. Stunned, I watched her leave the dining room, the whole scene replaying in my mind. My confusion only compounded on itself.

Several swallows of the cool water later, I straightened, pulling my pride down over me like a shield. I rotated my left shoulder several times, the tension there having become bothersome again.

"I'm alright," I said.

"If you're sure." I nodded, and he took the empty glass from my hands and set it aside before getting to his feet. "Let me take you down the main hall. Perhaps we can head up to the observatory after, if you're feeling up to it."

Vassago led me out of the dining room and through several stone classrooms. I delicately touched the edge of a candlestick here, peered into the contents of a bookshelf there. Everything appeared incredibly special while also being completely utilitarian. I worried that I was responsible for driving us into awkward silence as we came to the end of the corridor and a set of stairs.

"Your brother? He's an archmage?" I asked.

His gaze went flat. "Yes. What about him?"

"Your eyes ..." I stared at his face, perplexed at how the eyes I knew to be gold looked red again. A chill of warning tingled up my spine, but I couldn't look away. His dangerously cold tone felt like jealousy, which was just as confusing as everything else had been since we'd come inside, but at least I could relate.

"My brother is on holiday with his wife," he said, glancing away. When he looked back, his eyes were the same golden hue I'd known them to be, making me doubt what I'd seen. "He'll be back before the next term starts."

"Oh? How nice. It's just ... I've been educated only from books, so I thought it might be helpful to speak to him about what I'm doing wrong."

"Ah." He took a long inhale through his nose, his expression warming the slightest bit. "I'm sure there's some crossover in his work, as there is with mine. I'd imagine you will have much to compare notes about when he returns." He gave a tight, but gentle smile. "The second and third floors are staff and student apartments," Vassago gestured vaguely at the doorway as he turned us back down the hall toward a classroom. "And this is where I spend most of my time." He gestured for me to enter ahead of him.

My hand rose to my chest as I turned, taking in the whole room. It was masculine and comfortable, stocked with an eclectic mix of things but not cluttered. My mouth dropped open a little as I took in the floor-to-ceiling rainbow-colored glass that ran either side of an assortment of bookshelves and cabinets on the main wall. The thick glass allowed for brightness but wouldn't damage sensitive pages, equipment, or chemicals like regular windows. It was ingenious as well as beautiful, and I said as much.

"Thank you. I can't take any credit for that glass though. It was in place when I got here."

"I've never seen anything like it." I blinked and blushed when I caught him watching me. "I'm sorry, I never asked what you teach."

"I will be assisting those with a talent for the mystic arts."

"Oh." I looked over his worktables, feeling out of my depth. "What is that, exactly?"

"Many things, but I have a talent for scrying. Mirrors are best." He gestured to the large oval glass on one of the long tables, plus the broad flat tub of water beside it. "But any reflective surface will do. Divining, as well."

"Divination? Like telling the future?"

"Yes, in a way. The past and present as well."

"Telling the present? What does that mean?"

He turned and gestured to the next table over, the one with several seemingly ordinary objects on it. "I can locate lost things, if I have something that they are connected to that I can touch. A hairbrush, for example"—he picked one up—"or a piece of jewelry, could help me seek out someone if they were lost."

He paused briefly, then selected a crystal off the table. It caught the light as he held it up, sending sparkles across my dress and along the floor. He reached out for my hand, and I reflexively gave it. A smile teased his mouth as he placed the cool crystal in my palm and closed my fingers over it. "Keep that close. Just in case of emergency." He gestured as I stared at him, inviting me to sit on the sofa. It looked like the most comfortable piece of furniture in the room, perfect for lounging and reading.

"This place is ... beyond what I could have imagined." I sank into the cushion, confirming my suspicion.

"Can you see yourself here?" he asked, making my heart pound again.

"I'm not sure I'm qualified. Either to attend or to educate anyone on something that is mostly a hobby of mine."

"That remains to be seen," he said, repeating his words from the other night.

"Perhaps." I smiled, a flush warming my cheeks as he watched me with that same rapt attention. "I've loved experimenting since I was a girl. Learning how things work, what chemicals react to one another ... it's all endlessly interesting to me."

"On the contrary, I think those are the hallmarks of a good student, not to mention a wise teacher. You also practice alchemy?"

Nobody at the manor bothered to speak with me about such things, and I didn't want to sound like a fool so I chose my words carefully. "I try, yes. The notion that base metal can be transformed into something greater is fascinating, even though it's illogical. Ore is ore. But the idea that altering one compound could change an element completely is very compelling. For Lara's vanity, I was once tasked with trying to find the secret to eternal youth. Needless to say, I failed. I'm not versed in the more ... magical applications of it either, I'm afraid."

His teeth clicked together as he closed his open mouth. His attention had been wholly focused on me, making me feel like my explanation was the most interesting thing in the world. I frowned, still distrustful of my interpretations of his gestures. "Understandable."

"I also love toying with anything involving making flames turn interesting colors or pouring solutions together to see what happens. That's just good fun. It's what I have managed to succeed at best, as well."

"A thrill seeker then?" he teased, clearing his throat and straightening up in his chair, as though trying to regain his carefully organized appearance before he became too relaxed. "I do hope you've learned to wear gloves at least?"

"Yes, and spectacles," I capitulated with a nod, rushing to cover a yawn. Much to my mortification, I'd done the same thing partway through the interview with him about the necklace. "I'm so sorry. I promise you're not boring me. I tire dreadfully easily."

"No need to apologize. You've taken in a lot today already. Were you interested in doing a demonstration? Perhaps I could get some tea, would that help?"

He was already on his feet as I nodded. "I'm sorry to be an inconvenience."

"No trouble at all, please don't worry yourself. Grace is no doubt lingering in the kitchen on the off chance we'd ask for something," he said disappearing out into the hallway.

Something ugly flared in my chest. I was sure she was.

I propped my head on my hand, looking around the cozy room as I waited. As I surveyed the rows of books and oddities scattered throughout the room, my eyelids grew so heavy I couldn't keep them open more than a moment. I cursed my body's weakness silently, unable to fight sleep off any longer.

CHAPTER 6
GRETA

I BLINKED SEVERAL TIMES, trying to orient myself. There was a soft woven blanket covering my body, and a pillow under my cheek that smelled faintly of lavender.

As I sat up, I tried to stretch a bit, my muscles stiff from the way I'd slumped to one side.

I heard the quiet rasp of a book's page being turned, and mortification set all the way in as I realized I'd fallen asleep in the middle of my visit. Choking on my own breath, I drew the attention of the man sitting nearby.

"I hope you don't mind. I took a few liberties to ensure your comfort."

"Thank you," I managed, heart pounding frantically behind my ribs. How long had I napped? What did he think of me for having done so? I sat frozen for several seconds, trying to decide what the appropriate next step might be. My visit had turned into a giant mess.

Vassago appeared completely unbothered by what had happened. He looked relaxed in one of the broad leather armchairs across from the sofa, a stout volume of fiction between his hands. The soft leather cover was well worn around the edges, a favorite perhaps. And he was either wholly absorbed in the story or excellent at pretending.

"Did you rest well?" he asked finally, using a narrow silver ribbon as a page marker.

"I think so, yes. I didn't mean to—"

He set the book aside on a small round table, waving a hand in dismissal of my apology as he stood. "Please don't concern yourself. I rather enjoyed having a quiet moment to read." His gentle smile betrayed no hint of sarcasm. "You were asleep for about an hour. If you need more time, I'm happy to arrange one of the apartments for you?"

I sat up, shaking off the lingering drowsiness. "No, no. I'm fine, thank you." I napped at least once a day, my body simply required it, but I might never get over this beautiful man having brought me a pillow and blanket while I dozed on the sofa in his classroom. My heart had finally settled down, though it currently resided in my stomach.

He calmly poured tea for us both, the pot somehow still steaming. "If you're still up for a demonstration, I put together some things. If not, I'd be happy to have you back another time for that. I'm in no rush."

"I'd like to show you what I can while I'm here," I insisted, feeling like it was the least I could do.

"I didn't know exactly what you'd need, I just grabbed what I could find lying about."

"May I?" I asked, finding that trying to look over his shoulder at the table across the room was mostly useless.

"Please," he nodded. Standing, he offered me a hand to help me up.

Something passed between us where we touched, a sharp current that had me looking up into his eyes. They were soft still but widened just enough that I suspected he could feel it as well. He let go slower than I'd expected.

At the table, he shadowed behind me as I examined what supplies he'd provided. "There's no test," he reassured me. "And I'm no scientist. Is there something here that could be of use for you to demonstrate something ... entertaining perhaps?"

I smiled. I had everything I needed to put together some of my favorite tricks. I might not be the most skilled or talented, but I could entertain with a flame, a bit of washing powder, and some salt.

"Could I have a candle, please?"

Vassago gave the slightest of grins and stepped away. I noticed as he glided around the room that he moved like a cat. He was graceful and stealthy without any effort at all, his white hair so glossy it shined in the light when he moved.

He retrieved a lit taper from a silver holder on the table where the food had been served and brought it to me. After a beat, he turned to get something from a shelf. When he spun back, he had two pairs of round-lensed spectacles in his hand. He put one pair on and gave the other to me.

"Thank you. May I use this dish?" I held up a small shallow metal bowl once the glasses were securely over my eyes.

"Anything here is open to your use, Greta." His voice was dark, with an undercurrent of invitation I couldn't help but clench my thighs against. It was beyond shocking.

Blushing under his watchful gaze, I focused on pouring one of the powdered salts into the dish and then some of the clear, potent alcohol he'd left in a squatty jar. Using the taper, I lit the mixture. The alcohol ignited in a rush of orange that quickly turned blue.

"Ah! Yes. I remember seeing this with some of the monks I stayed with once. They did take it quite a bit further, however, and added gunpowder among other things. They made giant paper tubes that, once ignited, exploded into bright colors in the night sky."

I marveled at the thought. "I'd love to try that."

"You should, it was marvelous. Though, perhaps not in here."

I opened my mouth to explain that I would certainly not be experimenting with explosives inside the collegium, but the grin on his lips betrayed his humor. My face burned as he winked at me. It seemed there was no end of feeling similar levels embarrassment and emotion like I had when I was a teenager where this man was concerned.

We watched as the alcohol burned away and the blue flame guttered out. I wiped the dish out with a cloth, gritting my teeth as two of my fingertips burned against the edge of the iron.

"Are you alright?" he asked, concern etched into the creases of his eyes.

"Fine. It was just still a bit hot." As he stared at me as though gauging whether I was being truthful about the extent of my injury, I started again with a different powder. This time, when I lowered the flame to the alcohol, the flame turned a bright apple green.

"Fantastic," he enthused, smiling brightly, his canines leaving an indentation against his bottom lip. I blushed as I looked away, the faint edge of fear feathering against the unfamiliar flare of desire the sight provided.

I couldn't help but glow under his praise, proud of not only having performed an experiment correctly, but of my audience having received it enthusiastically. Henrik and Lara pressed me constantly to keep up with my studies but had no real interest in it themselves. Despite that, nothing was ever good enough for them. They were not impressed by colored fire or bubbling chemical reactions or even explosions.

Feeling buoyant, I pulled over the ingredients for one final trick. I spooned a third white powder into a bell-shaped jar, then poured in a small amount of a different clear liquid. Despite my light-handed pour, the combination bubbled up and over the rim of the glass, puddling around it on the table.

"I'm sorry," I apologized hastily, grabbing a fresh cloth to mop up the mess. My pulse pounded in my ears as my whole body braced for his reaction to the spill. The spectacles slipped off my nose, my anxiety shooting through the roof as they dove for the floor. I squeezed my eyes shut, prepared for the sound of breaking glass, but it never came.

A cool sensation passed along my back, then a warm hand covered mine as I blotted at the wood furiously, breath sawing in and out of my chest. When I opened my eyes again, I was surprised to find Vassago had moved to the other side of me.

"Greta." His voice was low and warm, wrapping around me like a calming embrace. "It's alright. It's only a bit of vinegar and bicarb soda, yes? Two things that are good for cleaning, if I'm not mistaken. That table could surely use a good scrubbing. You've done me a favor by giving me a head start is all." His reaction was so opposite of what I was used to getting, I couldn't do much besides stare at him in response. It didn't help that the strange current was there again, hot and prickly as it sparked between our hands. "Grace was rather curious why I wanted laundry detergent and several items from her spice cupboard. I'm thrilled to be able to report back to her that they were put to excellent use. Especially since some of them were rendered mostly useless for cooking and such by that rat."

I blinked at him again, pulling myself together once he finally removed his hand. "Rat?"

He frowned, head tilted. "Yes. A rather fat one who had been enjoying quite a good life under the stove and in the pantry. Grace worked on getting him out all morning, but she couldn't lift the stove on her own. Once I picked it up, he made a very bold last-ditch effort to avoid being caught, and charged us. Grace is not to be messed with though. Sharp reflexes." He made a gesture across his neck with one finger, the faintest of smiles on his mouth.

My lips parted, and a faint, "Oh," escaped as I went hot again, embarrassed all over at my misinterpretation of the situation. My mouth simply wouldn't cooperate as I tried to explain myself. "I heard … I thought … the sounds …" I gave up and just shook my head.

"You thought Grace and I—" He broke off suddenly and let out a rolling laugh. I focused on my hands, which were tangled in my lap. I didn't think I'd ever felt more mortified than I did in that moment. "I promise you, Greta, there's no woman in my life." He closed his eyes and sighed deeply. "Grace is my *friend*. And all but married to another man, besides." He looked through me then, leaning forward with his elbow on his knee, the pads of his fingers barely brushing my cheek so there was no avoiding his attention. I was too stunned to react. "Though I will say, there's a certain chemist I met recently that I find quite fascinating." He scanned me head to toe, eyes flashing red and the hints of his teeth showing. He sat back, suddenly subdued, and swallowed, eyes dropping from my face.

"Oh." It was hardly my most intelligent reply, but it was all I could muster.

Vassago carried the conversation for the short remainder of my visit. I was too internally scrambled to offer much more than some well-timed responses while I sipped. I hoped I wasn't missing anything vital, but my mind simply couldn't focus.

I was too caught up in the way his eyes seemed to flash red when he looked at me. At wondering if my little tricks were enough. I had no idea what the criteria even was to become a student, never mind a staff member. I wanted to hope that he'd been as impressed as he'd seemed, that his praise was genuine, but then I'd gone and ruined everything with my clumsiness, just like every other job trial before now.

"I'd be happy to have you back any time. I mean that." He stared at me long enough that I shifted uncomfortably in my seat. His jaw flexed several times, betraying some tension his demeanor hid. "Shall I expect you, say, Thursday? Come for lunch perhaps? That should give me enough time to secure some new supplies for you."

Surprise made my eyes widen, but I found myself nodding. "Yes, alright."

"When you're ready, I'll have the carriage take you back."

"That's very generous, thank you." I glanced around, finding the sun rather low. "I'm so sorry. I've overstayed my intention. And yours, I'm sure."

I hadn't meant for him to hear the last bit, but to my further embarrassment, he started to laugh. It was a low, rumbling sound that started somewhere in his broad chest and made my stomach feel funny. "Not at all. You're more than welcome to stay for supper as well. I'm sure Grace has prepared plenty. Her cooking is well worth it, I can attest. And I'll take as much of your company as I can get."

I didn't want to leave. I wanted to stay more than I'd wanted anything in recent years, which was a wonderful turn-around from how I'd felt earlier. Despite how frazzled I felt, I was more relaxed than I'd been in ages. There was no pressure here to be what Henrik and Lara wanted me to be, no looming threat of being scolded for existing outside the narrow box they liked to keep me in.

Regretfully, I declined. "I'm afraid I have to pass for now. I've been away longer than I said I would be. I really should get back."

We both glanced over as the raven returned, landed on the fence, and crowed a knocking kind of call deep in his throat. Seeing him made me unexpectedly happy.

"I'll send Clem to pick you up on Thursday." He studied me for a moment, then gave a gentle nod. "I look forward to your next visit, Greta. I apologize that we didn't have a chance to tour the observatory today. Though it's a very enticing reason for you to come back."

Disappointment flared. I'd forgotten all about it. Once again, it was my fault that something had gone off plan, and he was taking the blame. "I'd love that, thank you."

"Me too. Safe travels." He opened the carriage door, helped me in, and closed it behind me. "Give this to Henrik, if you please?" He handed me a letter sealed with what I assumed was his crest in crimson wax.

"Of course." I gave a gentle wave of my fingers as the carriage began to move, the raven, having observed our conversation from the fence, took flight with a loud squawk.

I watched the raven out the window the whole way back to the manor. He was a familiar dark streak in the sky nearly until the carriage pulled into the Belette's drive. My stomach was tight as I watched the vehicle leave and approached the front door.

Henrik was waiting in the entry for me and all but snatched Vassago's letter from my hand when I offered it. "What's this?" he asked as he broke the wax seal and scanned the words, glancing at me several times as he read through it. "You've been invited to return," he said, sounding mildly surprised.

"Yes."

He narrowed his eyes. "Remain on your best behavior, Greta."

"Sir." I bowed my head, unsure what else to say.

Henrik nodded sharply, then pitched the note into the fireplace as he passed by. I all but floated upstairs once he vanished into his den. Bea ambushed me the moment I walked into my room, demanding a full report of my visit, launching herself from the edge of my bed.

"Finally! I've been here forever waiting for you to get home. I even had to ask Caroline for snacks. And a new cake of soap because yours was looking pitiful, not to mention another towel. I'm going to bring you a new pillow as well, don't worry, I'll sneak it past Mother." She frowned as she rambled, scowling at my worn possessions. "Anyway, how did it go?" Her smile brightened, and she gripped my shoulders with her hands. "Tell me *everything*. Was it amazing?"

"It was so lovely, Bea." I blushed again, remembering my blunder but also the way the campus as a whole had made me feel at home. The sweet touches of concern and kindness.

"You like him." She clapped her hands excitedly. "And if he's giving you flowers and inviting you back, he likes you too."

"Let's not get ahead of ourselves." I sighed, relaying a very short version of my embarrassing misunderstanding about the rat.

"*Psh*. He likes you, and you're a shoo-in for d'Arcan. I'm so happy for you, Greta." Bea's eyes were moist as she pulled me in for a hug.

In truth, the place had grown on me so quickly, I worried I'd be left utterly devastated when the day came I was no longer invited to return. Until then, I promised I would do my best to enjoy every second I had there.

CHAPTER 7
VASSAGO

THURSDAY DAWNED WITH intentions of violence.

To start with, there was no coffee yet when I arrived downstairs. As I glanced out the front windows on my way from the dining room to my classroom, a stone kin man I didn't recognize landed in the courtyard. He was in his stone form, the large body nude aside from some tattered pants, showcasing skin that was a greenish-gray shade. His wings were out, bone spur points menacing despite them being tucked tight against his back. He paced nervously as though trying to decide where to knock.

I stepped out, the morning air heavy with humidity. "Can I help you?"

He spun, looking me over with a scowl. "You are not the archmage."

"No, I'm not." Something about the way he scanned me told me that he would have found me lacking even if I were.

"I need to see Magnus. He's not up in the observatory or patrolling his usual route. Do you know where I can find him?"

"Not at the moment. Is something the matter?" I crossed my arms as the stone kin man glanced around nervously.

"There's an issue that requires his attention. I need to speak with him. It's urgent."

"And you are?"

"General Gaius Caledon," he asserted, ego clearly making him feel it was vital that I know his rank. I was happy to play that game with him if it came down to it, especially because I outranked him. "He knows where to find me."

"What kind of issue, *General*?"

The way he fidgeted as he scowled left me unsettled. "None of your business, *demon*."

His disdain was obvious, but I didn't rise to his bait. I simply raised my eyebrows and smiled, momentarily showcasing the red in my eyes and my fangs, which seemed to leave him suitably uncomfortable.

Lucky for us both, Magnus himself arrived then, Grace in his grasp. He landed with a heavy blast of wind, and Grace ducked away quickly, clearly avoiding the visiting stone kin. Gaius turned his attention to Magnus, clearly glad to have a reason to ignore me.

"You're needed."

"Oh?" Magnus frowned at the visitor.

"Yes, and urgently. A significant demon horde has popped up beyond the edge of the city in the Dread Forest. They're already causing chaos. They are enough in numbers they could breach the city gate soon, and we all know that can't happen. As many soldiers as can be mustered have been called to help fight them." Gaius shifted on his feet. "We were hoping your archmage could join us as well." He clearly didn't appreciate having been given that particular directive.

Lower-level demon hordes had been a problem in Revalia for a number of months; my brother had helped the stone kin put several down already. The nearly mindless creatures the size of ten- or twelve-year-old children were only driven to do what they were instructed to, but were always bent on destruction. Left to their own devices and unhindered, they could destroy a city like Revalia in a matter of weeks. Plenty of damage could be done in mere hours if they weren't stopped, and that was all aside from the trouble that seeing such creatures would have on the human population.

Magnus agreed to join, and I offered my services in Rylan's stead, which earned me a change in Gaius's demeanor from disdain to surprise. I gloated for a moment over that victory, blessing the stone kin with another wide smile, being sure to show my teeth. It only made him frown harder.

Gaius left us after advising the location for the rally point, a cloud of dust swirling behind him.

"Can you get a message to your brother?" Magnus asked.

I agreed to try and told him I would meet him in the dining room, stopping first by my apartment to use the scrying mirror and grab my sword.

"Dammit, Rylan," I swore after several failed attempts to make contact.

I focused on an image of my brother's face in my mind and thought the information at him as firmly as I could, feeling my body fade into mist for a moment before solidifying back again.

I'd never wished to have an owl like he did, but it would have come in very handy for situations like this. If my message was not received, there was nothing I could do about it. As it stood, I was readily providing my service in his place. That would have to be enough.

Grace was doling out tankards of coffee and plates full of food when I got back to the dining room. "Eat up. I don't need to know the details, but I can tell bad news when I see it." She dusted her hands across her apron and returned to the kitchen.

"Should I know anything about Gaius?"

He sighed. "He and Grace have a not so friendly history."

"Oh?"

"Before she and I ... That is, when she was going into the city regularly, they had several uncomfortable interactions. But it's all sorted now."

"Mm." I smirked as he stumbled over his explanation.

"Don't start," Magnus said, shaking his head at my raised eyebrow.

"I said nothing, stone man. But it's about time something was finally done about all that tension boiling over between you. I assume you enjoyed a lovely night away?"

"*About time?*" he mocked. "You basically just got here, demon. And none of your bloody business."

"It was driving me mad, so I can't imagine how relieved everyone else will feel when they find out." He flicked a drop of hot coffee at my face, which earned him a foul hand gesture in return.

The rituals around preparing for battle were varied but never failed to calm me as well as the hilt of a sword in my palm.

"HERE." MAGNUS SAID, handing me a blade as we advanced on the large group of small demons that were scattered around the road on the outside of the city gate. Dozens of stone kin soldiers had arrived and were being given direction by Gaius. "I'm assuming the one strapped to your belt is not a Light blade?"

I shook my head. Light blades were rare; the metal of the blades forged with Heavenly essence from either the blood or feathers of angels. Such materials were strictly monitored by the councils but provided excellent effect against creatures like demons. "No, Rylan is the collector of that type of sword, I'm afraid. I've never had the pleasure."

"Use this one then. Yours will be useless."

I nodded, testing the weight and balance of the one he'd handed me. It was a good fit for my hand and similar to the one I carried. "Thank you."

It didn't take long for the fighting to start. The creatures screeched as they charged around creating chaos, most of them starting the moment they crawled out of a glowing rift in the earth. Stone kin soldiers dispatched them as quickly as they could, blood and gore staining the dirt and flesh beginning to stink as it baked in the sun.

Rylan flew in not long after we'd begun to battle in earnest. Our habit of fighting in tandem slipped over us as easily as a well-loved shirt. He twisted left, I went right. His blade plunged into the chest of a demon on the ground, and I swiped at the throat of one running at us. If he needed someone at his front instead of his back, or perhaps I needed to dodge a well-aimed blow, I could call the mist and blink out of my body only to reappear where I was best needed or just out of range. It was a dance we'd perfected in Hell, and our quarry was not that different here.

"I'm glad my message arrived," I grunted, tugging my borrowed blade out from between a creature's ribs. "Hang up the damned mirror."

"Come on, Vago, aren't you the least bit impressed some of our telepathy still works? I thought that was something we'd lost altogether. It's good to know that some time in close proximity has given it back."

"I'm happy it worked so you could still be useful while on your country holiday, but the two-way mirror is much easier. Hang. It. Up."

He darted off with the help of his wings and a blast of the electrical magic he possessed to take care of a cluster of little demons that had ganged up on a young stone kin soldier.

Somehow, the little bastards had started to get the upper hand and the stone kin were getting worn out, cornered and injured. If we didn't turn things around, this was going to go very, very badly.

"If either of you demons have been holding back, now's the time to show off a bit, yeah?" Magnus called out, he and Gaius grunting and thrashing as they helped a handful of stone kin soldiers get out from under a surge of the vicious little demons.

I inhaled, the stench of blood ripe on the air, every sensation in my body amplified. I'd mostly managed to compartmentalize since Greta's visit, but here, there was no more resisting my curse. I called it to me, revulsion heavy in my chest despite knowing this was needed.

A red haze descended over my vision and my fangs ached, begging to be put to use. Rage, incandescent in my veins, moved my body from one little demon to the next, my hand pulling at their coarse hair so their necks would be bared to me as the bloodlust curse I was haunted by took over. I tore through throats and slashed my blade, disgusted at myself even as I reveled in the warm splash against my face as their life drained from their severed arteries. Memories assaulted me as I tore through my victims. I blocked what I could as I moved methodically, blade and fangs taking down one after the next.

My curse dragged me through dozens of demons without flagging. When I finally regained some of my wits, I found I'd freed three separate groups of cornered stone kin soldiers and allowed them to regain dominance over the situation.

Breath heaved in and out of my lungs, and my arms moved almost of their own accord until suddenly, there were no more bottom-feeder demons to slay, and we were alone.

After what seemed like an awkwardly long silence where everyone stared between me and the absolute carnage around us in awed silence, Rylan grinned and clapped me on the shoulder.

"I'm glad I said something," Magnus chuffed with a grin, looking at several minor wounds on his arms. "You have my thanks."

A growly cheer went up through the lines of stone kin, but I couldn't rouse my excitement. The soldiers began to pile bodies for incineration, and after lending his power to expedite the process, Rylan left, wasting no time getting back to his wife and the peace of his manor.

Gaius approached, scowling. "Thank you," he said, voice tight. "There was a moment there …" His mouth curled in disgust and he shook his head. "I appreciate you saving my men and protecting Ophelia."

I said nothing but offered a slight bow, one hand wiping at the mess around my mouth.

Magnus gave a half smile as the other man stiffly walked away. "He'll learn."

"Ophelia?"

Magnus smiled. "Yes, one of the oldest of us left."

"She lives nearby?"

"Very. But her land is well warded and far enough inside the trees she was safe from danger." Magnus shook his head, mouth thinned as he glanced around, deep in thought. "This attack was too close both to her and Revalia proper for my comfort. They are getting bolder."

I followed his gaze to find several of the young stone kin men throwing glances at me over their shoulders, surprised gratitude on many of their faces.

"They see you," Magnus said. "Both of you. Helping us. For most, hearing that upper-level demons—princes at that—are aligned with our causes is laughable. But they've seen it now. They'll start to understand that not much is as it seems, and we have allies in unexpected places."

"Is that what I am?" I teased, fatigue beginning to make itself known as an ache in my muscles. "An ally?"

"Something like that," Magnus snorted, one of his massive hands patting me roughly on the back.

"I suppose that's not so bad, stone man."

I went back through the city gate on foot, needing some time to shake off the lingering sensations succumbing to the curse left behind. One of the soldiers loaned me a cloak to cover myself with so I wouldn't scare the wits out of anyone who saw me, covered in blood as I was.

I'd crossed into the neighborhoods full of large estates when a noise drew my attention. I paused, scanning the thin forest that lined the side of the road. As I sniffed, my guard went up as I found the faint scent of sulfur.

Just as I pulled the blade from my belt, three lower-level demons surged from the shadows. "How did you manage to get all the way in here?" I cursed, slashing out with my borrowed sword. One of the little troublemakers fell, but the other two were intent on taking me to the ground, both pulling on the cloak I now regretted wearing.

The grating screech they let out roused my rage, and I was able to fell the second with a quick stab through the heart as the third climbed on my back. He yanked back the hood on the cloak, causing my hair to spill out as I turned my head to the side. He leaned forward over my shoulder, but before he could so much as lift his blade, I opened my mouth wide and crushed through his throat, tossing him to the ground as a flash of his memories passed over me.

I was huddled over his body, his blood fresh on my mouth when a carriage drove by. I stayed there, hoping to have been disguised by the shadowy tree line. When I thought enough time had passed, I turned to be sure I hadn't drawn any attention.

My heart clenched as wide, intelligent hazel eyes met mine through the small window on the back of d'Arcan's carriage.

CHAPTER 8
GRETA

Dressed in a worn linen shirt and some hand-me-down men's trousers, I climbed into the carriage Thursday to discover Grace waiting inside. I was a mess of nerves as I took my seat, the days at the manor having crawled by as I waited for my next visit.

"Right on time!" She smiled at me and tapped on the ceiling with her knuckle to alert the driver we were ready to go once I got seated. "I must admit, I may make this a new part of my routine. Usually, I walk into the market on shopping days. I might get spoiled having Clem drive me around." She winked at me, my gaze pulled out the back window over Grace's shoulder as the carriage began to move down the road. "It's very nice to see you again, Greta."

Shock turned my blood to ice as ruby eyes stared back at me through the window. On the side of the road stood a man dressed in a heavy cloak. His face was largely obscured by the blood smeared across his skin, but he reminded me, unmistakably, of Vassago. And what were those creatures on the road near his feet?

"You too," I replied, feeling numb.

"Everything alright?" Grace's eyebrows pulled together. "You look pale."

"I just ... I saw something ..."

I blinked several times as the carriage turned the corner, removing the man from my view. I instantly doubted my own eyes, my insides warring over how impossible it was to have seen any such thing.

"Oh?" Grace turned and looked out the window herself, but it was too late. "Should we stop?"

"I ... I'm not sure. There was a man. Animals, maybe? Blood." Speaking his name aloud made it too real, too true, so I held it back.

"Ah." Grace tutted with her tongue and reached forward to pat my leg. "Sadly, there's been a sickness among the livestock this year, I heard several vendors talking about it at the market. Sudden and brutal. I hate that you saw something so terrible." Silence weighed heavily between us for several long moments. Finally, Grace cleared her throat. "I don't mean to be forward, but I owe you an apology. That mess with the rat? I had no idea it would look like ... *that*. Vassago told me what happened, and I'm terribly embarrassed."

"Thank you," I said, unsure what else could be said and too distracted to say anything coherent.

"Mr. Feland is a good man, Greta. You're the very first guest he's brought to campus since he arrived months ago." She leaned in conspiratorially. I swallowed and tried to focus on her words as my mind rationalized how it wasn't possible the man I'd just seen covered in blood was the same Vassago who had brought me a pillow and blanket when I fell asleep on his sofa. "He sees something special in you. And I can understand why." She winked, and I softened to her kindness, deciding that I'd perhaps seen a hunter perhaps, or ... anything, really, except him. "Well then. Tell me, are you tired often?"

Lara may have spent my life making me believe I was lazy, but I knew that wasn't true. I couldn't help my need for sleep. "Yes. I nap at least once most days. Doesn't matter how much I sleep at night, when my energy runs out, it's just gone—though I never have much to begin with."

"Hmm." Grace looked thoughtful, but her interest was lacking the judgment I usually got from others when they found out my requirement for sleep on a daily basis. "I'll bet that's frustrating. How is your hand?"

"Fine, thank you." She held one of hers out and I reluctantly offered mine. She examined the nearly healed burns as we bumped down the road. "Did Vassago tell you about that?"

She clucked her tongue. "It's best you know up front that there isn't much that escapes my notice. The archmage—d'Arcan's headmaster, Rylan—is quite adept at healing, but he's not always around. I try to be sure I'm well abreast of basic skills, given the students that come through my kitchen." Grace's words were firm but kind. She smiled at me again and I thawed a bit further. "I'm sure I have an ointment that he or his wife made up that might help, and I'll put together some energizing teas. You'll have to try them all and let me know if there's one you prefer."

"You don't have to go to any special trouble on my behalf, Grace. I'm not sure there's much to be done about my condition, honestly. I've been this way as long as I can remember, no matter the attempted treatment. I need more sleep than most people and more time to heal, that's all. I appreciate the concern, though."

"Well, I do like to tinker around with recipes, so it's no bother. If they help, all the better, if not, then at least we've got some new options in the kitchen, yes? Yes." She slapped her thigh with her palm, settling the matter. "And you're in luck. Today, we'll be arriving just in time for lunch. I left the girls to finish up for me. They're all adept learners. It's lovely to watch them flourish." She smiled, her pride evident in the way she glowed when she spoke of them.

"I can't wait," I admitted honestly. I'd been too caught up in moving furniture and shifting around the contents in the set of bedrooms Lara was preparing to refurbish that I'd worked off my simple breakfast in no time, and I knew better than to ask for anything else. As if to punctuate my hunger, my stomach let out an embarrassing noise.

She winked at me. "I'm so glad you're coming with an appetite."

I was learning that whatever I thought the response was going to be based on my experience at the manor, I should expect the opposite from these people. It was odd but welcome, to say the very least.

Grace filled the quiet between us with chatter she'd heard in the marketplace. Most of it made no matter to me—these were people and situations I'd never be involved in—but I appreciated her including me as though I had any idea what she was talking about. Almost like we were friends. It was an excellent distraction from what I'd seen, as well.

As we got out of the carriage, the raven flapped down to the fence from high up in a tree.

"Hello again," I said to him, getting the same close inspection as before. With soft caws, he fluffed his feathers. He let me get several steps closer than I had last time before shuffling a few steps along the top of the fence.

Grace stared at him. "Do you know this bird?"

"He greeted me last visit."

"Oh. Well, hello, I guess," she said, tilting her head as she watched him right back.

"Have you never seen him? Vassago said the same."

She shook her head. "No, but that means little. I'm not outside on the grounds much, and when I am, I'm not terribly observant. Shall we?" She gestured toward the door, and he took flight. A large shadow flitted across the very edge of my vision, disappearing beyond the roof of the observatory as Grace resumed her chatter.

She filled the quiet between us all the way up to the moment she left me at the large round table in the dining room.

"I'm sure Vassago will be along momentarily. Make yourself comfortable."

I hesitated, then offered, "I'm no cook, but I am skilled at washing dishes, if you need any help?"

"Absolutely not! You're a guest. Though perhaps if you get promoted to resident, I'll consider taking you up on that offer." She winked as she strode into the kitchen.

Instead of sitting, I took the opportunity to take a closer look at the animal carvings on the main posts throughout the room. Grace's mention of me becoming a resident on top of the strange encounter left me restless.

I'd studied the details of the owl and was captivated by the raven when I heard footsteps coming toward me from the hall. Turning as the sound got close, I found Vassago with a bright smile on his mouth.

I argued with myself once again, doubtful that there was any way this polished, well-dressed noble had taken any part of what I'd seen on the side of the road. And yet, when he smiled a certain way ... I shivered, trying to shake off the odd sensation fizzing in my veins.

Behind Vassago stood a virtual mountain of a man. If I'd ever felt too tall at the manor, I was positively small in comparison to either of these men—the one behind my host, in particular.

"I'm so glad you could make it, Greta. This is a ... friend." His eyebrows dipped, as though the word felt wrong.

"Yes, we're something like friends, devil." The man grinned.

"Right, yes. In any case, Greta, this is Magnus. Magnus, Greta. She's the chemist I mentioned."

"Pleased to meet you." He stuck out a giant hand for me to shake but changed his mind and pulled me into a brief hug instead, smiling broadly. "Which house do you claim, Greta?"

I glanced between the two men, confused. Vassago saw my hesitation and inclined his head slightly, indicating I could trust Magnus. I also had a niggling of recognition when I looked at him, which was odd. "Sorry?"

Magnus tilted his head to the side. "Which house? Gargoyle or grotesque?" I shook my head even more confused. "What is your family name?" Clever brown eyes searched my features as though he were trying to puzzle it out himself.

"I'm sorry, I don't know what you mean."

The massive man's face fell, surprise replacing the boisterous joy. "Who is your mother, child? Do you know her name?"

"Rowan." I barely whispered the name; the only thing I had left of her. I hadn't dared speak it in years.

Magnus faltered. It was odd seeing such a powerful man sag, but his whole body lurched as though I'd punched him. A sad smile lifted one corner of his mouth. "Oh, little Libelle. Is it really you?" His broad hands cupped the sides of my face, his own eyes moist. Air hissed between my teeth. Fear chased through my veins alongside several other messy emotions.

Vassago, who had been quietly watching from a reasonable distance, was suddenly several paces closer and appeared almost fuzzy around the edges. I blinked several times to clear my vision, confused as to how I'd not seen him moving.

"Rowan is my sister. I have missed her very much these many years. Oh, little niece. I am so happy to see you! I thought you were lost to us, the same as her. You must tell me everything."

And then I found I couldn't breathe at all thanks to the massive arms wrapped enthusiastically around my body, my cheek pressed into a chest that might as well have been made of granite.

"Easy, statue," Vassago chided gently, a frown on his mouth.

Grace popped out of the kitchen at that moment, doing a double take as she spotted me being smothered with affection. "Magnus, please don't break that lovely woman."

He rumbled a deep chuckle, loosened his grip, and took a step back, though his hands remained on my shoulders. "Saints be. I can hardly believe it. Grace, this woman is my niece! We must celebrate!"

"Right," she said, drawing out the word as she glanced between us. She narrowed her eyes thoughtfully at the large gargoyle, then clapped her hands together and strode back toward the kitchen with a broad smile. "I'll get the wine!"

CHAPTER 9
GRETA

ERVOUSNESS QUICKLY GAVE way to a surprisingly deep hunger for stories about a mother I barely remembered. As we made our way through fresh bread, stew, and a chocolate cake that might have been the most delicious thing ever made, Magnus relayed several of his favorite memories. It was far and away the most magical meal I'd ever eaten.

He'd also given me a brief explanation about the difference between gargoyle and grotesque—not much, all told—after I'd come to grips with the fact that such creatures as stone kin were real at all. While I'd felt a little numb during the conversation, something about what he said rang true within me in a way that I knew immediately he wasn't making things up. I'd always been fascinated by stories about beasts and creatures, while at the same time feeling an odd kinship with them, and it was thrilling to know that perhaps not every part of my favorite tales were fabrications.

"When you were born? Everything changed. Rowan never took her eyes off of you. She was so worried you would break, like a fragile little egg. You were little bitty, granted, but all babies are like that. And stone kin ones bounce better than most if dropped." He boomed another laugh, and I sank further into the warm nostalgia that both his stories and the wine had given me. It was the first time I'd had a real connection to any kind of family, even the hope of one. "Besides, we have wings! We're built for sterner stuff than that. But she wanted to protect you." He waved a broad hand as he chewed. "I was the same way with all of mine." He paused, tone going soft, his eyes crinkling at the edges like the idea brought him pain. "Have you been here, all this time, Libelle?"

"I'm not sure. We only come into Revalia during the summer months," I explained.

He frowned. "What should I call you? I knew you only as Libelle, but if it's Greta you prefer, I shall use that name instead."

I tested out both names out in my mind, seeing how they felt. I'd always felt Greta was harsh on the tongue, but it had been my name as long as I could remember.

"I don't mind which you use, but I'm far more likely to answer to Greta. Libelle is very beautiful, though." I found myself blushing, ashamed that I was ready to switch names on a whim just because of how it sounded to me.

Magnus glanced between Vassago and I. "When you say 'we' only come into the city during the summer, who is *we*?"

"She's a member of the Belette household," Vassago told him, lifting his wineglass. Vassago had been silent but watchful as Magnus took up my attention and told his stories. I appreciated that he hadn't seemed at all upset by the change in our visit plans. He and Grace had also both given me reassurance that Magnus was being truthful about everything as he explained about the stone kin. Grace and Magnus were also very obviously a couple, which put to rest any lingering doubts I had around the rat situation.

I was glad to be able to put several of the stressful thoughts I'd been dealing with aside, even if that meant being presented with something new, like being stone kin.

"Mm." Magnus's mouth pinched into a straight line. "Have they treated you well?"

I hesitated, weighing my words, but that seemed to be enough for both of them to come to a less-than-favorable conclusion. Which, honestly, wasn't at all wrong.

"They took me in as a child. I don't remember arriving, or much at all from the earliest years, though. They've kept me fed and housed, employed as staff. There are few luxuries in my life, but I'm provided for well enough."

Magnus sneered. "If you're a servant to them and not a beloved daughter, it is *not* enough." He pounded a frustrated fist on the table, apologizing when he saw me flinch. "Apologies. I'm not angry with you, please don't misunderstand. I can't believe you've been here all this time. You should have been cherished and taught so many things, not simply ... *tolerated* until you could be employed."

"It's alright." A warm sense of potential belonging flowed through me, made my worries fade into the background of all the noise in my mind.

"It's an incredibly difficult task to pull off, you being hidden in plain sight all this time," Vassago said, brows pulled together. "How has that been accomplished?"

I cleared my throat, glancing between them. "Since I was a child, one of Henrik's rules was that I remain unseen. I am not allowed in the city or around guests who don't already know of my existence." I slid a glance at Vassago, feeling the heat of a blush on my cheeks. "There's only been one time I failed with that one."

"Perhaps I should take back my apology for running into you that night," he teased.

"Henrik always said it was for my own safety. I'm not sure why, but perhaps if someone took or harmed my mother, they might very well be looking for me, too."

"*We* were looking for you, Greta. For her. I was. My sons and daughters, soldiers. Other stone kin. We've never stopped. I can't help but wonder what she was mixed up in. I've never once heard her name uttered alongside Henrik Belette's, either, so how you ended up with them is a mystery. For you to have been right here ... It breaks my heart that none of us knew." His large hand covered mine on the tabletop. He radiated sincerity. I'd never felt half as comfortable at the Belette house as I did inside d'Arcan's walls. The realization was profound, compressing my chest with emotion. "Though I will say, being unseen is somewhat of a common thing all stone kin are used to trying to be. Will you come back to d'Arcan soon?"

I glanced at Vassago, who grinned in a way that made me blush.

"She's welcome back as soon and as often as she'd like."

"Wonderful. I hope you come very, very soon." He heaved a sigh. "I regret leaving you, but I have an appointment I cannot miss. I am endlessly glad to have been here to see you today, niece."

His use of that word made my heart thump. "Me too."

Magnus stood, opening his arms. I rose and gratefully allowed myself to be folded into them. Magnus smelled like the air right before a rainstorm. I couldn't put words to why, but I suspected my mother had smelled much the same based on my body's inclination to relax in his grasp.

Once he finally let me go, Grace lovingly shooed us all out of the dining room. "Mr. Feland, why don't you take her somewhere with a cushioned seat for a while? Or maybe for a walk around the grounds? Clem will take her back whenever she's ready."

I appreciated her kind delivery, but the reminder that I had to leave soon saddened me. I didn't want to leave this welcoming place or the people. Especially not now that I knew I had actual family here. I'd spent nearly thirty years alone, just an orphan the Belettes had taken in who later became one of their maids. I wanted something *real* far more than I could express, especially now that I'd had the briefest taste of such a thing.

"Which do you prefer, Greta?" Vassago asked, offering me a

hand to get up from my dining chair. The brief contact sent a rush of heat through my body, a strange mixture of apprehension and lust. No matter where we were, he was attentive of my needs. It was the exact opposite of what I was used to and an incredible temptation.

"I could use some air," I admitted, my chest heavy. "But I'd hate to leave without having seen the observatory again."

"The observatory it is," he agreed, leading the way. "There's usually a breeze up there, and it's cool even when the sun is at its hottest because of the stone."

Despite the fact that we'd just finished eating, Grace reappeared with a basket that was as big as her torso. She handed it off to Vassago and, with a laugh, said, "You go on with this. Walking all those stairs is probably good for me, but I don't care for it. Enjoy your visit." She winked at me again before leaving.

"Shall we?" Vassago inclined his head, and I followed him down the hall and then up the stairs. And up and up.

His pace was sedate, and he kept up a conversation the whole time about the history of the building. As we crested the landing, my heart pounded for a reason other than the exertion of climbing all those steps.

"Oh my." I took in the large open space with awe, the marble pillars evenly spaced around the dome were perfectly glossy in the sunlight. Half of the roof was closed, providing shade, and the breeze he'd mentioned was indeed cool despite it being midday in the middle of summer.

"My brother's pride and joy," he smirked, setting the basket on one of the tables that ringed the room.

"I can understand why. These telescopes! They're magnificent. The stargazing must be unmatched."

"It is. Perhaps you'll be able to remain after dark and see for yourself. And once you perfect how to make those fireworks, this will be the best place to view them in the whole city." I glowed with the compliment he'd so kindly layered in. "Have a seat." He gestured to the collection of plush cushions piled up on the floor.

Once I'd gotten comfortable, he handed me a plate with an assortment of finger foods for us to share. I was stuffed, but it gave me something to do with my hands.

"Are those charts?" I asked, gesturing to the mass of parchment not only hanging on the walls but also piled up to the point of nearly spilling off a nearby table.

"Yes, Rylan has habitually tracked the sky for as long as I can recall."

My breath flowed easier as I relaxed into the cushion and nibbled on some sweet fresh berries. The room was massive, and even the smallest sound resounded with an echo.

"The rest of the building is beautiful but so unassuming. I wouldn't have expected this, even with being able to see the tower from anywhere in Revalia."

He grinned. "The marble is truly spectacular. The quarry had an abundance at that time. I heard there were several sculptors who traveled here to perfect their work."

"Oh? Perhaps that's where the statue in the maze comes from."

"The manor has a maze? I'm afraid I don't see much of the property beyond the study."

"Yes. I've always loved it." I flushed under his rapt golden gaze. He held a dark-red grape between his fingers and thumb, and I found myself unable to look away as he placed it in his mouth. The crunching noise as he chewed made my whole body tingle. I had zero self-preservation, because I continued, "There's a statue in the center, in a fountain. An angel."

"Oh?"

I found myself describing it, in detail, my arms going out as I described the wings, my body taking up the pose he stood in upon the rocks. He smiled in response, relaxed as he did that thing where all his attention was focused entirely on me. Feeling important was quickly becoming my favorite new sensation.

"I'd like to see that. The next time I visit, you'll have to give me a proper tour." Mortification set in. There was nothing quite like showing your entire soul to someone by accident. I worried that it would only happen again and again if I spent any kind of time around this man. "What do you know about angels and demons, Greta?"

I shook my head. "Nothing much, I suppose. That they are enemies, I guess. Though from what little I know of faith, I don't really understand why."

"I suppose, as with most things, it's kind of a long story. Shall I tell it?"

His voice was soothing as he told me about angels, how some had chosen to fall from the grace of Heaven because of a fundamental disagreement for which there was no compromise. How those angels had become high-ranking demons in Hell instead, each with their own unique talent and form. How stone kin had come to be as a defense against demons for humans. Then the origin of humans, including a story about Adam's first wife, Lilith. How she was made from the same clay as him, and when he tried to treat her as his lesser instead of the equal she had been created as, she sprouted wings and flew out of the garden. Lilith became the alleged mother of all demons, though the fallen angels could clearly not be included in that.

"There are many versions of those tales to choose from, of course, but that's how I know them."

I found myself blinking slowly against the quiet. I already missed the soft, warm cadence of his voice. "I'm afraid the day is already catching up to me," I said, failing to stifle my yawn. I tried hiding it behind a hand instead but needn't have bothered because my jaw gave a crack that echoed around the marble room.

"Are you in a rush to get back?" he asked, looking as relaxed as I felt, his lithe body reclined over several cushions, his back propped up on one that was folded in half so he wasn't entirely supine, one foot flat on the floor and his knee bent.

Any sculptor worth his salt would have been thrilled to capture such a pose.

I wasn't in any hurry to leave, but my employers were bound to be waiting for me when I got there. "No, I'm not."

"Good. Then relax here. You've no reason to leave yet."

I closed my eyes briefly, several disconnected thoughts swirling through my mind. "Libelle is a lovely name. I wonder if it means something in particular."

I heard the smile in his voice and turned my head, blinking heavily as he said, "I believe it means *dragonfly*. Are you a dragon, Greta? Have I just not provoked your fire well enough yet?"

"No." I smiled back, never ungrateful for his praise. "Not a dragon, nor can I fly." I frowned at the admission, remembering Magnus's face when he had described stone kin babies as having wings.

"We can discuss all that another time. Rest, little dragonfly. You're safe here."

The truth of those three simple words echoed through me as my eyelids became too heavy to lift again. I was vaguely aware of some quiet shuffling, then felt the warmth of a blanket being laid over me. I was powerless to stop myself from becoming accustomed to his quiet kindness and might die of loss should I ever have to go without it again.

CHAPTER 10
VASSAGO

I'D PLANNED TO leave my brother and his wife be for as long as they needed, especially after he had to fly in to help with the demon horde. Unfortunately, it had become necessary to speak with him, and I didn't want to waste time flying to his manor or energy trying to contact him telepathically.

Greta's last visit had left me feeling urgent about ensuring that she could be at d'Arcan as much as she wanted to. It had taken everything in me to send her home after our relaxing afternoon in the observatory.

After the incident on the road, I needed her to feel safe, craved being able to provide that for her. I also had a bizarre compulsion to touch her, to be as near as possible to her at all times. It was maddening. I was no mage but couldn't help but wonder if perhaps I'd accidentally invoked some kind of spell.

There were too many reactions on her part to ordinary things that left me convinced she wasn't being treated well. I hoped I wasn't responsible for any of her abrupt movements or tense stares, but knew the possibility was there after having seen what she had. There were dozens of ways to explain it away, and surely she'd rationalized however she could, but I'd seen the brief flashes of fear in her eyes.

Instead of the large mirror on the table in my classroom, I used the enchanted one in my apartment to try to contact my brother. I could only hope he'd finally unpacked the one I'd sent along with them.

After several long minutes, my brother's face swam into view.

"Saints, Vago, did you intend to make it sound like someone was shrieking?"

"Of course I did. How else would you hear it?"

"We just spent what felt like an hour looking for an injured woman in the house, only to find it was your mirror under a pile of cloth in my medicine case." He scowled, staring at me as though trying to decide whether I was serious or not.

I was. It was the most effective way to alert that a two-way mirror was active.

"Perhaps you should have *hung it* somewhere then, like I told you to not only before you left, but last I saw you. What do you have it standing on? Is it secure?"

"Secure enough."

I crossed my arms, seeing my brother's lie. "It's propped up on books, isn't it."

His mouth tightened, and he sighed. "Perhaps, but it's not in danger of breaking if that's what you're worried about. It will either fall into my lap or onto the carpet."

I pinned him with a stare, but he remained unbothered and just settled further into his seat. He was in his tower office by the looks of the sofa. I knew from experience it was one of the most comfortable pieces of furniture to ever exist, no matter how worn it was.

"How is the countryside?"

"Everything is fine. It's quiet here, which honestly took a bit of getting used to. I could ask you the same. Is everything running smoothly? Did you meet with the chemist you mentioned? Perhaps I should have stayed after the battle to catch up."

I smiled. There was nothing to do with this place that Rylan wouldn't find a way to worry about, even when he was supposed to be honeymooning. "I did. She's very talented. I've had her back to visit several times. Have you spoken to Magnus recently?"

"No, why?"

I hesitated, unsure if I should be sharing the news. "It appears as though they're related."

"Truly? She's stone kin?"

"Yes, his niece."

Calla's face drifted past the glass behind Rylan. "Who has a stone kin niece? Hello, Vassago. This is an incredible device, I'm glad you sent it! Though you did give me a bit of a heart attack when it went off just now. We could hear it all the way down in the library office." She waved her fingertips then disappeared from view.

"Hello, Calla. Apologies, I didn't mean to scare you."

"Our new chemist," Rylan answered her, "is Magnus's niece it seems."

"Truly? How wonderful! I can't wait to meet her."

"I haven't said I'm bringing her on yet," I argued.

"You didn't need to. I knew you would from the start, and anyway, I can see it all over your face. You like her," my brother smirked. I narrowed my eyes at him. "And you're not denying it." His head tilted to the side, and his smile faded as he stared at my clenched jaw. "Are you taking the tincture?"

"Of course I am."

"Is it helping? You seemed to be rather in a flare last I saw you, though you did have good cause."

I appreciated his careful wording. I trusted Calla, but the bloodlust curse was my secret to keep or reveal. "The effectiveness seems to be decreasing and I think it's giving me indigestion. Did you change the formula?"

"No. Not since we started making it for you, what, a century ago? And there's nothing in it that would cause reflux," he frowned, rubbing his chin thoughtfully. "In fact, several of the ingredients are used to resolve such a thing. Must be something you're eating." His eyes widened. "Don't tell Grace I said that."

I laughed at the horror in his face but understood the fear. Insulting Grace's cooking might mean never having the pleasure of eating it again. "My lips are sealed. But something is definitely off the last little while. I'm ... unbalanced." It was an incredible understatement.

"Mm. Have there been any other problems?"

"No, but in case there are, hang the blasted mirror. I don't want to rely on simply *thinking* things at you, should I need to get in touch."

"Alright, I swear I'll find a place for it. But I'm covering it up between uses."

"Do as you like, brother, but get it off the books and onto a wall somewhere."

"Yes, yes. Are you and Magnus getting along alright?"

"Magnus and I are fine. He won't have had a chance to tell you, but we also took care of the men responsible for Grace's capture." Rylan blinked once, then sat forward with his elbows on his knees. I heard Calla inhale, and his eyes flashed red as he processed what I'd said. "They were taken to the camp."

"When?"

"Shortly after you left."

"Good," Calla bit the word out.

Rylan ground his teeth together but nodded. Calla put her

hand on his shoulder, and he covered it with his own. "I'm glad it's handled, and they are where they belong. Is Grace alright?"

"She seems relieved, as expected. Magnus was insistent she get an apology." My lips curled at the memory of them all begging for mercy that would never be given. "Also, I'm fairly certain she and Magnus finally figured themselves out."

Calla made a squeak of a noise and clapped her hands together. "Good for them!"

Rylan sighed, a smile forming on his mouth as he relaxed. "Thank the saints for that."

"My thoughts exactly."

"That's quite the report," he said, giving a heavy sigh.

"I'm sorry to bring so much to you at once, but I have one more request. Would you mind showing me Calla's necklace? I've got a lead I'm following for the one I'm searching for, but I think seeing hers may help."

"Her necklace?" My brother frowned at me.

"The one I'm seeking is very similar."

"I'll get it," Calla offered.

"So, is this woman a chemist or an alchemist?" Rylan asked while his wife was away.

"Both. She's demonstrated a significant skill in chemistry, though I believe her current employers may have stifled her growth. She's opening up the more she's allowed to enjoy what she's doing."

"Maybe they didn't understand it." Rylan shrugged.

"Likely." I nodded, knowing that Henrik and Lara wouldn't know a good bit of science if it was right in front of them. The only thing they seemed interested in was gold. Something tickled at my mind, at that thought, but never fully formed.

"If you see her talent, then I'm happy to have her, in any case. And alchemy?"

"She's got interest, and with her skill in chemistry I'm convinced she'll figure it out. We'll try some things soon." I swallowed the acid that crept up and pushed forward. "She'd like to speak to you when you return. Your talents overlap in many ways."

"Of course. What about Lilith's book? If you're still taking the tincture, I assume you haven't found what you hoped inside."

"I'm making my way through as I can, but it's denser than I remember it being."

"A couple centuries and several new contributors will do that. Have you managed to get it fully into your possession yet?"

"No. And having to go to the manor to see it is not optimal. But this necklace thing may solve that for me as well. I do worry that Greta saw me ..." I shook my head.

"Saw you?"

"After the horde. There were stragglers, inside the city gates."

Rylan sat forward urgency in his expression. "Inside?"

"Yes. I've already told Magnus, and they're increasing patrols. No others have been found. But I had just put them down when the carriage passed by. Our carriage. She looked out the window ..." I pressed my lips together, her horrified gaze haunting my memories. It had been all I could manage to dispose of the bodies and fly back quickly so I could clean up before she arrived.

"She won't dwell," Rylan said, breaking me out of my thoughts.

"How can you be sure?"

"Because she won't be able to reconcile what she saw. It won't make any sense."

"That feels overly simplistic."

"Is she acting strangely?"

I considered. A flinch here, a suspicious glance there. "At times, I suppose, but we hardly know one another. There's no telling what she endures at the manor, either."

Rylan grunted, looking off to the side. The change in his face indicating his wife had returned. I wondered if all mate situations created such an outwardly visible bond.

"Here it is," Calla said as her hand and the jewelry came into view.

"Thank you." I leaned as close to the mirror as I could without touching it, committing the details of the metal setting to memory. It was a very unique style and matched the sketch Henrik had given me almost exactly. The only difference was the stone. Calla's was a moonstone, where the Belettes sought one made with a white opal. "At which jeweler did you find the matching ring?"

"Callihan's. It's the one over by the Straw Horse. Why?"

"I'm going to visit them again. They didn't have any memory of a necklace like this the first time I went by, but I think I may have asked the wrong questions."

"Alright." The suspicion was clear in my brother's tone.

"Everything is fine."

"As you say." Rylan sat back in his chair, watching me carefully, the same as he would have if I were occupying the room as him.

"And Calla? How is your magic coming along?" I asked.

Her smiling face appeared behind Rylan. "Nicely, thank you. Would you like to see?"

Rylan's pride in her was the only thing that kept him from getting cross with me for changing the subject, I was sure. "Of course I would." I'd never had a little sister, so I indulged her where I could. Besides, I really was interested in her progress; her earth-based magic was fascinating.

She turned and picked up a vase from a nearby table, one positively bursting with dark-purple calla lilies. "I'm getting much better with my control," she muttered as she began to focus, her hands wrapped around the bottom of the glass. The flowers all began to shrivel and droop, aging days in mere seconds. Then they reversed to their original vibrant states, full of life and dewy like they'd just been picked.

"I'm impressed. I'm glad you're making such excellent progress." I smiled at her, and Rylan's eyes flashed in warning. A fated mate's possessiveness was nothing to be trifled with, but I did love to poke at my brother at every opportunity.

"There's more tincture in my apartment," he said. "The small case on the table near the bookshelf."

I nodded, planning to double up on doses until my emotional state started to settle. "I'll be in touch. Enjoy your time away."

I waved my hand, severing the connection before Rylan could do more than open his mouth. Getting the last word was something I always strived to accomplish, no matter which of my brothers I was speaking to. It might have been petty, but it was a mission I rarely failed at.

I smiled as I tucked the sketch back into my vest and prepared to visit some merchants.

CHAPTER 11
GRETA

I COULDN'T STOP MYSELF from accepting Vassago's invitations to return. I felt powerless to refuse him, especially when he gave me that lopsided grin that made me feel like he could see straight through me. Like he knew exactly how desperate I was to continue coming. Besides, I didn't *want* to say no. I wanted to spend as much time at d'Arcan, and with him, as I could.

I left the Belette house with a heady mixture of excitement washed in fear again and again, visiting d'Arcan several more times over the next couple of weeks. Each time I walked through the front doors was more and more like coming home. With Grace and her helpers' enthusiastic welcomes, and Vassago's gentle smiles and increasingly common soft touches, my anxiety faded and comfort grew. The raven also always found a way to say hello when I was there. He was an odd fellow, but I found myself looking forward to his croaks and the dark streak of his figure following me in the sky when I left again.

Half the time when I got to the carriage, Grace was inside waiting for me. She'd gossip at me during the trip, and inevitably find an opportunity to feed me or have me try out her newest "energizing" tea blend. It never did help much, aside from being as delicious as everything else she prepared, but she seemed unaffected by my disappointing reports.

I never again saw anything disturbing out the rear window on the side of the road and I started to doubt that I'd seen quite what I thought I'd had in the first place.

Vassago and I worked side by side in his classroom with him showing me some of the unorthodox ways he communicated with people or how he located missing objects and different ways he practiced his craft. He'd fetch me ingredients and tools so I could continue to practice my chemistry, allowed me full access to his vast library of books to find recipes of interest or research my stone kin heritage. He was always calm and encouraging, even when I didn't get the result I wanted.

One of my visits, I attempted the experiment I'd been hung up on since before leaving the manor. Instead of watching from across the room like he usually did, Vassago lingered at the table with me. Nervous but also hyper-focused because of his nearness, when it came time to finalize the mixture, I flinched.

"Trust yourself," he said quietly, breath warm against my ear as his hand wrapped around mine, steadying the flask so I didn't lose any of the precisely measured solution.

I'd inhaled sharply, but thanks to his intervention, by my next visit, I'd grown a perfectly shaped purple alum crystal in the vial instead of cultivating another demoralizing failure.

If I was honest, Bea wasn't far off with her flippant assessment that I'd become enamored with the man and partially obsessed with seeing him, even though I didn't entirely understand why. But my chest ached every time I had to leave his general vicinity, and I could only breathe again once I was back on the campus grounds. Every time he brushed my skin with his I felt as though I might catch fire. More than once I'd caught myself daydreaming about what it might be like to have his mouth on mine, his hands on my skin.

The more time I spent away from the manor, the more foreboding curled in my gut every time I went back. It spiked every time I spotted Lara and Henrik talking quietly with their attention fixed on me. They never outright scolded me for visiting d'Arcan, nor did any part of my duties overtly change, but the tension in the house was palpable. Something was coming, and it had to do with me.

It all came crashing down when I was preparing to leave for d'Arcan one afternoon.

"Curse the saints, you haven't left yet," Bea said breathlessly, hauling me by the arm back toward the kitchen just as I arrived at the bottom of the stairs.

"What's happening?"

"My parents are looking for you. I was hoping the carriage had already retrieved you."

My heart sank. Clem was probably right down the street, but I didn't dare leave until he was in the drive. "What's going on?"

"I don't know." Bea shook her head, mouth tight. "But I had to sit through what felt like a suitor meeting with Ellis and his father earlier, so I have to wonder if it's something similar. There's a carriage out front I don't recognize."

"Ellis?" I inquired, and she beamed, her fingers squeezing into my arm.

"Yes, and it feels very promising. I tried to stay neutral, but it was *so* difficult. The last thing I want is some random smelly merchant for a husband when I could have Ellis—"

"Beatrice? Please bring Greta at once!" Henrik bellowed across the house.

We both winced. Bea took a moment to help me straighten my shirt and dipped in for a quick hug. "I'm so sorry. Good luck," she said, leaving me outside the den.

I approached the doorway with a heavy sense of dread. Flattening myself against the wall, I clenched my jaw as my employers bickered about me, not caring that anyone passing by the room could hear everything they were saying. They hadn't even bothered to properly close the doors to have their discussion. Henrik's side-swipe comments left just as much sting as Lara's direct ones. It seemed I'd gotten thoroughly spoiled by the kindness offered to me at d'Arcan.

I inhaled, trying to bolster my confidence, and knocked gently.

"I will not allow her to ruin this for us, Henrik," Lara whined, a catch in her voice. "We've waited so long for him to show."

"Shh, it'll be fine. He's said he doesn't mind her appearance more than once. I know we expected him sooner, but the money he's offered …"

Their voices traveled away from me as he soothed her. The fake sobbing she had a habit of doing grated on my nerves as I strained to hear more. I didn't understand many of Lara's complaints about my looks, but I was used to them. Knowing now that I was stone kin, it made sense why I was usually a head taller than most of the men who visited Henrik for business and just as broad.

Instead of their negative commentary, I focused on the way Vassago watched me move around a room, the intensity in his golden eyes and the draw I felt to him. The way he made me feel beautiful no matter what I was wearing and how his only response when I blew up something in his classroom was to check for my safety and promise to get me more supplies. Better ones so it wouldn't happen again. He was, in every way, the soft place to land they should have been but never were.

I knocked again, irritation an itch under my skin.

"Greta?" Henrik called, finally. "Please join us."

I inhaled a breath through my nose and strode into his office, joining them at the ostentatious round table that sat in the center of the room. I selected one of the seats closest to the fire, earning Lara's pinched-mouth glare in response.

"You will make proper eye contact with this man, understood? And I'm sure I needn't tell you that your best behavior is expected." Her icy eyes bored into me.

"Yes ma'am."

"Good."

After a brief moment, a butler appeared at the door. "Introducing Lord Otto Feiser."

We all got to our feet as he bowed, a tall, slender man who resembled a wet cat strolled into the room. "Welcome, Lord Feiser. Such an honor to have you in attendance," Henrik said.

His gaze raked over me, surprise and interest flaring in his beady black eyes. "The pleasure is mine," he said, taking Lara's hand in his and bowing, pressing his mouth to her prominent ring. He turned to me, clearly with the same intent. "You may call me Otto, if you like."

"Nice to meet you, Lord Feiser," I managed, insides churning.

I held still through his cringe-inducing performance of kissing my knuckles, then scrubbed the back of my hand against my skirt once he'd finally relinquished it. It felt slimy somehow, nothing at all like when Vassago had done the same thing.

"Please, have a seat." Henrik gestured to the seats around the table.

Feiser decided that two over from me was his preferred spot. Far enough for propriety and close enough to touch my hand on the table if he wanted. "I apologize for the delay in arriving. I assume everything is still in order, as we agreed?" His stare made me itchy. Out of habit, my eyes kept sliding to the table, and I fought to keep my head up as Lara stared me down, no doubt waiting to catch a mistake in my manners.

"Indeed." Henrik looked to Lara, who had on her most transparent fake smile. "We're honored you've entrusted us with this and will of course fulfill our agreement." My stomach twisted when Henrik met my eye, a lopsided smile on his mouth.

"Ah, wonderful." Feiser turned my way, folding his clammy hands around mine. "I still have some business to set in order, but we'll have ample time to get to know one another before the wedding."

I went cold all over. "Wedding?" I wheezed, refusing to accept that they'd done all of this with no discussion or warning.

"Lord Feiser has made a generous bid for your hand, though I must insist we're getting the better end of things." Lara smirked.

"It appears you've taken adequate care of her these past years. Has she kept her studies up?" Otto asked, a lascivious smile on his mouth.

"Yes, of course. We allow her as much time to practice as her work will allow." Lara nodded.

"Good, good. I was delayed longer than I hoped, but she's young enough yet to provide several children, so long as we start right away. Thanks to her training with you, she can obviously keep a tidy house, and she has other pursuits to keep her mind agile. I can't say nearly as much for several courtesans." He doled out compliments, but they were not genuine. How could they be? He'd offered to purchase me like livestock. "Not everything is about appearance, Duchess Belette, though I understand why you might be concerned."

I swallowed the insults, acid coating my tongue. "And if I don't agree?" My words were sharp, the sting of tears hot in the back of my throat.

"Your agreement is not required," Henrik said, eyes shifty as he looked away from me.

I stiffened my spine, digging deep for boldness as panic made my heart pound roughly behind my ribs. "Excuse me? What do you mean? You've never mentioned anything of the sort before. I'm of age to make my own decisions—"

"My dear, what he means to say is that while I have long since been promised your hand, there's no reason we can't proceed with some semblance of amicability." He lifted my knuckles to his mouth again, pressing in and leaving my skin dotted with condensation from his exhale. "I'm very happy with our arrangement, and I hope you'll feel the same. You're quite"—he scanned me head to toe, leaving me feeling unclean, somehow—"unique, and I'm certainly well-endowed enough to keep you satisfied and able to participate in the lifestyle you are accustomed to."

Bile rose at his clever wording, and I pulled my trembling fingers away from him, burying them in my lap. Betrayal raced angrily through my veins as I turned my glare from my would-be husband to my employers. The lifestyle I was accustomed to was that of a maid. An unacknowledged almost-daughter who never lived up to expectations.

"We didn't want to ruin the surprise," Lara said, chuckling nervously. "That's why we didn't mention it before."

"It's a good match, Greta. We're sure you'll grow to be fond of Otto, and he's agreed to let you continue your work here while he makes some final preparations to welcome you into his home."

How generous. The sarcastic thought raced across my mind, but I clenched my teeth to keep it from escaping my mouth. Anger flared hot, lighting up my cheeks and making my chest ache.

"No offense, sir, but I'm sure you understand this is quite shocking." I schooled my words carefully. "I've not been told of these plans. I'm flattered, but not sure I'd be a good match—"

"On the contrary." He winked at me, and I swallowed against the sour burn in my throat. "I believe we're perfectly paired. You're skilled and used to being protected from the outside world. Besides, I'm not one to back down from a challenge."

"Challenge?" I repeated, a numb feeling freezing my chest. Disbelief had given way to terror, but I remained rooted in my seat, afraid to move.

"Greta, you know our top priority is, and always has been, to keep you safe." Lara put on her sweetest tone, but the falseness grated at me. I had wondered more than once, especially in recent months, how many of their rules were actually in place for my safety versus their convenience. Their control. "We knew Mr. Feiser would return to claim your hand, as promised." She tipped her glass his direction. "Thank the saints I have friends who will humor me, otherwise you might have trialed with some household that would have *actually* hired you away." She laughed, the high-pitched noise riding on my frayed nerves.

"Safe," I repeated, feeling more and more disembodied by the moment. My shoulders had started to burn as well, a fierce ache I wasn't sure I would be able to ignore for very long.

"Yes, of course. Mr. Feiser is a good match. He'll take good care of you. Keep you safe."

They kept saying it, but that didn't make it true. How long this agreement had been in place also seemed a vital question. Never mind that Lara had admitted to keeping me captive here, that none of the job trials she'd set up were real, that she'd ensured I would fail one way or another and then had the gall to punish me for failing. My thoughts stuttered as I processed all this, my breath loud in my ears and my heart beating too fast.

"I have several affairs I must tend to yet before I remove you to my personal care. I'm satisfied that the Belettes can manage a few more months."

"And if I don't want taking care of?" There was a bite to my words, fear and anger coming together as a hot burn in my throat.

Lara made that scratchy tittering laugh again, and the men exchanged an annoyed knowing glance. Feiser chuckled heartily, upending his cup to guzzle the contents, but nobody addressed my question directly. That smarted as well, and my skin heated with a blush that was equal parts shame and anger.

"Please, take this as a good faith symbol of my intentions." He slid a small square box across the table.

I opened it to find a ring inside. It did not appear to be anything of significant value, just a silver band with filigree leaves. It looked like something found in a trinket shop, something that would turn my skin green in a matter of minutes. The insult of such a thing being my engagement ring cut almost as deep as my employers' betrayal.

Feiser frowned, clearly disappointed in my lack of reaction. "I can understand your hesitation to wear such an item, especially in your line of work." I'd disrespected him but was unrepentant, as they'd each done the same to me. "However," he continued, jaw set. A quick glance around the table showed similar expressions on all their faces. "I'm afraid I must insist. The material is uniquely durable. You should find no difficulty wearing it."

"I don't think—"

He snatched both the box and my right hand, jamming the ring onto my finger before I could protest any further. The metal was unusually warm where it rested against my skin.

"Oh dear. Isn't that the wrong hand?" Lara asked. "Greta, be a dear and switch it, would you?"

"For my people, it's customary to wear the engagement band on the right and the wedding ring on the left," Feiser said, waving her off.

"Ah! Well, it's a lovely ring! You've outdone yourself with her, for certain."

The jewelry felt heavier than it should, hotter. I couldn't wait to remove it from my finger, but it resisted even being adjusted or turned. It hadn't seemed overly tight when it first went on, but it must have been.

They all continued a conversation around me, though I was unable to hear anything distinct over the rushing of blood in my ears. Henrik's self-congratulations and compliments to the man about his business savvy were of no interest to me anyway.

I focused on the grain of the wood in the table instead of the fierce burn in my shoulders. I ran my fingertip over a dent I'd made as a teenager with the edge of a pewter cup. Bea and I had been playing a card game, and I'd gotten upset that she was winning. Not angry, just boisterous. My outburst and the deep gouge in the table had earned me a month's worth of extra cleaning as punishment. Bea had come with me every day to help, she felt so bad that I was punished for us having a good time.

"Greta?" Henrik's voice finally cut through the din.

"Sir?"

"You're excused," Lara rushed to say, her fear about me having an outburst was obvious, as well as her anger.

After one final glance at my intended husband—I gagged on the word—I got to my feet and crossed the room in long strides. It took all my effort not to fling the door open or slam it behind myself as a scream built in my throat.

CHAPTER 12
VASSAGO

"WHERE THE SAINTS is she?" I grumbled, stomping my way down the main hall, all the while cursing myself for such an outburst as I tried to contain the swell of emotions building behind my ribs. Greta had never not shown up when we agreed on a day for her to visit. Granted, she'd only come a handful of times over the previous weeks, but she'd always arrived as expected.

I paced my classroom, tempted again to scry for her whereabouts, then cursed myself for thinking such a thing. In my frustration, I flung one of the small books I kept notes in, and it knocked over a jar. The glass shattered on the stone floor before I could catch it. "Shit." I plunged my fingers into my hair, tugging lightly as my nails scraped along my scalp before cleaning up my mess.

I hadn't felt so ungrounded in decades. It was borderline obsessive how I felt about her; I recognized that. It shouldn't have made a bit of difference to me that she was missing one of our meetings.

I'd spent three days shifting books and supplies so she would have a whole cabinet and bookshelf to herself in my classroom. I hadn't needed to go out to find a plush velvet chaise that she could much more comfortably nap on, but finding one in a shade that exactly matched the sofa had provided me with an unreasonable amount of joy. I shouldn't have spent the better part of an hour staring out the front windows, watching for any activity at the gate, but I couldn't seem to help myself.

We hadn't even discussed yet whether she would join d'Arcan as a student or as a teacher, though she'd be here permanently one way or the other if I had any say in the matter. Rylan clearly assumed as much, and Magnus had handed me the key to his apartment over breakfast, claiming he had plenty of other places to find rest and if she needed it, she should make use of it.

I cleaned up the resulting destruction of my tantrum and forced slow breaths through my nose. This was not like me. I wasn't prone to emotional displays or childish behavior. But not seeing her, not having her close enough to check on, not hearing her laughter or smelling her soft lilac scent while she was curled up on my sofa napping made my chest ache. I knew it would be nothing at all for me to spend all the gold I'd stashed away over centuries if finding her a special ingredient or a custom crucible made her smile.

It was utter madness.

I paced my office as my thoughts trailed around in circles. Perhaps she'd lost track of what day it was. Maybe she couldn't get away. I eyed the mirror for longer than I should have, rubbing the alum crystal she'd made between my thumb and forefinger. Finally, I'd set it down and *tsked* at myself for being ridiculous. There was no reason to scry to locate her. She was fine. She was at the Belette manor where she *lived*, working, most likely.

I stomped up to my suite and took a double dose of my curse suppressing tincture, hopeful it would help settle me if only for a while.

My frustration only eased when Clem finally returned, carrying a passenger in the carriage.

Greta was unusually morose, her eyes puffy and bloodshot, as though she'd been crying. The sight made my insides burn. The rage was so instantaneous and intense, I wondered if Rylan's tincture worked at all anymore.

"I was beginning to worry you might not make it today," I forced a smile, but she flinched back with a blink, warning me that my anger was showing.

"You're not the only one," she said quietly, staring at my eyes. "Perhaps I shouldn't ..."

"No, please. Come inside." I forced the rage away, willing my fangs to recede.

The same damned one-eyed raven flew down in greeting, chattering away at her from the fence. The tight smile she gave made my heart squeeze in a painful way. It dropped away when the bird left as abruptly as he had arrived.

Something was very wrong. Everything about her was off, and it made me feel like I was crawling out of my skin. "Grace brought us tea. Go on ahead if you would? I need to have a quick word." I watched as she made her way down the hallway after throwing a tense glance at me, one fist clenched and the other rubbing at her shoulder blade.

"Was there anything out of the ordinary that you noticed?"

Clem squeezed his hat in his hands, turning it slowly as he considered. He was avoiding looking me in the eye, which, along with the prickle in my mouth from my fangs, told me my demon was out again. To their credit, most of the staff had seen it enough times between Rylan and I that they were no longer quite so affected, but I understood the instinct to hide from the predator when faced with it directly. "There was another carriage, sir. It wasn't one I recognized. She was noticeably upset when she came out of the house."

"Thank you, Clem. I appreciate your help." He bowed and hurried back to the horses.

I found Greta arranging ingredients on her worktable, hands trembling as she set vials out and adjusted things to her liking.

"Are you alright?" I asked, immediately regretting such a useless question. She clearly was not.

She met my eye but quickly looked away before offering me the lie. "Yes. I'm fine."

"You're late," I said, realizing as the words crossed my lips that it sounded like an accusation.

Her head snapped up, her eyes wide with tears already on the verge of spilling over. "I'm sorry." She buried her face in her hands, silent sobs racking her frame as I stood there, staring.

I approached her carefully. "I apologize, Greta. That's not what I meant—" I stopped, seeing the ring on her finger. It was her right, and the band was simple, but she'd never worn any jewelry before.

She was suddenly sobbing into my shoulder, trying unsuccessfully to inhale giant gasps of air, her fingers knotted in my shirt. One of my hands automatically went to the back of her head, my palm smoothing her wild curls down as I shushed her. I leaned my cheek against her silky hair, and my eyes slipped closed as everything in my body stilled. I was simultaneously the most at peace and least settled I'd been in years. I turned my face so I could inhale the floral scent of her, my lips resting against her forehead. The ache in my chest flared to life painfully hot, but I could easily ignore it for the calm that had settled over me with her in my arms. "Greta, I need you to tell me what's happened. Please, you're frightening me."

In truth, I'd never seen such a powerful emotion come out of her, and I had no idea how to respond. She was not passionless, far from it, but was generally so even-keeled, this kind of outburst left me feeling untethered.

I placed a hand on either side of her face, gently lifting so she'd look at me. Tears overflowed her gorgeous hazel eyes and sent lava racing through my veins. Anger burst down my spine, wings and fangs ready to release at the merest of thoughts. One hand instinctively moved to my belt where my sword should hang. Regrettably, it had become frowned upon in polite society to walk around with one's blade in full view, so I'd taken to leaving it in my room. I furiously reconsidered how much I cared about conforming to the standards of civilization. I wasn't human, after all, no matter how much I adapted. No matter how much I pretended to be.

She pulled back, the fear that crossed her face delivering equal parts shame and rage. I held fast to her arm, knowing I was risking her being even more afraid of me in my effort to soothe her.

"Who must I kill, Little Dragonfly? Who's upset you so? Just point me in the right direction, I promise I'll make it right for you. I could make it so they regret ever having been born, much less for offending you. I only need a name." There was darkness in my tone as I made the vow.

She collected herself with a sniffle and stepped back from me. I let her go, but reached out as she did so, grasping her hip with my palm. I wasn't sure whether it was for her or for me, but I wasn't ready to break contact. "I'm so sorry," she said miserably, pressing her palms into her eyes as if that would help stem the flow of tears.

"Don't apologize," I said, finding it increasingly difficult to maintain my calm. "Not to me. Please, explain before I decide for myself who's to pay for your unhappiness. It could end badly for some innocent soul."

"You'll do no such thing." Her tone was resolute, but she sighed miserably before crossing the room to fold herself into one end of the couch.

"I would," I promised again.

"I do believe you're offering seriously, but no, you won't. There's no need to put yourself in such a position for me." She took a deep breath, piercing me with those lovely hazel orbs. "They've matched me," she choked out, showing me her right hand. "I can't get it off." Her fingers tugged at the band, but it didn't budge. "It feels like it's burning, but it won't *come off.*"

Her words landed like punches, and I rubbed at my chest with one hand. "What?" Rage bubbled in my veins at the notion that someone other than me put a ring on her finger not only without her acceptance, but also without the ability to remove it. It didn't belong there. It was a vile stain on her hand, and I wanted it gone perhaps more than she did.

As I watched, the sadness within her turned to anger. "Marriage," she said, the word a curse. "They've promised me to a man in exchange for money. I mean, I'm guessing it's for money, though I don't even know for sure if that's what he offered, nor how much. It sounded like maybe it has been in progress for some time, now that I think about it. I thought ..." She shook her head, dismissing whatever she'd been about to say. "I thought I had more time, at the very least. I honestly thought your interest in me coming here was going to earn me my freedom." She dropped her face into her hands again, curls bouncing angrily against her cheeks.

I sat next to her, rage brewing hot under my skin. I forced my outward appearance to remain stoic, however. For her. Inside, I felt like I was being flayed into a million shards of flesh and bone.

"To whom have they"—the word *sold* begged to cross my tongue, but I didn't want to make her feel worse, or send myself into an unstoppable spiral—"*promised* your hand, Greta?"

I took her fingers into mine, gently tugging at the offensive band. It was as though it had fused with her skin when I pulled. It didn't move at all, not even to turn. Dread settled into my gut. There was some kind of magic at work here, and clearly nothing good.

She raised her head, swiping the tears away with her fingertips as though they annoyed her. "Some merchant, I think, but they kept referring to him as a lord. Otto Feiser? I've never met him

before. I don't understand what's changed. They've never mentioned anything about it before now. I thought ... I thought if I
had a prospect to get me out of their house, I wouldn't have to ...
But they made it so I couldn't, even if I wanted. And the other
jobs—" She choked on the words, unable to continue.

"Listen to me, Greta. You're of age and sound mind. This agreement is only binding to the men who made it. I'm guessing you did
not agree to any terms? Did you sign anything?" If she'd signed a
contract, things would be more difficult. I racked my brain for a
Feiser but came up empty. Though having a name certainly narrowed the options down for possible responsible parties.

"Henrik said my agreement was not required. But I didn't sign
anything. I don't think I verbally agreed to anything, either. I was
quite *dis*agreeable, as a matter of fact. Nobody was very happy
with me in that room by the end." Her brow pinched as though she
replayed every word of the conversation she'd had before arriving.

"Well done," I praised, loving that she'd used her backbone
during the discussion, though I was sure it had been at some risk
to herself. I was not surprised they didn't require her complicity.
My patience where Henrik was concerned had been thoroughly
exhausted, and I'd never met this Lord Feiser, but I was already
done with him as well. "How soon?" I asked, my quietness a mask
for my fury, not an indication of calmness.

The thought of her being paired with anyone aside from me in
such a way provoked my inner demon like nothing I'd ever felt
before. And that in and of itself was problematic for several reasons.

"He just said he'd return for me when the final arrangements
had been settled. It sounded like soon, though. Months? Like he
was already later in coming to claim me than he'd hoped." She
sagged. "I'm so sorry for dumping all of this on you. It's neither
your concern nor your responsibility."

I reached for her hand. "I'm happy I was in the wrong place at
the right time when we first met. It's a habit I hope to continue,

in fact." She mustered the smallest of smiles, and I forced myself to breathe over the swirling heat of my anger. "I'm certain there's a way for me to help with this situation, I only need to know what terms were laid out so I can best respond."

She took in a deep breath, the faraway stare in her eye communicating that she was debating her words. "I don't know about the terms. The ring though, I don't understand what's happening there. It's not too tight, but it feels all wrong."

"It is, Dragonfly. Completely wrong." It looked like a cheap ring, by appearance alone it was more insult to her than gift. But there was definitely something more going on. It was unique enough, however, be useful to me in finding out who had made it. I considered several options—some more self-serving than others—to solve this once and for all. "There is always another option. Don't fret over this, Greta. I will help you find a solution."

She brightened, but a thread of suspicion clouded her joy. "You would be willing to do that? You hardly know me."

I couldn't help but smile. She had grown used to people trying to keep her down, to make her feel small. I couldn't wait to see her truly blossom under the praise and encouragement she deserved. I craved it, in fact. So much, that I palmed her cheek, barely containing a groan when she turned her face into my hand. I rubbed my thumb along her cheek, blood surging at the simple touch.

"I know you well enough to say with certainty that you're a wonderful addition to d'Arcan in any capacity. You're passionate, knowledgeable, and not afraid to fail. It's the perfect combination. Along with that, it goes without saying that you are welcome to become a full-time resident here at the earliest possible time. As for the other part ... I'll speak to Henrik. I too am curious what this Lord Feiser has brought to them. Going purely off social conventions, I have reason to feel slighted, after all. You and I have an arrangement already in place. I've shown my intention with you and should have priority. They've shirked proper protocol by accepting his offer." Her brow pinched and she pulled away. The loss heavy in my chest, I let her go. "Please understand that I don't necessarily believe or agree with any of that, Greta. But I have to play the game they believe they are moving all the pieces around for.

"You are here of your own free will, now and always. If you should choose not to return, I would accept that. In the meantime, I will defend your right to be here first and above any kind of marriage contract they made without your consent or knowledge. As for the ring itself ... I'm happy to help you try whatever it takes to remove it."

She opened and closed her mouth several times before committing to what she wanted to say. In the end, she settled for a simple "Thank you."

"You're welcome."

"I'm sorry again for crying all over you."

I chuckled. "Don't be. I spilled wine on you, a few shed tears are nothing in comparison."

Mood lifting, but high emotions having taken their toll, she yawned behind her hand, then reached up to rub at her neck and shoulder. "Lara's favorite wine is awful, isn't it? Though you didn't have to go so far as to throw it on me to get rid of it."

I laughed outright at her poking fun of our first meeting. "Truly terrible wine, I've never tasted the like." I watched as she began to relax, thankful I could be there for her. Beyond thrilled she'd made it to my door today, I resolved to keep her here. "Do you trust me?"

She searched my eyes, and I resisted the urge to pull her flush to my body again as she worked through whatever she needed to. Finally, she gifted me the words, "Yes, I trust you."

I settled for taking up one of her hands and pressing my lips to her knuckles, wishing it were her cheek, her forehead, her mouth. "We'll figure this out. I promise."

I meant it. She was mine, and I was going to make sure she allowed me to keep her.

CHAPTER 13
VASSAGO

A FEW DAYS LATER, I was already seated at the table with Lilith's grimoire when Henrik strode into his den.

"Ah! Mr. Feland. I thought I saw your carriage arrive. I'll be with you in just a moment." His eyes barely grazed over me, he was so wrapped up in his own self-importance. I could feel the arrogance rolling off his skin from across the room.

He swaggered over to a table covered in liquor bottles that was near the desk where he normally kept the book. He poured himself a drink from the decanter before offering me one. I declined.

It took him several long seconds after opening up the desk to realize I'd already retrieved it, that it was in fact open on the table in front of me. I nearly burst out laughing at his comically wide eyes as he turned around slowly, probably frantically thinking up an excuse as he did so. Relief and shock were evident in equal measure as he spotted the large book in front of me.

"How did you—"

"You should be more careful with your valuables, Henrik.

Can't have just anyone walking in here and taking them as they please, can we?"

"Mr. Feland, I swear, nobody has ever—"

I waved my hand, stopping the bluster before it could truly get going. "It's alright, Henrik. I've watched you open that contraption at least a dozen times. It wasn't hard for me to figure out the right combination to get into it myself. Besides, this book is leaving with me today." He opened his mouth several times but made no sound. I thoroughly enjoyed seeing him squirm, and wished I had more cause to make it happen. "You should retrieve your wife. I believe she'll want to be here for this conversation."

"What conversation is that?"

I simply stared back, and he paled before scurrying off to locate her. They returned several minutes later, Lara clearly having rushed to put on a fresh dress and maybe even some cosmetics. The cloying scent of her perfume made me wrinkle my nose.

"Mr. Feland! What a pleasure to see you again."

I closed the book with a satisfyingly loud *thunk*. "Greta arrived at d'Arcan in quite a state during her last visit," I said without preamble. I kept my tone neutral, but the words had the impact I'd hoped for. I flicked my eyes from Lara to Henrik, waiting to see if they'd make an admission on their own. I'd hated that Greta was forced to come back here, to work for these people even a moment longer, but I had to ensure I had everything set up properly before taking her with me.

"I'm sorry she presented herself poorly—" Lara started. As expected, she shifted the blame from herself to Greta.

"It was not how she presented herself that was the problem, Duchess Belette."

"What, ah, seems to be the problem, then?" Henrik got even shiftier than usual then, as though realizing they'd made an error.

"She informed me she's to be wed?"

"Ah, yes!" Lara softened and clapped her hands together as though her smile fixed everything. "A joyous occasion, to be sure. She's been well matched, isn't that right, darling?"

"Yes, we received a very respectable offer from a man to make her his wife."

"Is that so? What are brides going for these days?" My skin tingled with the disgust I felt at such a notion. Common practice or not, I found it abhorrent.

"Not that it's your business, but Mr. Feiser bid an amount sufficient to keep us in the lifestyle we prefer, this manor included, not to mention allowing me to maintain my title," Henrik said vaguely. "It seemed wise to accept."

"Did it?" I raised my eyebrows, toying with an empty whiskey glass with my fingers as the joy slowly leaked from their faces. I braced myself to say the words that had already left a bitter coating in my mouth. Greta was not an object to be owned, but I knew these people saw her as such. "You dare to offer her out from under me when I had already made my claim? When we already had an agreement for her to come to d'Arcan at my whim, Henrik?"

He stumbled over several failed attempts at coherent words. "I'm afraid I wasn't aware there was an agreement involving Greta, Mr. Feland."

"After her first visit, you were given a message from me, were you not?"

"Yes, I believe I recall a message," he said, tentatively. His eyes darted to the fireplace and back, leaving me sure he'd burned the note.

"It outlined terms of an agreement where Greta is concerned. Clear ones, that your lack of response—as per the note's specifics—implied your agreement to. You going around me to match her with some merchant is a very clear violation of those terms."

Henrik puffed his chest out, cheeks bright red. "I'm afraid I can't speak to that, Mr. Feland. The note is, unfortunately, long gone. The timing of my agreement with Lord Feiser supersedes my arrangements with you. Besides, you were hired to find our necklace, not make our staff—"

I flung the necklace I'd had commissioned from Callihan's onto the table. I'd paid dearly for it, the speed required from the jeweler close to unheard of, but I was more than satisfied with the product. It matched every specification I'd requested and even the smallest details from the sketch.

The pair stared at it for a moment before Lara snatched it up, examining it closely with greedy eyes.

"I also have your signature here"—I slid a piece of parchment out from under the book, my copy of our original agreement—"stating that any violation of our original contract or addenda thereof, which that note"—I pulled out a second piece of parchment, one crafted much like the note I'd sent with Greta. Henrik paled even further, and I knew I'd hit my marks well and true. I wondered if he'd even read past my request to allow her to come to our following meeting—"was. Any violation as such renders all agreements between us null and void."

"Now, Mr. Feland, I must—"

"*Quiet.*" They both clammed up, the necklace gripped firmly in Lara's palm as though she were afraid I might reach out and take back the useless trinket. "I have fulfilled my end of our deal, despite your transgression. I have provided you a necklace. I will be leaving here with my book, as agreed, as well as Greta."

"You'd take a sickly, lazy maid—one who is already spoken for, besides—to practice chemistry at your prestigious school, but not honor my daughter with consideration as a wife?" Lara was incensed by my proposition. The more I got to know them, the more I despised them both.

"As I told you previously, *Duchess*," I said smoothly, refusing to rise to her baiting words while also giving her the honor of her ill-begotten title, "your daughter is lovely. From what I've seen, she surpasses you in wit as well as beauty, which I'm sure is to your great pride as her mother." She stiffened, unsure whether to react to the insult or the compliment, I was sure. "But I have no inclination to become her husband. I'm here to obtain a chemist for my brother's school." Speaking so degradingly of Greta made my teeth grind, but I knew better than to show these greedy people I found such value in her.

Henrik made a flourishing show of calming his wife.

"Mr. Feland," Lara begged, chuckling nervously and batting her eyes. I could see right through her act. She was something far different than the power-hungry schemer I knew her to be. "I'm sure this was all a misunderstanding. Mr. Feiser offered us a substantial sum to wed Greta, and we have agreed. I'm sure you understand what a delicate position we now find ourselves in."

"I empathize," I said, even though I did nothing of the sort. I didn't give a single damn what position they found themselves in. "But I feel I must remind you that Henrik was aware of the terms when he signed his name on the original contract."

"Perhaps we can come to a new agreement?" he rushed to say, just as I'd known he would. He'd clearly not shared all the details with his wife. I could understand him trying to keep the fact that he'd made a deal with an actual demon to himself, however.

"What are you proposing?" I sat back in the seat, prepared to be entertained as they floundered, and I still left with everything I wanted.

"You can, of course, take your book, as well as Greta. Though perhaps as a gesture of goodwill—"

"I owe you nothing further."

"Of course, of course. But you would be leaving us short an employee ahead of what we'd anticipated." I simply raised my eyebrow, annoyed that I was a little impressed by Henrik's boldness. "A hundred gold coins should minimize the impact of losing her so much sooner."

I gritted my teeth, forcing myself to breathe slowly and not let on how infuriating such a low offer was. Even still, I couldn't resist seeing how much bluster he had left in him.

"Fifty."

"Seventy, not a penny less." Henrik placed his palm flat on the table and leaned toward me, as though trying to intimidate me with his hard stare. It was all I could do not to laugh in his face.

"Seventy it is then."

The couple had the audacity to cheer as though they'd won something. I would be most interested to speak with this Mr. Feiser, to see what his offer had actually been. Accepting what they had was criminal. Greta was worth infinitely more than that and far more than the pair of them put together.

"It's been a pleasure doing business with you, Mr. Feland. I do truly appreciate all your efforts. Tell me, where did you find the necklace?"

I shrugged, knowing they would find no flaws in my careful wording. "With a local jeweler. Just a stroke of luck I went in to talk to them, I suppose. It's a unique piece. They were able to provide me with it without much trouble at all."

"After all this time! I can't imagine. Someone must have traded it not realizing what they had," Henrik mused.

"Mm."

"Such good fortune for us that they did!" Lara said, smiling wide. "I'll have Greta informed that she's to prepare her things." She all but skipped from the room with the necklace still gripped in her hand.

Henrik offered some awkward small talk, but I had no patience left for his babbling. "Where can I find this Lord Feiser?"

"Oh, I'm sure there's no reason to involve him."

"There's a ring on Greta's finger." I bit the words out, hating the way they felt in my mouth, unused to the sensation roiling under my skin. "One that doesn't belong there and which seems disinclined to be removed." Henrik blanched. He'd known there was an enchantment at play then. "I find it odd you'd have such intimate dealings with a man nobody else has heard of."

"He's quite illusive, does much of his business in far-flung realms. An illustrious businessman though. Greta will be well cared for."

"Are you refusing to tell me where I can find this man?" I asked, words coated in ice.

"Not a refusal, I simply don't know where to direct you! He is transient, Mr. Feland. I don't think he even has a home here in Revalia."

"If you were to send him a message, where would you have it delivered?"

Henrik must have finally seen the true threat behind my eyes, because he swallowed thickly, moved back, and paled even further.

"I am at his whim, Mr. Feland, I swear. I do not contact him. He is responsible for all of our communication. I anticipate he'll be back before the end of the season to claim her, but that's all I know."

"If he happens to avail himself to a visit before then ..."

"I'll send a messenger, of course," he hurried to answer.

"Lovely doing business with you, Henrik," I said, sarcasm thick on my tone. I handed over a pouch full of coins that had made Henrik sway on his feet, stars in his eyes. It was a disgustingly low offer, and I wouldn't forget how he'd traded her to me for the literal change in my pockets.

I excused myself from the den with the large book tucked under my arm, headed straight for the stairs. "Where?" I asked, and that was enough for him to direct me.

"Third floor."

I inclined my head and made my way up the steps, relieved to be finished with my dealings here.

CHAPTER 14

GRETA

"Sorry?"

"I said go pack. You're leaving with Mr. Feland." Lara had interrupted me scrubbing my second floor of the day to tell me to pack my things.

My heart skipped and then stopped. He'd done it, then. I'd been cautious not to allow myself to get too caught up in hoping something like this might happen. "Ma'am?"

Lara clucked her tongue at me. "You heard what I said. He'll be waiting. Go on!"

I put the hard-bristled brush into the bucket of soapy water, hastily drying my hands on my pants as I charged toward my room. The edges of the leaves on the detestable ring caught in the weave of towels, my clothing, my hair. I hated the damned thing, but there was no ridding myself of it.

Caroline had tried to help me remove it with soap, oil, and even a string. There was no getting anything between the metal and the skin of my finger, however, so I worried that the burn I'd felt that first day wasn't just imagined. She'd even tried a pair of pliers, but as she pinched, it was clear we were more likely to break the tools or cut my finger than break the band.

It was far from the simple metal it appeared to be, and that terrified me.

There wasn't much to speak of that was mine to pack, except some clothes and a handful of books. I gazed around the sparsely filled room, surprised to find I would miss it.

I opened the door to find Vassago on the other side, his hand raised as though he'd been about to knock. "Oh! Hello." I felt my face warm and set down the single small case I'd been carrying. On impulse, I darted forward, and wrapped my arms around his neck, giving a light squeeze. "I don't know what you did, but thank you." He pressed one hand into my back, his body warm against mine for several heartbeats until I stepped back.

"There's no need for thanks, Greta. It is my pleasure. Is this everything?"

"Yes. I made sure to bring in my notebooks yesterday, just in case." I frowned. "I never got to show you the maze."

He picked up the case and waited while I took one last look around my room.

"We can always come back," he offered, "if you need something or would like to visit someone. They'd of course be welcome at d'Arcan. It will be your home as well."

I smiled at the thought, something bright flaring in my chest. This place had been my home for a long time, but it also had never been.

With one hand on my lower back, Vassago walked with me down the stairs.

"Are we going straight to d'Arcan?" I asked.

"Yes. Unless you have somewhere you'd like to stop on the way?"

I laughed. "I wouldn't know. I don't get to visit the city."

"Never?" I shook my head. "We'll have to remedy that." He

bumped into my back as I stopped on the first-floor landing, eyes focused on Bea's open door. "Greta? Everything alright?"

"Yes, I just thought I might say goodbye." I was frozen, however, feeling like an unwelcome onlooker as the two interacted, oblivious to our presence.

Watching Lara be maternal with Bea had always fascinated me. She was never my mother, that boundary had been in place as far back as I could remember, but she'd always been wholly devoted to the young woman I considered my little sister. Often to the point of overwhelm, at least for Bea. Unfortunately for me, I'd sometimes also needed a mother, even if the only one available wasn't my own. Caroline and some of the other wonderful ladies on staff had taken up the role in their own ways, but it wasn't the same.

Lara had Bea trying out different styles for the ball, and currently, a large oval gem hung around Bea's neck. I couldn't stop myself from staring, even though I desperately wanted to divert my eyes to literally anywhere else. I also wanted Lara to leave so I could give Bea a proper goodbye hug, though she and I had made a point to do so the previous few evenings, just in case it was the last one.

"You found it," I muttered. "The necklace."

"Mm."

I could tell Bea wanted her hair down and Lara wanted to put it up. They were going to fight about it, and I wouldn't be around to make peace like I had many times before. I thought she should wear a single fishtail braid with the end tucked underneath. It was my favorite way for her to wear her hair, but that would be too close to agreeing with Lara for either of our liking.

I'd always wanted princess hair for myself, and to me, that meant either the fish braid or the waterfall that Lara sometimes did on Bea; a delicate wave of a braid crossing from one temple to below the other ear.

My hands reached up to touch the blunt ends of my hair where it stopped just below my ears. The unruly curls had been short far longer than they'd ever been long.

Lara had never once put braids in my hair. Nobody had. In fact, my curls proved too frustrating to manage altogether. I struggled with getting all the knots out, mostly because she only ever gave me brushes and combs meant to be used on straight hair. The bristles would get gnarled in the strands, half of my head frizzy and wild, the rest a tangled mess. On the last day it was long, the maid that normally helped me had been ill. Lara, angry that I wasn't ready in time to leave for some event, brushed it so aggressively I'd started to cry.

Her solution was to get rid of it altogether. She'd taken the fabric shears one of the ladies had left behind on my bureau while trimming the hem on a hand-me-down gown and cut all my curls off just below my ear. I'd cried all afternoon.

I'd been ten at the time, and already very aware of my place in the house. Her reaction had been meant to teach me a lesson. One I couldn't forget.

Especially because in all the years since, my hair had never grown back.

"Perhaps another time," I said finally, unable to hold back the deep sigh that had built in my chest.

"Mm," he repeated as his piercing eyes traveled my face. He quirked his mouth in thought, head cocked to the side, inquiry burning in his gaze. Vassago's brow crinkled, and he glanced from me to where my gaze was still locked on Bea and Lara. "What is it they have that pains you, Little Dragonfly? Their bond? Surely not their beauty or their brains, because you have them won out there by scores on both accounts."

I shook my head, feeling even more foolish than I had before because at least his suggestion about their bond was profound. Flattery aside, it felt silly that I was upset about a simple hairstyle.

I shifted uncomfortably, suddenly unsure whether or not he was wrong. I didn't need her to be my mother, but at some point along the way, for her to have at least been *kind* would have been more than welcome.

"It seems silly," I admitted, throat thick with tears I refused to shed. I wasn't even sure how to communicate that I'd needed so much more from Lara than I had ever gotten.

"Well, there's no accounting for taste," he grumbled. "None of that is your fault, Greta."

I twisted my fingers into the ends of my hair one last time and turned to face him. "I know." I forced my mouth to lift a bit, but he was not assuaged.

"I don't mean to minimize what it must have been like for you here, day after day." He directed his stare her direction again, at Lara fawning over Bea in a way that made her look decades younger, almost like a different person completely. "But I've met a lot of people in my life, and I can guarantee that you shouldn't waste your precious time or concern on people like your employers. Nor your tears." His thumb tracked along my cheek, chasing away one of the fat drops that had escaped. Something dark swirled in the golden depths of his eyes as his jaw clenched again. Everything in me went quiet as his lips pressed into the skin where he'd removed the tear. I released a shuddering breath, and he moved back, eyes widening.

As though shedding a skin, he shook his head and straightened his shoulders, one hand held out to me. "Come. You have an apartment to settle into, and I have an experiment for you to try. Magnus is likely to appear at some point over the next couple of days as well, so you have more actual family history to look forward to."

One of his hands lingered at my lower back as he walked us out of the estate. I stopped in the kitchen to say my goodbyes.

"I'm sorry," I said, as Caroline's arms wrapped around me. I wasn't sure what the apology was for, but I did feel a niggling sense of betrayal, like I was cheating somehow by leaving them all behind.

She grabbed both sides of my face with her palms, eyes shimmery as she stared deep into my eyes. "You don't apologize to anyone for living like you deserve, understand?" She released my face and gave me a final quick squeeze. "I'm so proud of you. Hear me?"

"Yes ma'am."

She turned her attention to Vassago. "You take care of her," she demanded, tone brokering no excuses. "She's special."

He smiled at her, and my body flared hot as he took my hand in his. "I plan to."

"Good." She nodded once, as though that settled the matter.

My heart was sore but also light as we left the kitchen and made our way out the front door. This time, when it closed behind us, it seemed final.

The relief I felt was as welcome as it was surprising.

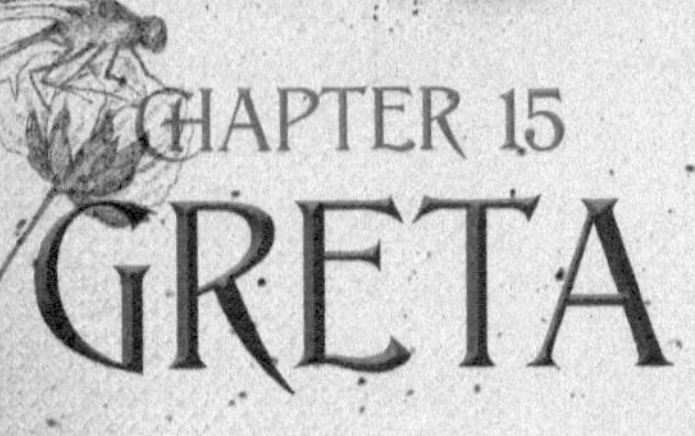

CHAPTER 15
GRETA

THE APARTMENT MAGNUS had vacated for me to take over was a luxurious suite as far as I was concerned. While my old room had a small bathing space attached, these rooms were appointed with proper bedding, a sitting room, and a bathtub that didn't appear to have survived a great war. I'd always known my things were shabby, but I hadn't realized how little comfort I'd become accustomed to until sinking into the soft mattress as I sat to have a look around.

Moving in was a simple affair, all I had to do was unpack my little case of clothes into the wardrobe, so I spent some time moving around the space, familiarizing myself with the flow of the room. I checked the water taps, pleased to find the hot side was immediately steamy. The bedding was lush and there were even several books left on the shelves that I hadn't yet read.

I placed the crystal Vassago had given me on my first visit on the bedside table before opening the window above it. A familiar croak echoed into the room.

"Hello there." I chuckled, slowly approaching the massive raven sitting on the sill. He turned his head this way and that, trying to get a good view of me with his one good eye. "I'm afraid I have no treats for you, but I'll see if I can get some from the kitchen, alright? Do you want to come inside?"

He threw out his wings for balance as he flared his feathers and walked sideways along the wood, making a ticking sound in his throat.

I reached my hand out, shocked when he allowed me to stroke the feathers along his head. That intelligent eye blinked up at me as I did so. I could swear he even smiled, though the idea of a bird doing that seemed ridiculous. After a few minutes of me talking nonsense to him and giving him gentle pets, he made a gurgling noise and took flight again.

I ventured down to the classroom afterward, feeling like I'd stepped into a whole other dimension I was so happy.

Vassago was on his sofa, reading a book. He brightened as I entered the room. "Are you all settled in?"

"Yes, I think so. That raven came to my window just now, if you can believe it. It's the strangest thing, it's like he's trying to make himself my pet." Lost in my elation, I paid little attention to where my feet were going and tripped over the edge of a rug. I flailed, but there was no righting myself. I had time enough to worry that I was going to hit my head on the wide edge of one of his worktables as I went down, but I never made impact.

In the span of a single breath, Vassago appeared on his knees in front of me, panic on his face and my name on his lips as he caught me mid fall, his shaky palm held up between my face and the sharp table edge. He was surrounded by gray smoke but also semitransparent, as though his body had started to vanish. I stared in wonder and confusion as he became solid again, his eyes crimson, pointed fangs where his canines should be. And he had wings. Broad ones, with white feathers.

"What ... are you?" I asked, knowing what I was seeing was not imagined. A trickle of fear licked through me. I knew now, without a doubt that it had indeed been him on the road that day. And I understood even less how this man, the one who protected me, cared for me, could possibly be the same creature with blood smeared across his face and a wild look in his eyes.

He hauled me to my feet, and held my body snugly up against his for a long moment, even his wings wrapped tightly around me. I felt his heart racing under my palm as he hastily checked me over, hands brushing along my shoulders, my hips, my face. He pressed a kiss to my forehead once he was satisfied, then tucked his wings away while his eyes and fangs also returned to normal.

"You're alright?" The deep concern in his tone chased away any vestiges of fear.

"I'm fine. Clumsy and embarrassed, but fine thanks to you." He nodded sharply but didn't answer my question. "Why do you have wings?" I asked quietly, blood rushing in my ears still. The way he'd checked me over, stared at me, kissed me, had everything in my body reaching for him.

He smiled grimly. "That is an awfully long story."

I plucked up my bravery before responding, transforming the swirl of emotions in my chest into something useful. "Then it's lucky I don't have to leave any time soon. And when I do, it's only to go down the hall and upstairs." He clenched his jaw and put an arm around my shoulders, ushering me over to the chaise he'd purchased for me. "Vassago." Every muscle stilled for a moment before he turned and handed me a mug of tea. He sat across from me with a glass of wine. "I need to know. I deserve the truth. I know what I just saw. What I've seen before and had no way of explaining."

"It makes me feel a certain way when you get stern with me, Little Dragonfly. Perhaps you should do it more often."

Vassago watched me over the rim of his glass. Everything in the room was suddenly too loud, my heartbeat the most offensive of all. It was an insistent throb in my ears each and every time he looked at me that way, when his voice dropped and he used that tone.

I sipped my tea, hopeful it would clear the sudden tightness in my throat.

"Lara once asked me if I held titles. I do. Several, in fact, but the one I've held the longest is Mighty Prince of Hell."

"What ... what does that mean, exactly?" I asked, throat dry despite the tea. I thought of our afternoon in the observatory, the stories he'd told me so casually.

The corner of his mouth twitched, and I had to resist the urge to sit back as he leaned forward, his elbows on his knees. "Once, I was in charge of legions. There were twenty-six under my command. Once, I was nothing more than a soldier among soldiers, fighting battles that quickly grew pointless and tiresome. My brother Rylan and I plotted to leave Hell together. He'd had enough, but I wasn't ready. It was the only time I ever lost a fight to him." He smiled, as though the memory was a fond one even though he hadn't been the victor. "You must never tell him so, but his timing was more correct than mine. There was no point in staying, though I did for several more years.

"Here though, on Earth, in Cyntere, in Revalia, something feels different. At the very least, using my skills to find lost treasures, to protect humans, to teach them, I have purpose. Once—" He broke off, shaking his head. "Long before any of that, I chose to fall from the heavens and became ... this." He settled back, draining the remainder of the wine in his glass.

As usual, he had a vest on, but several buttons on his shirt were undone. As it gaped, I couldn't help but stare at the tattoos that spanned along his collarbone and down his breastbone. They were white against his skin and almost iridescent, something that looked like letters in a language I didn't understand. I'd never seen anything quite like them. I blushed, fisting my hands as I realized I had my fingertips extended as though about to trace along their edges.

"If this is *after* you fell, what hope do the rest of us have?"

He choked, a rivulet of wine escaping the corner of his mouth. It should not have been half as tantalizing as it was watching him catch it and brush it aside with his fingertips.

Once he managed to swallow, he burst out laughing. I'd never heard him truly laugh before, if this was what it sounded like. This was a deep, rolling noise, one that made the hair on the back of my neck tingle, and a pulse throb between my thighs. This Vassago, the uninhibited one, was dangerous.

"Little Dragonfly, you underestimate yourself." He grinned once he'd stopped laughing, those golden eyes focused on me in a way that made it feel like he was looking through me.

"You're a literal demon?" I asked, instead of responding to his flattery. "It's not just a cheeky nickname from Magnus or a term of endearment?"

"Indeed." His expression fell, seriousness clouding his features. "Though where that overgrown statue is concerned, I believe it might be both."

I smiled, appreciating that he had an equal nickname for my uncle. "And the archmage?"

"Him too. Though it's not widely known, I'm sure you can understand why."

I could. "Is it a secret?"

"Not as such, but we also don't announce it. It's complicated with Rylan especially, being monitored as he is by the mage council. We don't want to jeopardize his ability to run this school. We have tried to keep ourselves spread out so we don't draw attention. There's no precedent for what might happen if we were all together. We never have been, at least not earth-side. Not for longer than a few hours at a time."

"How many of you are there? You keep saying *we*."

"There are seven of us, altogether. Rylan and myself, plus Seir, Sitri, Ipos, Bas, and Tap. Though any of them may have chosen another name, like Rylan has."

"And you all live on Earth?"

"No. Two of my brothers inhabit Hell primarily still, two others split their time between the two places. Only Rylan and Tap are here full time like I am. Though Tap's situation is ... complicated. Not like mine or Rylan's; we're free to do what we like. At least the last we spoke, that was the arrangement for them all. Things could have changed, I'm not sure. We don't stay in close contact."

"That's too bad. Do you miss them?" I could tell by the shift on his face this wasn't the question he'd been expecting.

"Not as such. I know I could find any one of them if I needed to, and we see one another now and then. We can get messages passed, though it often requires some patience in expecting a response. Everyone attended Rylan and Calla's wedding not long ago, but dispersed as quickly as they came. They seemed well."

I nodded, imagining such a gathering. "Your talents are all different?"

"You have a great many questions about my brothers, Little Dragonfly." His mouth pinched, eyes blazing red for several seconds as his nostrils flared.

"It's not every day I learn about a family of demons," I said, hoping to lighten the mood as he descended into full-on broodiness. Jealousy rolled from him in a hot wave. In truth, I wanted to hear the nickname he'd called me again. "I'm just curious."

He took a deep breath, the darkness clearing from his face. "Of course you are. Yes, we all have different skills and special abilities. All of us have wings. Some have horns, tails. A few of us have other forms entirely, not unlike the stone kin's ability to shift into a statue or a stone form."

"What was it that happened when you were surrounded by smoke just now? I think that's perhaps how you caught the spectacles before they broke one of my first visits. How you sometimes move far faster than you should."

"Yes," he confirmed. "That's the mist."

"Mist?"

He tilted his head to the side and closed his eyes, turning to vapor as I watched. It was a process my brain didn't want to accept, the way he grew more and more transparent until there was only a chair and smoke where he'd sat a moment before. He reappeared directly in front of me, making me jump. Cool tendrils brushed along the skin on my cheek, replaced by warm fingers as Vassago solidified and the mist evaporated.

"Oh," I said simply, stifling the dozen or so questions I still had before they could spill out. There was plenty of time to learn. I needed to pace myself. After all, I was learning all this just hours after leaving the only home I'd known most of my life. If I didn't exercise some caution, I might burn out or lose my mind entirely in a matter of days.

"Yes."

"That actually explains a lot." I studied him, the pieces falling together. The way his eyes sometimes flashed red or his fangs became more pronounced. His ability to move across a room in the span of a moment without being seen. "The other day ..." His expression fell. There was a tingle in my fingertips as my heart began to pound. "On the road. Was that you?"

He blew out a slow breath. "Yes, it was." The gasp that snuck out at his admission was louder than I'd hoped. "That's not a common occurrence, Greta. You must know that. There had been a situation, a fight. I was managing a threat when you saw me." His hands fidgeted, his face pensive.

"A threat?"

"Yes. There were some troublemaking demons that needed dealt with. A somewhat unique event, I swear it."

I stared at him, my mind sorting through every interaction we'd had so far. I nodded, unsure what else to say. I did not feel like I was in danger with him, but discounting what he could do was surely unwise.

I blinked as a realization set in. A *demon* stood between me and my former employers. This beautiful man, the one that looked like the angel in the maze fountain but was actually the opposite, had already proven he would keep me safe. From Henrik, from myself. From a life toiling as someone's purchased bride. Somehow, the threat of me falling for him was greater than it had been before, even with the new revelations about his nature.

His worry transformed into a confused scowl. "That's it?" he asked.

"That's what?"

"You don't have any further response to me telling you I'm a creature of Hell? Just some questions and *that explains a lot?*"

"Should I have a different reaction?" I laughed, realizing he was somewhere between shocked and offended I wasn't more bothered by the revelation.

"Most do."

"Does it come up in conversation often?" I frowned, wondering who he was talking to that it might come up at all.

"No." He chuckled, shaking his head as though I were being ridiculous.

I shrugged. "Well, you're still the same person you were earlier. Or yesterday. Last week. I'd be lying if I said having seen you that way wasn't fearsome, but you've never done anything to threaten or hurt me. Besides, it didn't bother you to find out I'm stone kin, and that's kind of the same thing."

The groove between his eyes deepened and then disappeared altogether as he unleashed another smile. "You, Little Dragonfly are ... unexpected. And I think you and my brother's wife will get along famously. Also, to be fair, I recognized your nature almost immediately. But no, it doesn't bother me in the least. You're one of the most compelling, loveliest creatures I've ever had the opportunity to meet. And I regret you seeing me in that moment more than I could ever express."

I took the compliment for what it was and smiled back. I couldn't wait. For the first time since I could remember, I felt like I belonged somewhere. Like everything I was had purpose. It was a heady, light feeling, and I happily floated on it as long as I could.

CHAPTER 16
VASSAGO

AFTER OUR CONVERSATION, I sent Greta off to her apartment to rest. Her exhaustion worried me despite her repeated assurances that she was no more tired than normal, and she'd been like this as long as she could remember. At the rate she napped, she could have given any cat a solid run for their money.

I'd made a casual record out of curiosity, and most days she visited, Greta only had around eight hours total of wakefulness. Perhaps a third of that was her either beginning to wear down toward a nap or trying to perk up after, as well. I couldn't imagine how frustrating it must be for her, but she never seemed upset about it. She'd accepted it for what it was. I decided to always strive to allow her to when she needed to, in hopes that would improve things overall for her.

Besides, today I wanted her to have some time to acclimate to her new environment, especially after what she'd learned. Her acceptance of what I was, having seen me at my worst, had impressed me but also left me worried. What else had she seen, been through, that such a revelation was so easily accepted? I suppose it should have put me at ease, but I was afraid she'd disappear from my collegium one night, never to return.

She emerged from her apartment at nearly the same time I did, looking refreshed and not at all terrified of me. I was even gifted a smile. Relief was a tangible thing, and a weight lifted from my shoulders, allowing me to breathe again. I was pleased that we were now only separated by a single wall instead of half a city, it made the ache in my chest feel better to know where she was at virtually all times.

"Hungry?" I asked.

"Starving."

Her enthusiasm around food never failed to bring me joy. "Shall we?" I offered my bent arm, and after turning an enticing shade of pink, she looped her arm through mine. I escorted her down the stairs and into the dining room, pleased to find Magnus already seated and Grace setting down several plates.

"Right on time!" she enthused, beckoning us closer. "I do love having a full table for supper. I hope you like chicken pie, Greta."

"It smells delicious," Greta replied earnestly, accepting my gesture of pulling out her chair.

"How are you getting on in the apartment, niece?" Magnus passed a basket of steaming rolls as he looked her over.

"The bed is like a cloud," she sighed dreamily. "The sofa too, actually. I can't wait to take a bath later, that tub is positively decadent." Greta stopped, clamped her mouth shut and pulled back the enthusiasm. I hated it. I loved the way her eyes danced when she spoke about something that excited her, even if it was as mundane as a bathing tub. "I've never had such a nice room, thank you." She glanced between the two of us as Grace took the empty seat next to Magnus.

"You are most welcome." Magnus preened a little, pleased with her complimentary words, but I noticed the jaw flex and fist clench that betrayed his rage. He hated that she'd made it to this age before getting something as simple as a comfortable bed. I noticed because I felt the same. "I always have several options for where I get my rest." His eyes drifted to Grace, and I raised my eyebrow, earning a slight glare. "I'd much rather you have use of it than me."

Greta poked at the pie on her plate, cautious before taking a small bite.

"Is there something wrong?" Grace asked, more concerned than I'd ever seen her. She clearly wanted Greta to be as happy here as the rest of us.

"No, not at all." Grace smiled, dipping in enthusiastically for another bite. "This is delicious, as always." At Grace's continued stare, Greta explained, "Caroline ... she's a good cook, but she's always been miserable at pastry. It was never flaky, always either gummy or over floured. It burned or was too thick and never baked through when she tried making pie. Whether for dessert or something like this. Those meals I had to hurry and chew through. But yours is just perfect, Grace."

"Well." Grace blushed under the compliment, and Magnus grinned wide as well, and they exchanged a look that confirmed without a doubt they'd turned a corner in their relationship. "I appreciate that."

Magnus had us all laughing with a story about his council meeting, though I could tell by the tightness around his mouth that the actual series of events hadn't been at all amusing.

"If you have time, you should come with us to the market one of these first days, Greta. I think you might find some things there you'd like. Perhaps some new ingredients for me to turn into tea?"

"I've never been to the market here," Greta said quietly, face turned down to her plate. "I was able to go a few times during festivals during our stays at the country house, though. A trip out sounds nice. I just don't want you to waste any more effort on my behalf unless you want to."

"Of course I want to," Grace chided gently, affronted, but still smiling. "You're a brand-new puzzle I want to figure out. I'm sure there's a good combination to be had to help re-energize you. Besides, finding out everyone's favorite things to eat and drink and the things that make them smile is a joy to me. Let me do it."

Greta's mouth twitched, and she nodded. "Okay. I'd love to go with you."

"I'll come along, too, if that's alright?" I asked, getting visions of the wonder Greta might have on her face traversing the stalls and shops in the heart of Revalia. I shook myself after a moment, realizing I was cataloging several items I wouldn't mind finding for her.

Magnus narrowed his gaze at me as though trying to work something out. "Why does she need energizing tea?"

"She tires quickly," I explained simply.

"Niece?"

Greta paused mid drink. "I've been this way as long as I can remember." She shrugged. "I need at least one nap most days. Lara brought a physician to see me a few times, and they offered teas or herbal tinctures. Nothing helped. Lara believed me to be lazy, but I just never feel totally rested. Though that bed is a wonder and may cure me," she joked, a chagrined lift to her lips.

"Any other ailments?" Magnus asked, rubbing his chin thoughtfully.

"I heal slowly, but my hand is nearly all better."

"It's been several weeks at this point," I countered. "But I've been pleased with your progress since I first saw your injury."

"I've always healed *well*, just slowly. And my hair ..." She stopped and shook her head. She tugged on the ends of her curls with one hand.

"What about it?" Magnus asked, tone soft.

"It doesn't grow. It was cut like this once when I was a child. It's never gotten any longer."

I digested this information, as did Grace, whose eyes were wide.

"What is that ring you're wearing?" Magnus asked.

Greta's eyes darted around the table, her hands folding into her lap. "A suitor's token," she said simply.

"It appears to be enchanted," I added. "It isn't removable."

"What?" Grace screeched, her silverware clattering against the table. "That's possible?"

"Unfortunately," I grumbled, noticing the embarrassed flush in Greta's cheeks. "We're working on a solution for that."

"I'd hope so. We've some strong metal cutters at the foundry. I'm sure Imogen would be happy to cut it off for you."

"Thanks," Greta bobbed her head. "Maybe we'll try that soon."

"Anyhow, how often do you stone sleep?" Magnus asked. Greta just stared at him. "Stone sleep," he said again, as though the repetition would spur her into speech.

"I'm sorry, I don't know what that is." Her voice was quiet, edged with shame. I braced, hating that she felt badly about something she had no control over.

His face turned a concerning shade of red as he held his breath against whatever it was that he truly wanted to say, then blustered through whatever had angered him, hands flailing as he ranted under his breath. "You are thirty years of age?" he confirmed.

"Yes, as far as I know. I celebrate my birthday in May."

"I'm sure there's a record. We can verify the date is the same," he said, thoughtful. "As I recall, that's correct, though. Rowan brought you to the circle for blessings around Beltane when you were brand-new. You don't recall your mother going into stone sleep?"

Her cheeks reddened as she shook her head, and I stiffened in response. Her voice was quiet, edged with shame. "I don't remember much, though. My memories are just a smile here, the way my mother's voice sounded there … I was very little when …"

Magnus softened. "Apologies, Greta. It is not your fault, but for a stone kin youth to not learn how to stone sleep … I can't imagine the troubles that might arise without doing so for such a prolonged period of time. It may explain your ailments." Grace rose to clear our empty plates, and Magnus reached across the table, covering her hand with his own. "I know you've been without her far too long. You were just a baby, really. One of us should've been called in to help you, instead …" He trailed off and visibly shook himself. "Alright, we'll have to start at the beginning then, yes?"

WE'D BEEN SHOOED out into the grassy area of the yard by Grace, who said she had to wash the dishes and finish preparing our dessert.

"Shall we all have a little stretch?" Magnus loosened the side lacings on his trousers and shirt, then reached his arms above his head. As he brought them down, he shifted into his stone form. He gained several inches in height and width, especially with his bony spear-tipped wings stretched out wide. His olive skin turned greenish gray, his mouth held massive tusk-like fangs, and his feet became lion's paws.

Greta looked on in awe. Impulsively, I shifted as well, trying to make her feel comfortable enough to follow our lead while at the same time revealing my true nature. The more she saw it without adverse reaction, the more I'd believe that she truly wasn't afraid.

"White feathers?" she teased, though her tone still held an edge of tension. My heart leapt in my chest, regardless. "How did you manage that? I thought those were reserved for—"

"I'm no angel," I confirmed, smiling through my fangs. "Not anymore."

"Yes, yes. He's a very lucky devil to have retained such pretty features and all that." Magnus rolled his eyes but winked at Greta, clearly also interested in putting her at ease. "Can you show us your beautiful wings, little niece? As I recall, they were some of the most unique our kind has ever been gifted."

"Aw, Magnus. You think I'm pretty?" I teased, batting my eyelashes, fingers delicately touching my chest.

"For the love of saints, demon. That's not what I said."

"But you're not denying it." I smiled wide, loving the way I got under his skin.

He sighed, shaking his head. "Greta?"

"I don't have wings." Her body was stiff, her voice low as though she were embarrassed to admit such a thing.

Magnus boomed a laugh as he folded his wings down and strode closer to her. "Of course you do, I've seen them. You were just a babe, but I remember them quite well."

Greta's expression morphed several times, from confusion to relief to sadness. Then, she pulled herself together as I watched. It was a truly magical process. Her back straightened, and a calm expression slipped over her features. She once again wore the unbothered mask I thought she'd left behind at Henrik's house. I hated it, but I understood more than most why she needed it. If she got excited about something like wings, only to be disappointed, it might break her spirit altogether.

Magnus shrank back to human form, and I did the same, tucking my wings away and relaxing my fangs. "Don't be nervous." He smiled, nodding gently in encouragement. "Just try. They're in there, you just need to will them to come out." Greta closed her eyes, focusing. "Think of the wind. What it feels like when you float in water—the air is much the same." Magnus encouraged.

She reached up and rubbed at the spot on her left shoulder that always seemed to bother her. "I get an itchy sensation, but there's nothing else," she said. "Sometimes it's more like a burn, but I've never had wings that I can remember. I've never shifted either, I have no stone form."

Magnus frowned again. "You used to, at the very least. I've seen both. Try again."

Greta fidgeted as she stood there, eyes closed and mouth pressed into a tight line. She made a pained noise and reached for her shoulder. "I can't, I'm sorry."

"Perhaps I could teach you a few tricks we have the younglings do."

"I'd rather not." She blushed fiercely, shame drawing her kind features into a frown as she rolled her shoulders back, distress pulling her eyes tight. "Not right now."

"There's plenty of time to learn," I said, stepping to her side.

"Of course. I'm sorry, niece. I didn't mean any harm. Just trying to help. If you can figure out how to shift, you can begin the process of learning to stone sleep. I'm just anxious for you to start."

She nodded. "I know. And I appreciate it. I just need some time, I think, get my head around things. Do you really believe I can get them back?" she asked, eyes impossibly round, hopeful. My heart clenched. She had given so much more than should have been required of her.

"You're in the right place, Greta." I took the opportunity to grasp for her hand and gently passed my lips over her knuckles. It gained me a raised eyebrow from her uncle, but I cared little. She was my concern, and in that, at least, he and I were aligned. "We'll help you figure things out. In your own time."

She brightened a bit, rubbed at her shoulder again, then dropped her hand as though she'd suddenly realized she was doing so.

"Are you alright?" Her head bobbed, but she twitched her shoulders up one at a time as though trying to shrug off a pain. I leaned in close to her ear to whisper, "Would you like one of us to take a look? I don't like that you're having pain, Dragonfly."

"No, thank you. I'm alright. It's always like this."

"But that's not normal, Greta," I argued.

"It is for me," she said with a finality that brokered no disagreement. I straightened, realizing too late I'd overstepped without intending to.

"I don't know what happened, but the demon is right. We'll help you figure it all out, one way or the other."

"I appreciate it. I do. I just … need some time. Excuse me."

Magnus and I exchanged looks of concern as she headed back toward the building.

"I didn't mean to …" Magnus pursed his lips, giving a rueful shake of his head.

Guilt sank into my flesh, burning as I watched her vanish inside. "It's alright."

"I don't like that ring," he grunted, arms crossed and a scowl on his normally jolly face.

"Me neither," I said. "Though, admittedly, for different reasons."

His mouth twitched. "Surely there's a way to remove it?"

I nodded slowly. "None of the conventional means have worked, but yes, I'm sure there's a way."

"Good. Doesn't belong there, and I don't like that she can't take it off. Who is this suitor?" I gave him as much information as I had, but he hadn't heard his name either. "I'll see what I can find out. I already don't like him."

I agreed wholeheartedly, and we made our own way back inside.

Giving her some space was my intent for the evening, but I couldn't shake the feeling that there was something Greta wasn't telling us. I was going to do everything I could to find out what.

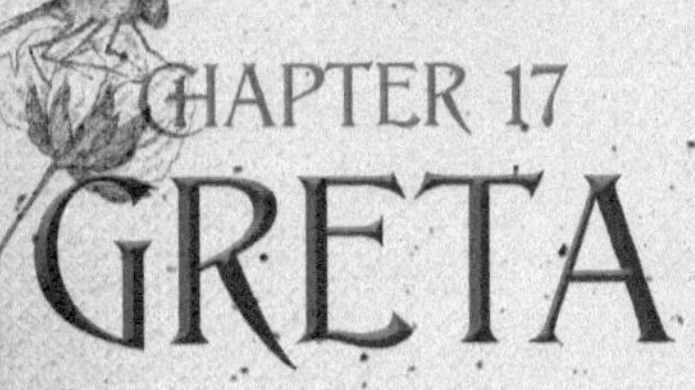

CHAPTER 17
GRETA

"**W**HAT'S THIS?" I asked, tapping my finger on the open page of Lilith's grimoire. Vassago had left it on my worktable, set to something he wanted me to see.

"Just an experiment that is outside my realm of expertise. I thought you'd excel at it, however," he said, working his way over from the sofa. He began arranging pots of ingredients on my worktable, clearly on a mission if he knew exactly what he needed to grab.

He was distracting me from my melancholy, I could tell. To my mild amusement, it was working.

After learning that I'd once been a proper gargoyle with wings and a stone form, and being reminded that it wasn't normal to feel the pains I did so often, I'd spent several hours pacing my new apartment. I'd tried soaking in the tub and lying on the bed, but sleep would not come as my mind spun. I was extra tired this morning because of it, but I appreciated his attempt at distracting me.

I read over the spell. "This is a recipe for the Elixir of Life." I frowned, looking at his skeptically. "*Nobody's* ever made this before."

He lit the small flame under my equipment with a flourish of his fingers and a flint. Jealousy warred with gratitude, because it would have taken me at least six tries with the striker to get it lit. "That's not true," he argued. "Someone has. Otherwise, how would we have a recipe?"

I tilted my head, eyes squinting at him. "I'm certain this is *well* above my skill level."

"And *I'm* certain you're underestimating yourself. But if you insist, perhaps we can try"—he flipped a few pages—"this one first."

I bit my lip, scanning the recipe. "Elixir of Health?" It didn't seem all that complicated, and if I went slowly, one step at a time ... "This isn't quite what I normally do, but I can try."

Vassago nodded once, a playful smile tugging at his lips. His quiet confidence made my blood warm.

"How is it you just happen to have such rare ingredients lying about?" I asked.

He shrugged. "My brother is a collector, as am I. One never knows when they might need something rare or unusual." He winked at me and pulled out an aged brown glass vial. The label on it was yellowed, the script all flourishes.

"Mm. How long have you kept this"—I consulted the label—"'oil of vitriol' while you waited for the right occasion?"

Vassago smiled widely, fangs teasing at his bottom lip as he ran his fingers through his long hair. "A while, Dragonfly. It's safe though, don't worry. It's as stable now as it ever was."

Oddly, my confidence was not bolstered by that endorsement, and I made sure to be extra gentle with that vial. After I collected the few remaining supplies, I studied all the pages for the spell carefully, making sure there wasn't an instruction several lines down or over a page that was important to the first step. Things like that were why I constantly failed at baking.

Because I was looking down, my hair kept falling out from behind my ears, getting in my face. I tucked it back repeatedly and grew increasingly agitated.

"Come here, Little Dragonfly." Vassago beckoned. I met him halfway, and he stepped behind me, confident fingers sliding effortlessly through my hair.

"What are you—" I barely contained a contented sigh, the scrape of his nails against my scalp sending tingles through my whole body.

Nobody ever played with my hair besides Bea, and when she had, it was more out of a fidget for her own comfort than to soothe me. I couldn't begin to count the mornings I'd woken up when she was a toddler with her fingers tangled up in my curls. That never helped with the brushing situation, but I'd always loved it.

Vassago pulled a length of silver ribbon from his pocket. As it brushed along my neck, I wondered why he always happened to have such a thing on his person. "There. Now it'll stay out of your eyes." His breath was warm as it feathered along my scalp. "We wouldn't want it to catch on fire, either, would we?"

"No." The word grated out of my throat, and I wished he hadn't been so efficient at what he'd been doing.

My fingers rose to inspect his work, and what I found made my chest squeeze. In those short seconds, with no effort or pulling at all, he'd braided my often-tangled short curls into a perfect fishtail plait.

He'd given me princess hair.

The blush rose furiously to my cheeks as he met my eye, long legs carrying him to the other side of my worktable as he somehow braided his own hair back without pausing a beat. Once his white locks were also safely braided and tied back by a silver ribbon, he placed both palms flat on the wooden top and smiled at me. The points of his canine teeth dragged along his bottom lip. "Think of all the amazing things we could do with such a rare, but versatile potion. Shall we begin?"

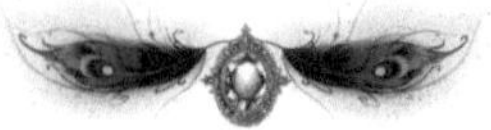

WE CONTINUED WELL into what would normally be a break for lunch, only pausing to accept Grace's offering of a basket and accept her gentle admonition for working too hard.

"You see that she gets a proper break, Mr. Feland."

"I've told you, Grace, you should call me Vassago. There's no need to stand on formality. You've done it before, I thought we were making progress?" She simply stared at him, one eyebrow raised, her hand on her hip. "Yes, ma'am. A break. A proper one, I promise."

"Good." Satisfied, she left the room with a sharp nod, though she threw a wink at me on her way. I appreciated that she was a force even the men in charge bowed to. It was beyond admirable.

We'd come to a particularly touchy part of the recipe, one that required all four of our combined hands to be steady and intense concentration. This was difficult for several reasons, not the least of which was that to accomplish what we needed to, he had to stand behind me. He was so close I felt exactly where every dip and curve between us met, and he frequently rested his cheek or chin on the top of my head. His stamina seemed limitless, but my muscles were growing shaky with weariness. Once we got past this part, though, I could eat and nap; everything should hold until we were ready to continue.

"Ready?" I asked, breathless, as I moved a spoon holding a volatile mixture that was in an odd creamy powder form across the table toward the crucible that held our whole morning's labors.

"Ready." His voice was low, sending an echo through my spine as it resonated through me.

I dipped the bottom of the spoon into the liquid inside the crucible, twisting it so the mixture would float at the top and dissolve slowly instead of sinking. Carefully, I set the utensil down on the table, an exhale that came from somewhere near my toes flowed out of me as the combination did what it was supposed to. At least, it did as far as I could tell. Nothing exploded, nothing caught fire and there was no smoke. That seemed positive.

Vassago's hands cradled my shoulders. "Nicely done, Little Dragonfly. I never doubted you." He pulled away with a wink, leaving my back chilled but my chest warm.

We made sure to wash up thoroughly before dividing the contents of Grace's basket. I sat curled up cross-legged on the floor, not trusting myself not to drop my plate. We'd spent more time than I'd anticipated holding something above the flame, above the dish, waiting. My muscles weren't used to such endurance training, and my arms currently were the same consistency as cooked pasta. I made short work of the sandwich and fruit, along with a large flask of water, flipping through a heavy book on alchemical theory as I did so.

"Are you alright, Greta?" Vassago asked, eyebrows drawn in concern.

"I'm fine," I assured him, but I caught myself rubbing at my shoulder again as he watched. It was always achy, always sore, but I was rubbing at it more and more without even meaning to. The itchiness had settled in deep, flaring as a burn more in the last several days than in most previous years combined.

"May I take a look?" he asked. "Please. I can't stand seeing you suffer like this."

I flushed hot. It was only a shoulder, but it was way more skin than we'd shared with one another. An argument formed on my tongue, but I stopped it. He was concerned, and if I was being honest, I desperately wanted some relief from the ache. If Vassago could help, I would gratefully take his aid. "Alright."

He set his plate on the sofa and crossed to where he could settle in behind me, his knees to either side of my head. I held my breath as he adjusted the collar of my shirt so he could open it more at the back. "Can you lean forward, please? Perhaps undo the top few buttons?"

I complied, and his fingers pulled at the shirt, the collar now settled somewhere under my shoulder blades. His fingers probed at the tight muscles with a gentle touch until he located a knot. His thumbs took up the work then, pressing in and under so that it made a slight crunching noise and a borderline painful sensation as he attempted to work it out.

All at once, the unpleasant sensation intensified. "Vassago?" I braced against the sudden discomfort.

"There are some darker spots here," he muttered, still working at the knot.

He probed a bit more and the pain flared. "Stop." The word came out as a gasp, and his fingers were instantly removed.

"What's wrong?" Vassago asked, hands roaming along my back, panic in his tone. "Have I hurt you?"

I shook my head, looking over my shoulder at him. I lifted my own hand, probing around to see if I could relieve the burn. "It's not you, there's a—" I sucked my breath in through my teeth as the burn became sharp, hot, like a knife at the edge of my shoulder blades where they ran near my spine. I tried to describe it, but the pain stole my breath. "It's like the itch I get sometimes but painful."

"Hold still if you can, Little Dragonfly. Let me see." His breath puffed against my skin as he leaned in close. I was folded in half, knees to my chest in a defensive posture. He touched something that sent an electric shock down my spine, and I whimpered.

"I'm sorry," he apologized. "Whatever's under the skin here"—he traced a loose oval around the region that hurt, all along that inside edge of my shoulder blade on both sides—"doesn't look like an infection, but there's discoloration. Bruising maybe. Nothing visible to cause that response though." I frowned. I had no idea about that, I'd never seen anything odd when I looked in the mirrors at the Belette manor, but mine were the older, cloudy castoffs. "This isn't quite enough to get a good look, Dragonfly. Can we perhaps pull your shirt up instead?"

"I suppose." I swallowed thickly, nerves strung tight at the thought of him seeing my whole back. I clutched the book to my middle as I bent forward over my knees.

His warm touch drifted across my skin as he pulled my shirt up from the hem with both hands. I braced when the pads of his thumbs crossed one of the raised areas that dotted my back, then another. The slow ascent of the fabric stopped, and a harsh breath left him.

"Greta." There was both empathy and rage in his voice. The fabric around my ribs tightened as he fisted it. Mist crept over my skin, preceding his touch. His warm hands mapped the patchwork of scars along my back. I had been braced against his exploration, but found myself melting into it after a moment, despite the low rumble of a growl in his chest and the heat of his body as he leaned as close as possible to mine.

"Who did this to you, Greta? I must know who has requested a slow, painful death by marking you in such a way. Was this Henrik's doing?" He spat the words darkly, jaw tightly clenched.

"Lara." Henrik had never approved of her methods, but he'd also never taken any actions to stop her. I closed my eyes, picturing her favorite punishment tools. The metal hairbrush with stiff boar bristles that never failed to create more knots in my curls than it helped. Any kind of stick she could find nearby. A broken spoke from the rails on my old iron headboard was her favorite though. It left the best marks.

"For what purpose would she harm you in such a way? There's nothing you could have done to deserve this. *Nothing*." I turned my head and found him practically vibrating with rage. His eyes were bright rubies, sharp fangs had extended, and heat poured from him in a heady wave. The smoky mist crawled along the edges of his form, shifting in a decidedly agitated way.

"Lara said she was teaching me."

He snarled a curse in a language I didn't understand.

"These are all old. She hasn't lifted a hand to me in several years. Not since I got taller than her and bold enough to stop her hand mid swing. I didn't know any better as a child."

He roared, and there was the sound of fabric tearing, followed by a grunt and a cool breeze over my entire back. "She will pay for this, Little Dragonfly. A hundred times over if I plan it right." He sounded distant, far too calm as he pushed the torn halves open, leaving them to dangle at my sides. "I'm sorry. I've ruined your shirt. I'll get you another."

I said nothing as he mapped every inch of my skin, his breath warm as he leaned close to inspect my flesh. I shivered under the contrast of his cool mist and heated touch and ached for reasons that seemed wholly inappropriate to what was happening.

It worried me how much I wanted him to punish her for what she'd done. It made me no better than them. It was concerning how I melted under the suggestion of someone being offended by my mistreatment. That I knew I would watch it happen and feel nothing but satisfaction.

But still, I said nothing.

"It looks like deep bruising," he said finally. "Perhaps from your worrying at it. But I want someone with more knowledge to examine it very soon. You need to be able to shift, to stone sleep. I need you to not be in pain. It's gone on far too long. I will take you wherever we need to go so you can get well, Greta. Anywhere."

"Thank you," I said, perilously close to tears. I found myself overwhelmed, particularly by his use of *we*. He was including himself in my problems, my life, and I strangely had less than no objections about that.

The mist retreated, and after gently brushing the space right between my shoulder blades—it was so brief I couldn't tell if it was fingers or his lips, though either had made me shiver in the best way—Vassago got to his feet and stalked across the room to a small cabinet. He retrieved several tins of salve, dropping one twice in his rush to get them. With a swear, he settled behind me again.

"I'm going to try these for now," he explained. "My brother made them for me. But I need you to tell me when you're getting the pains. Every time. Please."

"Okay." Under his gentle touch, the ache eased. "That's better."

"I'm sorry, Greta. I didn't mean to hurt you." His palms were hot against my bare shoulders, and I felt his lips brush against the back of my neck before he righted my shirt as best he could, tucking the torn halves back together.

I sat back, book still clutched to my front. "It wasn't your fault."

"Mm." He made a displeased noise before getting up and grabbing a small throw. He draped it around my shoulders, gathering it together at my front. He glanced up and stared deep into my eyes, a muscle ticking in his jaw as he moved several steps away.

"Apologies, I—"

My heart thudded in my chest, and a slight waver in my voice kept my words from sounding as confident as I wanted. "You don't scare me."

Vassago's hands were suddenly in my hair again, the braid loosened and his fingers gently combing through. "I'll buy you a dozen new shirts."

"This one has seen better days anyway." They all had, if I was honest, but what kind of man worried so much about a torn shirt? "What will you do about Lara?"

I heard the cold smile in his voice. "She will pay. They both will, and dearly. I will spend hours fantasizing about their punishments, in fact. But not today. Today my concern is you." I leaned my cheek against the side of his knee, my head too heavy to hold up any longer. "Rest, Greta. You're safe here with me, I promise. I'm not going anywhere."

Sleep came for me in earnest then, and I was powerless to stop it.

CHAPTER 18
VASSAGO

WITH MY FINGERS pulling through her hair, Greta had been deep asleep in no time at all. The heavy book on alchemical theory she'd been looking at after lunch landed on the floor with a soft thud as her cheek pressed into my thigh. She had responded positively when I'd braided her hair before, and I loved that such a simple touch eased her tension. The sensation of the silky strands against my skin certainly wasn't a deterrent for me and did a much better job at quelling the rage I'd felt seeing her scars than I expected.

I frowned. I didn't even recognize myself when I had the kind of thoughts I only ever had around her. I was almost painfully compelled to drag my mouth along her throat while I inhaled the concentrated scent that lingered at the curve where her neck and shoulder met. I'd kissed the soft space between her shoulder blades without even stopping to think about it. I'd wanted to lavish every part of her back with remnants of an old hurt with such affection.

It didn't help one bit that it was possible for me to determine exactly what had happened to her back if given the chance to sink my fangs into her flesh, to taste the memories in her blood. I would have to suggest it, despite my hesitation to invite my curse to rear its head on purpose, especially now that my rage had been provoked.

Lust, as always, was an enthusiastic companion to anger. I forced myself to sit back and breathe as I trailed my fingers through her hair. Once I had myself fully calmed, I lifted her onto the chaise and covered her with her favorite blanket.

While she slept, I went up to my room. I took an extra dose of my bloodlust tincture and retrieved a new shirt for her from my armoire. When I returned, I scoured my books for any mention of lost shifting ability, blocked wings ... anything that could be helpful. There was nothing much, though several high-powered curses were thought to have similar effects.

Before I realized much time had passed at all, she was sitting up.

"Is it ready for the next phase?" she asked sleepily.

"I'm sure it's well dissolved by now," I agreed, glancing over at her worktable. "Here." I handed her the shirt. It was one I rarely wore, as it was a bold blue, but I thought it suited her. She gave me her back to remove her destroyed one, and I also turned away to provide her some modesty. My blood surged hot, my ego unreasonably thrilled at how she looked in my garment when she turned back around.

Greta tossed aside the blanket, hastily drinking some more water.

"There's no rush." I chuckled at her enthusiasm.

"Yes, there is," she replied brightly, no trace of the heaviness we'd shared before remaining. "I want to see if we've done it properly!"

"As you wish, Little Dragonfly. Shall we continue?"

"Yes, please. And thank you ... for before."

"You're welcome." I rubbed my knuckles across my heart, trying to soothe the ache her words brought to life. Now that my rage had cooled, my concern was more for her than seeking vengeance on her behalf.

Though that would absolutely happen as well, and it would be spectacular. I could hardly wait, in fact, but I had lots of planning to do to ensure the Belettes' suffering was adequate. Someone had delighted in marking up as much of her lovely skin as possible. I was not always a good man, so I would find joy in repaying the dishonor in kind.

Together we read through the next and final set of steps, agreeing that we weren't missing anything and that we had everything at hand that we could possibly need.

"Alright," she said, inhaling slowly as she moved the whole container over the flame.

"Four drops of the essence of life. That's it," I told her.

"Mine? Or yours?" She blushed hot, an enticing pink color creeping over her cheeks.

"Yours. Mine is ... an unknown variable."

"Alright." She pricked her fingertip with a knife without hesitation, carefully squeezing out drops one at a time. Then we waited.

The mixture swirled lazily for several breaths. It was a shimmery silver, like someone had poured mercury into the glass. It continued to spin and swirl, darkening to red, then an odd greenish color, then settled on purple before emitting a tiny puff of steam and going still.

It was done.

Greta had perfectly executed a recipe that better-practiced alchemists had failed mightily at—and on her first try. One of only a handful of successes ever, if the records were accurate.

"You've done it," I breathed, a wisp of her hair moving with my exhale, as I was still standing right behind her.

"I ... Is that real?" she asked, reaching out a finger toward the container but stopping short of touching it. "The Elixir of Health. That can't be right, can it?"

"It's real."

She spun, smile brighter than I'd ever seen, her hands fisted as she bounced on her toes. "We did it!" A little excited squawk came out of her throat, then she reached up and hugged me.

I wrapped my arm around her, steadying her against me, and stepped us back away from the table to prevent any accidents from happening. The last thing either of us wanted was to see that flask crash to the floor. I wasn't sure I could get there, even with the help of my mist if it toppled over.

Whether or not I caused the way our feet got tangled up was a mystery, but Greta ended up with her back pressed against the supply cabinet, my forearms flat against the glass. Her chest heaved and cheeks flushed as she gazed up at me with wide eyes.

"Are you alright?"

"Yes," she whispered.

There was no missing how her eyes tracked my mouth, the way I was steeped in her scent or how my heart kept trying to reach for her directly through my chest. It had been the sweetest torture to spend the day pressed up against her from behind, able to smell her hair and feel the curves of her body line up with the planes of mine. And now, with her dressed in my clothing, after what we'd been through earlier, I hardly had any restraint at all left.

"Greta," I warned.

"It's okay. I want—" She swallowed, my eyes following every movement of her throat and the way her tongue darted out to wet her bottom lip.

I cupped her cheek with one hand, warring with myself as every impulse in my body screamed at me.

Her eyes became glazed, half-closed, and I lost all hold on my control. I dove in like a man starved, plundering her mouth with my own. I swallowed her noises of surprise, growling back as she pressed herself against me instead of retreating.

She tasted like the berries we'd had with lunch, and I marveled at the softness of her body under my hands, my lips. I teased at her bottom lip with one fang, swiping at the tiny droplet of blood I'd made rush to the surface with my tongue as she sucked in a breath. To my great pleasure, she didn't pull away as a brief collage of her here at the collegium danced across my mind. If anything, she hovered closer, asking for more in the way her eyes lingered, half-closed, her hands fisted in my shirt.

"Vassago." My name was music on her lips, speaking to the darkest parts of me. The neediest. The most dangerous.

"Greta." I pressed my lips to hers again, but gently, taking my time exploring. I mapped the way her cupid's bow formed perfect points on her lush upper lip and a tiny scar caused an imperfection in her bottom one. The way she reached for me the way I was for her. The way she hesitated, but just barely, when I requested she open for me by swiping along her lips with my tongue.

As I kissed her deeply, she followed my lead, making another of those incendiary sounds. I lost myself in her, and it was glorious. When I finally swam back out of the heady moment, we were both panting, tangled in one another's arms against the cabinet.

Guilt crashed in as I stared down at her, shame that I'd allowed myself to take advantage like that. "Forgive me, Greta, I—"

"I wanted this," she cut me off firmly.

I sucked in a shuddering breath and lowered my forehead to hers, blood surging again. "If I'm taking advantage, I'd never forgive myself. I shouldn't have—"

"You aren't. You didn't. You *wouldn't*." She sounded so confident I had no choice but to believe her. "You're the noblest gentleman I've ever met, which might not be saying much given my restricted exposure, but you're allowed to feel things too. Just as I'm allowed to want something for myself. And I've never wanted anything like I wanted this." Her breath eased out of her then, and her eyes widened as she realized the confession she'd made.

My heart squeezed in my chest. "I don't deserve you, Dragonfly."

She gave a slow smile. "Of course you do."

Which naturally, was further proof I did not, but I said nothing. I just allowed myself to linger there, in that moment, for a little bit longer before crashing us both back to reality.

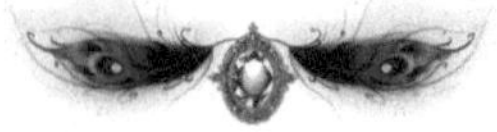

"THE MORE RECENT the injury, the better the chance it can be put to rights. My daughter Lovette is a very talented healer. She's mended wounds I believed beyond all help. I'm sure she would be honored to help." Magnus had joined us in my apartment for a drink after supper and examined Greta's shoulder with concern.

"It's probably been too long," she lamented, rubbing at the offending muscle out of reflex.

"Perhaps, but you never know. Worth a look in any case, little niece. It would be good for everyone to meet you, as well. And I'd be willing to bet Imogen has a special tool to rid you of that ring once and for all, as well." His eyes slid to mine, and I shook my head. The pinch of his mouth indicated he'd had no luck finding Feiser either. "Are you up for a trip to the conclave?"

"Conclave?"

"It's what we call our little settlement in the forest just outside of Revalia. Neither the labor camp nor the military outpost are part of it, though neither are very far. We have a miniature town there pretty much, disguised and hidden among the forest. Our kind doesn't always feel comfortable integrating with the human population of a city. We're here a lot, but it's also nice to have somewhere to go to be among ourselves. Besides, there are things we fabricate and do that are best kept away from prying eyes. Humans get overwhelmed seeing creatures with wings, besides."

"Are your children there?"

Magnus beamed. "Some of them, yes. Lovette and Imogen have

been there on and off since the fall. Coltor hasn't arrived yet, but word is he's on his way. My eldest, Tormund, is the one we see least of, but he'll likely join us eventually. Lovette's twin, Lionel, is finishing a long journey, but we should see him by winter. I'm hopeful we'll all be together soon." He grinned like he was keeping a secret, but I had a strong suspicion he was trying to get them all in one place so he could introduce them to Grace.

"Do you think she would have time to see me?" Greta asked. "Are there many injuries to be tended?"

"Of course she would." Magnus laughed heartily, his tone just this side of offended. "There's always flesh to be mended, but she'll make time for you. When would you like to go? Soon, yes?"

"We can't leave the school unattended." I pondered how best to arrange things, but Magnus was one step ahead of me.

"You wouldn't be gone more than a few days, I don't think. But surely one of us with wings could travel between if need be."

"I appreciate that very much, Magnus." Greta gave him one of her soft smiles and he beamed.

"It is my pleasure, niece. Now, I have a much less fun place I think you should also visit, so keep in mind that you like me when you get there."

"What is the less fun place?" she asked, nerves making her voice rise.

Magnus shook his head. "One of the eldest of our kind, Ophelia. I think you would benefit from a visit to her, but she's unpredictable. Calla visited with her and learned a great deal. But she's not keen on company, and if she's in a mood ..." He shivered.

The mountainous man being scared of an old woman seemed preposterous, but I knew as well as he did the oldest of us often only got scarier, more unpredictable. More powerful.

"If you think it will help, I'm more than happy to go." Greta nodded.

"Then you'll need salted licorice. The more the better."

I tilted my head at the suggestion but believed him. Even with demon-kind, when the most ancient got to a certain point, it was dangerous to approach them. Many had felt the wrath of a deteriorating elder, and most of those were lucky to have survived.

"I owe Greta a trip to the markets anyhow. We can get supplies."

"I'll inform them you're coming to the conclave as soon as possible. And I'll speak to Ophelia as well." Magnus finished off his drink and got to his feet, bowing out on a promise from Greta that she didn't mind if he retrieved a few more things from the apartment while he was here.

"I should go with you," she said, covering a yawn with her hand. "I could use a good soak before I get in bed. Good night, Vassago."

"Good night, Dragonfly." I watched her go with regret, but immediately set to making plans.

CHAPTER 19
GRETA

GOING TO THE market was an event I realized I wasn't prepared for once we got there. Several days after creating the elixir, we'd finally ventured out, and to my dismay, the noise alone had me on edge. People shouted numbers and orders and wore angry expressions as they bickered over products. Aggressive, loud voices seemed to surround me in all directions.

There was a raven hovering above us, making a knocking noise as it circled, and I was certain it was my bird. He'd been making a point to check on me at least once every day since I'd moved in, tapping impatiently with his beak if I forgot to open my window before breakfast. I'd started leaving little treats for him, scraps from my meals, mostly. In return he'd brought me several gifts. Each and every time I went outside, I was sure to find him nearby. He liked to follow me from one end of the grounds to the other. I wasn't sure why he'd adopted me, but his friendship was appreciated.

"I've got you, Dragonfly," Vassago whispered close to my ear, his arm protectively around my shoulders as he steered me through narrow alleys and around the busiest stalls.

Grace contributed to the noise, well-practiced at her routine and one of the loudest voices when she needed to be heard. "It was seven last week, and six the two before that!" She scoffed at one of the vendor tables, her finger waving in the merchant's face as she demanded a better price. "I'll pay no more than seven, or I'll find a new vendor," she threatened. "There are a dozen others who will gladly take d'Arcan's business."

"Of course, of course. Seven, a special price only for you. As long as you're taking the same number of crates?" the merchant responded, clearly disappointed that his price increase was not quietly accepted by her.

Vassago chuckled, his breath tickling along my cheek. "Let's move along, yes? Grace has this well in hand."

I nodded, overwhelmed by the crush of bodies in the main square.

He signaled to her that we were going a certain direction, and she waved back that she understood but never broke stride in her negotiations as she moved from one spot to the next, collecting everything she had on her list.

Vassago directed me onto one of the side streets, which was still busy but far removed from the bustle and noise of the central market square.

I made eye contact with several smiling merchants as I walked past their tables, which I quickly realized was mistaken as an invitation. One draped me with a bright-blue scarf she claimed was made from a fabric that came from special worms. That was not a detail I personally would have used to peddle silk, but it did feel wonderfully cool and smooth against my skin. Flustered, I handed it back, but I trailed my fingers over a similar one in green as we moved past her stall, loving the richness of the emerald color.

Several men and women offered me little treats to taste, and each seemed to hit more flavor notes than the last, all unique and nothing I'd ever experienced before.

"Which is your favorite?" Vassago asked with a grin, taking the little paper cones they'd given to me from my hands.

"The third one for salty. For sweet, the first. I love them all though. There's nothing here I wouldn't eat."

"I'd have to agree with you." He chuckled, staring right through me.

My cheeks heated as I stared back, taking in the clean lines of his silver vest and trousers, the way his hair was held back by two thin braids he'd formed on the sides then linked in the back with one of his ribbons. It should have been pretentious, out of place. But his regal beauty fit in wherever we went.

My eyes were dazzled by the colors and sparkle on the tables, my stomach thrilled by the selections everyone wanted me to sample. By the time we'd made a full loop down both sides of the alley and were headed back into the main square, Grace had finished her business and was coming toward us with a bright smile.

"How are you getting on?" She looked at my empty arms and clucked her tongue. "Nothing at all yet?"

"I'm not sure where I would start, to be honest," I admitted. "Though, I don't have any money."

"Of course you do," Vassago said smoothly.

"No, I don't." I frowned, eyebrows coming together in my confusion.

He shook his head, a playful grin on his mouth. "You do, Dragonfly. Ask for something, anything at all, and it shall be yours."

"I wouldn't want to take advantage." The blush crept up my throat and onto my cheeks, deepening as he stared down at me with his head tilted, the tip of his tongue resting in the corner of his mouth as though he were planning to taste me again. I hoped he was.

"You can't abuse something freely offered."

Grace linked her arm with mine. "Come with me, Greta. I need a cup of tea, and there's a place just here"—she pointed to the building ahead of us with one hand, making sure Vassago understood her intent—"that makes the best muffins. Then I'll take you to my favorite street for shopping, and you can choose all the little trinkets your heart desires to take back to the collegium, yes?"

I followed along because I had no choice, and Vassago said he'd be right behind us, that he was going to go get the salted licorice Magnus had suggested for Ophelia, as the vendor was nearby.

"I prefer the blueberry ones with the big granules of sugar on top," Grace said as she maneuvered us into the line for the counter. "But they have an apples-and-cinnamon kind with this brown sugar topping that's lovely too. I keep saying I'm going to try to make them, but I never get around to it. It's just too easy to get my fill when I come here instead."

"I think the apple for me," I said, mouth watering at the thought of the warm cinnamon flavor.

"Wonderful. Go on and get us a table, yes? I'll get our order in."

I sat down at an iron table set for four, waving Vassago over as he strolled in through the door with a large white paper bag bearing the candymaker's stamp. Grace was just behind, carrying a plate overflowing with a variety of muffins. She gestured, and he accepted a steaming pot of tea and cups from the woman behind the counter.

Grace took up the conversation, as she had a habit of doing, describing how more than one merchant knew better than to try the price gouging that first had done and what she'd do if she had to trade which vendors she gave d'Arcan's business to. Vassago chimed in where it was appropriate and smiled kindly the whole time, though I worried something was bothering him. I couldn't quite put my finger on it, but he no longer seemed as open as he had the rest of the morning.

The blueberry muffins were good, but the apple was as delicious as I'd hoped. Grace had even picked out some others to try—one made from bananas and one a lemon flavor with tiny sweet black seeds in it.

It was an entirely ordinary thing, sitting at that iron table sampling those delicious muffins and drinking mediocre tea, but it was one of my favorite new memories.

AFTER FORTIFYING OURSELVES, we took a slow meander down Grace's favorite market street. On the way back to the carriage, we walked the long way around so I could see the library as well as the cathedral. Both were stunning feats of architecture, and I couldn't wait to visit the insides of them. She pointed out several other important locations throughout Revalia as well, albeit all from a distance. The observatory at d'Arcan was a constant compass point, however, being the tallest and most recognizable building in the city.

Vassago frowned, fingers trailing down my arm as he focused on someone at the end of the street and took several steps away from me in their direction. I saw nothing more than the normal crush of people, but something had drawn his very serious attention.

"Stay with Grace. I'll be back." He looked at Grace, who nodded seriously, but turned on a bright smile as she led me to the next table. I glanced the direction he'd gone several times as we shopped, but he was nowhere to be found.

When we got to the end of the street, Vassago came around the corner, one hand tucked into the gap between buttons in his vest like he did when he was nervous or intently focused.

"Everything alright?" I asked, off balance by his unusual mood shift and behavior.

"Yes." His lips lifted, and he reached for the items I'd purchased. "Just saw someone I thought I recognized."

"Did you find them?" I asked as we shifted down to the next table.

He shook his head slowly, eyebrows coming together, as he leaned across me to trade a coin for a new leather pouch. His white locks drifted across my shoulder, his body pressing into mine as he did so. It was a distraction technique, and an effective one. "No, Dragonfly. He turned one too many corners before I could find out for sure." He linked his arm in mine, the carriage within view. "Shall we?"

I nodded, and Grace took up the conversation all on her own as we traveled back to d'Arcan, gushing over the choices I'd made. "It's always a bit hard to see straight when you're new to the market," she nodded sagely. "The vendors were all on their best behavior as well, I didn't see any that tried to take advantage of your lack of experience with bartering. Not like that food vendor. And did you see the candler?" She scoffed and launched into a recounting of how she wasn't having any part of the vendors increasing their prices.

I listened and nodded, feeling guilty when we arrived back at the collegium and I realized I hadn't been paying attention.

"I'm glad you came. And you made excellent choices. I hope you'll join me again. The vendors switch every few weeks, so there's always something new."

"I'd like that," I said. Grace patted my hand and veered off toward the kitchen while Vassago and I continued up the stairs.

All told, I'd chosen two books and a pot of lilac-scented hand cream to bring home. It felt odd spending money that wasn't mine. I'd never really had any to speak of, but for Vassago to hand over coin on my behalf ... I wasn't sure I liked it.

Once we were standing outside my apartment door, I found myself fidgeting, nervous about how to start that conversation.

"Are you alright?" he asked.

"Yes."

His eyes narrowed on me. "You can speak freely with me, Greta."

"I just—The money you spent."

"What about it?"

"I feel strange that you did it."

"You shouldn't. You ask for nothing, and I have ample coin to spare. It's my pleasure, truly, to use it on you." He leaned forward, pinning me with that golden stare that turned my insides to liquid. "But I can also understand why it might feel strange. I'll have to discuss numbers with my brother, but I'm certain we can come to an arrangement where a salary is concerned."

"Salary? So, am I to be faculty?"

"If you wish to be. I think you have much to offer the students should you choose to teach next term."

My heart thudded gleefully behind my ribs, pride and excitement bubbling over. "I would love that."

"Good. Then we'll need to make up a contract with our mutual terms. Until then, I'm happy to set aside some coin for you, for your time, so you have your own money." He frowned. "What did your employers do before? If you were not allowed to go into the city at all, did they purchase things for you?"

Shame quickly replaced the buoyant feelings. "I was given meals, boarding, and clothing. I received an hourly wage as well, but it was not much. They would hold my money until I made a supply request, then use my earned coin for that." Vassago's eyes flashed red and a muscle in his jaw ticked. "I didn't *need* anything else, but it would have been nice to be able to choose some things for myself once in a while. Bea was good about asking for things I mentioned, though." I smiled, remembering the time she'd gotten me some hair pins, and another where she'd found me a vial of rose oil. Her biggest triumph had been convincing Henrik that I was better served by a new pair of suede trousers and several linen shirts than the stiff shift dresses many of the maids lived in day in and day out.

"They are in your debt, Greta. Should you ever choose to make things right, I'd be honored to stand at your side to deliver the justice they deserve." His smile lacked all warmth, his teeth pointed and eyes a fierce ruby shade.

I worried for myself, because seeing him like that set my heart racing and had my thighs clenching together. My head bobbed as I struggled to swallow over the sudden rush of desire, and opened my apartment door, seeking an escape. "I appreciate that," I said, not sure what else I could say to calm him.

I knew he wasn't wrong, but until I met him, I'd been completely powerless to do much about it myself. "I'd like to go to Bea's ball," I blurted. It had been on my mind for days, but I wasn't sure how to bring it up.

"Ball?" he asked, shocked out of his anger. "When is it?"

"When they normally do their end-of-summer celebration. It's to announce her entrance into marriage eligibility." I couldn't help but grimace, even saying those words tasted bad.

"I'll be happy to escort you to her event." He nodded, vicious smile widening. I knew him well enough to know he was quietly plotting seven moves ahead for such a thing now that I'd mentioned it. "Sweet dreams, Greta."

"Good night." I took one step inside, then froze. "What ..." Tears filled my eyes as I took in the room.

Placed neatly on the square coffee table were things from all over the market. The emerald scarf made by the special worms. A box full to overflowing with several of the treats I'd sampled. Another book I'd regretted leaving behind but had wanted slightly less than the two I'd chosen. A new hairbrush with bristles spaced far apart that wouldn't pull so badly through my curls. Some delicious varieties of fruit I'd never seen before. A braided bread I remembered having during the solstice holidays as a child but hadn't seen in years. A dozen little things I'd lingered over for barely a moment, or maybe briefly touched.

I spun, finding Vassago still standing in the hall right where he had been.

"What have you done? And how? When?" I asked, though the questions came out on a laugh. Shock warred with pure elation at the novel experience of receiving gifts. He'd been a wonderful companion the whole day, following along patiently, explaining something here, holding something there. But he'd done so much more.

He'd paid attention. To me. To everything. The whole time.

"These are just some trinkets, Little Dragonfly. Take them as mementoes of your first visit to the city. Inconsequential, frivolous perhaps. But they brought you joy." His brow furrowed. "I worry that you've had far too little of that in your life. The coin I spent today means nothing in the grand scheme. I would spend a hundred times that to see you smile like you did while we walked around the market. I would take you back tomorrow, and the day after, stopping only when you've had your fill. You need only ask."

My throat clogged with emotion, rendering me speechless. Instead, I stepped right up against him, and threw my arms around his waist. He pulled me in close, both of his hands splayed wide along my spine. He breathed deeply, his mouth lingering in the curve of my neck.

I pulled back only enough to put my hands on his face and kiss him. He grunted in surprise, his grip on me tightened as he tasted me slowly right there in the quiet hall.

The way his lips moved against mine was intoxicating, and time was of no consequence as we mapped one another's mouths. One of his hands slid to grip my ass as he pressed me against him, his sharp fangs pricking my bottom lip. He followed the sting with a swipe of his tongue before diving back in again, his other hand cradling the back of my head as he took everything he needed from our embrace. It was like he was drawing out my very essence, drinking from my lips as he rumbled a soft groan and caused every nerve in my body to stand at attention.

When we finally broke apart, he ran gentle fingertips down my cheek as I remembered how to breathe, eyes bright red and canines vicious. "Get some rest, Greta."

He kissed my knuckles as I moved away, still able only to nod.

I wondered if I would survive this man or if that was even necessary as long as he was going to keep kissing me like that.

CHAPTER 20
VASSAGO

"**W**HAT BUG HAS crawled up your backside, demon?" Magnus growled at me over breakfast.

"What do you mean?" I grumbled, setting my cup down harder than I'd meant to, coffee sloshing over the rim. I'd spent a restless night pacing my apartment. My curse was riding my nerves hard day in and day out, no matter how much tincture I took.

I needed to tell Greta about my ability to see into memories as well, and I worried about putting yet another burden on her shoulders. We'd crossed several lines we couldn't uncross, and it was only fair to her to be honest about what happened when I consumed as little as a single drop of her blood. I just wasn't sure how to broach the subject, nor prepared for the potential negative reaction she might have to it. My gifts were a never-ending source of frustration for me, despite the incredible outcomes they had the potential to provide when used properly.

Not to mention the man responsible for putting that forsaken ring on Greta's finger was a ghost. Nobody knew anything about him other than he was wealthy and rarely came to the city. I'd done plenty of asking around while we were in town, and nothing had come of any of my leads. It was odd. More than, in fact. Add to that the glimpse I'd gotten of someone who was the very image of the man I'd long searched for ... and I was out of sorts.

Nobody else had that specific auburn hair; the look on his face showed all too clearly he'd been up to no good. It had been decades, but I'd never forget him. He was responsible for Lilith's book disappearing from my possession the last time around, not to mention my hateful curse. If he was in Revalia, I would find him and end the decades-long feud we found ourselves in by ending him. Besides all that, I still hadn't located the actual necklace I'd been hired by Henrik to find.

Between the three, I was beyond agitated. I hated not being able to locate something I was searching for, despised the feeling that I'd failed. All of these things added to that had made me want to climb out of my own skin with anxious rage.

"*That*," he said, pointing at the mess I was cleaning up with a napkin. "You've been stalking around here all morning like someone stole your favorite toy."

Greta was in the kitchen with Grace, which I was thankful for. He wasn't wrong, but nobody liked to have their bad mood pointed out to them. "I didn't sleep well," I said, hoping that would be enough explanation.

"My sympathies." He sipped at his tankard of coffee, head tilted to the side. "What's happening there? Your hand."

I dropped my hand to my lap, annoyed that he'd noticed I'd been pressing the heel of it into the space over my heart. "My chest hurts."

Magnus stilled. One eyebrow went up slowly. He glanced at the closed door of the kitchen, making sure we were alone. "What do you mean your chest hurts? Did you fall out of the sky or something? Have a wound left from the day we battled the demons?"

I blew out a breath and sat back in my chair, annoyed with myself that I'd not only let the discomfort get to me, but also that I'd let it show to others. "Just what I said, stone man. Something under my ribs is burning. Not from an injury, either. It simply won't leave me, no matter what I do. It's nothing."

"I see." Magnus gave me a solemn stare, compassion in his expression. That quickly melted away though, and his booming laugh rang out throughout the dining room.

I sighed, regretting having said anything at all. "Dare I ask? What exactly are you laughing about?"

"You. Well, you and your brother. In complete denial, the both of you."

"Denial? About what?" I barked the question more testily than I'd meant to, which only made him laugh harder. One of his meaty fists thumped the tabletop, making our plates jump.

"Oh, I wish he were here!" He wiped the tears in his eyes the laughter had brought forth.

"Speak clearly, Magnus." I gritted my teeth and delivered the words with a growl. I felt my fangs prickle in my mouth, and I had no doubt my eyes were red.

"Saints and stars, you are a mess today, aren't you?"

"If you aren't going to be helpful ..." I pushed my chair back, ready to get up and walk out before Greta came back in and I did something unforgivable. I'd already been unable to do much more than grunt *good morning* at her. Perhaps I needed to take a quick flight somewhere, lose myself in the woods for a while—

He waved a hand at me. "It's a mate bond waking up, you daft demon."

I squinted at him. "Surely not." A mate bond was a blessing, and I was cursed. It was as simple and as complicated as that.

Magnus sighed, leaning forward on the table with his hands laced together as though preparing for an interrogation. "When did the chest pain start?"

"Weeks ago."

"Elaborate, Vassago." He unlinked his fingers and gestured for me to keep going with one hand.

"During one of my visits to the Belette manor." I scrubbed a hand over my face, heart thumping as the reality of what he'd suggested began to sink in. It made a certain kind of sense but was also terrifying.

"Go on," Magnus prompted, the lopsided grin on his mouth unreasonably infuriating.

"The first time I met Greta," I relented, and he began to laugh again as inside my body, everything churned. "I physically bumped into her that night. After that ..." *Everything had changed.* I was terrified to begin with. My chest truly did hurt, the burning had only gotten worse, and now? Now I had the fizzy sensation of hope to contend with as well.

"Rylan performed a spell to confirm that he and Calla were fated. Perhaps you could go visit him, and he could instruct you how?"

I shook my head. "No. I'm no mage. No matter how similar divination seems, spell casting is not my strength. I don't doubt you're speaking truth, statue. It just ... complicates things."

"Does it? Seems to me that simplifies quite a lot."

All the bluster of my bad mood evaporated like steam as the idea of a long future with Greta by my side settled in. No more guilt over my desire to kiss her, to hold her. To make her mine in every way.

Unless, of course, she didn't feel the same.

I flared my nostrils and forced several slow breaths. The rush of frustration chased away all my fleeting good feelings. My balance was terrifyingly off, and I needed to get it back.

Magnus checked the kitchen door again. Whatever they were doing in there had consumed their attention in the same way this conversation had ours. I was intensely curious what they were talking about, no matter the irony of me certainly not wanting to share what we were discussing with them.

He cleared his throat, jovial expression replaced by a serious stare. "It's my duty to remind you that she's my niece. One that I've had regrettably little exposure to due to unfortunate circumstances. She is my sister's child, nonetheless, and therefore under my watch in Rowan's absence. If you do anything to hurt her—"

"I would never, Magnus." I shook my head, melancholy at the thought of something bad happening to her. "If I did, I would hand you the blade myself, for whatever good it might do you."

"Even if it didn't kill you, I could make it hurt. A lot."

"Yes, Rylan's told me all about the odd beginnings of your friendship. I applaud your valiant efforts to rid the world of him, but it seems we're all stuck here for the long haul."

"One can hope, demon." His grin was borderline malicious. I'd never felt like I'd understood him better than in that moment. "So long as we have an understanding. And we do, yes?"

"Quite."

He sat back, relaxed once again, and picked up his tankard. "What will you tell her?"

"I don't know yet. She's dealing with a lot already."

"She's strong."

"Yes, very. It's just one of her many attractive qualities."

"Good. I'm sure the pair of you will figure out your way." He smirked, shaking his head. "I'll be damned. I'll be excommunicated from the clan for sure. Collecting demon princes as in-laws? Unheard of."

I couldn't help but grin. The world had become a very strange place indeed.

GRETA SPENT MOST of the day with Grace and the four sisters that lived at the manor, familiarizing herself with the ins and outs of the campus beyond the classroom.

While she often downplayed her role, Grace managed all the inner workings of d'Arcan. Without her, we'd have no clean linen, nothing to eat, and the whole of the campus would be mired in dust and grime. To have been accepted into her most sacred work-space, the kitchen, was a sign Greta had been wholly accepted by Grace. Not that there had been any doubt their friendship would blossom quickly but seeing it in such obvious motion was lovely.

Greta being preoccupied for the day left me plenty of time to work myself up, calm myself back down, and come to some kind of internal peace with what I wanted to say to her all while touching on a few new leads for the actual necklace Henrik hired me to track down and the mysterious man I'd seen at the markets.

While the counterfeit necklace had passed with flying colors with the Belettes, the real one was obviously important, and I wanted to know why. There had to be a reason they needed it badly enough to hire me, and the fact that it matched Calla's heirloom seemed uncanny. Unfortunately, none of the jewelers, pawnbrokers, brothel madams, or seamstresses had seen it nor anything like it.

All through dinner, Greta shifted her shoulder restlessly, clear-ly fighting off an ache. Though she did not feel her discomfort should be announced, it gave me one final valid reason to get the conversation done with.

"Thank you for today," Grace said, beaming as she collected our dishes.

"I should be thanking you," Greta said, rising to help.

"No, no. You go on. I've got a helper." She winked, handing the stack of plates to Magnus.

I raised my eyebrow as the two of them loped off to the kitchen. "Care to join me for some wine?" I asked, unreasonably nervous.

"Sure." She forced a weak smile.

I followed her out of the dining room and up the stairs, my fingertips lingering at the small of her back. The burn in my chest had settled substantially since I'd come to terms with the label it deserved. However, seeing her in discomfort brought it roaring back to life.

"Is it bad?" I asked, once she was comfortable on my sofa with a glass of my favorite white wine in hand.

"I think perhaps I overused it today. Grace and I folded what must have been a month's worth of linens. It was good for me though."

"I ..." My nerve faltered, but I pulled the threads of my bravery together as I sat on the edge of the coffee table directly in front of her. Her eyes widened and she swallowed her mouthful of wine in one hard gulp. "I have something I need to discuss with you, Greta."

"I'm sorry. I know you asked me to tell you when it was bothering me, but I'm so used to it being a dull ache I didn't—" Her voice held an edge of fear, and I regretted being the cause.

I took her wine and set it on the table next to me, then held both of her hands loosely in mine. "No, no. I'm not upset with you about that, though I do want you to tell me when it's bothering you. What I was going to say is it's possible for me to learn what happened to make it hurt in the first place. There's a way."

"There is?" Hope flared bright in her eyes, her fingertips squeezing mine.

"Yes. My ability to see the past takes several forms. I can use my divination equipment, or I can ... see it. In memories."

Lurching forward, she asked, "Can we do that?"

I nodded, bracing myself for the hard part. "We can, Dragonfly. But I haven't told you what that requires yet."

"I don't care," she said, voice low but firm. "I want to know. I want to fix it."

I tightened my fingers around hers, bringing one of her hands up to my face so I could kiss her warm palm. My heart thudded behind my ribs, nerves battling with affection. "I'd love nothing more than to make it as though it never happened," I admitted. "But there are things I cannot take back if we try this. I need you to understand exactly what's going to happen."

"Okay." Her voice went breathy as she studied my face, the sound sending a thrill through my veins.

"If we do this, we will be bound, Greta. I will be able to find you, no matter where you go, at least for a time." The idea sent a surge of lust straight through me, the ache in my chest blazing to life. "I need to be clear though: there's no way to predict which memories I will see, how far they'll go back, or how vividly they'll come through. I may not see what we're looking for."

"If there's a chance you'll be able to tell me what happened and how to fix it, I want you to. I don't care about any of the other stuff. I trust you. I understand the risks."

"I don't know that you do, Dragonfly." My hands trembled, blood rushing hot through my body. "And I haven't even told you what I must do yet." I let go of her hand and allowed my fingers to trace along her jaw.

I tried to remember myself as the haze of desire took me over, so I focused on Greta's face to keep myself grounded. She was fearless, and her trust in me would be our undoing.

"I don't care, Vassago. Truly, I don't. You wouldn't hurt me." She gave me a gentle smile, a breath of the lust I felt echoed in her words. She frowned. "Tell me how it works. Tell me what you're so afraid of."

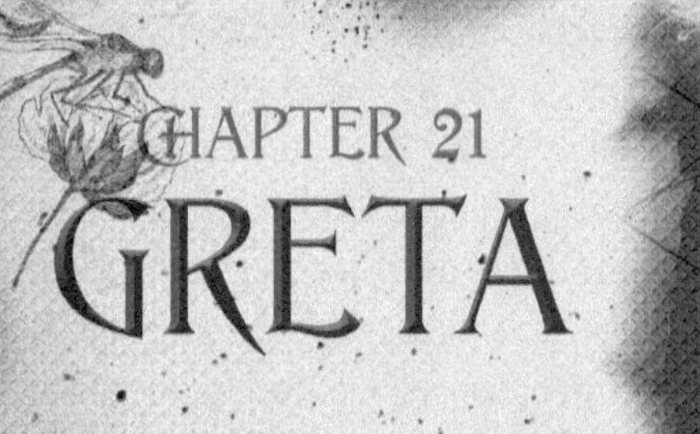

"IN ORDER TO see your memories, I need access to your blood, Little Dragonfly. I have to bite. I have to drink. It's there your secrets are kept."

I heard the words, but the way he'd somehow moved closer to run his warm fingertips up and down the column of my throat as he spoke was mighty distracting. My heart raced so hard I was sure he could hear it. He pressed down right on the pulse point at the base of my throat with his thumb, his golden gaze flashing ruby as he wet his lips. His eyes drifted from where his hand now gripped me around the neck to my mouth, my eyes.

"Greta. I need your words. I need to know you understand. That you are willing."

I exhaled, thighs clamped together against a fierce ache that only seemed to grow the more he spoke. "What happens if you lose control?" My eyes wanted to close, my whole body somehow tensed as tight as it had ever been and relaxed, tingling as it anticipated his touch.

"I will not lose control," he insisted, gravel in his voice.

"Okay."

He dropped to his knees on the rug in front of me. I reached for him, sliding to the very edge of the sofa seat, holding on to his shoulders. "Okay what? You must say it. Please." His voice held an edge of pleading, the sound teasing down my spine.

"I understand. I want this. I trust you." I couldn't recall exactly what he'd asked for, but I thought I had it all covered.

He leaned in close with a low groan, doing that thing where he hovered with his lips brushing the curve where my neck and shoulder met.

His touch sent warm shivers dancing along my skin as he teased down my shoulder before gripping my throat with his right hand, pulling me closer with his left arm wrapped around my back. I thought he was going to go straight for it, but instead he opted for torture.

His mouth dipped, and he sucked at my collarbone, making me squirm against the insistent pulse between my thighs. He left a trail of soft kisses all the way from my ear to my chin and then his lips were on mine, hot and demanding.

I couldn't stop the sigh that left me as I dissolved under his touch. It was all I could do to keep up with the elaborate dance his kiss had become, the way his tongue teased at mine and his teeth nipped just enough to bring the tiniest edge of pain before he soothed it away again. I became breathless, boneless, held up only by his solid grip around me, drunk on his kiss and unready to be done with it even as he pulled away.

"I am unworthy, Dragonfly."

His hand snaked up around my throat again, the gentle pressure somehow fanning the flames of my desire even further. Gently, he tilted my head to the side. The softness of his lips brushed over my neck several times. My body quivered under his touch and the featherlight caress of his warm breath. Even through the heady haze of my arousal, I recognized his careful motions for what they were. He was hesitating.

"I trust you," I whispered, finding his gaze with mine, tensing as it flipped from gold to red in a single breath.

"Truly a gift," he muttered.

His mouth widened, and he licked a hot path along the pulsing vein, his thumb and two middle fingers tightening against my throat. Air still flowed, but my pulse thudded too loudly in my ears, the slight oxygen deprivation and blood flow constriction enhanced every sensation.

My moan was what alerted me to the fact that he'd bitten me. It was not a sound I was used to hearing nor making, but my body clearly understood the odd precipice he was helping me walk between pain and pleasure even if I lacked experience. There was a bright sting under his warm mouth, but that discomfort twisted, becoming intense arousal. He removed his hand from my neck after one final squeeze, and the gray I hadn't even noticed forming around the edges of my vision cleared away as I inhaled an unhindered breath. His arm snaked around my back but went down low. He gripped my ass with sure fingers and yanked me all the way up against him as he drank deep, a groan rattling out of his throat.

My legs were splayed wide, my center pressed up against his torso, the seam of my trousers pressed right where I ached the most. A tightness began to form low in my gut, a sharp throb that came closer to the surface with each gentle pull he made with his mouth. All at once, the feelings surged into one overwhelming peak, and I cried out, trembling in his grasp.

He growled low in his chest, the way his fingers clutched at me desperate. The tug on my veins became sharp, and a cold sliver of fear chased away the arousal.

"Vassago." He buried his head further into my shoulder, and panic started to take hold. I tugged at his hair. "Vassago!"

With a gasp, he withdrew his fangs and stared, the wild look in his eyes the same as I'd seen that night on the road.

"Forgive me," he said.

"It's alright." I saw him come back to himself and put my hand on his cheek. He turned into it, closing his eyes. "I'm okay."

He sank his face into the curve of my neck again, lathing over the wound his teeth had made with his tongue, planting gentle kisses all around where he'd bitten. The pleasant warm sensation returned, curling low in my stomach.

"Tell me to stop, Greta. To go." He nipped at my jaw and drew gentle fingertips down my spine, giving me a whole new set of tingles. "I should leave you be. I said I wouldn't lose control, but—"

"I don't want you to stop." I allowed the words to flow as they wished, no censoring myself like I always did. "I want you to touch me."

He growled, wrapping one hand in my hair as he forced me to focus on his face. "This was not my intention in asking you here tonight. I do not wish to do things you'll regret tomorrow. Or ever." He looked impossibly sad then, and I wanted nothing more than to comfort away his melancholy.

"I could never regret you, Vassago." I stared deep into his eyes, the color swirling between gold and ruby as some of my blood stained the corner of his mouth. It was wholly true. There was nothing at all about the weeks I'd had with him I would take back or do differently. I'd lived more completely and freely during my time with him at d'Arcan than all of my previous thirty years.

"Nor I you, Dragonfly. For you ... For you, I would lose all control. And I would never be able to bring myself to regret a single moment."

His hand traced gently down the side of my face and then he grinned. And it was like everything in my chest finally opened up, allowing me to breathe again, feel everything I was supposed to. He exhaled deeply, his eyes slipping closed, and for a moment, he became the mist. He was everywhere and nowhere; tendrils stroked their cool breath along my face, my arms. It was odd but also comforting, because I could tell it was him even if I couldn't see his normal form.

The mist evaporated, and Vassago returned. He tightened his grip on me and stood, taking long gliding steps to the bed. With space between us, doubt about my lack of experience began to crowd in, but he was too fast for me to get very far down that road.

"I need your words again, Dragonfly," he requested, hovering above me as I clumsily undid the buttons on his shirt.

"I want this," I said firmly, hauling my own shirt up and over my head.

He inhaled sharply and crawled over me, fighting with one of his sleeves before resting a hand along the side of my face as he delved deep with another impossibly intoxicating kiss.

I unlashed my trousers and wriggled them down my hips. His long white hair dangled, tickling my bare shoulders as I used whatever I could reach to get the pants all the way down my legs. He broke the kiss and provided the final assist, sliding them off the rest of the way as he dropped to his knees at the edge of the bed. I found myself being slid toward the edge, his hands around my ankles. He placed each of my feet on either shoulder and leaned in.

Out of reflex, I shifted my legs together, but seeing him between them, a hungry look in his eyes made them relax again. "Greta?" He stilled, warm palms wrapped around my calves.

"Don't stop," I begged.

His eyebrow quirked up, as did his mouth. His control was slipping again, his fangs resting on his full lower lip, eyes ruby as they watched for my reaction. One of his hands gripped my thigh, his thumb leaving an erotic indentation in my flesh.

"Eyes on me, Little Dragonfly. Use your words. Tell me what you need."

"You," was all I could manage as he started to plant light kisses up the inside of my leg. "I think sometimes that all I've ever needed is you."

"You shall have me then," he said, the words deep and rumbly in his chest as he left gentle nips and kisses up and down my legs. "How could I deny you anything?" He paused only long enough to breathe over the place I ached most for his attentions but never indulged me. One forearm landed over my hips to hold me in place as I wiggled and bucked in protest. "Hold still, Greta. Be patient. Trust that I'll take care of you."

His corporeal form also remained this time as the tendrils swept up and down my legs, driving every nerve to the point of hypersensitization. Several came up as far as my arms, brushing along the sides of my breasts and over my ribs.

I had a hard time keeping still between the cool glide of the mist along my exposed skin and Vassago's mouth coming closer and closer to where I needed it. My legs wanted to jerk, my fingers grasped at the sheets. I was perilously close to begging.

All at once, I got what I wanted.

Vassago's tongue lashed the length of my opening as the mist restrained me. I hadn't expected the smoke-like substance to have any kind of strength to it, but I was well and truly pinned by the tendrils at my wrists and across my middle. Tiny wisps reached up and out, some coming over to tease across my nipples, which were so tight they were painful, others drifted into my hair, pulling gently.

I gave in to a throaty moan as Vassago's mouth wrapped around my clit and sucked, sensation rocketing through me. He was everywhere—fingers, mouth, mist. There was no beginning or ending to his form, and I felt him in every part of me.

Warm palms pressed against my thighs, forcing them wider as he buried his face further into me. He alternated between licking at the tight bundle of nerves and plunging his tongue inside me, all while the mist plucked and teased and drifted over my heated skin. When he added his fingers, I knew I was done for. I whimpered as he sank one of his long, graceful fingers into me, a low hum coming from his chest as he withdrew and added another. The mist clung to me, kept me from squirming out of his hold as he flicked the tip of his tongue at a pace that had me close to screaming from the intensity.

When he turned his head to the side and bit into my inner thigh, I said his name ... or at least I thought I did. The dam of sensation burst, and I moaned out as my body began to spasm around his fingers. He licked where he'd bitten before returning his focus to the sensitive bundle of nerves and didn't gentle his ministrations until I couldn't stop twitching against the riot of sensation and screamed again.

"Look at me, Dragonfly." He rose from between my thighs with glazed-over eyes, the tip of his tongue running along his bottom lip. "You're one of the most delicious things I've ever tasted. Sweet like honey." He put his fingers in his mouth and sucked, and I clenched my thighs together as my arousal gave another pulse.

The mist had lightened its grip after shifting me closer to the pillows. It was an odd feeling to be pulled along the sheets by something incorporeal. Vassago loosened his pants, pushing them indecently low. He was lean and tall, clearly built for activity very different from classroom work. I stared at the indentation in the muscles just below his hips as he stood at the end of the bed, looking right back at me. His hair was loose and wild around his face, the normally straight white locks curled up at the ends from the moisture his mist put off. It made him softer, though there was nothing at all soft about this man.

"Your words, Greta."

I shivered at the demand, unused to this side of the demon and helplessly fixated on his impressive naked form. "I'm yours, I trust you," I said. And I meant it.

His pants dropped to the floor before he prowled over me, the mist swirling in crisscrosses over the both of us. "As you wish, Little Dragonfly." He put his mouth to mine and notched his impressive length at my entrance.

I had only a breath to tense before he was deep inside me with one smooth thrust, a pinch of pain bright but negligible as the pleasure rushed in behind it. His eyes widened and he froze, pulling away from the kiss. After a painfully long moment where he just breathed and scanned my face, he lowered himself to his forearms, bracketing my head with his hands.

"Greta." There was a world of questions in that one word. I knew what he was asking, but I didn't want everything I was feeling to be reduced to that. I couldn't. "No other man has seen you? Feasted upon your flesh, had the honor of seeing you flush with passion? No man has seen you come well and truly apart under his touch?" He groaned. "No other man has been inside you, Dragonfly?"

"No."

His eyes closed and his nostrils flared as he breathed in deep. "Fuck." He dragged the word out but didn't move at all. I couldn't tell by his inflection how he meant the word, but shame was the first emotion to flood in. I knew that thirty was well past when most people had their first sexual experience, but I hadn't lived like most people. For some reason, my impulse was to explain that I wasn't wholly ignorant of romance.

"There was one boy who worked in the stables at the country manor ... he and I kissed a few times, fooled around a little, but—"

"*Greta.*" He sounded almost pained. "I do not want to hear about anyone else," he said softly, shaking his head slowly. "It makes me feel very much like committing violence, and I don't want to be that way just now."

"Sorry." I felt awkward, unsure what to do. I lay there under him, more exposed than my lack of clothing could ever make me. The fullness of him stretching me was riding the edge of discomfort, though pleasure hovered close. I just needed him to move. "Vassago, please. I know what I chose." I would beg if that's what it took for him to stop thinking and *move*. "I choose you. I would always have chosen you."

His eyes slipped closed, and he leaned his forehead against mine, teeth sunk into his full bottom lip as the mist redoubled its efforts where my most sensitive areas were concerned. He moved his hips slowly, my body aching with a sharp burn as it learned to accommodate him. It only took a few thrusts for his glide to ease.

He shuddered, holding my face with one hand as he leaned in to kiss me again. I tasted the sharp iron of his blood; he'd bit his lip that hard. The other hand gripped my ass, pulling that leg up around his hip. I tried to angle my body to meet his, the sensation of him rubbing my inside walls enough to have my body tightening up once again.

Vassago plundered my mouth, his tongue plunging in and out at a pace that matched his thrusts. The mist flowed over my skin in a frenzied pattern as I began to moan, my inner muscles contracting as his controlled thrusts drove me close to madness.

I arched as much as I could against the weight of his body and the grip of the mist, calling his name out as he wrung wave after wave from me.

He quickened his pace before giving one final hard thrust. He throbbed inside me as I tried to hang on to the rush I was coming down from all too quickly.

"I do not deserve you, Dragonfly," he said, eyes closed and forehead pressed against mine. "But I swear to do everything I can to be worthy."

CHAPTER 22
VASSAGO

T HE WHOLE WORLD narrowed to the small apartment, the cocoon we'd made in my bed. Time ticked by sluggishly as we stared at one another, worry settling in deeper the longer I gazed down at her. My chest had stopped burning at some point, which was a relief for so many reasons, but a new concern for others.

I'd lost control.

She'd brought me back to myself, but I'd heard the fear in her voice.

As we lay there, I sorted through the wash of memories I'd gotten from Greta's blood, coming up with less than I'd hoped for. There was more happiness mixed in than I'd expected, but what I'd seen hadn't gone back very far.

I played over every moment of our coupling, my blood stirring again with desire despite having just been slaked for the first time in many years. I regretted my haste but promised myself I'd make up for it.

"Are you alright, Little Dragonfly?" I asked, unable to keep myself from hearing it from her own lips.

"Yes, I'm fine. Perfect, in fact."

"I would have done things differently had I known." My sigh was deep and heavy.

"I wouldn't." The gentle smile on her lips did not erase my concern, but it did ease it. I reached up and ran gentle fingers through her tangled hair, unable to keep my hands from her in one way or another.

"What do these mean?" she asked, tracing along the edges of the tattoos that ran underneath my collarbone and down my sternum.

"They are my rank and class as a prince of Hell and commander of legions," I said. It wasn't the full picture, but finding a way to explain further was too complicated. It didn't matter besides, I'd forfeited my place when I left Hell for earth.

"Instead of a pin or ribbon for a uniform?"

"Kind of like, yes."

"That seems rather ... permanent."

"Indeed." My skin tingled under her touch as she traced them all in turn, left to right across my chest, then down my breastbone.

"What if you get demoted?"

I laughed. "That's not how it works in Hell, Dragonfly. Not for demons like me anyway."

Her hand finally dropped, a soft smile lingering on her mouth. "They shimmer, kind of. It's pretty."

"Mm." The quiet wrapped us up tight, muffling the noises of the night outside my room. It was peaceful, at least until my thoughts left me unfairly agitated. "The boy," I asked, needing an answer despite the question tasting like ashes in my mouth. "Was he kind to you?"

I tried to relax my jaw, my face, but I knew my expression dared her to say something provocative. I'd have accepted anything at all as an excuse to justify the irrational rage I felt at the mention of someone else touching her. As permission to find him and be sure that he understood what a grave mistake hurting her had been.

"He was," she said, taking all the momentum out of my plans to avenge her honor. Relief was there, as well. "We'd known each other a long time. It was just … curiosity mostly. There weren't many opportunities for me to have friends, let alone find someone to take as a lover—" I couldn't stop the groan that came out more like a growl. I was not comfortable with this discussion even if I wished to be. "I have never wanted to be like *this* with anyone else," she said plainly, putting her palm on my cheek as she stared directly into my eyes.

I tightened my arms around her, my mist doing the same and curling around her protectively. She snuggled further into me, and I pressed a kiss into her hair. "What did you see?" she asked. At my confused silence, she added, "In my memories?"

"Not what we hoped for."

"Oh." Disappointment was profound in the single syllable. "Does it change? Like if we were to try again, would you see something new?"

"Yes, probably. But it's unpredictable. I could sample your blood fifty times and never get what we're looking for. Or I could have seen it the first try. There's no way to request what I'm shown or sift through what's there. I'm presented with what I'm presented with."

She yawned. "That's okay. We'll try again. It might not matter anyway, right? If Magnus's daughter can help?"

"Perhaps. Go to sleep, Greta. We'll talk about it tomorrow. Everything is clearer in the daylight."

Her breathing slowed into an even, deep cadence and I found myself relaxing as well, falling into some of the deepest, most peaceful rest I'd had in a very long time.

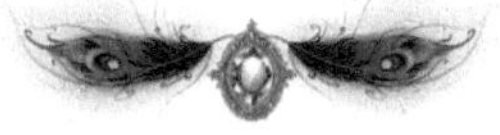

AN INSISTENT TAPPING roused me from my deep sleep.

I cracked one eye open and found the large black bird perched outside my window, head tilted as he searched with his one good eye for Greta. The object of our mutual affection was curled on her side next to me, hands fisted near her chest, wild curls splayed over the pillow. The scent of her was everywhere, on my skin, in my sheets. It stirred everything inside me that was protective, possessive. I'd spent most of my time earth-side avoiding such entanglements, but with her ... everything was different.

Greta stirred as the raven tapped on the glass again, more insistently this time. "I don't have any treats for you this morning, bird," she grumbled, and while I hated that he'd woken her, I was glad to get my first opportunity to see her all sleep rumpled as she stirred.

"Shall I tell him?" I asked, leaning over to kiss her temple.

"Mm. He probably won't believe you. He's quite pushy. If I don't have anything in my room for him, I try to take something out to leave in the courtyard for him to find after breakfast."

"Well, I see why he's so insistent. You've spoiled him," I joked, sliding out from between the sheets and tugging on some pants.

"He was like this when I got here," she laughed.

Now that I was good and awake, the pressing issues we had to discuss were pressing at my awareness with ferocity. Not the least of which was explaining to her that I was feeling the sensations of a mate bond.

I regretted having gotten carried away before telling her everything, worried that she might not be pleased with such an omission on my part. But I wouldn't change a single thing that happened between us. I felt calm, truly at peace, for the first time in ages. I was selfish, perhaps, but unrepentant where she was concerned.

"Greta, we need—" I was interrupted by a new knocking, what I could only assume was a meaty fist on the outside of my door.

"Demon, you awake? Grace is serving breakfast, and I have news."

"I'm awake, stone man. What news?" I glanced at Greta with regret, her eyes were wide as she sat up, clutching the sheet to her chest.

"Ophelia has agreed to meet."

"Indeed? When?"

"This afternoon. Come downstairs, we can discuss it face-to-face instead of me speaking to a blasted door."

"Alright. I'll be down in a moment. Shall I retrieve Greta? This concerns her as well." I winked at her, getting an eye roll in response as she threw back the sheets and pulled on her pants. I watched without shame, sad that she was covering up all that glorious skin. I ached to get my hands on it all over again.

"Yes, that's a good idea. Hurry up, would you?"

"I'm not one of your soldiers, quit ordering me around. I'll be down momentarily." He snorted, his heavy footsteps moved away from the door and Greta sagged, a breath filtering out from between her lips. "You have nothing to be ashamed of, Dragonfly."

"I know," she sighed, pulling on the shirt I'd given her, which she'd had to search for since she'd flung it across the room after removing it. "But I've never had an uncle to disappoint, and I feel like I'm sneaking around behind his back right now."

"You kind of are," I teased. She tilted her head, eyes narrowed. Before she could move away, I gathered her in for a proper kiss.

"I'll meet you downstairs," she said once we separated. "I want to clean up first."

"Alright. But Greta, there's something else I need to speak to you about."

"Will it take long?" she asked.

I frowned. "It will take some dedicated attention."

"Lots of that going around today it seems."

"Indeed."

She closed my door behind herself, leaving me to contend with the bird, who was now looking at me in an oddly accusatory way.

"Go on with you," I said, flinging the pane open wide. He flapped away to avoid being struck, but I would have put down good money he was simply making the rounds so he could go to her window instead.

"SHE SEEMED ALMOST enthusiastic," Magnus shrugged as he ate a slice of toast with a fried egg on top in a single bite. "She was much the same when Rylan and Calla visited."

"Do you trust that?" I asked, glancing at Greta who was quietly sipping her coffee with attentive, wide eyes.

"Yes. Her mood swings are a slow progression most of the time, but I'll of course be going with you as well."

"I appreciate it." Greta gave him a gentle smile.

"Of course, niece. It will be good for you to meet one of our most respected elders in any case. But make no mistake, she can be incredibly dangerous. If you are afraid for any reason once we are inside her home, take heed of that instinct."

Greta's eyes grew even rounder. "I will."

"You have the candy?"

"Yes, I got as much as I could, as you suggested."

"Good. That helps."

After breakfast, Greta went up to her room to bathe and change. I lingered behind with Magnus, his face set in a grin as though he was well aware of my intention to speak with him.

"I can admit when I'm slow figuring things out. She's my mate," I said plainly. The mirth fell off his face for a brief moment but returned as he leaned toward me across the table with a broad smile. I held up my hand when his mouth dropped open. "We haven't discussed what that means yet."

"Of course." He put on a serious expression, but the grin gave away his good humor about the situation. "Welcome to the family, devil. Perhaps we'll have no choice but to be friends now," he teased.

I didn't respond, but the words landed warmly in my chest.

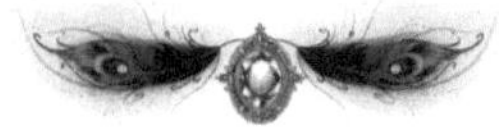

WHEN I GOT upstairs, Greta's door was open. I tapped on it, appreciative of the invitation but mindful of a whole new set of rules forming between us. I wanted to tread carefully. "May I come in?"

"Yes, of course," she said. She was at the window, feeding the raven something out of her palm, when she smiled, and the simple act caused my heart to beat faster. "We're going to see a stone kin sorceress, right?"

"Yes. And she's likely to know many things others have forgotten, so if you have a specific question, be sure to ask. We have many talented allies, and Magnus is confident—and I am too—that we can find someone else to help if need be."

She brightened and smiled. "That's good."

"Are you preparing her properly for her visit?" Magnus interrupted, head poking through the open door.

"No, we hadn't gotten to that yet. But honestly, I'm not sure I am myself. I've never had the honor."

Greta invited her uncle in, and he sat, dominating the conversation instantly with stories about Ophelia and her unique talents. "We all move slowly around her for good reason, Greta. She seemed very amicable today, but it's important you are cautious."

"Does she know who I am?"

Magnus shook his head. "No. She doesn't like to know who's coming beforehand, we only ever get permission to come or not."

"Is she far?"

"No, she lives just outside Revalia in the Dread Forest. Her area is warded, so when we get close, you may get a sense of sadness or fear. Don't be alarmed."

"Okay. Thank you, Magnus."

"It's my honor, niece."

And then I lost them both to tales of her family, and there was no interrupting the statue, even if I wanted to. She deserved to hear it all. Seeing her face light up was well worth the delay in me speaking with her about mate bonds.

I was still wrapping my own head around such a thing, and I was glad for the reprieve, but my desire to be wholly honest with her would not allow me to put it off for long.

CHAPTER 23
GRETA

WE'D CLIMBED IN the carriage while Magnus flew ahead, my anxiety about meeting the elder stone kin only growing as we made our way through the city.

As Magnus had warned, once we arrived at the edge of the forest, my thoughts turned panicky. I wanted nothing more than to turn around, flee back to d'Arcan and the safety it provided. Even the horses hated what they sensed in the forest, slowing to a stop, whinnying as though thoroughly spooked.

Heavy wings beat above us as a hut came into view. Cheerful flowers in boxes outside the windows and smoke curling from the chimney offered a striking contrast to the foreboding sensation crushing in on me. It looked like a fairy-tale house, but perhaps the one where the witch invites children in and they never reappear.

"Come. The feeling will ease soon," Vassago said, opening the carriage door and reaching back for my hand. He helped me out while Magnus approached from where he'd landed nearby. "Thank you, Clem. You can take the horses beyond the tree line to make them more comfortable."

"Sir," Clem responded, sagging with relief before immediately turning the nervous horses back down the skinny dirt lane.

"Ready?" Magnus was missing his usual smile, clearly nervous despite having reassured the both of us that everything was as prepared for our visit as it could be.

"Yes."

Vassago just nodded, one hand at the small of my back and the other carrying the candy he'd purchased as we approached the door.

Magnus knocked, a specific series of taps that was obviously a code. After a brief delay, the door swung open, revealing a squatty little woman with shrewd bright-blue eyes, snow-white hair, and a severe frown. She eyed Vassago up and down, narrowing her gaze as it flitted from him to me. It only softened once she settled on Magnus.

"Thank you for seeing us today, Ophelia," Vassago said smoothly, offering the bag. "We appreciate it very much. Might I offer you a token of appreciation?"

She sniffed, appraising him with those clever eyes, then snatched the bag from his hand. He lowered his arm slowly, a patient smile on his lips.

"Salted licorice?"

"Yes, we heard it was your favorite. I bought out the whole of the candymaker's stock for the week."

Her mouth twitched, never fully forming a smile, but the ghost of one teased at the corner of her mouth. "I suppose you'd better come in." She gestured with her arm for us to enter, tapping one cheek with her finger as Magnus passed her. He dipped down to place a chaste kiss on her cheek, a low chuckle in his throat. She even graced him with a smile.

"He gave you the licorice, but I hope I remain your favorite?" he teased her.

"It would be disgraceful to have a demon as my favorite, wouldn't it?" she said with an exaggerated whisper, then winked at Vassago. "So, I suppose you'll do."

Magnus laughed aloud, and the fact that he was more relaxed helped put us all at ease.

The ancient gargoyle followed us into her little hut, and the crushing sensation lifted once we were on the other side of the threshold. It took a moment for my body to regulate again, my adrenaline waning as an overwhelming sense of comfort took the place of cold fear.

"Your wards are much more potent than they were several weeks ago, Ophelia. Is everything alright?" Magnus asked.

"Fine, fine. Just some nosy neighbors and travelers getting too close for my liking. That little demon horde didn't help matters either. I wanted a little bit more security. You know how I don't care for company." She looked directly at me when she said this, but her tiny smile told me she didn't necessarily mean me. Maybe. It was impossible to tell for sure, but she seemed pleasant enough. "Sit down, demon," she instructed, waving her hand at Vassago. "I'd like you in the seat next to me, if you don't mind," she said to me.

"Of course," I responded, sinking into the cushion she'd indicated.

We'd come through a small kitchen and dining area to the living room. There were large, deep pieces of furniture arranged in a half circle facing the fireplace, books scattered all over, and potted plants in the most unlikely of places. The home was lived in, loved, and smelled like freshly baked bread.

I blinked, realizing that now that I found myself inside, I wanted to stay much more than I'd wanted to turn back at the height of my panic when we crossed the wards.

"Your generosity and willingness to meet with us is appreciated, my lady." Vassago gave a flourish of his hand, bowing at her before settling into the plush seat next to me.

"*Mmph*," she grumbled at him, clever eyes scanning his face. "I suppose it's only fair since you helped keep those little terrors away from my home. Have I thanked you for that?"

"Not as such. But we haven't had the pleasure of meeting before now."

She only grunted in response, eyes twinkling. It would seem even she wasn't immune to his charms, especially when he had them turned up to full power. Magnus's mouth twitched. He met my eye, and I felt the rest of my apprehension melt away with his amusement. She was an interesting lady, I'd give her that.

"In any case, it was my pleasure," Vassago continued smoothly, ignoring that she'd never actually given words of gratitude even after dangling it like that.

"You're very like your brother," she said suddenly, head tilted as she looked at him.

His eyebrow raised. "Oh?"

"Yes. The pair of you could be twins."

Vassago smiled, the points of his slightly elongated canines pressing against the inside of his bottom lip. "How's that?" he asked.

I too was curious how she'd arrived at that estimation, because I knew as well as anyone that he and his brother were basically opposites when it came to appearance, despite not yet having met the archmage.

"You both bring me the most interesting women as company, for starters. How is it that you both happen to be fated to truly extraordinary stone kin mates? Seems odd for demons, even if you are some kind of royalty. There are a great many parallels in your lives, are there not?"

Everything stilled. Vassago's eyes slid to mine, his smile faltering. Magnus busied himself with straightening the cuffs of his shirt, eyes cautiously traveling between the three of us. He was clearly enjoying the show while remaining uncharacteristically quiet.

"Mate?" I asked, voice barely a squeak.

"Yes, yes." Ophelia busily poured healthy dollops of whiskey into fancy porcelain teacups before adding an equal amount of steaming tea. At our silence, she looked up, though there was no shame or repentance in her expression. "No need to rub it in with those of us who aren't so lucky, hmm? I assume you're here for a reason?"

"Several, it seems," I managed to say, heart lodged in my throat.

"Yes, my dear. That's usually how it goes. And you? What's your story?"

"Oh, um, I recently moved to d'Arcan to practice chemistry."

"And before that?"

"I was employed by the Belettes. I lived with Henrik and Lara since I was a toddler—"

Ophelia flapped a hand impatiently as she dropped into her chair, the full teacup in her hand nearly sloshing its contents over the edge. "I don't care about the impostors you lived with. Tell me, who are your parents?"

I sipped at the tea concoction, the fire the whiskey put in my nose and throat slowing my response. I finally managed to cough and clear the tears from my eyes after several attempts at swallowing over the burn. "Rowan," I coughed again, sucking in a deep breath to soothe my burning throat before trying again. "I don't know her surname, but my mother's name is Rowan. I ... I never knew my father."

"Yes, I thought so." The old woman smiled, revealing several missing teeth, but there was a sparkle in her eye. "You look like her." The compliment hit me square in the chest and my heart thudded painfully. She said it reverently, with kindness.

"She's been missing for decades, much like the Noctuas." Magnus frowned, voice soft. The way he spoke about them, he seemed to take every mystery that existed within the stone kin community as a personal failing. I wished I could reassure him that not all these things were his responsibility, and likely none were his fault.

"Yes. So many of us vanished without explanation. Entirely too many families have met such painful, unnecessary separations." Ophelia tossed back the contents of her cup, only looking away from me when she had no other choice. The attention was not unexpected, but it was slightly uncomfortable. Vassago was a solid presence at my side, and I knew Magnus would protect me if it came down to that, but it was not lost on me that this tiny woman was seen by both of these powerful men as a threat.

She nodded firmly, pulled herself out of her seat, then gestured for me to follow her. "Come."

I followed her to a little nook behind the kitchen. She approached a table full of assorted items, and rapidly rearranged them. Crystals and herbs, sand and salt. Everything went to a specific location only she understood the reasoning behind. She stopped, glanced at me, turned a piece of white ocean coral ninety degrees, swapped the positions of a chunk of amethyst and a square bit of rose quartz, then handed me a small bell.

"Ring it," she instructed blandly, looking perplexed as she examined the layout of the table. I did as she asked, gripping the wooden handle as the clapper clanked hollowly against the side of the bell.

"Foolish, foolish. Of course. May I see your palm?" I held one hand out for her, and she peered close to the skin. "Yes, there it is. Your demon's mark. And this?" Her lip curled in disgust at the sight of the ring.

I wasn't sure how to address it exactly, but managed to say, "Unwanted. But it won't come off. The more we try, the harder it clings."

She turned her head toward Vassago. "Surely not yours?"

"No, no." I rushed to tell her. "My former employers accepted an offer for my hand. This was his token."

"Bad magic," she shook her head. "I'm afraid I don't know much about that kind of thing, but I can tell it's rotten. Here." She handed me a tightly rolled bundle of papers. "Hold this. Now try again."

I obeyed, and this time the bell's tone was crisp and resonated through the small room in a way that should have been impossible. The instrument was no bigger than the palm of my hand and somehow, the little shake I'd given it made the dishes in the kitchen cabinets rattle.

"Good, good," Ophelia muttered as she tossed open the window. "You've made a friend at that school in recent weeks, haven't you?"

I itched to look over my shoulder at Vassago. Though *friend* was an unusual word for whatever it was we were. Especially now. Even more so with her declaration about us being mates. And me having his mark. I wasn't even sure what that meant.

"A friend?"

"Not human." Ophelia's mouth curled into a smile as the heavy sound of wings beating came close, and a large raven landed on the sill. It cocked its head to the side so it could look at us with its good eye, clicked a few times, and blinked as it took us in. He dipped down on one leg almost as though trying to bow.

Ophelia cooed over him, stroking his beak and the feathers on the top of his head. "Hello, little beast. Aren't you lovely? Yes, I know, the wards are bothersome, but so are unwelcome visitors, you see." She looked from him to me, and I felt awkward standing there, subject of, but excluded from, their conversation. After several low comments, Ophelia turned back to me. "Your raven's name is Belmont, though he doesn't mind that you call him *bird*. He likes when you leave him eggs best—three-minute is his favorite, though raw is fine too. Berries run a close second. He's doing his absolute best to help the cats rid the barn of rodents. He likes you."

"I like him too. Hello, Belmont." I stumbled over my words, feeling awkward. But as I tasted the name, something rang in my mind, a sense of rightness settling over me. "Thank you for the gifts you've left for me," I said, making sure to look at him instead of Ophelia, reaching my hand out so he could choose whether or not to accept a few beak strokes. "The red glass is my favorite. I keep it near the window with my crystal so I can see it when I wake up in the morning with the sunlight behind them." He lifted his beak and made a long cawing noise, making me flinch. Close up and contained in the small house, his voice was *loud*. "I'll be sure to ask Grace for more eggs."

The bird made the knocking sound in his throat, feathers splaying at the praise and promise of his favorite food.

Ophelia chuckled. "Yes, yes. You'll be a truly spoiled bird in no time, well done. You know what this means?" He chattered at her. "Very well, you'll have your wish, I'll see if the demon will help me post the official request. Help yourself to my berry patch while you wait. There's likely plenty of rodents in the brambles you can help with too." He turned and flew back out the window, headed toward the rear of Ophelia's house.

"Sorry, official request? For what?"

Ophelia pinched coarse salt, then some crumbled herbs, and put them both in the tiny cauldron hanging over a candle on the table. After a beat, she added a broken piece of clear crystal to the pot as well. All she said in response was, "We've much to discuss." She put her hand out, and I reflexively offered mine, sucking in a quick breath when the pain from a quick finger stick registered. "Just a drop of blood for this next part." Ophelia squeezed my finger over the cauldron, one of my knuckles bumping the outer edge of the rim as she yanked my hand.

I peered over my shoulder, and Vassago wore an intense frown, gray mist curling around the edges of his body. He looked ready to pounce, his weight balanced and ready to leap to my side if necessary.

"You're more well-behaved than your brother," Ophelia muttered. "He was halfway across the room by this point."

Vassago's eyebrows drew together, and the corners of his mouth pulled even further toward the floor. "I *am* the more cultured of the two of us," he said, voice unnaturally neutral.

It was interesting to watch the exchange between them, mostly because he was generally good-natured and happy. It also spoke volumes about the respect he had for this petite old woman. It was fascinating, and I couldn't explain how, but I knew I wasn't in danger from her.

Ophelia let go of my hand, and I stuck my throbbing fingertip in my mouth to soothe the sting, finding a little burn mark on my knuckle where it had bumped the edge of the small cauldron.

"Here we are," she crooned, pleased as the mixture in the cauldron began to emit a yellowish-orange smoke.

I gasped as the smoke formed a portrait of my mother. So many years had passed since I'd seen her face, my memories were scant at best, but the image immediately brought tears to my eyes. I recalled her features upon seeing them again, like I'd never been without them at all; the tilt of her smiling eyes, the crinkle in her nose. I reached out a hand but pulled back, afraid to disrupt the likeness. I wanted to stare at her for as long as possible.

I blanched as my mother's smile widened, and she looked right at me. I fought the overwhelming urge to run toward her for a hug. I thought she was about to fade out, but instead she moved to the side. A second figure appeared, a man. One with a bright smile and kind eyes. A brutal scar ran from one temple to under the ear on the opposite side of his face. He dipped his head, holding both sides of my mother's face as he planted a gentle kiss on her mouth. He looked at her lovingly, longingly. She gazed up at him as though he was her whole world. I sucked in a breath when he turned forward again, smiled, winked at me, and then waved his hand, disrupting what little was left of the smoke. Then, they were both gone, and I felt overwhelmingly bereft.

Vassago's peaceful presence warmed my back, and his fingers laced into mine. I swiped the tears from my eyes and breathed out heavily. Having a chance to see her face again was both the best remedy and worst curse for the hole in me her disappearance had left behind.

Ophelia took a deep breath and used an arm to sweep everything on the table into disarray before opening the window again.

I turned, finding Magnus beside Vassago. His eyes were misty and one of his hands gripped the front of his shirt. He gave me a sad smile. My heart clenched, he clearly loved his sister and missed her fiercely. He'd needed to see her again as much as I had.

"Well. That went much nicer than the last time I had visitors like you, I'll say that, but that fellow at the end is a puzzle, wouldn't you say? I need more whiskey. Always more whiskey when I have company like you lot."

She stomped off toward the kitchen, chuckling when I called out that I would like one as well.

CHAPTER 24
VASSAGO

GRETA GRIMACED AS she swallowed down the last of her cup. I worried that she might have gone ahead too brazenly drinking the whole thing in one go, but I wasn't going to judge.

"Candy?" Ophelia offered. Greta was the only one to accept a piece from the bag, though at the first taste of the potent flavor, she looked as though she regretted her choice. Her eyes went wide with panic for a moment, and I realized she'd swallowed it whole. "Shall we start at the beginning, perhaps?" Ophelia queried. "You know nothing of that man? Your father?"

Greta shook her head. "No, I never met him. Not that I can remember, anyway."

"As far as I know, there are no records of him either," Magnus offered. "Rowan was careful. All I ever knew was that she'd met someone and she was happy. I didn't know his name or where he was from. Nothing at all. Toward the end of her pregnancy, she stopped speaking about him altogether." Magnus frowned. "I got the impression something had happened, but she never told me anything more about it. I didn't push. She had her secrets and I had mine. Then she disappeared. I wish more than anything I'd asked questions, even if she'd withheld answers."

"It's not your fault, nephew. She had her reasons." Ophelia leaned in, patting Magnus's hand. The relief in his eyes was palpable. I gave him a hard time at every opportunity, but I could tell he didn't hear that very often and carried much he wasn't responsible for. Ophelia turned back toward Greta. "What are your talents, girl?"

"I practice chemistry."

I squeezed her fingers. "She's being far too modest. She excels not only in chemistry, but also in alchemy," I corrected, pulling a small vial out of my inner vest pocket.

Ophelia reached her hand out for it, eyes squinted in disbelief as she read my tidy script on the label.

"Elixir of Healing?" Ophelia paused, head tilted to the side as she uncorked it and sniffed. "You made this?" she asked Greta.

"Yes, with his help."

"And where did you get a recipe for such a thing?"

"Lilith's grimoire," I offered.

Ophelia's eyes widened in surprise. "Indeed? That's quite a claim, demon." She squinted at us. "Whose blood went into the mixture?"

"Hers," I assured her.

"May I see it? The book?"

I'd only just gotten my hands back on the book and was apprehensive about it traveling beyond the walls of the collegium. "I left it at d'Arcan, but you're welcome to—"

"Go get it."

"Sorry?" I was stunned by her immediate and unwavering demand but knew better than to reject the request outright.

Magnus shifted uncomfortably, watching the conversation. Our eyes met, and he raised one eyebrow.

"Go. Get. It." Her tone was sharp and brooked no argument. "Bring me the book. I need to see it."

Torn, I looked from Greta to Magnus. He gave a slight nod.

Ophelia burst into laughter, and that was slightly more terrifying than her stern tone. My heart thudded, unsure if this mood change was dangerous or if she was genuinely mirthful.

"As if I'd hurt my"—she glanced skyward, a thoughtful finger on her chin—"several-times great-niece. She's safe with me, and she needs my help. Go get your little book, demon, or I'll be forced to revoke all hospitality where you're concerned." She laughed again, seeing me fighting with my darker urges. The ice in her voice forced every demon feature to the surface with no effort at all. "That mist you have is fascinating. I'd love to have a closer look one day. Now, are we to be friends, or not? Your fangs don't scare me, little prince."

I breathed deeply and forced a smile, trying not to allow her words to be too hard of a blow to my ego. "Of course." I mentally calculated how quickly I could get there and back by flight, deciding that the span of minutes I'd be gone were reasonable, especially with Magnus here.

Greta was much calmer than I felt. "It's alright. She's not going to hurt me." She even smiled. I tried to reassure myself with her demeanor that she wasn't worried about being here alone with the sorceress.

"Certainly not," Ophelia muttered, getting to her feet and heading toward the door. She opened it, clearly inviting me to leave.

I cupped Greta's cheek with my palm and stole a quick kiss. Magnus grunted, but his delicate sensibilities were not my concern. He'd heard Ophelia as clearly as I had when she confirmed Greta was my mate. "I'll be back as quickly as I can."

"We'll be fine," she repeated.

With a nod, I got up, my feet leaden as I strode toward the little sorceress.

"Hurry back, demon," she said. "I've got bread in the oven. I expect you can return in time to eat some warm."

I tipped my head politely but offered no response, my wings out and spread wide the moment I was clear of her doorway.

HUMAN SIGHTINGS BE damned, I flew the most direct route I could take across the city back to the collegium. I'd broken out in a cold sweat somewhere along the way, and drops trickled down my spine as I rushed through the hallway toward my classroom.

Hurried footsteps chased me, but I didn't pause. "Mr. Feland? Is everything alright?" Grace's panicked voice echoed along the stones of the hall.

"Fine, Grace. I just need to get something."

"Oh, good." She slumped against the doorway as I retrieved the book from a secure box disguised in the floor under my desk. "I was worried for a moment. You have a very concerning look on your face. Magnus has told me some stories about Ophelia ..." She shook her head. "Can I help?"

I pulled the book from its hiding place and secured it in a bag I could fasten across my body. "Not with this. We'll all be back later," I assured her, and left again as quickly as I'd come, hoping she wasn't too put out by my haste.

Landing at the hut was disorienting, the potent foreboding wards mixing with a flood of relief. I knocked on the door, and Ophelia answered within a breath of me raising my hand.

She smiled widely, walking away from me. "Excellent timing, demon. I've just taken the bread out."

Greta was laughing at something Magnus had said, eating a slice of steaming bread with honey on it. "That was fast!" she said as I sat next to her, pulling the bag over my head. "This is delicious, Ophelia, thank you."

"So polite," she graced Greta with a smile. "May I have it, please?" She held her hands out, palms up. I handed the tome over, reminding myself that it was in good hands, and I was right here with it. "Oh my."

She took it over to an angled book stand at the back of the room, immediately flipping through the pages. We all watched as she muttered to herself, finger tracing the ink on the parchment as she scanned the elixir recipe. "Come here, Greta."

Greta got to her feet and joined Ophelia, Magnus and I following behind. There wasn't much standing room in the corner where she had her stand and several bookshelves, but we all squeezed in.

Ophelia pulled the vial from her pocket and tipped it upside down for a second before removing the cork. She took Greta's hand in hers and smeared the wet side of the cork over a burn on her knuckle.

"What happened there?" I asked her.

"I bumped it on the cauldron."

"Just a little burn," Ophelia confirmed. "Let's see now ..." Her words trailed off as the flesh began to change from a deep red to normal color. The skin was brand-new within a breath. The old gargoyle smiled broadly.

"It works," Greta sighed the words.

"Of course it does." I chuckled at her immense relief. "Did you doubt it?"

"Yes." She nodded. "It wasn't an easy thing to make, but it also wasn't terribly difficult, all things considered. Rare ingredients aside, and the fact that I needed Vassago's hands as much as my own to get everything done, I don't understand how so many others have failed at it. Why did it work for me?"

"Because you're The Alchemist," Ophelia said with a shrug, as though that explained everything. She dropped Greta's hand and began to flip through the pages of the grimoire again, skipping whole sections and stopping to read other pages in their entirety.

"It's been a long time since I've seen this book. There's much here that wasn't written before." I twitched. I'd said the same to Rylan not long ago. "Lilith's secrets were always both deeply coveted and highly regarded. It's an honor to have one's recipes included here." Ophelia paused, having come to a section near the back that had troubled me as well.

"That section's been encrypted," I told her. "I haven't had an opportunity to make an effort to translate the code."

"Encrypted?" Greta asked.

"Disguised with a secret language," Magnus explained. "I'll have to see if Imogen will teach you some of ours. Or Lionel. They both excel at keeping our messages from being read by prying enemy eyes." He smiled proudly.

"No, I know what that means, I'm just confused. They're not disguised."

"What do you mean?" I asked, stepping closer. The letters on the page were not like anything I'd ever seen, not even during my decades in far-flung monasteries looking for ancient relics. No human language even had a similar alphabet. It wasn't angel script either, nor stone kin or that of old Hell.

Ophelia moved back a step, watching Greta with keen eyes and a lopsided grin.

"There's no encoding," Greta frowned. Her finger traced under the words. "This is a recipe for a fertility tea. It says, 'For best result in conceiving a child and having a prosperous harvest season, consume this tea every night the week before Beltane. Combine equal parts rosehips, elderflower, hawthorn, meadowsweet, and lemon balm. Steep three minutes and strain. Serve with honey from a local hive or lemon.'" Her eyebrows came together. "See? It's right here."

"Oh, you demons do find the most extraordinary women." The little gargoyle all but bounced on her toes. "They're part stone kin, so that's in their nature of course, but *saints*, they're unique."

"Do you know what language that is, Ophelia?" Magnus asked.

She nodded slowly, cocking her head to the side as she watched Greta absently rub at her sore shoulder. "I think so. Greta, was the cauldron hot when you brushed it?"

"I suppose so." A blush rose to her cheeks at the intensity of Ophelia's attention. "You had just lit the candle, but it was a small pot."

Ophelia crossed to the table and grabbed the bell. "Touch this please?" Greta gently pressed her fingertip to the side of the bell, then quickly snatched it away again. "Go ahead and use the elixir as I did before, demon."

I frowned as I followed the instructions, Greta's burned skin mending as we watched. She gave the unwanted ring an ineffective tug before dropping her hands.

Ophelia reached up toward Greta's face, but Greta was so tall she had to lean forward to bridge the gap. The old sorceress moved her hair, examined her ear, which had the slightest of tapers to it near the back edge, then patted her cheek. "It would appear that you're part fae, my dear."

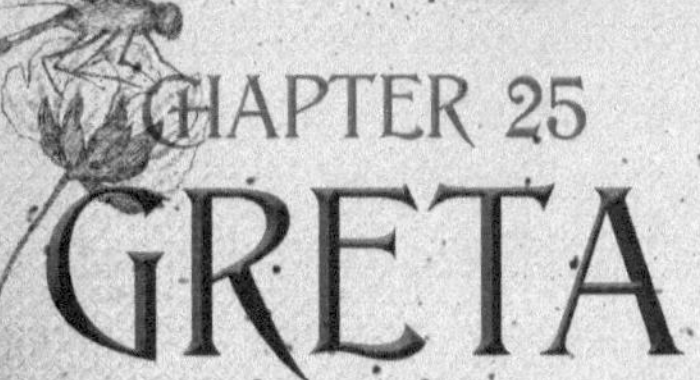

CHAPTER 25
GRETA

"F AE?" I ASKED. "Like fairies? From children's stories?" We'd gone back to Ophelia's living room, more bread and whiskey with a splash of tea making the rounds. Magnus was quietly absorbing everything, and Vassago relaxed into the seat beside me, glancing back at his book now and then.

"All stories have some seed of truth," Ophelia said. "The fae are much like the stone kin or demons. A whole race with their own kingdoms and politics. There's always been rumors of doorways to their realm existing here, but it seems our Rowan may have managed to find one."

"You think Rowan's gone to the fae realm?" Magnus asked.

"It's one of several possibilities. A likely one, given the portrait, wouldn't you say? Did you notice that handsome man's pointed ears and extra-sharp canines?" Her eyes drifted to Vassago, then back to her nephew. "I'll admit, the impressive scar on his face was a little distracting, but they were distinctly unrounded."

"Perhaps." He frowned, rubbing at his chin with his hand.

Ophelia's attention returned to me. "Come sit in front of me. I want to see what you keep digging at on your back."

I glanced at Vassago as I stood to obey her request.

"There's some discoloration under her skin," he said. "When I was examining it, it flared and caused her pain."

"I see." Ophelia gestured with her hands, and I sat at her feet. She pulled up the back of my shirt without hesitation. I startled under her cool touch, braced for the bite of pain that had come before or some commentary on my scars. The ache was its usual dull, insistent throb. She pressed her whole palm to the area that hurt, and it warmed, riding the edge of pain but never crossing it. Suddenly she gasped. "May I show them?"

I nodded. Vassago and Magnus both straightened in their seats. She beckoned them to come forward.

"That's *not* what it looked like before," Vassago said, tone stern and bordering on defensive. "There were just small pockmark scars there, some darkening. How have you lit up her flesh on the inside like that?"

"What?" I squeaked.

"That's one of my favorite little tricks, demon. Does it hurt, Greta?" Ophelia asked blandly.

"No, not really. It's just warm."

"See? There's no danger. It just helps me get a better view."

"I could see these," Vassago said, and I felt his fingertip brush my skin. "But they were a bit darker, not like this." His voice went whispery, regret riding the edges. "I would have acted with far more urgency had I known."

"I've been this way as long as I can remember," I reassured them as well as myself. "Urgency wouldn't have changed anything."

"Years like this? Decades?" Ophelia sounded angry.

"Yes," I admitted.

"What is it?" Magnus asked.

"Her wing ways. They're sutured closed. Never mind that she's been bound. Though the two … may or may not be related."

There was a general sense of discomfort at her pronouncement, noises of displeasure rumbling out of them all.

"Bound?" I asked.

"Some kind of fae magic, if I had to guess. It's not ours, nor yours I would assume?"

"No," Vassago said, sounding appalled that she'd asked. "This hideous curse isn't demon mage craft."

"There's no way for her wings to work, not like this. It would be excruciating to try. Can you shift at all, Greta?"

"No."

She grunted in frustration and dropped my shirt.

"She said she's never stone slept either," Magnus added.

"Never?" Ophelia gasped, clearly distressed by the suggestion of such a thing.

I shook my head as I returned to my seat next to Vassago. "I became a ward of the Belettes when I was a child. I never knew anything about the stone kin, let alone that I was one."

"What a hateful thing to have done. Closing the wing ways? Blocking shifts?" Ophelia launched into a rant not unlike the one Magnus had given about not knowing what such a deprivation could do to a stone kin body as she stalked over to the book and brought it back, offering it to me instead of Vassago.

"You're the only one who can read the fae entries, Greta. I'm betting there's an answer here for you."

"I'm not a witch or a mage," I lamented.

"No, but you are The Alchemist. I would bet your skill will allow you to undo what's been done if you can find the right recipe."

My stomach bottomed out. "Why do you keep saying it like that?"

Ophelia's smile became broad. "Because that's who you are. We've waited a long time for you, Greta. You are incredibly unique. Your gift allows you to transform things in ways the rest of us cannot. In ways *nobody* else can. Do you understand? The elixir recipe wouldn't have worked for anyone else—your blood was likely the key. You have an incredible talent and responsibility, my dear."

"What does that mean though? What will I have to do?" Nerves on fire, I worried that I had yet another set of expectations to live up to, and I couldn't possibly meet any of them, let alone all of them.

She shook her head. "That I cannot say. It's up to you to choose your path."

"Can I come back if I need your help?" I asked, afraid to not have the sorceress to guide me on what seemed like an incredibly important journey. One she clearly knew far more about than anyone else.

"Yes, of course you can. Send Belmont ahead to ask when you'd like to visit. I will give him my answer."

"Thank you."

"Oh! Hold on a moment." She dashed into the kitchen and came back with a pen. My body jolted as she opened the heavy book and flipped to a certain page, then began to mark out measurements and make new notes. "Sometimes, my dear, recipes change. They can be improved on. Corrected. Simplified." Ophelia's script was clear and precise as she altered a handful of recipes. "But it has always been an honor to be included, as I said." She slammed the book closed, a satisfied smile on her mouth. "I have no doubt you'll have success with any of the recipes inside, if you only set your mind to it."

"I suggested the Elixir of Life the day she made this one," Vassago grinned. "But we needed to bolster her confidence a bit first."

"Yes, yes," Ophelia nodded enthusiastically. "That would be a marvelous choice. Do try that one soon."

Stunned, I handed the book to Vassago, who seemed relieved to have it back in his hands, and stood. I had to bend nearly in half, but I embraced Ophelia in a hug. I heard Magnus and Vassago both inhale, but she just chuckled and patted me on the back.

"You seem like a good girl, Libelle. You'll come see me again, but you have other things to do first. Know that we will all do what we can to keep you safe. Take your mate back to the mage school and rest. Study that book. Find whatever answers it can provide. Make the most complicated of recipes. Failure is not to be feared, just keep attempting until you succeed. Go visit our kin so you can reclaim your wings."

I nodded, too stunned to do much else, and allowed Vassago to usher me out to the carriage. Belmont announced himself from a nearby tree on our way, a familiar dark shadow the whole way home.

I FELL ASLEEP on the way back to d'Arcan, the very last of my energy sapped by the wards. As soon as we were on the main road, I simply couldn't keep my eyes open. Vassago served well as a pillow, my head tucked into the soft space between his shoulder and chest as we bumped along the dirt through the city. It was beyond comforting to have his arms wrapped solidly around me and his steady, strong heartbeat under my ear.

When I woke, I was in my own bed, my stomach grumbling noisily. As delicious as Ophelia's bread had been, it wasn't enough to pass for a meal, and the whiskey had needed a little more to soak it up besides.

I looked over to find my raven perched on the windowsill, watching me quietly. "Hello, Belmont." I smiled, glad I finally had a real name for him.

He gave a proud *caw*, then took off again. I guess he just wanted to be sure I was okay.

I exited my apartment to find Vassago's door standing open wide. I walked across and rapped my knuckles on the wood of the frame.

"Grace brought up lunch for us, Dragonfly. I've been waiting for you."

I flushed hot at the sound of his voice, the memories of our time in his room the night before washing over me. My blood cooled, however, at the serious look on his face. "Oh?"

He gestured for me to take a seat and began doling out the hearty offerings Grace had left for us. "Did you get enough rest?"

"Yes. I must have been out like a rock." I smiled, realizing the unintentional pun I'd set up, and he grinned back at me. "I don't remember anything after the carriage turned onto the main road. I can't believe you carried me all the way up here and I didn't wake up." It still astounded me that he could maneuver my body with such ease, but he'd done it more than once and never seemed taxed.

"It was a busy morning." He handed me a plate but continued to stare instead of picking up his own food. "I'm sure you have questions."

I set my plate down on his low coffee table. "I do." I started simple. "What was she talking about in regard to Belmont? That you could help with the paperwork?"

Vassago smiled. "My brother Tap is in charge of recording and monitoring all familiar bonds."

"Familiars?"

"Yes, animals devoted to mages and such. I'm assuming that Belmont asked to be yours. Or something along those lines."

"Oh." I wasn't sure what I'd been expecting, but that certainly wasn't it. "Do I have to do anything? I've said it several times today, but it bears repeating. I'm not a mage."

He shrugged. "I don't think that matters for what fate has planned for you. As for the bird, I honestly have no idea. Pretty sure Ophelia's going to do the formal paperwork part, and I just have to pass it along."

"I see." I didn't really, but it was pointless to speculate how we were going to cross a bridge we hadn't yet arrived at. I pushed around some of the food on my plate, my stomach empty but also knotted.

"Ask your question, Greta. I can see you thinking it. I'll answer as well as I'm able."

I took in a breath, willing myself to be brave. "What exactly did she mean when she said you were my mate?"

"It means I am getting a tremendous gift." He settled back in his chair. "A mate is one's perfect match, in theory. My brother and his wife are mated, Magnus and Grace as well, to some degree. I never envisioned that kind of future for myself, to be honest." He smiled, an introspective private kind of tilt to his lips. "But you will always have a choice. If you don't want this, want me, then I will find a way to accept that. And the more you learn about me, the more you may hesitate."

I tilted my head. "Why would you think I wouldn't want it? Or you?"

He reached out and took one of my hands in his, tracing the lines in my palm with a fingertip, mouth pulled into a sullen frown. "You know what evil I'm capable of, Dragonfly. You've seen it. Been frightened of it. Of me. And rightfully so." His eyes squeezed closed and his forehead dropped.

I swallowed, throat suddenly dry. Flashes of moments crossed my mind, a compilation of moments where fear had overridden my sense of who he was. But they were few, and I knew they were not illustrative of even a tiny fraction of who he was.

"You don't scare me," I whispered. "And you had reason to do those things."

He looked up at me, gaze soft. "And I will likely have such reasons again, at some point." He cleared his throat, seriousness pulling at his mouth. "You have a choice. Fate isn't in charge here. If you have hesitations, we will honor them." He pulled a long silver ribbon from his pocket and laced in through my fingers, the satin sliding smoothly over my skin. Then he wrapped it around both of our wrists, somehow tying it in a perfect bow with just one free hand. "Do you feel the bond, Dragonfly?"

I considered what he might mean. "What does it feel like to you?"

He rubbed at his chest. "A burn here. An ache. It's worse when I'm far from you or worried. It's better when you're close. It was gone altogether for a while last night. After ..." He tilted his head.

"After?"

"Yes, Greta." His eyes sparked with mischief, and he ran his tongue along his teeth as he closed the gap between us, on his knees between my feet once again. Mist swirled lazily around his body, some wisps reaching out and caressing me at what seemed like their own will. He laced his fingers with mine on the hands he'd tied together, holding them over his heart. "After I tasted your essence, both from your neck"—he ran the fingers of his other hand lightly over the spot he'd bitten, eliciting a shiver that somehow traveled from there all the way to my toes—"and from between these incredible legs."

His eyes slid closed as he ran his free hand along my thigh from knee to hip, and the mist wrapped itself around me like a wide rope. He pulled me toward him with a sudden jerk, both with his hand and his mist, forcing my legs wide as I pressed up against his torso. "After I sank deep inside you. After I felt you tremble beneath me in pleasure."

His hand swept up my spine, fingers tangling in my hair and tugging so that my head fell back, exposing my neck to him. A breath of cool mist wrapped itself around my throat, the slight constriction unexpected but enticing. I felt the fast beat of his heart under the back of my hand as he pressed it into his chest, my skin on his. "After you imbedded yourself undeniably, irrevocably in my soul. *After*, my darling. Having you so completely has satisfied the bond, if only temporarily." He pressed his open mouth to the spot he'd bitten, and my pulse jumped under the wet warmth of his tongue, the sting of his quick suck. "I will always recognize those two distinct parts of my life, now. Before you, and after."

I found myself unable to breathe for a moment as I processed the incendiary words, his touch, the tingle in my scalp. My body responded mightily to them, and I wanted nothing more than to repeat everything he'd mentioned. There was an insistent pulse back in my core thanks to the gleam in his eye and the hint of fangs on his lip. He'd let go of my hair, wrapped his arm around my center, and held me against him as I collected my thoughts.

After another quick suck at my throat, enough to bring the blood toward the surface of my skin but not keep it there, he exhaled a warm breath. I shivered, and a chuckle rumbled in his chest as he placed light kisses all the way up and along my jaw. I felt the mist retreat, missing the way it glided along my skin.

"Do you feel it?" he asked. I was still putting my thoughts back together, tongue not responding to my efforts to speak. "The bond."

"Yes," I managed finally. "In my chest too." It was not an eloquent answer, but it was an accurate one. There'd been an odd sensation beneath my ribs since we first met.

"Thank the stars." Vassago exhaled as though he'd been holding his breath, worried I might not feel what he was. He leaned in for one thorough, reassuring kiss, then sighed as he undid the ribbon and put it back into his pocket before returning to his seat. "Eat, Dragonfly. Then we need to scour that book for anything that might help you and pack. The sooner we see Lovette about your wings the better."

I could barely breathe, let alone focus on food, but I did as he asked. I had a feeling I would need the energy too much to argue.

CHAPTER 26
VASSAGO

"CAN YOU CHANGE it to something like a teakettle noise? The shriek is far too human." My brother scowled at me through the mirror, rubbing at his ear.

Greta and I had spent the afternoon in the classroom, translating as many entries in Lilith's book as possible. She'd lost steam after several hours, however, and had gone off to rest before dinner.

"Would you hear it as well if I did?"

He frowned. "Probably not."

"Then no. And you still haven't hung it properly, I see. If it breaks, I'm not going to make you another." That was a lie, I absolutely would, if only for my own convenience, and he likely knew that.

"You're impossible," he sighed. "If it didn't make such a horrific noise, perhaps I'd be more likely to commit it to a permanent location."

"I'm a realist, *Stolas*. And any wall will do. Besides, you won't be at the manor forever. In a perfect world, I wouldn't even need to contact you."

"So why are you?" One corner of his mouth tilted up, along with his eyebrow.

"Have you ever encountered a merchant named Feiser?"

Rylan considered, rubbing his chin with his thumb and forefinger. "Doesn't sound familiar. Why?"

I did the best I could explaining the convoluted arranged marriage situation between him and Greta, not to mention the ring that couldn't be removed no matter the tactic.

"An enchanted ring? How horrible."

I clenched my jaw the same as I did every time I saw it on her finger. "Indeed."

"I will check my records just in case, but that's not a name I think I've heard before. What business is he in?"

I started to respond, but realized I had no idea. A successful merchant, who had long-standing dealings with Henrik, but nobody had ever heard of? The more I thought about him, the more I was convinced there was something deeper going on. I shared my thoughts with my brother, who also seemed suspicious.

"It's not a common magic that can be done, rings and such," he argued. "It's been a very long time since I've seen it in person, as a matter of fact. Usually, it's overzealous young lovers promised to others who seek it out. They're always convinced their love is the strongest in all the world and that's the cure for their parents' alternative marriage arrangements."

"Oh? And how does that usually end?" I teased, knowing what he was going to say.

"Much of the time? Badly," he chuckled. "I can think of a handful that worked out, but that kind of passion tends to burn bright and strong, only to go out quickly. Many have resorted to removing the finger when the relationship ends because it's difficult and expensive to dissolve the enchantment." I stiffened. "I do think that there have been mages who practice making such things regularly, but it's treacherously close to going against the council's regulations on things like love spells. It's a dangerous business to be in for very long if your work gets too well-known."

"Traveling and cost would be the least of my worries. Do you think you could trace the enchantment to a particular mage if you were able to handle the ring?"

Rylan sighed, eyes distant as he thought about it. Eventually he shook his head. "No, I don't think so. It would certainly be worth a try, but that's not one of my strengths. Perhaps one of the stone kin have a talent?"

"Perhaps." I was disappointed to hear that, especially after Ophelia had said something similar. "I will ask. And in that vein, you should be aware that Greta and I will be away for a few days. Magnus will be flying back to check up on the place, make sure it hasn't burned to the ground or something disastrous. He can't bear to be away from Grace for long, anyway. She, Clem, and the girls will be here of course."

"Where are you going? It's a bit early for a honeymoon." He smiled broadly, mirth faltering when I just raised an eyebrow. "It *is* too early, isn't it?"

"Of course it is." I huffed a breath, but my heart beat perilously fast behind my ribs. Greta was my mate, and we'd already consummated the bond. It wouldn't be unheard of to do such a thing, though I'd given little thought to an actual wedding. "We're going to the stone kin conclave. We need to visit with their healers."

"Oh? Is everything alright?"

I gave Rylan the abbreviated version of events he'd missed since we'd last spoken, including our visit to Ophelia. "Magnus says his daughter can help."

"Only if you find a way to cancel out the magical bindings, correct?" Rylan argued, frowning again. "Bonds that have been in place for decades, ones that are clearly very powerful. I could meet you there, if you like. Calla will be alright here for a day or two."

I could see the pained hesitation as he considered it. I understood completely why he would be torn about doing such a thing. I shook my head. "No, if you came, which you're not going to, you would bring her with you. Not only because she's the stone kin one, but also because there's no reason to leave her alone. Where is she, by the way?"

"She's helping Mrs. Brisbane with a project in the kitchen. And Greta? When can I meet her?" There was nothing quite like brotherly tit for tat.

"She's resting. Your offer is appreciated, Rylan, but your presence isn't required. Ophelia seemed to think Greta could manage on her own, we just need to find the right entry in the book."

"Which is partially written in *fae*. Saints, your simple summer alone at d'Arcan has gotten significantly complicated, hasn't it? We should come back. There's too much going on—"

"You're fine where you are," I insisted. "If we need you, I won't hesitate. But for now, we have it managed."

Rylan sighed again. "Remember when you got irritated with me for not calling upon your talent to help me find Calla? Even though she wasn't missing, but rather that she wasn't supposed to exist at all?"

"Possibly." I did indeed recall that conversation, I'd been sitting in the very chair he occupied now, in fact.

"In case you've forgotten, I'm an archmage. A powerful one at that."

"Modest as well."

"*Vago.*" The word came out thoroughly exasperated. "You have a magic problem, do you not? Does it not make sense to call upon my aid?"

"Are you versed in fae magic, brother?"

"Not in particular, but I'm sure I could help—"

"If we need you, I will call you," I promised. "Presently, I wanted you to be aware that I would be away from d'Arcan for a few days, nothing more. The school will be in good hands in our absence."

"Fine." He threw his hands up as if I were the most infuriating creature on the planet. I reveled in having won another round of our sparring. He narrowed his eyes. "I knew you liked her straight away, just for the record."

"Nobody asked."

"If I wanted to show up for a visit at the conclave, I could, and nobody could stop me. Not even you."

"You think rather highly of yourself, don't you, archmage?"

"I don't have to, I have friends who reassure me of my positive traits. Have you made some of those yet, brother?"

"As a matter of fact, I have. Has anyone told you lately you're a pompous ass?"

"Not in several hours at least. And you? Has anyone noticed yet how you avoid getting dirty at all costs or walk around like an old codger's cane is up your ass?"

"Fuck off, Stolas. It's not my fault as eldest I had to be the one to set a good example. Even Ophelia remarked on how much more well-behaved I am than you. How the rest of you failed so miserably to become properly cultured is beyond me."

"I'm plenty *cultured*, you self-important prick. And Ophelia drew my mate's blood. There was reason for me to act the way I did."

I smirked. "She drew *my* mate's as well, and I didn't charge at her ... or whatever it was you did to be so memorably unruly."

He sighed and pinched at the bridge of his nose. "I do so enjoy our talks, Vassago."

"That makes one of us."

He smiled. "Your mate?"

"So it seems."

"Congratulations."

We stared at one another through the mirror, dissolving into laughter at the same time. The bickering struck a particularly sensitive place in my chest, one that didn't see much use since we'd all gone our separate ways outside of the legions of Hell. Some of our seven-way sibling arguments had been so full of incredible insults they should have been recorded for posterity.

"I do miss our weekly brawls," he smiled. "Was excellent for the mind and body."

"You'll hear no arguments from me. I loved beating you every week without fail."

"There was once," he reminded me. "I bettered you once. The one time it mattered."

"So, you did," I capitulated. There was a companionable beat of silence between us as my memories with my brothers swirled around in my mind. I never really considered how much I missed them, but having Rylan close recently had made me unusually nostalgic.

"With the fae and portals to other realms involved, you should probably reach out to Seir or Tap," Rylan suggested.

I nodded, the notion having already crossed my mind. "Yes, it's on my list. There's a raven who's taken to Greta. What I gathered from the conversation he had with Ophelia is that he was petitioning to become Greta's familiar. So, I actually have several reasons to get in touch with Tap."

"Is that so?" Rylan smiled wide. "Archimedes will be pleased to have some company, I think. I've never seen ravens lingering around the grounds, though, so I have to wonder where he came from."

"Agreed. He took up residence immediately, like he's always been here, but I'd never so much as glimpsed him before he announced himself to her. His life has been well-fought, I think—he only has one good eye. He's admirably dedicated to her, though. Has been, from the moment he arrived."

"How wonderful." Rylan smiled knowingly again. I wasn't as convinced. His owl had been an annoyance for us all since they'd bonded. "And your bloodlust?"

"Managed. For now." I sighed, worried about the concerning progression. "I'm still searching the book for a possible cure.

Greta's ability to read fae is likely to be most helpful where that's concerned."

"Indeed."

"I think I saw the man who cursed me in the city center," I reported.

Rylan sat forward, elbows on his knees. "The book thief?"

"Yes. It was only a glimpse the other day when we were at the market. He slipped down an alley or around a corner before I could get close."

"Have you seen him since that day?"

"Not once." Dread mixed with anger curled in my gut. I wanted nothing more than to find him and wring a reversal of my curse from him before removing his head from his body so he couldn't wreak any more havoc on people's lives. "Magnus has been made aware and has his men watching for him."

"Good." He relaxed back in his seat. "I assume there haven't been any more issues with the creatures popping up where they shouldn't be?"

I shook my head. It had been unusually quiet according to Magnus, which only added to my concern about being away from Revalia proper for too long. "No."

"There doesn't seem to be any kind of pattern for where they're deciding to show up. It's odd. I've reached out to our brothers about it."

"And?"

Rylan shook his head. "They don't have any information but are seeing what they can find out. But you know how secretive the inner workings are. Always have been."

I exhaled, an ancient agitation rising from its resting place deep inside me. "Indeed, they never did like telling anyone much of anything at all. Magnus knows I'm available to help if he needs me. And you."

"Yes, of course. Safe journey, brother. I'll be interested to hear what you find in that book."

"I'm sure we'll be fine, especially with Magnus as an escort. And Greta did perfectly with the Elixir of Healing, after all. If there's a recipe for a cure in that book, she can make it. She's going to attempt the Elixir of Life soon."

"Did you say *Elixir of Life*? Surely I misheard you."

"No, you heard correctly. She got the Elixir of Healing on her first attempt, so I see no reason she won't succeed." I couldn't stop the proud smile that took over my face at the admission. My brother stared at me, open-mouthed and stunned. "Give my love to Calla, would you?"

"Vassa—"

I severed the connection, reveling in the fact that I'd likely left him swearing on the other end.

CHAPTER 27
VASSAGO

I'D GONE DOWN to the classroom so I could gather a few things to take with me to the stone kin encampment, expecting to find it empty. Instead, I found Greta poring over Lilith's book, supplies lined up on her worktable.

"What are you working on, Dragonfly?"

"I think I may have found something." Her eyes squinted as she traced down the paper with her finger.

"Oh? How can I help?"

"I'm not sure yet. The name is strange, but I feel like it's something I need to try." She gestured vaguely to her midsection with her hands, demonstrating as best she could where the drive was coming from.

"Of course. Are you hungry? I'm afraid if you start now, you'll be in the middle of something when you should be stopping to eat." I'd learned when Greta was motivated, it was best to go with it. Her energy stores were too fickle to delay.

She peered up at me, eyes bright. "I think I might always be hungry." Her cheeks colored, as though the admission were embarrassing.

Or perhaps not completely about food. I could absolutely relate. The way I felt when she looked at me like that was borderline criminal. It made me incapable of refusing her anything.

"I'll take care of that, then. Can't have you working on an empty stomach." I winked at her, and the color in her cheeks deepened. It was a ridiculous temptation. "Be careful."

"I'm always careful," she muttered back, already lost in the recipe again as she slid on a pair of spectacles. She was adorable.

I headed for the dining room, taking my time approaching the kitchen as the sounds of Grace and Magnus's mixed laughter rang out from behind the door. Grace popped out with plates in her hand, the mountainous man grinning as he stepped out right behind her.

"Good evening, Vassago," Grace greeted me with a wide smile.

"Grace." It was impossible not to smile back at her.

Magnus smirked, parking himself at the table with three of the plates he'd carried. "Demon."

"Statue."

"Will Greta be joining us?" Grace asked.

"She's actually in the middle of working on something. May I get a plate to take to her?"

"Of course. Come on, I'll get you set up."

"It can wait a few minutes. Please, eat while your food is hot." She waved me off. "It'll keep."

Magnus shook his head, warning me off from trying to argue further. He looked to be pacing himself with his first plate, trying to make it last so he could have more time at the table with her, if I were to hazard a guess.

I followed her into the kitchen, and Grace efficiently set a plate in each of my hands. "Thank you."

"I'll be along in a bit with some nibbles and fresh tea."

"You're too good to us, Grace."

She smiled. "Go on. Get it to her before she's got no hands to eat with. I know well enough how that goes."

Greta had a flask in one hand when I returned but struggled with the striker for the burner she held it over, spectacles abandoned on the tabletop.

"I'll help light the flame, but only if you come eat first," I bargained.

"This little contraption hates me. I'm convinced of it." She dropped the tools with a huff, sitting heavily on the chaise.

"I'm not sure such an object like that torch striker has emotions, Dragonfly."

She settled the plate on her lap, shuffling the roast chicken and vegetables Grace had provided around, mouth a tense straight line. "Well, something's the matter with it. Makes no sense how easily you get it to work. I could do it exactly the same as you and never get a flame from it." She stabbed her food in frustration, chewing the bite with much more enthusiasm than necessary.

We ate in silence, her rushing through the meal and me too unsure what to say that I ended up saying nothing at all. When she was done, I put my plate aside and lit the little wick under the glass as promised.

"Thank you," she said softly, still glaring at the striker.

"Of course." I threaded my hands through her hair, efficiently putting it up into a braid that sat close to her scalp. She smiled up at me as I tied a ribbon at the bottom to hold it in place. "What's the recipe for?" I asked, returning to my seat so I could finish my own food.

She methodically worked through the items on her table. "It's purifying. Or cleansing? I'm not sure which word is the most accurate. It just seemed like the one I should try. I don't know how to explain it."

"You don't need to, Dragonfly. I trust your instincts. You should too."

She grew quiet in her focus. I kept her company as she worked but tried not to distract her. I returned the dirty plates to the kitchen, brought back a pot of tea, and even had time to read some of my book before she finally let out a strong exhale.

"I think it worked." Pride shone in her smile as she held up the flask to the light.

The liquid inside was somewhere between white and silver, glittery and iridescent, not unlike my tattoos. "What do you do with it?"

"I have to drink it." Her smile finally slipped, concern pulling the corners of her mouth tight. She frowned, looking around the room. "Did I forget a flame?"

I checked as well. "Not that I can see. Why?"

"I smell something. Like metal burning."

"Probably from the elixir," I suggested. "What happens when you drink it?" My fingers gripped the arms of the sofa, apprehension at her blindly consuming a potion driving hard on my nerves.

"Any ill-intended enchantments should be nullified." Her eyes drifted to the ring on her finger.

"Mm." One could only hope.

"I'm supposed to take it during a new moon," she frowned further. "But I don't know when that will be."

I'd lived with my brother long enough to have picked up tracking lunar cycles. "That's only three days from now."

She perked up again. "Really? I'm clearly not terribly observant. I would have guessed weeks. I think ... I think I should take it at the conclave. I want to be close to people who could help me if ... Well, I don't know what could happen other than it acting like poison."

The terrifying suggestion dropped between us, heavy as it landed in the quiet.

"That's not going to happen, Greta."

"I mean … it could." She swallowed.

"I won't allow it." There was a gravity to my voice, a command. She blinked, but instead of flinching away from it, just gave a weak smile. She would be the end of me, I was more convinced every day. But I'd love every single moment of my demise at her hand. "We can pack up tomorrow and go whenever you're ready. There's no reason to delay, especially if it will help you."

"Okay." She was breathless, pink-cheeked again. Panic that something was wrong lit my nerves up, and I allowed the mist to blink me across the room. "Oh!" she exclaimed as my hands cupped her cheeks. "I'm not sure I'll ever get used to that."

"You seemed ill, Dragonfly. I didn't want to waste precious moments getting to you if you were about to fall."

She ducked her head. "I'm fine. Just nervous. Until very recently, I didn't know anything about stone kin, let alone that I was one. I can't shift or use my wings. I can't even stone sleep. I feel terribly inadequate, like an impostor almost. I don't know how to explain it." She sagged, the sadness etched into her face stabbed at me.

I knew I couldn't make her doubt vanish immediately, but I would do my best to make sure she understood that the nonsense her previous employers had no doubt spouted had never been about *her* inadequacies.

"You are anything but, Greta. Case in point, you just created a fae potion nobody else could even translate. You must never tell him I said so, but Magnus is nothing if not a good man. He'd never let anyone make you feel badly if he could help it. You are his family. That means everything to him. I have no doubt he'd defend you to his own kind, even if that left him injured or worse." I leaned in for a taste of her lips, heartbeat thudding in my ears. Somewhere in there, I'd stopped talking just about Magnus.

"I know." She closed her eyes, released a breath, and settled more comfortably into my grasp. "I really am very excited to meet everyone, but I can't help being nervous. It's shocking to me that

I've got so much family there after thinking I had none at all for so long. It's just a strange place to be. My emotions are ... messy."

"I understand." I held her loosely in my arms, reveling in the way she felt pressed up against me. She leaned her cheek into my chest, taking a deep breath and relaxing in my grip. It was a heady responsibility, to know I was providing her comfort. Her arms crossed along my back, her hands wrapped around my sides.

We stood there for an untold amount of time, neither of us willing to be the one to break the little bubble of quiet comfort we had. I think we both worried it was the last we'd have for a while, so we clung extra tight for as long as we could.

When she finally pulled back, I carefully tucked the potion as well as a vial of the elixir into a padded case before taking her by the hand and leading her upstairs. Her eyes communicated both trust in me and curiosity as I led her into my room. She perched herself on the very edge of my bed as I turned on the tap in the tub, adding shavings of a scented soap I'd found on our trip to the market that created a lovely layer of frothy bubbles to the water.

I took her by the hand again, pulled her gently to her feet, then held her with one arm around her waist. On an impulse, I waltzed her slowly toward the bath, her feet clumsy at first, but picking up the rhythm after the first turn.

I was struck with an intense curiosity then, for what she'd look like in a proper ball gown. I smiled, planning for an outing where I could have the honor of getting her such a dress, maybe some matching shoes. Cosmetics, hair pins—whatever she wanted. Her sister's ball provided the perfect opportunity to adorn her beautiful form with finery, and I was absolutely going to take it.

Her heavy breath as I dipped her, the way her eyes fluttered closed, and her pulse throbbing in her throat all had my cock thickening inside my trousers. My mist embraced her, helping keep her suspended in the reclined position as I used one hand to unfasten the buttons on her shirt, then her pants. When she was free of the garments, I pulled her upright once more. Her eyes were hazy, her smile soft as she allowed me to look my fill.

It seemed blasphemous to break the potent silence, but I couldn't help myself. I groaned as I palmed her ample ass in one hand, pressing her body flush against me. Her hands flew up to hold my face as she joined her mouth to mine, our breath mingling as she nipped and tasted, her tongue teasing along the tips of my fangs. Greta's soft lips worked mine until I could scarcely breathe, my desire a throbbing ache that her hand grazed at least twice with purpose. There was a gleam in her eye as she reached for my pants a third time that had me struggling to remember my intentions.

Before I could change my plans, I scooped her up and set her into the tub. Her arms remained up, reaching out for me to join her as I settled her in. I shook my head as I removed my shirt. Confusion had her brows drawing together while I rubbed soap into a cloth. I ran it down each arm, over her shoulders, and across her chest. She allowed me to manipulate her limbs to my liking as I washed and rinsed her whole body. No inch was spared. Greta all but purred as I moved on to her hair, bracing her back with one hand as the other threaded through the thick locks as they floated among the bubbles.

Only then did I join her.

I stripped and slid into the tub, her eyes glittering with mischief as she repaid me in kind. I'd thought I was on the brink of madness before, but I'd been wrong. So wrong. I had underestimated how much more torturous her touching me would be than me touching her.

She balanced herself on her knees over my lap, gentle hands scrubbing at my skin with the soapy cloth. Her breasts brushed against my chest, the soft skin of her inner thighs teasing along the outer edges of mine. Her pussy brushed against my cock several times, and it was all I could do not to grab her hips and drag her down where she belonged. Instead, I fisted my hands and shoved them under my thighs, allowing her whatever time she needed to touch and explore the way I had.

My skin tingled, her touch somehow hotter than the steamy water. Her fingers threaded through my hair, and she pressed up against me with all of herself. I inhaled sharply as she pulled tight, bending my head back to get the strands wet. My throat was fully exposed to her, at risk, and she didn't disappoint when she leaned in and nipped at my pulse point, the very place I'd bitten her. We were melded together as she scrubbed in the shampoo, my thoughts reduced to the steady throb of my need and the beat of her heart against my chest.

She smiled when she was finally done, her hands twined around the back of my neck. She stole several slow kisses, her eyes roving over my face before she reached a hand down, positioned my cock at her entrance, and sat, fully impaling herself.

My head fell back again, the pleasure exquisite as her body held mine in a tight embrace. I wrapped my arms around her but allowed her to control the movement, her breath coming in short pants edged with a low moan. She rocked, water sloshing over the rim of the tub as she found the rhythm that felt best. I watched her face change. Her mouth relaxed from a tense line to half-open, her eyebrows from knitted together to soft as she found her pleasure.

Sharp need rode hard down my spine as she began to rock faster. My fingers dug into her hips as my hips thrust up to meet her downward sway. I felt when she began to tip over the edge, her muscles gripping me tightly, her breath more moan than anything else. When she shuddered in my arms, I kissed her with everything I had and rumbled in my throat as I spilled inside her.

We sat for several moments after, just breathing. I worked the remaining tension out of her scalp and neck with my fingers, too pleased as she turned into a puddle against me. Then I pulled a towel around our bodies before letting the cool water out and turned the tap on warm to quickly clean us both up.

Greta smiled at me as I dried us off, then hustled her under the covers of my bed. "Thank you," she whispered as she settled into the pillow, her voice the first real break in the silence other than our breathy moans since we'd left the classroom.

"The pleasure is mine, Dragonfly. Indisputably." My fingers toyed with her curls, pulling through the damp tangles. It took no time at all before her breathing evened out, and I knew she'd fallen asleep.

My world had tilted again. Everything I thought I knew was suddenly on its head. The only thing that made any sense at all anymore was her, and I'd be twice damned if anyone would ever take her from me.

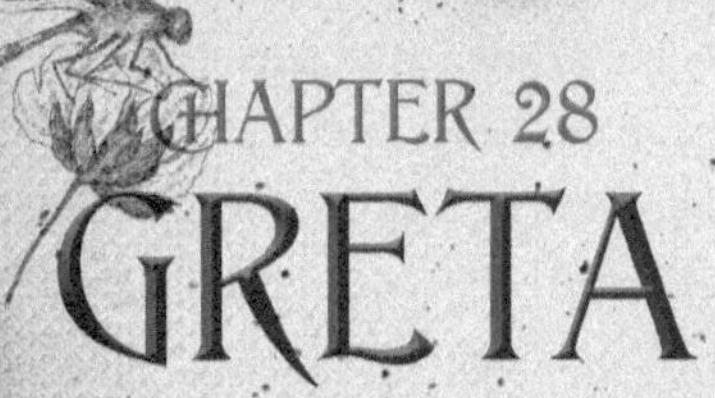

CHAPTER 28
GRETA

THE STONE KIN conclave was only about an hour's travel via carriage from d'Arcan, but it might as well have been an entire world away. I marveled out the small window as we drove deeper into the woods, unable to see enough to completely satisfy my curiosity.

"I've never had the honor of visiting here, though I was briefly at the soldier encampment," Vassago said, similarly entertained as we got further inside the dense tree line that marked the covert settlement. "It's quite marvelous."

The stone kin had managed to keep an entire tiny town to themselves, hidden among the trees and rocks. It was an astounding feat that left me open-mouthed and unable to swivel my head fast enough to see everything I wanted to.

As the trees became less dense but taller with more canopy cover, I saw there were as many buildings built between the massive trunks and in the branches or even balanced between rocks as there were on the ground. Everyone moved around the small village center with purpose and ease. It felt nothing like the tense bustle of Revalia. Half the population was in their stone form, and there were no sideways glances when someone decided to take flight. It was a place gargoyles and grotesques could wear whatever skin they were most comfortable in without having to worry about fallout from being spotted by humans.

The social rules of the city could certainly be oppressive after a while for a people that could fly and change form. Their existence in a city like Revalia would seem magical, and to some, evil, despite their purpose as protectors against exactly that.

Magnus landed beside us as the carriage stopped, a heavy gust of air from his wings chasing up dirt and leaves. He was all broad smiles and enthusiasm as he greeted people walking by, our arrival a definite point of interest for the residents.

Vassago opened the door and stepped out first, reaching up a hand to help me down. "Come, Little Dragonfly. I have a feeling you're about to meet an entire flock of relations."

Clem wasted no time hopping down out of the driver's seat and unloading our bags. Before I'd so much as looked around at the steadily growing crowd, our things were piled up behind us and he was tipping his hat to Vassago, the horses already turned back toward the city.

My stomach flipped anxiously as I walked toward my uncle, several people already having stopped to stare at us newcomers. A familiar knocking sound had me gazing toward the sky, and I found Belmont doing slow circles above us.

Magnus opened his arms wide, taking several long strides toward a woman dressed in linen shirt and trousers, like I was. She had bright-blue eyes and short golden hair, and was several inches shorter than I was, leaving her downright petite. Stone kin ages were difficult to guess at, but she was clearly quite a bit younger than him.

"You arrived faster than I thought you would, Father."

The pair embraced, and I felt an unexpected rush of sadness mixed with wonder. It was truly lovely to see Magnus glowing with pride and love as he looked at her, but I felt a strange stab of longing for all the years I'd lacked something like it.

"There was no reason to delay." He gestured toward us, walking her closer with one arm draped over her shoulders. "Allow me to introduce you. Greta, this is my daughter, Lovette."

"Pleased to meet you," I said, reaching out one hand for her to shake. "Oh!" I exclaimed as I was unceremoniously pulled into a surprisingly tight hug by the unassuming woman.

"Cousin," she said, letting go of the embrace but grabbing onto my hands. "I'm so happy you're here." She smiled widely, as she looked me up and down. "And you too, demon." Her smile became a smirk as she took in Vassago, who stood casually off to one side of me, fingers absently combing through his hair, the length of which was draped over his shoulder. He was the picture of calm and collected, though he seemed amused as he watched our interaction.

"The honor is mine." He lowered his upper body into a deep bow, making her laugh.

"Father did say you were something else." Vassago's eyebrows went up, and Magnus tried to appear innocent. "He wasn't exaggerating."

"He also said something about me being pretty the other day, so I'm going to take that as a compliment," Vassago smiled.

"That's *not* what I said, and certainly not how I meant it," Magnus grumbled, but his smile never faded.

Lovette laughed. "Come on. We can do proper introductions later," she said the last with a loud voice as she tucked my arm into her elbow.

Several onlookers grumbled, taking that as a cue to continue along their way while Magnus and Vassago gathered our luggage and Lovette led me toward the far side of the village center.

"That's the meetinghouse," she said, gesturing at the largest building. "If you happen to need a quick bite between meals, there's always something to be found there. Just be careful," she warned, smile broadening. "That's where the old men like to hang around to drink ale and trade battle stories. They love new ears, too, you might get stuck for several hours while they reminisce about how wonderful they all are." She winked at me and tossed a glance over her shoulder towards her father.

"Hey," he grumbled, "I'm not all that bad."

She laughed, the sound bright. "If you say so, old man."

Magnus scoffed. "And here I thought you enjoyed being my favorite."

Lovette laughed and patted my arm before pointing at a long, rectangular building situated behind the meetinghouse. "That's the infirmary, where I spend most of my time."

"Are all these houses inhabited?" Vassago asked. Nearly all the little buildings were dwellings.

"Not all, but most are used a majority of the time. They are not usually claimed like human property, though my apartment is one of the exceptions. Basically, if the bed is open, anyone is welcome."

Vassago made a thoughtful noise. "Is there no commerce done here?"

Lovette shook her head. "No, not really. There's a mercantile for small items, but only things that need to be acquired with urgency. We keep a robust communal food store, and ample supplies for the infirmary. Forge aside, we rely mainly on Revalia for our goods."

I frowned. "That seems complicated."

Lovette turned us toward a small side road that was lined with little cottages. "It's not so bad. Nearly all of us are in and out of the city at least every few days. It's a short flight, after all. We haven't had to relocate in many years, but stone kin memories are long. Most of us remember having to tear down entire settlements overnight and find somewhere new to go. Keeping too many things on hand can be problematic. "

"How terrible," I lamented. Picturing having to uproot a whole community in a single night left me dizzy.

"It hasn't happened in a long time, and besides, we're a hardy lot." She opened the door on the third small cottage down the path. "This one is yours."

"Thank you."

There was a low fire lit in the small hearth, the entirety of the cottage comprised of a bed and a small table with a single chair.

"The toilet and shower are in the cottage one over. You should have it mostly to yourself." Her eyebrow went up as Vassago casually set the luggage down by the table. "It's worth warning you that there's been rumblings of a celebration for your arrival."

"Celebration?"

"It's not every day that one of us who we believed to be lost reappears. Most of us love any reason to throw a party," Magnus said, hovering outside of the doorframe. "You arriving at the conclave gives everyone a very good one."

Lovette came close, examining my face and hair, her eyes pausing on the faint marks on my neck left behind from Vassago's bite. She took my hands in hers again and looked at both the backs of them and my palms. She ran a thumb over the horrible ring, her smile never faltering. "An excellent reason," she muttered. "How are you feeling? Do you need to take a rest?"

I was still well energized, so I shook my head. "I'm fine, thanks."

"Good. Come with me, I'll introduce you to my sister." Vassago stepped back as she pulled me toward the door. "I'm sure you two can keep yourselves occupied for a while?"

Vassago's mouth dropped open in amused surprise, and he looked at Magnus. "Certainly," he replied, politeness too ingrained to disagree. "Have fun, Dragonfly. Be sure to rest when you need to." He dipped down and kissed my temple.

"I'll take good care of her," Lovette promised. "We'll see you later." Once we were away from the little cottage, she squeezed my arm. I was no child, but the emotions surging through me made me feel like one, as did her enthusiastic words. "I'm so glad you're here. We have much to show you."

OUR FIRST STOP was at the far end of the encampment. The trees were closely packed together and seemed older, the shade they provided dense. A cool breeze blew through the branches, the leaves making a calming music. I smelled some kind of nearby water as well, which was likely responsible for the temperature drop.

I marveled again at the intelligence of the conclave placement and design as we approached the smithy building, complete with roaring forge fires.

"She's a little scary at first, but don't worry. Imogen is friendly." Lovette giggled, and we stood just outside the broad double doors to watch for a moment before interrupting.

I stared in awe as a tall, broad-shouldered woman with a long, dark braid hanging over her shoulder shaped a red-hot piece of metal into something resembling a blade with a hammer. When she stopped to dunk it into a vat of cool water, Lovette called out. "Hello in there! Can you take a break?"

Imogen looked up from her work and smiled, teeth bright against her soot-smudged face. She peeled off her heavy leather gloves, leaving them and the blade in progress on an anvil.

When she stepped out into the daylight, I inhaled in surprise. She was definitely Magnus's daughter. I found most of his features in her beautiful face, but they were softer on her, more rounded. I wondered what their mother had looked like, and whether Lovette resembled her more than she did Magnus.

"Libelle?" Imogen held a hand out. "I'd love to hug you, but I'm a mess."

"I think it's Greta, actually," Lovette corrected her, a smile on her mouth as she glanced between us.

"Either is fine," I said, my hand still clutched in Imogen's warm palm. "Though I'm much more used to Greta." Her deep-brown eyes were kind, and her hair was a similar shade of brown as mine. "It's so nice to meet you." Imogen's eyes dipped to the ring on my finger, my hand still loosely held in hers.

"Are you finishing up?" Lovette asked.

Imogen sighed. "For today, yes. There're plenty of projects that need my attention, but they'll keep."

"Perfect, then you can bank the fire and go get cleaned up. We have lots of catching up to do, and you know the ladies will all be more than eager to start celebrating the moment they think an appropriate amount of time has passed."

"All too well." Imogen's eyebrows drew together as she let go of my hand. "That's an interesting ring. The metal is ... unique."

"Is it? I don't actually know what it's made of. It seemed cheap when I was first presented with it, though I don't think so anymore. Maybe you could help me take it off?" I perked up, hopeful she had a tool in her shop that could remove it.

Her head tilted to the side. "Sorry?"

"It's stuck. Nothing we've tried will get it to budge. It's a long story, but my former employers matched me, and this is his token. I don't want it, never did, but I can't seem to rid myself of it either."

"Hmm. Let me see." Imogen went back inside the shadowy workshop. When she returned a few moments later, she had a wicked-looking tool in her hands. "Is it tight?"

"Yes. It's almost like it's fused with my skin."

"Oh," Lovette said. "In that case, before she gives it a go, may I?"

"Sure."

Lovette peered close, poking around the edges of the green-and-gold leaves. "It's not burned or infected that I can tell, but there's no gap to be had at all."

"We can try to cut it, but I don't want to hurt you." Imogen took my finger between hers, a sharp pair of nippers at the ready. She pinched the needlelike blades down on the edge of the band and squeezed. She grunted with the effort, her teeth clenched, but the blades didn't so much as bend the edge of the ring.

"That's the same problem we've been having," I admitted, disappointed, but not surprised.

"It's magicked," Imogen muttered. "Until the spell is removed, you're stuck with it I'm afraid."

"That's alright." I dropped my hand to my side. "I think I may have found something that can help with that part. But I didn't want to use it before we arrived."

"Come on, I'll show you the rest of town while my sister washes up." Lovette took my arm again and walked us back toward the meetinghouse after Imogen promised to join us as soon as she could.

We made our way down the opposite lane that we'd walked up on our way to the cottage. All along the way, I admired the houses nestled in the trees, the rope ladders, bridges, and charming nature of the whole compact village.

I got a quick tour of the infirmary, which had more than a dozen beds evenly spaced throughout the main room, but no patients. Then we saw the meetinghouse, which was basically one giant dining room with a fireplace Magnus could comfortably stand inside at each end. There were three pairs of men moving the long wooden tables around and two pairs of women moving in an efficient dance together as they swept and mopped the worn floors.

Lovette grabbed up a plate of snacks on our way through the kitchen. "That's really all there is to it. Can you hold this, please?" She offered the plate to me.

"Oh. Sure." I took it, and she snatched up a pitcher of ale and a stack of glasses as well.

There was more activity than there had been earlier, all centered around the main square. People were bringing over baskets of fruit and trays of sweets to go on several tables that looked like they'd been moved from inside the meetinghouse. Ribbons and lights were being strung up on poles, everything a very organized kind of chaos.

"Here we are," Lovette announced as we walked up a set of stairs at the back of the infirmary. "This is my place." She opened a door, and several women's voices sounded off in excitement. I mostly could only see Lovette's back as she pushed her way into the room, the several new voices challenging for space. "Back up, the lot of you! Didn't I tell you to wait? That we'd meet downstairs in just a bit? Give the poor girl a moment to breathe!"

Lovette scolded and tutted like a professional as she waved the cluster of women back into the main part of the living room, turning around several times to give me a tight, reassuring smile.

Once I had a chance to really look around, I found five other women, all of them enthusiastic to say the least about meeting me. They chattered all at once, and I tried to do my best to follow the conversations, but mostly just nodded, trying not to become overwhelmed.

"Leave off!" Lovette shouted, making everyone stop at once. "Nobody can understand a thing you're saying. *Please.* One at a time, yes?" She set the pitcher and glasses down on the low coffee table, then took the plate from my hands and did the same.

I was approached by them calmly and in a single file line after that. They all gave me a thorough once-over, each of them touching my hair, my face, my shoulder. I received a hug, some kind words about my mother, and a small gift. It was an unusual experience, but mostly very sweet.

"Alright, out. You've had your introductions and gotten to gift her before the rest of the clan, good on you. There'll be plenty of time for more later, yes? And I'm sure you all have plenty to do, besides. Don't think I haven't warned her about the shenanigans we love to get up to whenever there's a good reason."

"You didn't!" one complained, though they gave a group groan. "You've spoiled the surprise!"

"Some people don't *like* surprises, Jorna. Ever think of that?" Lovette shooed them all back out the door as nicely as possible, sagging against it once they were all gone and it was closed again. "Sorry about that. The aunties do love a new niece to fawn over."

"That's alright. They all seem very nice." The silence in their absence was resolute, a hum remaining in my ears from their noise.

The main room of Lovette's apartment was one open space for living, dining, and kitchen. She walked around, opening several windows wide. "Mostly they are." She chuckled as she plopped down into a well-loved sofa that reminded me of the ones back at d'Arcan. "Though they do have a thing against my preference for the breeze, for some reason. Please, make yourself comfortable." She gestured toward the mate to the sofa she was sitting on. "I don't mean to jump right in, but Father mentioned you have some things you'd like me to help with? It might be best if we have a chat before things get too busy."

"Oh. Yes. We visited Ophelia—"

She leaned forward, sampling a slice of cheese. "Isn't she great? The men are all terrified of her, and I just want to squeeze her."

"She was very helpful." We'd definitely warmed to one another the later it had gotten during our visit. I gave the short version of my issues, and not being able to shift. "She said something about my wing ways being sutured closed."

Lovette's smile vanished. "That's ... I'm so sorry."

I shrugged. "It's been like this as long as I can remember. But she and your father thought maybe you could help with that."

"I'm sure I can, but it's not going to be easy. Or painless."

"I wasn't expecting it to be."

She nodded, getting to her feet to answer a knock at the door. "That'll be Imogen. But yes, we'll do our best." Lovette gasped. "Oh my goodness! Hi! Come in!" I turned, the greeting alone telling me it was in fact, not Imogen at the door. A petite brunette leaned in for a hug with Lovette. "I didn't know you were coming!"

"Rylan insisted. It's not every day we're invited to visit, after all."

Lovette clucked her tongue. "You're always welcome here. This is your place too."

I stood, accepting the newcomer's outstretched hand. "You must be Greta?" I nodded as she shook it, her palm and smile both warm and familiar. "I'm Calla. So pleased to meet you."

CHAPTER 29
VASSAGO

"So, what should we expect from this celebration then?" I asked, pausing as a familiar form came into view on the main path. "You're joking."

Two large birds swooped low over our heads, disappearing into the trees before I could get a good look at them. I didn't need to see them—I could guarantee one was an owl and the other a raven. At least they'd keep one another occupied for a while.

Magnus chuckled. "Well, it's not every day we invite a demon to the conclave. Guess they figured why not two? Get it all done at once."

I watched as my brother loped up the road, his face locked in a smug smile. "Who's in charge of invitations? That sounds like very poor logic," I argued.

Magnus only laughed harder.

"It's alright, Vago, you can admit you're happy to see me." Rylan grinned. He was every inch my opposite in his black-on-black-with-red-trim attire and dark features, but for some reason, all I could hear in my head was Ophelia claiming we were like twins.

"Feels like I just got rid of you. Where's your lovely wife?" I asked, not wasting a chance to needle him.

"Off finding your chemist, I assume. I left her near the infirmary."

"You just *left* her there? After all we went through to get her back the last time?"

He reached out and punched my arm. "Knock it off. She's half stone kin, I doubt she's in much trouble here. Us on the other hand ..." He playfully threw a suspicious look at Magnus.

"I'm offended, demon. Does our friendship mean nothing to you?"

"It means plenty to me, it's *them* I'm concerned about." He gestured widely with his hands.

"You're welcome here. And just hug, the pair of you. Or fight. Whichever it's to be, have done with it so we can move on with our day," Magnus grumbled playfully, pushing us both at the shoulder.

I found myself smiling and did indeed embrace my brother. No matter how cross I pretended to be, it was always good to see him in the flesh.

"Are you here to satisfy your damnable curiosity?" I asked.

He chuckled as we followed Magnus back the way he'd just come, toward the meetinghouse that was now buzzing with activity. "I'm here because I was invited to the conclave for a celebration."

"So, this has been in the works a while," I said, looking accusatorially at Magnus. The three of us were quite the curiosity as we walked through the stone kin settlement. People stopped what they were doing to watch us pass.

"He was only summoned last night," Magnus admitted.

"Quite a trip on such short notice! How did you travel?"

"I flew us, as you had my carriage," he said, the *obviously* silent but heavily implied. "Anyhow, you have a magic problem. I can help with that. Not to mention you brought up having made a very rare elixir as though it were an unimportant sideline detail."

"So ... yes?"

"Yes," he grumbled. "I'm *intensely* curious about several things we've discussed lately. So here I am."

"Wonderful." I smiled widely as we joined the chaos that was unavoidable in front of the meetinghouse.

As we assisted with moving around tables, stringing up lanterns and other manual labor, the stone kin seemed to become less and less apprehensive about our presence. Having Magnus there with us certainly helped, but once they decided we weren't there to sow discord, most became cautiously friendly.

A group of women began to gossip in frantic whispers at one point, and they set off on a new project without a backward glance, leaving us to finish up the tasks we'd been directed to do. As we were finishing up the last strand of lanterns between tall trees, d'Arcan's carriage came back into the square.

Magnus tilted his head, a roguish smile spreading across his face as Grace climbed out. He immediately jogged over to greet her and collect her single bag. He leaned in and kissed her soundly, lifting her off the ground with one arm around her waist as she squealed in surprise and laughed.

"Would you look at that," Rylan muttered, an amused grin on his mouth.

"You've missed quite a lot of that sort of thing," I admitted, dusting off my hands.

"They look happy."

I nodded. "Seem to be."

Magnus gestured around, Grace tucked protectively under his arm, as he led her back toward us. She brightened but seemed uncharacteristically nervous as she glanced at all the stone kin who were now watching her instead of us.

Rylan opened his arms wide. "Hello, Grace."

"Archmage," she greeted him, returning his hug. "Mr. Feland," she said, head inclined my way.

"We've talked about this," I reminded her, one eyebrow raised.

"Habits." She smiled back, but I knew better. Her formality was a dead giveaway that she was nervous. Couldn't say I blamed her, she was a lone human amongst dozens of monsters. Friendly ones, for the most part, and she was involved with one of the largest and oldest, but still.

"We could have just brought you with us, you know. Saved Clem a trip."

"I wasn't planning on coming," she admitted. Her furious blush and glance at Magnus told me that he'd done something to convince her.

"I was going to fly you here later either way," Magnus growled, the serene smile still plastered on his face. He was enamored by her. A fool in love. But still afraid to see the scowl of disapproval she wore.

It suddenly occurred to me that we all might look like that, and all the levity left my body. Rylan certainly did whenever Calla was in view, and Magnus did at even the mention of Grace. The thought that I did as well made me sputter on my own breath. Two demon princes and a gargoyle knight all struck silly with hearts in our eyes over our mates? It was ridiculous. Laughable even.

I was still wrangling with the notion when Greta came around the corner of the infirmary, arm in arm with Calla. I couldn't even recall what I'd been upset about when she looked my way and smiled, I was too busy drowning in my adoration of her.

"I DON'T LIKE this," I grumbled, heart thumping almost painfully against my ribs as Greta prepared to consume her cleansing elixir. "We could always wait until tomorrow. What if it puts you out of commission for the celebration?" I paced up and down the aisle between the infirmary beds, and Greta was seated on the trunk at the foot of the first bed.

Everyone stood around nearby, except for Grace. She was trying to be inconspicuous from a spot halfway across the room, which naturally drew the very attention she was trying to avoid.

"Then our kin will be thankful for a reason to continue celebrating another day," Imogen said dryly. "He's a worrier, yeah?" She made a questioning face as she looked from me to her father.

My fangs dropped instantly, and a feral noise rumbled through me.

"Vassago," Greta said quietly but with steel in her voice. I snapped my head toward her, finding a disappointed frown on her beautiful face. "I'm going to be fine. They're trying to help."

I inhaled slowly, squeezing my hands into fists. "I know."

Rylan looked up at me with a knowing smile. "The mate bond can be quite troublesome, can't it?" He patted my shoulder, and I found the gesture partly patronizing though he meant it to be soothing. I recalled all too well the trouble I'd dished out to him intentionally over Calla, and I knew turnabout was only fair play. "We're not going to let anything happen to her."

"It's not up to you, though, is it?" I snarled. He opened his mouth, but I continued before he could speak. "And that's the problem. She's taking a potion nobody knows anything about from a centuries-old grimoire put together by a woman scorned. One could argue *the* woman scorned. From a fae recipe no less. Nobody else can even read the damn thing to verify the correct ingredients or measurements." My hands had begun to tremble with the notion something terrible might happen. It gripped me with a terror I had no idea I was capable of feeling. Greta reached for me, tucking my hand between hers.

"You want to make her better?" Lovette asked, boldly stepping up to my side. "Remove the binding, have me try to undo the sutures?"

"Of course I do but—"

"Then trust me," Greta blurted, leaving Lovette with whatever she was about to say caught on her tongue. I felt the words like a physical blow. "I knew the recipe was the right one the moment I saw it in the book. I know that I made it properly. So trust *me*."

There was no way for me to sensibly argue with that. I'd been the one pushing her all this time to listen to her instincts, to believe that she could do the hard things. How could I be the one doubting her now?

I sagged before bringing her hand up to my mouth and kissing her knuckles before releasing it again. "I do. I trust you, Dragonfly."

"Good." She glanced at Rylan, who gave a shallow nod. After picking up and examining the flask, she gulped down the contents. The infirmary was suddenly so void of sound it was as though someone had sucked all the oxygen out. "Tastes like I rolled some old coins around in my mouth." She coughed, accepting the water Lovette handed to her, and greedily drank it down as well.

"Will we have to wait long, do you think?" Calla asked, her eyes—as well as everyone else's—fixed on Greta. She looked around nervously, and her fingers twitched on her thigh.

"Alright?"

"I'm fine."

I sat beside Greta, pulling her toward me with one hand. I rested my lips on her forehead, breathing in the soft floral scent of her hair. With my eyes closed, I willed the wild energy coursing through me to quiet. She was my peace, but it was not my turn to be coddled.

Everyone was quiet as we waited, Lovette shifting supplies around restlessly at her work station.

"Oh." The exclamation originated with Calla, but quickly rippled through the rest of the group.

"Greta?" Magnus asked quietly.

When I opened my eyes, Rylan was staring at Greta intensely, hands held out loosely but with his electric power at the ready.

"Vago, could you step away, please?" My brother delivered the words in a tone so gentle it struck fear deep in my heart.

I glanced from him to Greta, who looked exactly like the elixir had in its bottle. She was surrounded by shimmery white, bathed in an ethereal glow from her hair to her toes.

"I'm fine," she said, as though reassuring herself as well as us. "It doesn't feel like anything at all." I stood, taking a single short step away from her side as she marveled at her skin, turning her opalescent arms over and back again. As she examined herself, the pearly sheen began to shift. It darkened, swirling into gray smoke as it settled like a layer of clothing on her form. "How does it not feel like anything?" she mused, smiling despite the terrifying transformation happening with her as a source. A complex mandala began to glow over her midsection.

"Is that ...?" Lovette gestured, eyes wide with awe.

Rylan walked around to the side of the bed, nodding. "A seal. A powerful one." He glanced over at me. "And you told me not to come. That I wasn't needed."

I scoffed and rolled my eyes, crossing my arms so I wouldn't be tempted to reach out for her again.

"Would you mind standing, Greta?" Rylan asked, electricity building around his hands.

Greta got to her feet, the shimmery smoke clinging to her form now a deep green, the seal a golden circle that took up her whole torso. The complicated tangle of geometric shapes and mysterious symbols inside turned almost lazily, as though her heartbeat propelled them. It reminded me of the insides of a clock.

My gut lurched as I stared at her. A thought turned around and around in my mind, getting louder as it repeated itself.

"Greta. I think I could see what we're looking for," I said, hoping she'd understand what I meant.

"Yes," she said, nodding firmly.

I glanced around at our significant audience and took her wrist in my hand, drawing it up near my mouth. "We must be quick, Little Dragonfly. I don't want to waste your elixir."

"Yes," she breathed again, eyes her own and hazy with lust as she looked at me, my lips brushing against the soft skin just below her palm.

My brother said something, but I couldn't hear the words, only his familiar low timbre. Someone else crowded closer, even more voices tried to intrude as I breathed in her scent, felt her pulse under my fingers, and gave myself over to my full demon form.

As my fangs plunged into her flesh, the press of panic from the others surged around me, but I paid it no attention. I snapped my wings out wide, the buffer they offered as well as the shroud of my mist buying us some space and privacy as I wrapped her inside them with me, the soft sigh she made and the way she leaned against me soothing every bit of agitation in my soul.

I wrapped my other arm around her waist, anchoring her body against mine. I slid my knee between her legs, supporting her as she sagged and gave a soft moan, her forehead heavy against my chest.

Greta's memories washed over me in a series of flashes. Some were inconsequential moments of her life—scrubbing a floor on her hands and knees, her hair tied back with a frayed kerchief. Kneading bread dough with the cook at the Belette manor, smiling. Running through the grass somewhere with Bea in the midday sun. A shed full of odds and ends that must have been where she practiced chemistry at the country estate. A youthful smile with slightly crooked teeth, that I immediately knew belonged to the boy who had kissed her first, the one who had her attention and affections before me.

I growled and pulled her tighter against me, ignoring the muted yelling coming from all around us as her blood flowed into my mouth and I drank it down in shallow sips, seeking, searching. Willing the right memory to come into view so that we could begin to solve things once and for all.

Then it was there.

The face of a man I knew all too well, his auburn hair flared around him and that damnable grin on his mouth. And he was casting a spell on the small child that would grow into my mate.

CHAPTER 30
GRETA

I LOOKED UP INTO Vassago's eyes, my breath a soft gasp as he licked the place he'd bitten and then kissed it, the wound sore but already finished bleeding.

"Did you—" I stopped mid-sentence, finding the answer I sought in the hard set of his mouth, the blown-out pupils in his ruby eyes. Even his mist seemed tense, hardly moving at all as it slowly disappeared.

"I'll kill him," he said resolutely, relaxing his wings only after pressing a thorough kiss to my mouth. I tasted the iron tang of my blood on his tongue and the promise of violence it held.

A rush of daylight and a barrage of voices pummeled me as he removed our cozy cocoon. He shifted his stance so he was mostly in front of me, snarling back at the aggressive tone both his brother and Magnus were shouting with.

"I'm fine!" I yelled, but I was drowned out by the booms of the men's voices.

Calla caught my eye, as did Imogen. Lovette was quickly behind and even Grace had made her way closer. On a short nod, we all yelled at once.

"It's okay!"

"Hey!"

"Shut it!"

"Quiet!"

It was a garbled message, but our combined volume and serious tone drew their attention. As if prompted by our noise, four beating wings resounded through the space, a third body sailing toward us and landing with grace at Calla's feet. It was a cat, but one with wings. Made of stone. I blinked several times, but that didn't change. Calla reached down to pat the feline stone kin's head.

Imogen cursed, ducking with her hands over her head until the birds settled.

A massive black owl perched himself in the rafters, and Belmont paced along the footboard of the bed next to the one I stood in front of, cawing loudly, then making that knocking sound. The stone kin cat, clearly annoyed, growled and hissed. The bickering stopped and silence rang throughout the infirmary once more, even the birds obeyed the quiet.

I looked down at myself, finding the golden seal had turned partially black. The circle was completely shaded, and nearly half of the other symbols were dark as well.

I shouldered my way around Vassago. "I'm fine. He wasn't hurting me. He would never. Besides, I think it's working?"

Rylan leaned down. "We won't know for sure until it all changes, but yes, it appears so." He frowned, relaxing when his mate put her hand on his shoulder. "That was reckless, Vago."

Vassago stared at his brother, his hand resting against my lower back, thumb drawing slow arcs against my spine. "It wasn't."

"But—"

"My curse is managed well enough!" he bit out. "I would never risk harming her. Not like that."

Belmont called out again, upset by the tension that surrounded me, though I wasn't the target. Then Rylan softened, as did

Magnus, and I wondered what exactly he meant by his curse, though I kept my mouth shut.

Rylan held a hand out to Belmont. "It's alright, friend." Belmont considered this, his head twitching back and forth for several moments before he resumed his shuffling. His eye turned toward the group as he resumed quiet monitoring of their movements. "Apologies brother." Rylan continued, "But still, your previous history, ours together ... Surely you can understand why I was concerned."

"I can. But even with the changes of late, I am not the same because of her. Just like the pair of you are not the same as you once were." He stared at them each in turn, and his point was clearly received the way they stiffened under his glare.

Magnus frowned still but gave a terse nod and stepped back.

"It's nearly gone," Calla commented quietly.

Everyone watched as the last of the gold slowly turned black, like a stick of incense burning away. I still felt nothing, despite there being a layer of smoky mist clinging to me, a strange magical seal slowly rotating against my middle.

I was disconnected from my body for a moment, the reality of my present too incongruent to the memory of my past for me to comprehend them as having both happened to me.

When the final symbol was solid black, I held my breath.

Despite the magical binding being incorporeal, my ribs were being slowly compressed.

"The seal," Calla said, stepping in front of me and reaching forward as if to touch it. "It's rotating backwards."

"That should have made it go away, right?" Vassago asked. "What does backwards mean?"

"I'm not sure. With high-level magic, anything is possible," Rylan said, still frowning as he crowded close to his mate, studying the arcane symbols.

"I saw how, when, and by whom it was placed, but that explained nothing. What good is my talent when it doesn't give me everything I need it to?" he groused, fangs bared as he cursed a gift he felt was incomplete.

"But we can find him," I reminded him.

"Yes, Dragonfly. We can. And I will. You were very small when it happened. Doing something reprehensible like that to a child is unforgivable." I was beyond grateful that the memory had been kind enough to show him the man responsible, but I wasn't sure it actually helped us solve anything. "I can't wait to locate him and repay his exceptional cruelty. There's much of that for me to do, it seems. I didn't get all the context around why he did such a thing, but it doesn't matter. Thank the saints you didn't try this on your own at d'Arcan."

"As I said before—" Rylan started.

"Yes, yes. It's perfectly wonderful that you came, brother. Very useful. Helpful, even."

Between the aggressive presence of two demon princes and a curious witch, plus the feeling that I was being corseted by something that shouldn't have any form, I found it exceptionally hard to inhale.

"Getting tighter," I puffed out. "Hard to breathe."

I wasn't sure what Vassago saw on my face then, but his eyes went wide. "*Stolas.* Help her." Panic edged his tone, and one of his hands latched onto one of mine as the other unsheathed his sword.

A low hum came from Rylan's hands as he pushed his magic toward the seal. It sparked and sputtered, a metal-against-metal sound echoing around the room. My chest compressed even further, and my vision began to darken around the edges as I sipped and panted through increasingly shallow breaths. Belmont made a noise I'd never heard before, clearly distressed.

"Stop," Calla said, putting her hand on Rylan's forearm. He lowered his hands, and I began to panic, my breath only able to flow in tiny sharp gasps. "It's earth magic. Not the same as mine, but of the earth all the same. It has a certain odor to it. Rusty, almost. Can you smell it?"

His nostrils flared as he scented the air. "No, beloved. But I believe you." He gestured for her to take over.

"Potion tasted like coins," I forced out. "Sounded like swords."

"Yes, I heard that too." A quick look around showed not everyone had experienced the same. "Whatever this magic is will likely disagree with his demon powers, but it may accept my earth magic since it's similar." She met my eye, giving a reassuring nod before placing her palms against my sides. Her eyes closed, and warmth flooded into my body through her hands. "Try to breathe with me." Calla's voice was calming, low. I felt grounded despite the absolute panic stabbing through my veins. "In"—she inhaled slowly as the heat around her hands expanded—"and out. Again. In ... and out. Good. Morticia?" She turned to the cat, who took up a post next to me, her head butting against my leg. I was a modicum better once she touched me as well.

My vision was still a little gray around the edges, but I could get enough air in that I was no longer worried about passing out.

"This can't be solved with a blade," Lovette told Vassago, edging her way to Calla's side.

"Not even one made with Light?" Magnus asked.

"No, I don't think so. Can you get my dagger please?" Calla asked her mate. "It's in my pocket sheath."

He reached down into her skirt pocket, much farther than should have been possible, and pulled out a dagger. I wasn't sure how the mechanics of what I'd just seen worked, but I wanted to find out. Calla removed one of her hands from my side, the invisible bands instantly tightening.

"Sorry," she apologized to me, seeing how I was affected and putting it back. "Would you do it?"

Gently, Rylan prodded the tip of her dagger at the center of the seal. It flared gold and gave terrible shriek that was so high-pitched it felt like my ear drums were being pierced by icy needles.

"No," she said quickly, shaking her head. "That's not going to help."

Vassago frowned but sheathed his sword again, letting go of my fingers and stepping back next to Rylan.

"I don't have the same kind of talent, but perhaps I can help too. Alright, Greta?" Lovette asked. I nodded, tears filling my eyes. I didn't care who helped or what they did if it made this feeling go away.

Calla softly guided our breaths in and then out again as her magic flowed into me. Lovette gripped my hand between hers, a brightness about her smile alone that put me at ease. I understood immediately why she was a healer once she took hold of my hand. She could dampen fear, panic. I felt oddly detached as I focused on simply drawing in and letting out what little breath I could manage, the rest of it just ... gone.

Imogen also stepped in, sinking to her knees as she scowled at the seal itself. "It's a puzzle. We need to solve it so it will unlock, right? That's the whole point of this kind of thing. To be as permanent as possible?"

"Yes," Rylan confirmed.

"But we can't read those symbols," Lovette mused. "That's nothing I've ever seen or studied before."

"I can," I said, the simple words taking far more energy than they should.

Rylan coached Imogen from over her shoulder. "Solve from the outside in. Everything should line up when it's right, like a well-stitched seam. It may form another symbol."

"Right." Her fingertips guided the tiny symbols around in a circle. "This is so odd. There's something here, clearly, but also there's nothing actually here. I'm just touching the air."

"Welcome to the world of mage craft," Magnus said dryly.

Rylan nodded solemnly. "It's definitely unusual, and a complicated piece, but you've got the right of it. Keep going."

It took Imogen a few tries to figure out how many layers she was working with, how the rings liked to move. There were seven bands of symbols within the larger circle.

"You're okay," Calla reassured me. "Is it helping?" I nodded, glad for the improvement. "Good. Keep breathing with me, okay?"

I looked down at the seal, trying to focus on what the little symbols were. "Elements," I told Imogen. "The first one is elements." She nodded, quickly rearranging them as I described which was which. When the first band was in the correct order, it locked into place with an audible hiss.

"That's promising," Calla said, moving her hands a bit higher on my ribs. I was able to breathe a fraction better and eyed her gratefully.

"Hurry," Vassago ordered gruffly.

"Planets next." I described them to Imogen, the second course locking in. We continued through the rest, until all the rings were locked. The end image was a seven-pointed star, the lines of it made up of the small symbols.

"Now what?" Imogen asked, backing up again.

"Can we break the damned thing open with our hands?" Magnus asked, arms crossed and jaw tight. Grace was at his side, a quiet but empathetic onlooker.

I almost smiled at the simplicity but had a feeling I had the answer. "Open," I said, using what I believed to be the proper pronunciation in fae.

The star pulled apart from the center, and the whole thing vanished before my eyes.

"Oh good. That's—" my throat closed around the words, my body frozen as my body cycled between white hot and freezing cold.

One after another, a barrage of memories flashed through my mind. My mother and I, cooking, laughing, when I was just a child. A disorienting image of me floating above her as she clapped, her hands outstretched and pride on her face. The two of us getting into a carriage with a well-dressed man she clearly trusted—a man who seemed familiar but I couldn't put a name to. Her scent in my nose as she hugged me tightly, tears in her eyes. My mother's voice carrying on the wind, but her nowhere in sight. A man with a terrible laugh and red hair standing over me, doing something that made me hurt. Me crying on the steps outside the Belette's country manor.

I screamed then, unable to do much else as my fingertips changed to greenish gray, the pain in my shoulders so intense I couldn't think past it. The cursed ring dug deep into my skin, flaring hot.

Vassago barked demands at everyone around me, fangs out and eyes blazing as he gripped me roughly up against his body. "Make it stop! I've got you, Dragonfly. How can I help you? Please. Anything. Do something!"

Rylan stepped forward and made some furious gestures with his hands, but to no effect. Calla was right behind, her green magic wrapping around me but nothing truly improved the pain until the magic had run its full course.

When it finally let go, I sagged, drawing in breaths so deep I got lightheaded. Belmont knocked, nodding his beak in agitation before taking flight again and leaving the infirmary through the open door, the owl not far behind. My eyelids became nearly impossible to lift then, my body exhausted. "I need to rest," I whispered.

Vassago's frown was intense as he bent his knees slightly and swept me up in his arms bridal style, crossing the infirmary without a backward glance. "We're done here."

"Wait!" Lovette exclaimed, clearly worried.

"I'm tired," I said, but even my voice was worn out, and didn't travel far enough to reach her.

"She needs to rest," Vassago said, not even turning his head as he strode with me in his arms out of the infirmary and down the dirt path through the conclave. I was out cold within seconds as I swayed in Vassago's arms.

WHEN I STIRRED, I found myself lying up against him in the cozy hut, pillows propping him up against the wooden headboard as he read a book. My head was positioned with my ear directly over his heart, the steady thumping beat the perfect lullaby as his fingers pulled through my hair.

"That was a rough one, Dragonfly," he said, voice rumbling through his chest. He kissed my forehead, concern in his golden eyes as I blinked and stretched. "I was beginning to worry."

"How long was I asleep?"

"A few hours."

"How many is a few?"

He shifted so he could sit all the way up, leaning to set the book he'd been reading on the floor next to the bed. "Four."

I gasped. I never slept that long except at night. My naps were usually an hour or so, and the idea that I'd slept away half the day horrified me. "I'm sorry, I—" Vassago's arm banded around me, forcing me to stop mid turn as I went to slide off the bed.

"Greta." His voice was all power, galvanizing me to the spot. "You are the only thing that matters. Right now, tomorrow, ever. If you're tired, you rest. You don't apologize. There's nothing to be sorry about, and if someone makes you feel like there is, they can take it up with me. Do you understand?"

I blushed head to toe, the concept of being first, cared for, *loved*, welcome if totally foreign. "Yes."

"Good." He pulled me back against him, lavishing me with his full attention as he examined my face inch by inch before dipping in with a gentle kiss that was just as comforting as it was enticing. "Are you feeling better? Any pains?"

"I'm fine," I assured him, testing my limbs in demonstration. "When you bit me … who did you see?"

He sighed, sadness in his eyes. "I have much to tell you Dragonfly. But first, are you hungry? Grace can't seem to help herself even here—she dropped off several things to tide you over since you missed lunch."

I nodded, though my empty stomach had knotted up. We grazed on the variety of finger foods she'd left on the small table, Vassago's eyes tracking my every move as he began to speak.

"The first time I encountered Lilith's book, I was still commanding legions in hell."

I stopped chewing and looked up from my plate. Vassago seemed unusually introspective, and that carried a gravity that demanded my attention. He paced in front of the hearth, long hair curtaining the sides of his face when he peered down.

He continued, "Lilith herself had it then, and it was quite a bit simpler, smaller. Unfortunately, it went missing not long after that. The second time I came across it was here on earth, in a little church in a tiny village in the realm of Vincara. How the priest there managed to get his hands on it I'll never know, because he kept that secret to his grave, but he was all too happy to entrust it to me after learning what I was and who the book had originated from." He smiled. "It will never not amaze me how humans disregard the pieces of their origin stories that they don't care for."

I would love to have further explanation on that, but it could wait. "What happened to the priest?"

His eyes flashed my way, the nostalgic memories he'd begun to lose himself in vanishing. "He led his small but dedicated congregation for many years. But the book … it's always managed to wander away from me." His fist tightened. "The man I saw in your memories is a talented trickster. The last time I found myself with the book in my possession, he stole it from me. But he did so only after putting a powerful curse on me that I didn't even notice until it was too late. A curse I still carry. I'd long believed him to be some kind of demon or even an angel, but as he bound you with fae magic ..."

"He's neither of those things."

"No, I don't believe so. And honestly, that explains quite a few mysteries, while leaving several new ones, not the least of which is how he knows you and what happened to your parents. And why I think I saw him in town the day we went to the markets. And how all these things are connected." The room was heavy with silence as his gaze went distant, his jaw clenched. "I told you I'd kill him, and I meant it. He's evaded me for the last time."

I should have argued with him, made some plea for mercy. But I had none to give. This fae had stolen much of what my life should and could have been from me, binding me with a powerful magic for reasons only he knew. Once he gave us answers, I'd have no qualms with Vassago ending his existence. I knew that said something about me, but I couldn't muster anything inside myself to care.

"I saw my mother."

He straightened, grasping one of my hands between his. "You did?"

"Yes. And a man in a suit. I can't put my finger on who he is just yet. There was another man, with red hair. I think I saw a little of what you did." Vassago's jaw clenched and his eyes flashed red. His fingers tightened around mine. "What is your curse?" I asked. "You mentioned it earlier, said that it's managed."

"My brother has supplied me with a special tincture to dampen the effects of my bloodlust curse for many, many years." I waited, watching as the muscles in his jaw ticked and his fingernails dug deeper into the wood on the footboard of the bed. "I slept in the crypts of monasteries on and off for the better part of two centuries, learning to master my new impulses. That tactic was not entirely successful, but it was necessary to keep others safe." His shoulders sagged, and he sat next to me on the edge of the mattress. "If I don't have a safe outlet where the rage can consume me, for that urge to be satiated, innocent people die. I lose all agency to my curse, no matter what I do, how powerful I am. Nothing satisfies it except blood." He swallowed, shame in his eyes as they dropped from my face to his lap. "And it does not discriminate. Young, old, innocent, or guilty ... it must be fed. It has served a purpose now and then, like the day you saw me on the road. That day, it helped me defeat an enemy, but those instances are rare."

I was torn between the desire to comfort him and the instinct to pull away. Regret poured from him, a deep sadness stole all his usual joy and bravado.

"Is that ... When you've drunk from me, is that—"

"*No*, Dragonfly." He shook his head fiercely, taking one of my hands between his, horror in his golden gaze. "That's entirely different and has always been part of my talents as a creature of Hell. Though I do wonder if the fact that you are fae has helped in some way."

The sincerity in his words echoed through me. He had never lied to me, and I could see no reason for him to start now. "What is his name?"

"I don't know. I've never even heard him speak. He hasn't reappeared in decades."

"What does he look like? So I know if it's the same man I saw."

"He's got auburn hair. Green eyes, a devilish smile." He grinned, shaking his head. "I realize how ironic it is for me to use that particular descriptor, but he always smiles as though he's up to no good. Which it seems he often is."

"Yes. I got a flash of someone that looks like that standing over me. Have you been expecting him to come after the book?"

"It's certainly not out of the question, as I assumed he was the last one in possession. If he lost it to another after all this time, I thought he might already be dead." He frowned, as though losing the opportunity to kill this mysterious man himself was disappointing, but it quickly vanished. "But it would seem he's found me in Revalia, after all this time."

Silence fell between us, my thoughts heavy and sluggish as I tried to sort through everything that had happened, everything I had learned.

"I think I want to clean up," I said into the quiet. My stomach churned and every inch of me itched.

Vassago stared at me, gauging my state. Finally, he nodded and took my hand, leading me out of our small hut to the one next door.

CHAPTER 31
GRETA

"SHALL I LEAVE you in peace?" Vassago asked, hovering near the door. "I can stand outside, make sure nobody bothers you."

I looked around as I considered his suggestion, finding no tub. There was only a walled off area for the toilet and an open wet room with a pipe rigged up to spray water from above.

"No, I don't … I don't want to be alone," I admitted.

"Nor do I want you to be, but I didn't want to seem overbearing, especially if you need some space to digest what I've told you. Do you need space, Greta? Some time? It would be understandable if you do."

I stared at him. The tall, confident demon unusually wary, somehow smaller. My heart squeezed. "I'm not afraid of you, Vassago. Nothing you've told me has changed the way I feel. You wouldn't hurt me."

"Wouldn't I?" he frowned again, eyebrows pulling together. I knew what he meant, that night he'd teetered on the edge of losing control. But I'd been able to bring him back.

"No. You wouldn't."

He approached slowly, a spark of hope back in his eye. "Shall I wash your hair, then, Dragonfly?" He plunged his fingers into it and gave a gentle tug. "I'll do yours if you do mine?"

The underlying heat of his words went straight to my core. "Yes."

"Mm." He planted playful kisses on my mouth, my cheeks, my neck, all while walking me backwards toward the wet room.

"Why do you always carry ribbons with you?"

He smiled as he reached out an arm to turn on the taps, testing to be sure the temperature was to his liking before sliding his hands up against both sides of my jaw and bringing his mouth to mine in a slow, tender kiss that had me boneless by the time he pulled away. He sipped and tasted, gentle in his ministrations as he lavished me with careful affection.

And that's what it was, I felt it in my bones. He was telling me I was precious. Desired. Cared for. I had been so starved for such a thing before I met him that I couldn't help but soak every ounce of it up.

"When I went into the catacombs of the Vincara monastery to sleep, one of the monks thought it would be helpful for me to have some measurement of the time that was passing. Every single week, he brought me a new length of ribbon. Always silver, always exactly the length from the tip of his middle finger to the inside of his elbow. He'd open the door of my little cell and place it in my hand. Even in my sleep, I felt the gentle weight. It gave me something to focus on. Marked my progress, such as it was. When he died, I was allowed to braid one into the cord of his burial robe. I've left one with every person that I've lost along the way." His mouth twitched into a smile. "I never did figure out where he got such a massive coil of silver satin ribbon, nor where he stored it. If there was more after I woke and left the monastery. It was an extravagance beyond imagining for a monk in a desolate place, but I was always grateful. I keep them in my pockets, in drawers.

Use them as bookmarks. I fear the day I use up my last one, but they have served me very well."

My chest squeezed, knowing he'd casually used several in my hair. "That's beautiful. I wish I could have met him."

He gave me a soft smile and kissed me reverently. "He would have loved you, Dragonfly."

We fell into that quiet space again, the bubble that fit just the two of us. He carefully undid the buttons on my shirt as I worked on his, the pair of us getting one another undressed in a way that felt far more intimate than it should have.

"Under the spray," he said, voice so low it rolled along my skin.

The water was just barely the tolerable side of too hot as it washed over me, the stress of the morning melting away under the heat. Vassago's fingers threaded through my curls, the muscles in his arms bunching and rolling as he worked. I reached out and traced along the edges of his tattoos, the ink ethereal the way it shimmered no matter the light.

My hands slid down to the ridges of his stomach muscles, and they tensed under my touch. "Careful," he warned and turned me around, putting himself under the water while he lathered shampoo in my hair. Once I was rinsed, we traded again, and I carefully worked the suds through his nearly waist-length white tresses.

"Mm," he growled pleasurably, low in his throat. "You could do that every day, and I would never complain. I understand why you enjoy it so when I play with your hair."

I sighed, loving the way my whole body tingled as his fingers worked against my scalp. "It's incredibly relaxing."

"Perhaps you could practice braiding mine, too. We can trade."

I smiled, enjoying the way he crushed our bodies together so he could get us both under the water at once. He then turned what should have been an efficient washing into something far more intimate simply by dropping to one knee.

"Give me your foot." He placed the one I raised on his knee and ran the soap up the inside of my leg, then down the back, repeating this all the way around. "The other." He repeated the process, fingers sweeping dangerously close to my center as he worked around my thighs.

I took the bar and lathered up his arms, down his chest and stomach, only to be turned around again so he could work on my back. His hands caressed my ass lovingly, but he went no further. I did the same, admiring the network of faint scars and the rest of his tattoos as I washed the broad expanse of his shoulders.

"Let's get you rinsed," he said breathily, his thick arousal pressed against my stomach. I did my best to breathe slow and intentional, much like Calla had instructed me. That only lasted until the soap bubbles were headed down the drain, because he kissed me again, and breath no longer mattered.

My back hit the wall, and he hiked one of my legs up over his hip as he stepped into my body, his length hot and pulsing against my belly as he thrust his tongue against mine. Tiny needy noises rattled through my throat, but no matter how I reached, he brushed me off, maintaining all control.

"I know, beloved. I know," he said, before maneuvering his kisses along my jaw and down my throat, which only fanned the flames.

Finally, his chest heaving, he stopped torturing me, and my plea came out coherently. "Please," I moaned.

"Eyes on me, Dragonfly." He stared straight down into my soul as he manipulated my body to where he needed it and slid into me, the teasing he'd been doing having left me slick and ready.

My eyelids fluttered as my body gripped him, the feel of him rubbing against that spot at the very front of my channel making me whimper.

"You were made for me, Greta. You take me so well. So perfectly."

There was something about this refined gentleman having a dirty mouth that set every single nerve of mine on fire. I wanted to be everything he claimed I was, reveling in his praise as he drove me closer and closer to my climax with every brutal thrust.

He reached down and picked up my other leg. I locked my ankles around his back, leaving him to balance me between his hips and the wall with one hand around my neck and the other gripping my hip. His mouth settled against that spot where my neck met my shoulder, the one that belonged to him.

"Please," I begged, every cell throbbing as my core clenched around him. I knew that a peak beyond all compare would consume me if he indulged in a bite right now. "Do it."

"Needy, Little Dragonfly?" he smirked. When he stopped, though, it made me moan in agitation. "I'll take care of you, I promise. Are you watching? Do you see how perfectly we fit together? You are *mine*, Greta." His thumb slipped over my aching clit and circled, sending shocks of pleasure ricocheting under my skin.

"Yes," I agreed, desperate for the release he was holding just out of my grasp.

Vassago smiled, fangs out in full, eyes a bright ruby that I knew should scare me but only left me burning with need. I sucked in a harsh breath as he bit down, then screamed as my orgasm racked my whole body. He only sipped a handful of times before pulling free to roar into my shoulder, his cock spasming inside me and forcing another tremor out of me as well.

He stood there holding me up, the both of us panting as the water continued to cascade over us.

The quiet bubble descended again as he quickly put me through another careful wash once I could trust my legs to hold me up, then bundled me into oversized towels. We lingered in the steamy room, combing through all the knots in my hair, and sharing wordless kisses, prolonging the peace as long as possible. It wasn't that we didn't want to tackle our responsibilities, it was that it was so nice to be in that room, only us.

Too much noise waited for us on the other side of the door.

WE ONLY HAD long enough to get dressed before someone was knocking on the door of our hut.

Lovette had come with Calla to be sure I was doing alright after such a long rest. Despite finding me in suitable health, they insisted they take me to the infirmary for a quick once-over, on the assurance that if anything was amiss, they'd find him immediately.

"Your presence has been requested at the forge, besides," Lovette informed Vassago as I tugged on my shoes.

"It has?"

"Yes," she laughed. "My father and your brother are there. They requested you join them." She smiled, then it widened when he rolled his eyes. "Don't worry, the celebration will start soon enough, and we'll all be plenty distracted by food, drink, and music. Nothing much will matter for several hours at least."

"Sounds lovely," he said, and we left the hut as a group, splitting off once the main square was in sight.

The infirmary was much busier than I imagined. Dresses were being handed around, flower crows and ribbons being stacked and draped on the empty beds.

"What's ...?" I couldn't even get the question to form as I watched the flurry of activity.

"For the celebration," Flora, one of the ladies I'd met in Lovette's apartment, said, smiling widely at me as she held a silver dress with ornate beading and embroidery against my body. "Yes, I think this one will do nicely."

"I thought we wanted her to try the blue?" the one Lovette had called Jorna complained, rushing over with a similar dress but in a deep sapphire color.

"No, the silver is better," one of the ladies in charge of ribbons nodded, barely looking over her shoulder.

"See? Here, put this on." Flora shoved the dress into my arms, and out of reflex, I accepted it.

"Oh. Thank you, but I—"

Lovette reached out and pulled both Calla and I into a supplies room at the front of the infirmary, shutting the door behind us.

"Listen, Greta, you don't have to do anything these busybodies tell you," she said, her smile wide as she delivered the words. "But that will be absolutely stunning on you. It's not often those gowns come out of the aunts' strongboxes. Special occasions only." She winked at me, reverently touching the beadwork. "Though keeping them well maintained is one of their favorite ways to pass the time."

"Are you feeling alright?" Calla asked, genuine concern in her eyes.

I touched the silken fabric of the dress, reminded of Bea and her well-stocked wardrobe and that time was edging ever closer to her ball. "I'm fine," I said, taking a deep inhale as proof. "I'm sorry if I worried you. I don't usually sleep that long when I nap, but I am tired often."

Lovette nodded, taking the dress from my hands.

"Magical residue," Calla nodded knowingly.

"Partially, yes." I shifted, allowing them to pull the dress over my head.

"It's perfect," Lovette said, having arranged the dress on my body atop my clothes. She turned me toward a cabinet that had a large oval mirror sitting on top.

The gown was beyond gorgeous, the smallest movement making it shimmer in a different way. The threads and fabric were silver, the beading both iridescent and metallic. Each tiny detail in the flowers and vines was unique and important.

"Oh." A lump formed in my throat at the sight of it on me, tears threatening out of nothing less than pure joy.

"That's the one," Lovette said with a firm nod. "Come on, let's get you changed for real."

The next hour blurred into a frenzy of activity as I was fussed over. My chin-length hair was braided tight against my head around ribbons and flowers by no fewer than four of the aunts at once, and I was beautified beyond recognition by a room full of women who had accepted me as their own without question.

There were so many people bustling around between the gown- and ribbon-stacked beds, I had a hard time keeping track, but Calla and Grace were getting similar treatment. Being a guest for a celebration certainly had its perks, if that's what aggressive and affectionate pampering was.

By the time the infirmary had emptied out, I felt unrecognizable but far lovelier than I ever had before.

All the women in the conclave, young and old, had come through the infirmary to choose a dress at some point. I'd met so many of my kin, there was no chance of me remembering even most of the names. I was filled with a joy that was bright and bubbly but unfamiliar at the same time.

Lovette had ended up with the sapphire gown, and it was stunning paired with her eyes. Calla had found one in a deep, saturated red that looked like it had been reserved especially for her. Even Grace had been hustled in. Despite her protests, she left with a gown in an emerald shade that had made Calla laugh and Grace blush. I wasn't sure of the joke between them about the color, but it didn't matter. Everyone's joy was infectious, and it was impossible to worry surrounded by such intense beauty and happiness.

Imogen was the last to arrive and change, and once she emerged from the little side room in her earthy-brown dress,

Lovette clapped her hands excitedly and dragged us all down to the square in front of the meetinghouse, where a glorious party was already underway.

I floated with them, gripping the moment so fiercely it had no choice but to become a treasured memory.

CHAPTER 32
VASSAGO

"**Y**OUR RANGE IS improving," Rylan said thoughtfully as I set down the case I'd used my mist to blink back to our hut to retrieve.

"It is." I intentionally held both forms at once. His eyebrow went up.

"Mm." My brother smiled but kept whatever thoughts he had about that development to himself, accepting the small opal ring from my outstretched hand. "And yours." I slid it off my finger and handed it over as well.

Most of the time, I wore the larger opal on my right index finger and the smaller one on my left pinky, but after our recent revelations, I'd decided the smaller one belonged to Greta. Once properly enchanted, even if our blood bond waned, I would be able to find her, no matter the distance. Given what Rylan and Calla had gone through, I was taking no chances with her.

"You understand the human implications of rings," Rylan asked.

"Of course I do."

He studied my face for a moment, long enough that we were able to hold an entire conversation only using subtle shifts in our eyebrows and the set of our mouths. Finally, he nodded and smiled, approving of whatever it was he'd seen there.

Magnus was proudly admiring Imogen's work, including several new Light blades. She was there as well, standing off to the side, a flush in her cheeks as her father gushed proudly over her talent.

"Do you like the one I loaned you, demon?" he asked me.

"Yes. It's well balanced. Feels much like my regular sword. Is that one of yours as well?" I asked her.

She shook her head. "No, that one came from Tynan I believe. He was forge master for many years before I took his place."

"Ah. I like it fine," I answered.

"Would you like to keep it?" Magnus smirked.

"I thought the agreement was I would do just that until further notice?"

"It is. I'm just wondering if you'd rather take one of these instead. A gift."

"A generous one," Rylan said, and Imogen gave a polite head bow.

"It's my pleasure," she replied. "Much like the dagger I made for your mate."

Rylan smiled, though whether it was the mention of Calla or the blade he was grinning at, I wasn't sure. "Have you taught Greta to fight at all?" he asked, placing both rings on a cloth atop the nearest table.

I shook my head. "Her energy isn't adequate for that yet, I don't think. Though perhaps soon."

"She should be armed," Magnus muttered, nodding as he examined the options. "Imogen has offered any that speak to you, demon. I'm sure you will not take such a gift for granted."

I turned to look at her, finding a proud smile on her face. "Truly?" I asked.

"Yes. For both you and Greta. You should be properly equipped. It is the way of the conclave to take care of its guests, stone kin or not."

I understood the gravity of what she was offering. A new blade, one with no other owner was special, but one imbued with Light? A blade forged by stone kin hands was rare. But one specifically made to kill creatures of Hell? Invaluable.

"Greta should make her own choice." They all smiled at my assertion, which left me shaking my head as I tried them out one by one. When I took the third one off its pegs, a surge ran through me, and I froze. I looked around for the source of the electric sensation, glancing at my brother who just stared back innocently.

"Wasn't me," he put his hands up. "I don't even have my magic out."

"Ah. That's the one then," Imogen chuckled, taking it from me so she could match it with a sheath.

"The one I loaned you works well enough, but this one is yours." Magnus clapped a hand on my shoulder.

"Thank you," I bowed my head as I accepted the gift from Imogen.

"You're welcome. If you'll excuse me, I need to go get ready."

"Of course."

She hugged her father, and Magnus squeezed her briefly, dropping a kiss on the top of her head before allowing her to leave.

"Alright then. Shall we?" Rylan asked, wasting no time.

He began to mutter over the rings, face hard with focus as his hands twisted in precise, controlled movements I didn't understand but surely had profound symbolic meaning. His talent was interesting to watch, even if I never quite understood the way it worked. I supposed it was the same for him with my ability to locate things with nothing more than a hairbrush or a mirror.

The rings danced as he lowered his hands over the top of it, reciting his spell in perfectly annunciated syllables. The tips of his thumbs and forefingers were touching, the gap they made a perfect triangle. A surge of golden energy wrapped around the jewelry, then dissipated in a small ripple of electricity. The air around us felt charged even after he stopped, a side effect from Rylan using his power.

He picked up the rings and handed them back to me. "That should do it."

"That's it?" I took them, surprised.

He frowned. "Yes, that's all. What were you expecting?"

"I don't know. Not ... that."

My brother rolled his eyes at me and began poking through my lock box. "Well, what you do isn't often glamorous either. You will need to put your blood on those, you know. Yours and hers. And you're welcome."

"I'm well aware how to prepare an object I want to employ for scrying capabilities, *Stolas*."

"Just checking, brother. You'd be surprised what things slip one's mind when their mate is taking up all the available space in their brain."

"Mages are such odd creatures," Magnus muttered, watching us with his arms crossed.

"You adore me, Magnus. I know you do," Rylan teased.

"I may, archmage, but you're still strange."

Rylan laughed, clearly getting agitated as he swiped through the hidden compartments of my case.

"In the smallest pocket on the left-hand side," I told him helpfully. I slipped Greta's ring onto my pinkie so it would be safe until I could put it on her finger where it belonged. "You have my gratitude," I said, giving a little bow.

He smirked and shook his head as he dug around. His eyes

scanned the vial of healing elixir with undisguised awe and fascination. "Explain."

"I found the recipe in Lilith's book. Greta came to me doubtful of her capabilities, so I had her try as an experiment in trusting herself. It was a step down from my original, loftier goal, the Elixir of Life, but she succeeded. And I have no doubt that she'll make the other in due time."

He tilted the vial as he held it up to the light, but never removed the cork. "May I keep this?"

"I suppose I can trust you with it. I left one with Ophelia, after all. Do you have specific intentions for it?"

He tucked the little vial into his inner vest pocket. "No, but one never knows when they might need one of the rarest elixirs ever made. Some similar items Ophelia gave to me came in very handy not so long ago." He narrowed his eyes at me. "There's another vial in here, somewhere, isn't there?"

I grinned. "Of course there is. As you said, one never knows, do they?"

"If you've done what you came to do, we should be going," Magnus said. "Stone kin celebrations wait for no man."

"I'll meet you there." I fastened my new sword on my belt and locked up my case, holding it tight and reveling in the way both of their eyes narrowed as I blinked away into the mist.

WHEN I GOT to the square in front of the meetinghouse, the sun was making its descent, and tankards of ale and cups of wine were already freely flowing. There was meat roasting on open spits and an array of dishes covering several of the long dining tables. The area immediately surrounding the central fire pit was reserved for dancing, and a diverse collection of benches and stumps were collected in clusters beyond that for sitting. The transformation from just that morning was tremendous.

Rylan approached me from one side and handed me a wooden mug full of ale. "It's something else," he chuckled, taking a drink of the brew.

"Are all the women …"

"In gowns? Yes." Rylan laughed harder. "They could have warned us. I'd have at least brought my best shirt."

I glanced down, finding nothing wrong with my usual clothing, but I did feel slightly underdressed in comparison.

A trio of women approached, each with a devious smile and a fistful of ribbon. "Have a seat, gentlemen," they ordered, dragging Magnus over as well when they spotted him on the fringes, chatting with one of the other soldiers.

"What's this?" Rylan asked.

"Ceremonial plaits," one of them replied, trading around ribbon colors until they were all satisfied.

"I have my own, if you like?" I offered, pulling a set of silver ribbons out of my pocket.

"Ah! Beautiful. Those are perfect." The woman snatched them from me and set to work.

"What's the ceremony?" Magnus frowned.

"Traditional clan welcome," the woman working on his hair muttered, giving no further response.

We each got a single close braid along each side of our head, a colored ribbon threaded through and used to tie the two together at the back.

"Jorna," Magnus said calmly, but she wasn't having any of his questioning.

"All done!" She patted the top of his head like he was a child and the three of them roved off as quickly as they'd come.

We'd barely stood when I saw her. From the way my brother held his breath, I could tell he'd spotted his mate as well. Magnus rumbled low in his throat.

They moved as a pack, our women and their cousins, each luminous in their finery. I'd mused not all that long ago about getting Greta into such decoration and dress, and seeing her so made up and bedecked had my pulse racing. It was everything I knew it would be and more.

"Here you are," Lovette said, going on her toes to kiss her father's cheek. "I told you we'd deliver them safely."

Magnus took Grace's hand and spun her around, and Rylan simply wasted no time pulling Calla to his chest and kissing her soundly.

"You are truly lovely," I said, throat tight as I took her in. I bowed, offering her my hand. She put her fingers into mine, and I lifted them to my mouth as I straightened. "Radiant."

"They did your hair too?" She laughed, brushing along the braids above my ears.

"There's no arguing with the aunties," Imogen said.

"Look," Calla tilted her head and gestured. "We all match."

She wasn't wrong. Greta had been put in silver to match my vest and ribbons, Calla in red to complement the red trim Rylan had on his black clothes, and Grace's green dress matched the emerald shade of Magnus's shirt.

A hush fell over the gathering as a short, stout woman built much like Ophelia climbed up on a table and banged two metal cups together.

"Kin, friends, and honored guests! We, the stone kin of Cyntere, welcome you to our humble conclave." There was a cheer, and I saw both Grace and Greta blush at the sudden rush of attention this put on them. I tucked Greta closer into my side, offering silent strength. "Today, we celebrate! Two of our own have been returned to us, and a third joins for the first time. Such gifts must be honored." A raucous noise went up, and this time, even Calla ducked her head. Grace looked to Magnus, but he just beamed down at her. "Welcome to you, now and always. Let us begin!"

She bowed and stepped down, and we were all pushed closer to the flames by the crush of bodies. Musicians began to play from near the meetinghouse, and as I turned Greta around in a strange kind of waltz, I realized we were being ushered toward the massive tree that stood at the entrance of the square.

Everyone danced their way there either coupled up or skipping and spinning alongside us. Many of the women had long ribbons tied around their wrists, so as they raised their arms they fluttered on the breeze when they moved.

"Magnus, what exactly is the traditional welcome?" Rylan asked, but Magnus and Grace were ushered to the side by the crowd.

"Welcome home, Calla Noctua and Greta Aurichal. Welcome, Grace Jardin!" the short woman intoned, a broad smile on her face as she took up another stump much closer to the massive tree.

As we got closer, I found an owl and a raven perched in the lowest branches. Archimedes, Rylan's massive black owl, fluffed proudly, and Belmont made that knocking sound in his throat, turning his good eye on Greta. Morticia, the stone kin cat, sat on one as well, swishing her tail back and forth as she watched, seemingly bored with the whole occasion.

"Your parents would all be so happy that this day has come. Rylan Stolas and Vassago Feland, we welcome you as well and thank you for all you have done for the stone kin." I bowed, unsure what else to do as we were arranged as pairs in front of the woman. "Hello, Magnus," she said in a bored tone, raising a round of laughter through the crowd.

"This is a special day indeed, as these new members of our clan have all also found other parts of their souls on this plane. It is a *gift* to be soul bound, even once in a lifetime, but to find one's true mate is rare indeed. We can only hope that such a rare and special event taking place between you is a portent of good things to come! Now, I ask all six of you here before me, do you accept what the fates have given you? Will you treasure your mate, dedicate your mind, body, and spirit to them, until the fates so choose?"

Greta looked up at me, the same tension I felt reflected in her eyes, but I could also see her answer there. "Yes, I will," I said, gripping her cheek with my palm.

"Yes," Greta said. I was sure the others echoed the same, but I didn't look away from her to see.

"They will!" the stone kin woman cheered. "The clan accepts your answers and will record your bonds into our history for all to see, from now until eternity. My beloved brothers and sisters, let us welcome them all properly into our clan!"

The stone kin around us all raised their voices in what sounded much like a hymn. It felt like a fever dream in a way. The singing was much more than just song with the way the sun dipped below the horizon and left us in the glow of the flames and the lanterns, highlighted by the sliver of new moon peeking out among the clouds.

"May you always be the victor of your battles, and may your lives be long," The woman shouted over the last notes of the ethereal song. "May you bask in the love of your mate until the fates see fit to part you. Blessings to you all."

I closed my eyes and put everything I had into a kiss while Greta's hand knotted in the back of my shirt as applause and whoops of celebration rose up all around us.

The stone kin woman said something that made the crowd split off in a burst of raucous energy, but I was too lost in Greta to pay attention. I stared into her eyes, taking every ounce of adoration and love she offered in that moment, holding her against me as the chill of the evening breeze lifted my hair.

I held both sides of her face with my hands, kissed her forehead, and then pulled her against me, looking over her head toward my brother and his wife, then beyond them to Magnus and Grace. They were all doing the same, holding on to the moment like we were.

I didn't know much about stone kin traditions or how anything worked among them as a people, but I was fairly certain we'd just been married, or something very much like it.

And I wasn't upset about it in the slightest.

CHAPTER 33
GRETA

"I HAVE SOMETHING FOR you," Vassago said, steering me away from the crowd toward a quiet spot in the trees.

"Oh?" My fingers went nervously to my hair, testing to be sure all the little flowers and ribbons that had been woven in were still in place. I regretted not seeing how the ornate braid the aunts had given me for the event had been accomplished. Perhaps Vassago could puzzle it out for me to attempt to replicate later if he helped me take it down before I went to sleep. While beautiful, it would likely knot terribly overnight with all the little bits and bobs.

"Yes," he said. He pulled a ring off his pinkie, hands abnormally unsteady as he presented it to me. "For you." He held the ring up between his thumb and forefinger.

My gut twisted. "Oh. You don't have to just because—"

"Of course I don't, Dragonfly. This was going to be yours even before ... all that. Which for the record, was a surprise to us all." He swallowed, something like worry crossing his face. "I would like for you to have this, but I only want you to accept it if you want it. It will keep us connected if we are ever separated."

I looked at the small round opal stone atop the simple band. It was beautiful. "Won't the bites also do that? And my crystal?"

"Yes, for a time. But these have been spelled. Rylan performed the magic. They will be more permanent—assuming you wear it, of course—and work both ways. You'll be able to find me if you need to."

"It matches yours," I pointed out, gesturing at his hand.

"Yes."

"Won't people think ... I mean, it will look like ..."

A slow smile spread across his mouth. "Have I given you the impression I'm letting you go, Dragonfly?" He emphasized his words by pulling me even more snugly against him. "That I'm anything but honored to be seen at your side, whether here or at d'Arcan or anywhere else? Unless you want me to, of course, in which case ..." He dropped one arm to his side, a neutral expression on his face. The shift from his adoring gaze to this distant, unfeeling one was like a thousand little knives piercing my skin. "I'll honor your wishes, first and always," he said quietly.

"No, no! It's not that, it's ..." I tried to find the right words. None of how I'd gotten to this moment made any sense if I was honest, but that didn't mean it wasn't right. "I would be honored to wear your ring, Vassago. For people to assume that I'm your— That we're—" The word didn't want to come, no matter how loudly it might have been rolling around in my brain. "I just ... I don't know how to see myself in this extraordinary life. One that you've been instrumental in giving me. It still feels like it fits oddly at moments, no matter that it's everything I've ever dreamed of. It's still new. All of this. You."

The smile spread across his mouth again, slow and gentle. Feral. My heart rate immediately spiked seeing it, the points of his fangs pressing into his bottom lip, the tip of his tongue resting in the corner of his mouth.

"I understand. I do, Greta. But know that it is truly my honor. Mate bond aside, as far as I'm concerned, you're mine and I'm yours unless or until you decide that's not what you want." The thought of refusing him after having experienced what we had made my chest feel like it was collapsing, and I was sure that my horror at the suggestion showed clearly on my face. "It won't bother me at all if people assume you're my wife. In fact, I'd prefer it."

My eyes widened as he said the words, but I loved the way they sounded.

He took my reaction as permission and slid the ring onto my finger. I held my breath, feeling as though this simple action was as profound as the entire ceremony we'd been through, even if that had been altogether unexpected.

"I need blood to seal it," he said softly. "Yours and mine." He lifted my hand once I nodded my agreement, the sharp tip of his fang bringing a drop to the surface. He repeated the gesture on himself, pressing our fingertips together before guiding my finger to his ring and placing his on mine. They flared bright white at the contact, but no remnant of blood remained on the stones when we pulled away.

"It's beautiful." I breathed the words, turning my finger side to side to see the array of colors within the gem. There were slashes of red and green, a bright teal blue and a sunny yellow.

I wanted nothing more than to tear Feiser's unwanted ring from my flesh, but short of cutting the whole digit off, I was sure it was impossible. I'd held out some hope that removing the binding would undo whatever kept it attached to me, but that had not proven out. In fact, it had dug itself deeper once the binding was removed.

Seeing my frown, he pulled me close again and swallowed all my worries back up with a kiss, causing my whole body to flush hot. Vassago took my hand, pulling me toward the revelry.

"Let's get you fed, then perhaps you'll honor your husband with a dance?" I made a strangled noise, which just made him laugh as he walked me back through the crowd, paying attention to everything around us but intent on only me. He leaned close to my ear, his lips brushing my throat and making me shiver. "Anything, for my wife."

AFTER TRYING NO fewer than a dozen dishes, each decadent and delicious despite the simplicity of their appearance, I simply couldn't eat anything else. Magnus was contentedly tossing back virtual platters of food, a serene Grace at his side. Rylan was much like Vassago, selecting the best bits and giving them to Calla to sample.

Everyone we saw offered us congratulations, many leaving small favors at our tables when they passed, introducing themselves again briefly before flitting off for more dancing or ale.

When I pushed my plate to the side, Vassago took the opportunity to sweep me off for a dance, and we happily mingled with a dozen other couples as he twirled me around the fire.

"I'm not very good at this," I admitted, having stumbled more than once.

"You're doing wonderfully." He dipped me low, my back arching. "We'll be doing this again soon yes?" he asked. "I'm happy to practice any time you like."

"Bea's ball is in a few weeks, I think."

"I can't wait." He grinned, and I could tell there was some deviousness there, something motivating him that I hadn't yet guessed at.

"I miss her," I said, realizing the fact as I gave voice to the words. "She'll be so sad that she didn't get to see this."

"You can visit her whenever you like, Greta, or invite her to d'Arcan. I'd happily escort you to meet her out in the city somewhere if you prefer." We started another circuit around the flames, my body getting properly winded from the activity. "I'm happy to make the arrangements, though I cannot guarantee I'll be civil with your former employers. As far as I'm concerned, they have a debt to settle. One I'm eager to collect on." The flash of red in his eyes made me shiver, though, not even remotely out of fear.

We danced, drank some fancy wine that Magnus had located from the stores, and sank into the joy of the event.

The moment the first yawn cracked my jaw, Vassago started making our goodbyes. "Come, Dragonfly. You've had a busy day."

We slipped into the shadows, the arm he slung around my waist a helpful crutch as my tired legs carried me down the road. Belmont called out, a streak of black wings in the sky as he and Archimedes chased down their dinner, Morticia a funny cat-shaped member of their trio.

Once we were back in the little hut, Vassago crushed me up against the door, his hands cradling my face, his mouth on mine. "I will never grow tired of you, Little Dragonfly. I'll never have enough," he swore, dropping to his knees as he pushed the heavy skirt of my dress up to my waist. "I have been going mad all night, wondering if you taste any different now, wife."

I gasped as his hot mouth pressed against me, his fingers pulling the flimsy cloth of my underthings aside. The noise I made when his tongue swept along my seam, then plunged inside me was somewhere between a moan and a shriek. I gave over to his demands immediately, pleasure coursing warmly through my veins as he feasted on my flesh.

The scrap of lace I'd been given to cover myself ended up nothing more than shreds of cloth on the floor, his greedy mouth affixed to my cleft as I melted into a boneless, sweaty mess against the door. When he added two fingers, plunging them in and out of me while he sucked on my clit, I rocketed out of my body altogether.

"Vassago!" I cried out and grabbed onto his hair with my hand. He growled and pushed me all the way through the orgasm to the other side, having to catch me as I slid down toward the floor.

He scooped me up again, licking his lips. "You taste like mine," he said low. I shivered as he peeled the dress carefully away from my shoulders, letting it fall to the floor in a pile. He stripped efficiently, pulling me atop him on the mattress. "Take what you need, Greta," he said, stomach muscles tensing as I positioned myself over him. "I am yours."

My breasts in my hands, I shifted until his proud cock brushed against my lower lips. I made a noise and sank down, bending my knees until I was seated fully. Vassago groaned, eyes closed and head tilted back. I leaned forward and kissed the spot he loved so much on me, the tender juncture between his neck and shoulder. I nipped with my flat teeth, making him hiss as I rocked my hips.

His hands pressed into my thighs as they traveled upward, his grip tightening the more I tilted up, the harder I pressed my teeth into his skin. He leaned his head up and took one of my nipples into his mouth, teasing the achy bud with his tongue and then suckling hard so all the blood prickled at the surface.

I rocked faster, chasing the peak that was building. Following my lead, he began to thrust up from below like he had in the tub, allowing me to set the pace but helping me along.

"I can't ..." I moaned in frustration, the edge I was reaching for just out of my grasp.

"Look at me," he said, and I opened my eyes to meet the bright gold of his. "There you are. Take it, Dragonfly. Take your pleasure from me. Shall I help you?" He sucked his thumb into his mouth and then pressed it where we were joined, against that bundle of nerves that sang when he began to make small circles against it.

Tingles sparked at the base of my spine, prompting a moan, and my pace faltered. "Take it," he said firmly, and I tilted my hips, leaning backward just enough so he could rub against that soft place on the inside of me with every thrust.

"Show me your fire, Dragonfly." He gritted the words out as I disintegrated into nothing more than violent sensation, his cock throbbing inside me as he grunted and found his own release. "Saints," he panted. "You'll kill me. It will be the most honorable of deaths." He pulled me down against him, our sweat mingling as he kissed my face, my mouth. "Let's get you cleaned up. You deserve your rest, wife."

Before he even returned with the warm wet cloth from the bathing room, I'd faded fast. After he gently washed us both, he pulled the covers over us and tucked me close to his body. I floated off as his breath puffed warmly against the back of my neck.

IT WAS VASSAGO'S tense tone that snapped me out of the soft dream I was having, though his words had my pulse pounding in my throat. There was nothing quite like being woken with urgency to leave you simultaneously anxious and groggy.

"Greta. Wake up. You have to get up and dressed. Quickly."

"Why?" I asked, sitting up, the heavy fog of sleep still weighing me down.

"I have to leave for a while." He strapped his new sword sheath to his belt, already fully clothed. I reached for a pair of clean trousers and a shirt from my bag. "I don't want you here alone," he explained. "Lovette is outside. She'll take you to her apartment. Calla will join you." Vassago pulled me in for a thorough kiss, then hastily gathered a few more things from his case.

"What's happening?"

"A demon horde has popped up inside the walls of Revalia. We have to take care of it expeditiously."

"Okay."

He threw the door open to reveal Lovette and Imogen standing outside, talking in low, strained voices. Imogen was fully armored and in her stone form, her long dark hair braided back. She shoved several weapons and a wooden box into Lovette's arms, effectively ending whatever discussion they'd been having.

"Thank you," he said, but I wasn't sure whether it was to them or me. "We'll be back as soon as we can." He kissed me again then let his wings out and burst into flight right from where he stood, Imogen hugged her sister before throwing out her wings and taking to the air right behind him.

I flinched from the suddenness of it but marveled at how smooth they'd both made the transition seem.

"Come on. It's late still," Lovette said, clutching the items to her chest. "Some of the clan was still up celebrating, in fact. They'll be head sore and cranky when they get back no doubt."

I yawned, finding the sliver of new moon still high in the sky. Despite the hour, I wasn't sure I would be able to go back to sleep after an awakening like that.

Lovette dumped the items Imogen had given her on the kitchen table before vanishing into her room. When she returned, she handed me a pillow and blankets. I sat down on one end of her comfortable sofa, still feeling out of sorts from the abrupt awakening. Calla knocked a moment later and was offered more bedding and the other couch. We all looked at one another, exhausted and lost.

"Where's Grace?" I asked.

"My father was going to fly her back to d'Arcan on his way to deal with the horde. She wanted to check on the girls. He said he would try to talk her into coming back with him later. I hope she comes, there's much I'd love to discuss with her. Imo too." A gentle smile crossed her face, and I hoped Grace knew that his daughters seemed to think of her warmly.

"Here," Lovette said, bringing me one of the weapons. "I assume you have yours?" she asked Calla, who nodded. "Good. Imogen insisted that you have something on your person. So. Now you do."

I looked down at the leather sheath. Curious, I gripped the handle and pulled out the short dagger she'd given me. It was utilitarian, but clearly well made. "Thank you." I slid it back inside the sheath and set it down on the floor at my feet where I could easily grab it if I needed it.

"Get some sleep if you can, the both of you. Try not to worry though. The danger is in the city, we're safe here," she said, and went into her room.

"Does this kind of thing happen a lot?" I asked Calla as we tried to get comfortable.

She snorted softly. "No, I wouldn't say a lot, but enough that I'm learning not to be as afraid about it. But I remember all too well the first few times Rylan vanished like this. It was terrifying. He jumped right out one of the observatory windows once before I had a good grasp of what it meant for him to have wings. I was paralyzed. It took several long moments for me to get my wits about me." She paused to yawn. "I understand why they wanted us here together but do think they should have taken me with them. I can hold my own just fine," she groused. I stared back, unsure what to say and curious beyond measure what this lovely woman could do if she thought she could hold her own in battle with them. "Don't worry, Greta. They're fierce," she assured me on a sleepy sigh. "Especially together."

That made me feel the tiniest bit better, and I knew Vassago was a force, even if he didn't always want to be. "Have you seen them fight?"

She was quiet for a moment but eventually answered, "Yes. I was taken once, and they came for me. All three of them. I've seen Magnus hurt, if you can imagine such a thing, and had my mate come home to me covered in blood. But they always come out the victors. Once Vassago arrived, their odds only improved. Besides, they had all of the conclave and outpost to recruit for help with this. The fact that the horde appeared within the bounds of the city is a concern, though. They haven't done that before. It's hard to keep such unusual things quiet when there are little demons running around causing chaos and blood being spilled in the street."

We stared at one another for a moment before she apologized, a chagrined look on her face. I wasn't upset though, if anything it helped me understand even more why Vassago had done what he had in the road that day. Those creatures were inside the city gates.

"If you tell me not to worry, I won't," I said, smiling despite the situation.

"Don't worry." She chuckled softly. "Get some sleep. They'll be back as soon as they take care of things. And if there are injuries, Lovette will need our help, so it's best we get as much rest as we can."

Before long, her breathing leveled out and my gritty eyes were closing again. The couch was oversized and very comfortable, and I was in the company of women I trusted. I knew we could keep one another safe.

CHAPTER 34
VASSAGO

I LANDED NEAR THE market square a few moments before Imogen and several stone kin. My brother stood in full demon form with his sword drawn as he evaluated the situation.

Lower-level demons were boiling out of a volcanic-like fissure in the street and causing destruction on anything they could get their hands on. Pots of flowers, shop windows, signposts. The glowing portal allowing them to come through temporarily had to be under the direction of a very powerful force.

We'd flown ahead of Magnus, who was to deliver Grace back to d'Arcan and make a quick patrol with several of his soldiers on his way to join us. Sentries were posted at a distance all around the conclave for security, not to mention all around Revalia proper. The network of stone kin monitoring the city had been the ones to alert him of the problem.

He managed the goings-on of troops in both places, and it made my head spin thinking how he managed it all. I'd hated doing it for well-organized legions that could go no further than a single shadow realm in Hell and had no other function.

We'd left our mates safely tucked away in Lovette's apartment, together and under a watchful eye, but I still felt ill at ease about it. The timing felt too coincidental.

Magnus landed with a heavy gust of wind, more stone kin troops just behind him. "Saints. We've got to be quick about this one, yeah?" Magnus grumbled.

"Those business owners won't thank us for dallying," Rylan answered.

"Let's get busy then." Magnus shouted several commands at his troops, many clearly blinking away the effects of too much ale from the celebration as they fell into order at his direction, fanning around the square so that as many of the small creatures as possible were contained.

"Ready?" Rylan asked, the hint of a grin on his mouth.

"As I'll ever be," I replied, giving my new Light blade a turn with my wrist. It felt good in my hand.

"She'll serve you well," Imogen commented, before running directly into the center of the mass of little demons, arms pumping, a broadsword in each hand.

I reached into the deep well inside me that I kept my rage contained in, summoning the bloodlust that had hovered near the surface so often recently. To my surprise, it hesitated briefly, but once stoked by the notion that my mate could be in danger as well, it flared to bright life. My fangs dropped fully down, my jaw aching as I prepared myself for the onslaught of memories that would wash over me with every drop of blood I tasted.

After another quick look to my brother—he had his wings spread wide and glowed with threads of golden electricity—I called my mist, and we descended into the madness that battle was and always had been.

Blood spattered the ground and everyone nearby as my new sword was quickly and properly christened. Rylan and I stood back-to-back, our well-choreographed technique dispatching dozens of the little demons at a time. The new blade in my hands sang as it sliced through the air, flesh, bone. As before, once the curse had taken a solid hold of me, I forewent slashing with only my blade in favor of using my aching fangs on hastily bared throats. Flashes of inconsequential memories assaulted me over and over again as I worked from one body to the next. I dodged blows and blades as Rylan and I danced around one another, making short work of as many demons as possible, all the stone kin soldiers doing just as much to dispatch the chaos.

Entrenched in my mission, I wasn't able to stop when a flash of red hair crossed my vision, but it niggled all the same. There was a great roar and the sound of a ghostly laugh, but I was lost to the lust, and the only thing I could do was continue to destroy the enemy.

RYLAN'S CHOICE TO wear all black made much more sense to me now. I looked down at myself with disgust, the silver and white of my clothes splashed with rust and crimson. It might never be the same no matter how much I scrubbed, which was a shame. These were some of my favorite pieces. The closer to daylight it got, the more concerned I became about my state being seen by the townspeople. Bakers and other craftsmen arrived before daybreak, so we were rapidly running out of time.

"Just a few more small things to incinerate," Rylan said, face spattered, but dark clothing hiding all evidence of his work. "Then we can head back."

"Do you think the humans will believe it was just a mob that got out of hand?" Magnus asked, similarly decorated with splashes of color and gore.

The smashed windows and charred stains on the cobblestones would be difficult to explain away, but with the help of the stone kin, several shops had been pilfered of their food and drinks and goods that were not in short supply, bottles and wrappers left scattered among the debris.

"People believe what makes sense to them," Rylan said. He wasn't wrong. "There have been rumblings of unrest for some time now. A group of dissidents who went on a little rampage to satiate their need for justice will be easily accepted. The magistrate will help with replacing the missing goods and glass."

"Thank you both," Magnus said, clapping a hand to our shoulders as he walked past, directing his exhausted troops with final orders.

"Sir!" A young woman rushed up to Magnus, pointing at the fringes of where we'd fought to keep the demons contained. "It's General Gaius."

"What about him?" Magnus's concern was plain as he trotted after her.

"Alright, let's finish, shall we?" Rylan asked, approaching the last remaining piles of lower-level demon carcasses. He extended his arm as well as his magic, turning the flesh and bone to less than a dark smudge on the street in a matter of minutes.

We did one final sweep of the area, passing stone kin catching their breath and staring off into the distance as they processed the events of the night. Rylan charred away anything that might be blood, removing the battle from the market square as well as he could.

Magnus squatted down over another massive gargoyle. I recognized Gaius from our meeting before, but it took a moment. This man was pale, panting through what must have been excruciating pain.

"No," Magnus argued. "You need a healer. We cannot move you if you go into stone sleep here."

"I will not lose my wing as well!"

"Fuck your wing and your *pride*, Gaius!" Magnus boomed. "If you don't go now, it will be your life that you lose. You've already lost far too much blood."

"What does that matter? What good am I to the clan like this?" Gaius laughed, the sound humorless and pitiful.

"You have much to offer yet," Magnus said, staring at him hard in the face. "Whether you believe it or not, you do. I know it." He stood and turned, facing the three nervous soldiers hovering nearby. "What caused this grave injury?" he asked.

They looked between each other, hesitating long enough that Magnus had started to growl in displeasure before one, the female, began to speak. "There was a man. He and the general were fighting—"

"You hold your tongue! You know nothing of what you speak. My business is mine."

"And your business got you in the deepest pile of shit I've seen since the covenants battle," Magnus barked.

"You know nothing, same as them, Magnus. Many good stone kin were lost that day. This is not the same."

"Agreed, Gaius. You lost a brother, and I lost a wife that day." Magnus sighed. "What did this man look like?" He turned his attention to the young woman.

Her eyes widened as she glanced over to find Gaius staring her down. "He had long red hair, green eyes. He smiled ..." Her brow pinched, and she shook her head. "I didn't hear him speak at all, but he was a very talented swordsman. General Gaius said something about the council? I'm sorry, I didn't hear anything further."

Rylan glanced at me, eyebrow raised. My instincts were instantly on high alert. I'd begun to wonder if I was imagining things.

"The three of you, take him to the infirmary at the conclave. If you disobey my direct order for any of his misguided whims, there will be consequences. And I will require a full debrief later."

The three young stone kin, including the woman who'd fetched him, all muttered their compliance, grabbed onto the fallen general, and took flight. His protests were loud, but they seemed happy enough to ignore Gaius rather than face Magnus's wrath.

"You!" he called out to another. "Follow them. Take these." He gestured to what I realized were Gaius's limbs. One forearm, and one lower leg, both already discolored to a deep gray with black streaking down from where they'd been severed. The young woman flinched but did as she was told.

"How many lost?" Rylan asked.

Magnus shook his head. "None."

"Injured?"

"That need care? Only a handful, thank the saints. But nearly all will be giving over to stone sleep the moment they get somewhere safe."

"Send the worst to d'Arcan so they don't have to travel far. The observatory is open to them."

Magnus nodded. "Thank you. I'm going there myself, I want to check in with Grace. I'll be sure to look around. We'll join you back at the conclave soon." He turned to leave, but I stopped him, a hand on his shoulder.

"The red-haired man ... I saw him in the city the other day. I cannot say for certain, but I suspect he's someone I've been chasing for quite some time." Magnus nodded slowly, and I explained my history with him, the book, even my curse. That Greta had seen him in her memories as well. "He's mine," I asserted, the words bitter in my mouth. "For what he did to Greta. And me."

"Fair enough." Magnus nodded. "If we catch him, you get first rights."

"We'll find him. We'll figure it out," Rylan said confidently. "We always do."

"Always as in the one time it's happened before? Granted, that was a very important occasion, but it does not a pattern make," I groused, frustrated that this man was running around causing more havoc, not at my brother.

"Then we'll make it one, yes?" Magnus rolled his shoulders back and extended his wings.

Residents had started to filter in, calling to one another as they discovered the damage to their shops, the missing items, and broken windows.

"We need to leave," Rylan said.

As the sun crested the horizon, we took flight, two demons and one massive stone kin, the demons headed for the conclave and the stone kin general headed for d'Arcan.

Strange times indeed.

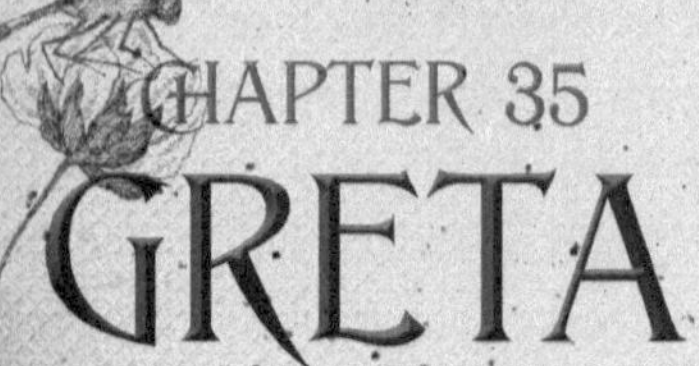

CHAPTER 35
GRETA

I BLINKED AWAKE IN the gray light of predawn to the sound of Belmont tapping on one of the windows and cawing as quietly as he was able, which, sadly, was not quiet at all.

We'd woken sometime in the middle of the night to help Lovette tend to some injured stone kin, the night feeling somehow both terribly short and unusually long.

"Good morning, Belmont," I greeted him, eyes still closed. A soft *whoo* joined Belmont's knocking sound, and Calla grumbled into her pillow. "I don't have any treats just yet." I rubbed my eyes and sat up, finding them both perched in the same window.

"Yes, treats are in short supply for you as well, Archimedes. I thought you left with Rylan?" The owl fluffed out his feathers, turning his head to watch her as she folded up her blanket. "Is everything alright?" Tension stilled her movements. He made a series of noises that seemed to put her at ease. "Good. Well, if you see Morticia, send her my way, yes? I expected her to come up last night, but she never did." He hooted. "Of course she did. Well, I'm glad you're all well fed, but she was missed. I'll get you all something later, alright?" He *whooed* and flew away, Belmont following him.

I watched the interaction in awe, wondering if she truly understood what he was saying. It would be wonderful to actually know what it was Belmont was trying to communicate without all the guessing.

She caught me staring and smiled. "He's Rylan's, but we've been practicing. I can hear him pretty well now, almost as well as Morticia. I can teach you some tricks maybe, if you'd like?"

As I was nodding that I would appreciate that, Lovette walked in the front door, bright and shiny despite the rough night.

"Did you both get some rest?" she asked. "I got a little nap after we came back up but couldn't stay still for long. I get that way when there are patients downstairs."

Calla and I both agreed that we had while Lovette made some very strong coffee. Cups in hand, we ventured down to the meetinghouse where breakfast was set up buffet style. We grabbed a plate on our way to the infirmary, the conclave eerily quiet in the half-light of dawn.

Lovette dusted her hands off after putting the remains of a baked sausage roll in her mouth. "Well. I'm ready to have a look at those stitches if you are."

"Oh. Now? What if someone else is brought in?" I stumbled over my words, unsure if I'd ever really be ready for someone to undo magical stitching that had been in place for decades, though eager to be on the other side of the process.

"I think we've seen everyone we're going to, if I'm honest. Most are probably in stone sleep in the city if they haven't returned here by now. We've got time and opportunity. But if you'd rather not …"

I stared at her kind face, heart pounding. My protests were foolish, I knew, but I had no idea what I might be facing on the other side of having them removed, if she could take them out at all. "No, I should. We should. I want to be done with it, but I'm also terrified."

"I understand." Lovette patted my hand. "I promise to be as gentle as possible."

Calla hovered nearby. "Rylan's the healer, but—"

"Please, stay. I couldn't have made it without you yesterday."

"Of course." She squeezed my hand as I picked a clean bed and pulled my shirt up my back, pulling it off altogether after a moment's hesitation. I'd seen a lot of flesh since arriving; the modesty of my kind much different than that of humans. While I had no plans to parade around in just my skin, this was a small step toward becoming more comfortable with that. But my scars were another thing entirely.

I heard them both make small noises and shrank into myself. I sat cross-legged in the middle of the mattress, my back facing the side of the bed where she plonked down a wooden stool with a padded cushion on the seat. I hugged a pillow against my torso, clutching it tightly between my arms.

"You've been through a lot, haven't you?" Calla said softly. She untucked her own shirt and showed me her back. I made a noise similar to the ones they had, finding a network of finger-width scars. "When I was first at Rylan's manor, I had no memories. There was a man Rylan trusted, the man he'd left in charge while he was at d'Arcan. Both he and the housekeeper mistreated me. He hurt me. When Rylan found out … Well, the man is dead."

"And the woman?"

She shrugged, and dropped her shirt again, taking a seat on the opposite side of my bed from Lovette. "Fired and exiled. I'm sure she had a difficult time finding work after what she did."

"As she should," Lovette tutted.

"I'm guessing Vassago has seen them?" Calla asked, a smile on her face.

I blushed, unable to stop the reaction from happening. "Yes."

"And does he care?"

"No. Though he did seem upset at first."

"If he's anything like Rylan, he wants to make it right for you. Make whoever is responsible for them sorry. At the very least, allow you to. And you've seen his too?"

"Yes."

"And were you horrified?"

I thought about the first time I'd run my fingers over his tattoos, finding the raised skin and webs of scarring on his smooth flesh. "No. But sad for him, that he'd gone through so much."

"Exactly. It's no different."

Lovette hummed quietly as she pulled over a tray of tools. "Did you know that scars are revered among our people?"

"Hmm?" I was surprised by the question, but I'd heard what she said.

"They tell your history. What you've survived. You shouldn't be ashamed of your marks, Greta. I know that it's an odd thing to say to someone who grew up surrounded by humans, not knowing what she really was, but those scars prove you lived through something. You survived." She patted my shoulder, and I found my eyes had filled with tears.

"Thank you."

"Any time. Lean over for me?"

"Ophelia did something when we visited, lit up my skin from under so she could see better?"

"That's the first thing I asked her to teach me," Lovette chuckled, examining a scalpel that had my skin prickling with nervousness. "It's dreadfully handy. Ready?"

"Yes, I'm ready. She taught you?"

"Oh yes," Lovette said, her breath warm as it brushed along my back. "Ophelia is a wonderful mentor. Many of us have had the great honor of her tutelage." The way she said it made me believe there was some joke there I wasn't in on. "I see ..." She tutted with her tongue as Calla inhaled sharply. "Horrible. Alright. I have to make a cut." The tools rattled around as she chose one, her other palm flat against my spine. The fear disappeared under her touch, but the pinch and burn of the cut was still bright. "Now the tweezers."

I felt the tool as it burrowed into my skin. I choked a sob into the pillow while Calla sat next to me, holding onto my arm in support.

Lovette made a frustrated noise. "It's a fine thread of some kind. It keeps slipping. I'm sorry, I'm trying to work quickly—"

"It's alright," I said, the pain not a normal ache but far from unbearable.

Calla frowned, watching Lovette work. "May I?"

"Of course."

She stood, and I felt her fingertips join Lovette's against my back. Something slithered under my skin, making my stomach pitch and roll. I tasted coins again, deep in the back of my throat.

Calla frowned in concentration. "I'm going to try to draw it out."

"Okay."

I inhaled and focused on my breathing as the pain flared hot, and something foreign tugged and moved inside my flesh.

"Greta, you alright?" Calla asked.

"Mm-hmm," I muttered.

"Change of plans," Lovette said. "Go ahead and lie down. We need to make a bigger incision."

I squeaked nervously, but did as she asked. A cold swab brushed over my skin in the space between my spine and shoulder blade. Whatever it was offered some numbness, but the cut still burned. Lovette pressed a cloth against my skin as well to catch the blood.

"One, two, three, *go*," Lovette said, and my vision went white. I screamed into the pillow, eyes welling with tears.

"I'm sorry," Calla repeated over and over as the pair of them worked in tandem, the strange slithery sensation going on and on as they worked, a hot smell reaching my nostrils.

"Saints and devils," Lovette swore, the sensation finally stopping. I let out a breath that was part gasp and part sob. "All done with that side."

The relief that had started to wash over me evaporated when I was reminded that we were only halfway done.

"Want to see?" Calla asked. "If not, I'll throw it all out."

I turned my head and found an unwieldy tangle of thread barely as thick as a strand of hair. It was bloody, with pieces of my flesh stuck to it, but also rusty in places.

"Does it feel better?" Lovette asked, efficiently cleansing my wound.

"I'm not sure yet."

"That's fair."

"It's braided with a metal," Calla said. "It was burning you as we pulled it through."

"I'm allergic to iron," I muttered, momentarily lightheaded.

They looked at one another and nodded solemnly, then shifted to the other side of the bed. I braced myself as well as I could, glad that if nothing else, they knew what to do this time around.

I was screaming into the pillow because of the incision when my heart skipped several beats. Without reason, I relaxed a bit.

"They're back," Calla said, glancing over her shoulder.

The pair moved their hands as fast as possible, the slide of the thread through my body more distinct on this side, perhaps because now that I knew what it was, what it looked like.

"It's caught. Hold on, Greta. I just need to—" Lovette yanked, and I cried out again, the pain a strange mixture of seeing stars and wanting to vomit. Both Calla and Lovette increased the pressure they were using, keeping me immobile so they could work. "Almost done. Just a little more, I promise."

"I imagine he'll be none too pleased if he heard—"

The footsteps on the stone floor were heavy, the growl feral. "What are you doing to my mate?"

CHAPTER 36
VASSAGO

T HE SOUND OF Greta's pained shriek echoed through my bones. My fangs descended, and a harsh growl rumbled through my chest. Rylan glanced at me, and we increased our steady walk to a run as we passed the meetinghouse and turned into the infirmary.

"What are you doing to my mate?" I demanded, finding her prone and in pain while Calla and Lovette held her down, bent over her back. Rylan grabbed a fistful of my shirt, keeping me from rushing ahead.

"Think, brother," he said calmly. "They wouldn't—"

"Helping her," Lovette said with a grunt, falling back against her stool with a mass of thread in her grip.

Greta let out another noise, this one more a muffled sob. I blinked across the room to her, making Rylan swear as he looked at his empty hand. The women stiffened but didn't stop what they were doing.

Calla pressed a cloth firmly against Greta's skin, which was lit up inside like Ophelia had done. "All finished." She gave me a tight smile. "See?" She removed the cloth and all that remained was a clean incision on each side of her spine. Where the stitches had been in her flesh was now normal muscle and bone.

"You did this to her while we were *gone*?" I demanded, tone icy as I looked between them. To their credit, neither flinched from my red eyes or fangs.

"There was no danger in performing the procedure without you here," Lovette frowned and applied some loose gauze bandage.

"I'm alright," Greta insisted. "It already feels better."

Two tangled nests of wire sat on a metal tray. I smelled her blood and old rust. "Iron."

Calla nodded. "Yes."

My jaw clenched at how much discomfort that would have caused for her. Iron, imbedded in her skin when she was part fae? Closing up her wing ways so she couldn't shift, heal, sleep properly ... it was sadistic. That trickster had no idea what was coming to him. I would make his death *slow*.

"We'll want to check your wing function as soon as you feel up to it," Lovette said, wiping her hands on a clean towel. "But it's not urgent."

"I just want to lie here a few minutes," she muttered, but I saw her eyelids fluttering. "Thank you both."

"Of course."

I nodded to Lovette and sat on the edge of the bed after pulling up the sheet. "Do you want a blanket? Or your shirt?"

"I'm okay."

"Alright." I stroked her hair, the need to touch her driving hard on my nerves. I would much prefer to pull her up off the bed, to crush her to my chest, but she seemed comfortable.

"Are you hurt?" she asked, eyes wide as she looked at the state of me.

"No, Dragonfly. I'm fine."

"Is it done? Are there more injured stone kin coming? There were some, earlier, but—" She stopped, interrupted by the sharp clang of something falling on the floor.

"Put me down, you insolent children! I'll have you punished for this! Latrine duty for weeks on end, the worst patrols—"

"They're only trying to help you," Rylan interrupted calmly.

"Who asked *you*, archmage?" he barked, all too happy to redirect his rage.

"I'm here to help, General, but if you'd like me to leave ..."

"I don't care what you do," Gaius groused.

The other stone kin arrived with his severed limbs, and Lovette said several colorful things before flying into action, Calla on her heels as she collected supplies.

I made eye contact with my brother, and he patted his chest, where I assumed the elixir was contained in a pocket. I nodded, turning to Greta. "He's missing some pieces at the moment," I told her.

"Use the elixir," she said without hesitation.

"My thoughts exactly." I pressed a kiss to her cheek and rose, ready to help with the frantic scramble taking place. "Besides, we need some for you, also."

"I'm just going to rest a bit," she muttered.

"I won't be far."

"Fix my wing first," Gaius commanded. "I can manage the rest as long as I can fly."

"We'll go in the order that I say we will," Lovette said cheerfully, combating his intense frown with her bright smile. "Here we go." She lined his limbs up to his body, getting everything as close as possible to how it should be. "How on earth did you manage to get yourself in such a predicament?"

"You wouldn't understand."

"Try me. I'd bet you'd be surprised what I've seen come through this building."

Rylan offered the elixir, but Gaius shook his head. "Not drinking any mage's potion."

"No need to be stubborn," I said, unreasonably offended at his refusal. He'd made use of d'Arcan at his will plenty of times. For him to refuse my brother's offer was a grave insult after the kindness he'd been shown. "It wasn't made by a mage. It was made by her." I gestured to Greta, now asleep on the nearby bed. "Ophelia kept referring to her as The Alchemist. If that means anything to you, I'd encourage you to use it."

He watched me cautiously. "Ophelia?"

"Yes."

"The Alchemist?" Lovette breathed over the word. "My father didn't mention that." Her mouth quirked, and she shook her head. Rylan handed her his vial. "Elixir of Healing?"

"What does that mean?" Gaius demanded.

"Just what it sounds like. You should let me use this." She held up the little bottle for him to see, but he was unimpressed.

"Will it fix my wing?"

"It will fix your everything, I'd imagine," she said.

Without warning, he reached out and snatched it from her hand. Before anyone could intervene, he'd popped the cork and downed the contents. "Fine. Happy?"

"You absolute fool," I snarled.

"What is the *matter* with you!" Lovette howled, punching him fiercely in the shoulder.

"That hurt! And you said I should!" He looked between us, genuinely perplexed at our reaction.

"We have no idea what consumption will do," I explained. "Especially that quantity. It's to be used topically."

"Topically?"

"On your skin," Rylan said, tone dark and deadly. He was glaring down at the injured stone kin general, sparks of magic floating around him out of anger.

"That's alright," Lovette said, her usually bright, friendly tone shockingly cool. "Since he decided to be rash, we can just do this the old-fashioned way. Then you'll go off to stone sleep, and we'll hope for the best. You'll get exactly what you deserve, I suppose. If it works, it works. If not, you'll be no worse off than if you'd never taken it. Unless you're dead." Wasting no time, she pushed him over on his side. She then pulled his damaged wing out straight, causing him to howl, and set to work with tight, precise stitches on the delicate fleshy membrane.

"If I can't fly, I'm as good as dead anyh—" He gasped. "Saints and devils, you're doing that on *purpose!*" he yelled, twisting as though trying to escape but trapped in her grasp.

"Hold still, and it won't hurt as much." Lovette sniffed, her steady stitching pace unaffected by her patient's movements.

"I could cauterize the stumps," Rylan offered, eyes narrowing as he suggested it. My normally easygoing brother had been offended and apparently wanted to show Gaius the mistake he'd made. "Perhaps while you tell us in more detail exactly what happened?"

"That's kind, but the tissue must be living for the limbs to have any chance of reattachment once he goes into stone sleep. Hold. Still." She jerked against Gaius's wing, and he roared again. "I have this well in hand if you'd like to go get something to eat?"

I looked over at Greta, and Lovette nodded, indicating that she'd take care of her as well.

"We won't be long."

"Take your time." Her smile was genuine when she flashed it at me, but I'd seen the wrath in it already and perhaps respected her more for it.

She might be Magnus's sunshiniest daughter, but I'd never want to be on her wrong side.

GAIUS WAS A grumpy-faced statue in his infirmary bed when I returned with a plate of celebration leftovers for Greta.

She stirred at my light touch along her back, sending my pulse skyward when she smiled at me. "Feeling better?" I asked.

"Yes," she said. "Can you pass me my shirt, please?"

"If you insist," I teased.

For the moment, we were alone in the big room, except Gaius, of course, and he wasn't aware of much, right then.

She ate while I gave her a brief summary of what had happened in Revalia.

"Is it odd that he was hurt so badly when nobody else was?" she asked, pausing with an apple slice halfway to her mouth.

"It is." Rylan and I had discussed as much with Magnus when he arrived back. He'd been cryptic but assured us he was looking into things where Gaius and the mysterious man were concerned. "Are you ready to test out your wings, Dragonfly?"

She nodded. I helped her to her feet, and we joined the gathering of people standing beneath a row of tall oaks. Imogen, Lovette, and Magnus all lingered there, smiling encouragingly at her as we approached.

"If we make you nervous, we can leave," Imogen offered. "But we thought perhaps you might benefit from some help this first time."

"That's alright, you can stay." Greta blushed, which told me perhaps she'd be more comfortable with less of an audience, but also worried she'd need the help. "How do I make them come out?"

"For me, I think of how they look when they're spread wide, the feeling of wind under them," Imogen said, holding her arms out to the side, her wings snapping out wide behind her a moment later.

Greta's face was stern with concentration but nothing happened.

"I get a tingle in my wing ways," Lovette said. "I focus my attention there. You might have trouble with that approach since I'd imagine it's rather sore, just now."

Greta turned her back on us all and went through several motions. She did like Imogen had demonstrated, holding her arms out wide. Her head tilted to one side, and she pulled the back of her shirt up.

I stiffened, the sight of her scars still inciting my fury with Lara, though they detracted nothing from her beauty. The others seemed wholly unaffected, and I was proud of Greta for not being so modest that she hindered her progress.

"That's right, get the feel of the wind," Imogen nodded encouragingly.

I wished I could see her face, but I didn't want to break her concentration by walking to her front. Then, she made a surprised sound and stepped one foot to the side to catch herself as her center of gravity shifted.

Her wings unfurled like those of a freshly hatched butterfly as they opened and gave one slow, gentle flap. They shimmered with iridescent color, nearly translucent, and they were slightly oblong instead of the regular inverted V shape.

"Wonderfully done, little niece!" Magnus boomed.

"Dragonfly wings," I muttered, simultaneously awed and horrified by what I saw. They were gorgeous, unique in every way, but they were clearly not as developed as they should be.

"What?" Greta asked, eyes glossy as she looked over her shoulder at me. I hated that the experience had been painful for her.

"Your wings. They're lovely. Like opal glass." I stepped closer, finger outstretched to stroke along one of the edges. I stopped before touching her though.

"That wasn't so hard. I was afraid because of how it always hurt before, but this wasn't bad."

"You did perfectly, beloved." Blood pulsed loudly in my ears as I examined her new appendages along with the others.

Lovette stepped close, a frown on her mouth. "Were they always like this?"

Greta's left wing was bent at the stem where it joined her body at her shoulder blade. It looked uncomfortable, awkward. I inhaled through my nose as understanding dawned as to why she constantly worked at that muscle. It took several seconds for me to swallow my rage, my fangs refusing to retract.

"These are just as I recall," Magnus said proudly. "Nobody else has ever seen the like. Just beautiful. At least now we know why," he muttered the last, her fae father still a secret.

I glanced around, finding that we'd drawn attention from the rest of the conclave as well, several small gatherings of stone kin had stopped to gawk and point at her unique wings.

Magnus continued, "They were always this shape. But they used to be more solid in the middle. They have always been somewhat translucent with this coloring, though. I don't remember you ever being able to fly properly, but that's normal for children. Lots of hovering off the ground and tumbling back to earth. They seem thin ..." He stopped, frowning with concern.

Greta swallowed thickly, eyes turning to the ground as she focused on making them move. The muscles that controlled them were weak, and the wings only gave a cursory twitch. She grunted and reached over her left shoulder.

"This one will need mending," Lovette said. "It was probably broken before you were bound and it healed wrong. All these years ..." She shook her head. "I'm so sorry, Greta. I'll need to re-break it. But if you can go into stone sleep afterward, it should heal up without any lingering issues."

Everything stopped, the only sound my own blood rushing in my ears. The idea that her bone had to be snapped to correct the way her wing hung sent me into a spiral of rage. This had been done *to* her. The red-haired man had bound her with magic, broken her wing. Made her forget it all. Then he'd left her without proper healing, for decades.

"You were just a child," I growled, not meaning to say it out loud. "Four, maybe five years old. That's all. *I will. Kill. Him.*" I repeated my vow, more certain that I would be his end now than I had been before. His trespasses against me paled in comparison to how he'd sinned against my mate.

Magnus roared. Greta flinched back from the boom, and he sucked in a deep inhale. "I'm sorry, little niece. I am not angry with you. But whomever was responsible for this should be *destroyed*."

The appendages drooped then tucked into themselves before disappearing back inside her body. We all followed her lead, shifting back to our human forms so we wouldn't tower over her quite as much. It felt like bragging almost, being fully in my other form while she showed us her beautiful broken wings.

"Would you please fix it, Lovette?" Greta said, my brave mate marching right back into the infirmary.

Lovette answered in the affirmative but didn't move. Her normally soft face was bracketed with tension. "I'll need help. That's one of the strongest bones in her body."

"I'll fetch Rylan," Magnus offered.

I stood there, vacillating between righteous rage and nauseated worry.

In the end, I joined them in the infirmary and held my mate's hand, not quite stifling the roar that built in my chest, hot and wild, while they broke her wing and put it back together again.

I even managed not to kill anybody once she let go of my hand and I lost the grounding touch she provided.

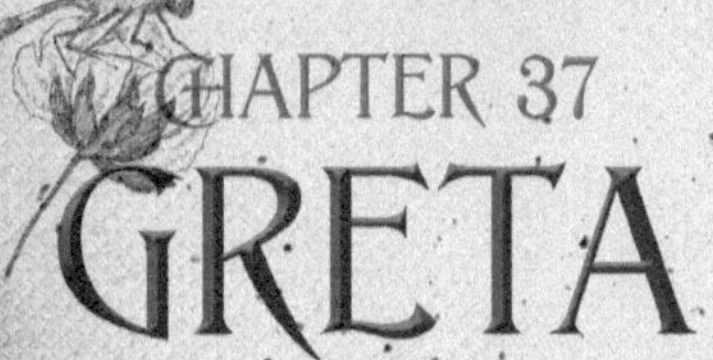

CHAPTER 37
GRETA

'D LEFT THE infirmary with Magnus for a crash course in stone sleep.

I couldn't help but feel anxious. Vassago had given me a solid kiss and sent me away with my uncle, promising to be nearby if I needed anything. He rubbed over the stone of his ring with the pad of his thumb, sending a warm tingle through me from mine.

I suspected he needed to safely burn off some of the rage keeping his eyes red and fangs extended.

Magnus had immediately brought me to one of the huts way out by the forge where there was a nice breeze and no other people. He gathered up a pile of plush cushions, pointing to the middle. "Sit there."

I did as he asked, muscles stiff as I dropped onto the cushions. My shoulder ached still, but the sharp bite of pain that had come when three of them gripped me and broke that wing bone was long gone.

"Is this going to hurt?" Since everything else had so far, it felt like a valid question.

Empathy softened his sharp features. "No, little niece. Regaining balance can be difficult for those unused to the sensation of waking up from stone sleep, but the process doesn't cause any discomfort. It's like a firm hug. Quiet, peaceful. Waking up is disorienting sometimes, even for those of us who are well-practiced. Regular sleep can sometimes leave the mind a little foggy, yes?"

I often woke up still groggy, no matter how well I'd slept, so I knew that all too well. "Okay." I planted myself on my knees on the center cushion.

"Picture yourself in the place you are most serene," he instructed.

Closing my eyes, I envisioned the maze. My favorite bench, the statue of the angel with his wings spread wide and placid smile. The perfect view of the starry night sky. The vision quickly shifted to Vassago's bed, the pair of us cuddled close in a tangle of limbs.

"Untether yourself from this body. Allow it to slip away from you." The low timbre of his voice paired with the cool breeze from the open windows and the comfort of knowing I was safe helped me to relax. I tried not to fall into my pattern for when I was simply falling asleep, as that's not quite what we were trying to accomplish.

"If you feel heavy, that's good," Magnus coached. "Embrace the sensation of weight in your limbs. Invite the stone to take you over."

I had no idea what that meant and began to worry I was trying too hard. "I'm sorry," I apologized, feeling silly and like I'd failed all at the same time.

"No apologies needed, brave little niece. It's not your fault you were never taught. Most start training around ten years old, so they can have it mastered by fifteen or so. You weren't old enough to start training when your mother ... went away."

"Five years?" I gasped. "It's going to take *years* for me to learn?"

"It's a skill like any other and takes time to master," he said gently, reaching across the cushions to pat my shoulder. "But no, I don't expect it to take you much time at all to learn. Your body is desperate for the restorative sleep it provides. And look, some success already! You're an apt pupil, to nobody's surprise."

My two smallest fingers on my right hand were a greenish gray color up to the first knuckle. The joints moved a little stiffer than normal as I flexed them. Unlike when they'd flashed to stone once the binding was removed, there was no discomfort.

"See?" he praised. "Wonderfully done. Shall we try again? Perhaps it would help if it were darker in here."

Magnus went around the round room, dropping cloth shades over the windows. The breeze still flowed through, but the waning afternoon light was significantly dimmed.

He slid one of the cushions over for himself and sat, getting his oversized form into a meditative pose as he coached me through some relaxation. It was next to impossible for me to get my mind to stop. At every turn, I scolded myself for wondering if I was doing it right, if I'd started to change, if this was the time I turned to a statue for a proper rest. The inside of my head was a maddening place to be.

"Greta. Stop thinking." Magnus chuckled.

My cheeks flushed hot, embarrassment rushing through me. "Sorry."

"It's alright. You're not in trouble, little one. This is about you resting. If we can get you to cross over into proper stone sleep, you'll heal faster. Your body will have a chance to repair itself and at least some of the damage it's taken on all these years. You'll likely awaken more rested than you've felt in a very long time. You just have to stop trying to be in control."

I had literally less than zero idea how to stop trying to be in control and grumbled as much.

"I know, little niece. It's a big thing to ask."

Panic suddenly shook away any semblance of relaxation. "What happens if I get stuck? Will I be trapped a statue forever? But ... sentient?" Horror chased the panic through my veins, and I found myself scrambling to my feet. "That sounds terrible, I don't think I can—"

Magnus crouched in front of me, hands heavy on my shoulders as I drew in one ragged breath after another.

"If you get trapped, I can pull you out."

"You can?"

Magnus nodded, his expression comforting, the weight of his hands grounding. "I can. And if for some reason I cannot, there are others who certainly could. There is no danger here, little niece, only hope."

My shoulders dropped away from my ears, and warmth replaced the cold tingle that my panic had sent coursing under my skin.

"Okay." I breathed out through my nose and returned to my cushion. Magnus did the same, a slight grin on his mouth. I closed my eyes, focusing on my heartbeat and the steady sound of my breathing as I tried to force myself into relaxation. It helped that I was genuinely tired after the burst of energy the adrenaline had provided.

"Get comfortable," Magnus waved a hand. "Perhaps imitating how you'd normally prepare to rest will be helpful."

"Even if I just fall asleep?"

"Even then. If that happens, you'll get a nap, and we'll try again later. This is not a test you're going to pass or fail. I promise, I'm only trying to help."

I adjusted myself on the plush cushions, lying on my back. I smiled, finding a fairly accurate map of the night sky painted on the rustic ceiling in whitewash and charcoal.

"Which is your favorite?" Magnus asked. I glanced over, and he was lying down as well, ankles crossed at the end of his long legs, arms butterflied under his head.

"Constellation? Probably the three tails." He grinned and I looked back at the sky.

"Calista," he said.

"Sorry?"

"That's her name. Do you know the story?"

"I have a feeling the one you're about to tell me is different than the one I know."

Magnus chuckled. "Rylan is the expert, what with his detailed records of the night sky. You'll have to make do with me and my storytelling, however. My children would all be rolling their eyes right about now."

I had a feeling his storytelling ability was just fine. "Please," I asked, finding my eyelids growing heavier. "I'd love to hear it."

"Well, legend has it she was jilted by her lover. You know how it goes, she's hopelessly devoted to him, but his eye wanders. Shameful, if you ask me. One day, she follows him into the city while he's running his errands and finds him chatting up a girl at the candler. The next day, same thing, only it's one of the smithy's daughters. She's unsure whether to think he's being unfaithful or perhaps is just chatty. She tells herself he's only being friendly at first, but then the third day, she actually catches him exchanging a kiss for his midday loaf at the bakery. Infuriated, but not about to be shamed for his actions, she invited them all to tea."

Every blink stretched longer as his smooth, deep voice elaborated on a slightly different version of the story I had told Bea dozens of times. Knowing I wasn't long for consciousness, I tried to follow his instructions—to let go of my body, allow the heavy sensation of stone wrap itself around me as I drifted off.

I RAISED MY arms above my head, every muscle in my body bunching and releasing in a huge cat-stretch as I slowly climbed back into consciousness. My body was heavy still, warm from the sunshine pouring in over me and the blanket someone had covered me with.

"There you are, Little Dragonfly."

I turned to the side and found Vassago lounging against the wall near where Magnus had lain as I fell asleep, a book open against his bent knee. His serene smile was impossible not to return. "Hello."

He closed the book, setting it aside. "Good morning."

I pushed myself up to a seated position, brain a little swimmy. "It's morning?"

"Quite. How do you feel?" His head cocked to the side, his brilliant gold eyes fixed to my face as I assessed myself.

My shoulder was absent of any aching, and I felt rejuvenated enough to have slept a whole week. "I feel really rested, actually."

His smile widened, and he climbed to his feet. "I'm so pleased to hear that. Magnus had nothing but glowing praise when I relieved him earlier. I've missed having you in my bed though," he lamented, my blood warming instantly. "I don't sleep well when you're not there."

I looked down at my hands for any evidence of the green-gray coloring that had been there the night before during my first attempt. All I found was my normal lightly tanned skin tone and some chipped fingernails that could use a trim.

"You did well," he said, a proud smile on his lips.

"I did?" My voice rose into a surprised screech, prompting Vassago to laugh as he approached me with his hand out. I accepted it, and he pulled me to standing.

"Gloriously. This morning when I arrived, you were a vision. Lying on your side, totally at peace ... your stone skin is no less attractive than this version of you, wife." His eyes flashed red for the briefest moment as they dipped down my body. He cleared his throat and turned away, offering me his elbow. "How is your wing?"

I looked over my own shoulder, feeling silly as I did so because I hadn't stopped to call my wings out yet. I closed my eyes and tried to feel for the tingle that Lovette described, thrilled when I found it. My wings came forth, any discomfort that I was used to feeling completely gone.

"Is it straight?"

Vassago smiled widely. "She did good work, Dragonfly. It looks perfect. Does it feel okay?"

"Yes, it feels fine." I practiced moving them, the strain on my underdeveloped muscles significant but bearable.

"Wonderful. Are you hungry?"

My stomach rumbled in agreement. "Absolutely."

He flashed his teeth again. "Let's go show you off then." We ventured down the long lane toward the meetinghouse, his fingers laced with mine.

"You should be prepared," he said, slowing his speed as we approached the building.

"Prepared?"

"Magnus is very proud you managed a full stone sleep your first night. There may be hugging or patting or some form of aggressive pride and affection." He frowned, eyebrows pulling together. "If it's too much, I'm happy to step in."

I laughed, unsure how serious he was being. "I'm sure it'll be okay."

"I've warned you," he said again, at my side as we went through the door.

Magnus looked up from his plates, a beaming grin transforming his focused face.

"There she is! Greta, you did so well. How do you feel? Are you hungry? Do you need anything?"

Vassago growled in warning, and Magnus rolled his eyes at the sound, but did return to his seat and tamped down his exuberance.

"You're very much like your brother at times, demon. Ophelia was not wrong about that," he muttered.

"I would love some breakfast," I managed, making eye contact with Lovette, who nursed a cup of coffee across the table from her father.

Vassago kissed the top of my head before going over to the tables of food and selecting several things for both of us.

"Don't let him run roughshod over you, hear? You just tell him to hush and let you eat." Grace winked at me from her seat next to Magnus, and he blustered, pretending to be offended. I knew better though; that was the way this pair communicated more often than not.

They all tried not to stare, but I felt the curiosity.

"So. How did we do?" Lovette asked.

"It healed perfectly, thank you. I was always a slow healer before, but everything seems great."

"Perfect. I'll take another look if you like, but it sounds like you're all set."

Magnus puffed his chest out proudly, telling the group how I'd gone right off into stone sleep like I'd been doing it my whole life.

After breakfast, I let Lovette check me over once again. "Is Gaius well?" I asked, seeing the empty bed.

Lovette snorted. "He'll survive. He was taken to a nearby hut. The elixir helped, but his limbs were already mostly stone when he got here. There was a strange poison or something ..." She frowned thoughtfully and shook her head. "I'm afraid their function was permanently debilitated, though they were successfully reattached, which is hopeful."

"There's more elixir. It could be used properly this time. We have another vial—"

Lovette placed a warm hand on my shoulder, shaking her head. The gentle smile on her face felt like a warm hug. "Vassago gave it to me already, we've tried everything we could. You did more than your share, Greta. He's got to do the rest for himself." Her expression changed, a hint of spiciness in it. "With my help, of course. I've yet to fail a patient, and I'm not about to start with him."

I thanked her for all her help, and she wrapped me in a tight hug. "Absolutely my pleasure, Greta. Come back soon, okay? We have plenty more to talk about."

"I will. You are always welcome to come to d'Arcan, too. I think your father would like that, actually. And Grace."

After that, all that was left was to prepare to go back to d'Arcan. Our whirlwind of a visit had come to a close.

Imogen knocked on the door to our hut as we were packing up.

"I'll give you a moment," Vassago offered, stepping out the door as Imogen came inside, a cloth bundle in her arms.

"The aunts sent a gift for you," she said, setting it on the bed.

"Oh?" I untied the ribbon and pulled back the covering to find the silver gown. "I thought these stayed with the clan?"

Imogen smiled. "Usually, they do. But it's tradition for brides to keep theirs."

My mind stopped functioning for a moment at the word, which made Imogen laugh. "Congratulations, cousin. This dress is yours. Wear it well."

"Thank you," I breathed, suddenly overcome with emotion. I'd never owned anything as lovely and felt honored they'd trust me with such a precious heirloom.

"And this ..." She frowned as though considering her words. "My mother gave this to me for safekeeping many years ago. I didn't think I'd ever find its owner until you got here. I can't explain how she knew or why she put me in charge of it, but I know it belongs to you." She held her hand out, dropping the contents into mine. As I got a good look at the item she'd given me, I was lost for breath.

It was a necklace. One like Calla wore. The opal in it matched my new ring, and it was a perfect fit for the piece that Henrik had hired Vassago to seek out. The one that Bea now wore around her neck.

Imogen pulled me in for a hug, then turned for the door. "When you're ready to choose a blade, let me know. It would be my honor to make one for you. And come visit whenever you like, okay? There's still plenty to learn about being a proper gargoyle."

"I will," I promised. I put the necklace on, the heavy pendant warm against my skin when I tucked it inside my shirt.

I marveled at the gown a moment longer, then packed it safely in my luggage, knowing I was leaving the conclave a vastly different version of the Greta that had arrived and all the happier for it.

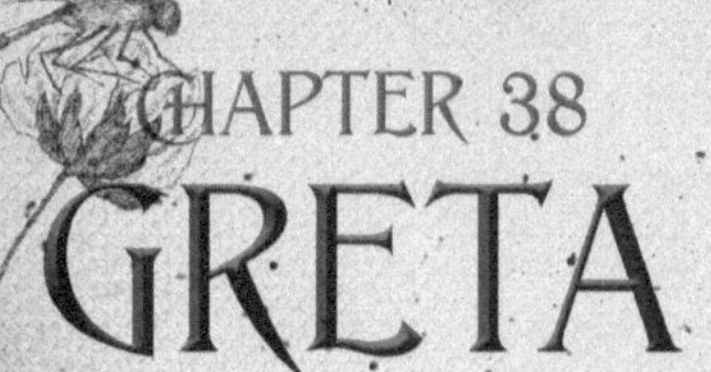

CHAPTER 38
GRETA

I HAD JUST FINISHED up making one of the fae elixirs when a messenger from Belette Manor arrived. Vassago had been gone most of the day, attending to some business in the city with Magnus, and I'd been left to my own devices in the classroom.

In truth, while I missed his supportive presence, it was also nice to have some quiet time to work with just my thoughts. I worried that we were becoming too intertwined, and I think he sensed I needed some space to spread my own wings ... metaphorically speaking.

I'd spent several days after our return from the conclave exhausted, everything that had happened and trying to jump back into the routine at d'Arcan more than I was ready to handle. After plenty of naps on the sofa, most of which curled up on Vassago's lap, I had finally recovered and was diving in to my alchemy with both feet.

Leaving the dark-green liquid in its flask on the worktable, I followed Grace out to the hall where one of Henrik's butlers waited.

"Greta," he said, inclining his head slightly before handing off a parchment invitation. "You look well. Miss Beatrice asked me to make sure you received this personally."

"Thank you very much, Colman. It's nice to see you."

"And you. You seem well?"

"Yes, thank you."

"May I return with a response?"

I broke the familiar crimson wax seal and read the invitation with a surge of excitement. "Please let her know that Mr. Feland and I will happily attend."

"Yes, he said as much, but she was insistent I get your answer directly."

I frowned. "When did he give a response?"

"Just now. He's at the manor having a rather ... *boisterous* conversation with my lord."

I narrowed my gaze at the messenger, gauging how much he was likely to share with me. "About what, Colman? Anything important I should know?"

"Your name came up a time or two. As did a ring and a man named Feiser."

"Indeed? Thank you." I could only guess at what Henrik was thinking if his intent was to summon Vassago for a dressing down. He'd not recover from such a thing, especially now with tensions running so high.

"Miss." Colman bowed again, a light smile playing on his lips as he spun on his heel, leaving as quickly as he'd come.

Two weeks. That's all the time that was left until Bea's ball.

I couldn't believe it had been such a long time since we'd spoken. We'd never been apart so long before. Guilt surged in that I hadn't had much more than a passing thought about her since I'd left the manor with Vassago.

"Something exciting?" Grace asked, finding me in the hallway several minutes later, still staring at the invitation.

"A ball," I said.

"Oh! How wonderful. You'll need a dress then." She nodded sagely.

"I'm not sure there's time for a new dress," I frowned. Money was no issue, as Vassago made a habit of leaving handfuls in my pouch at every opportunity, despite my weak protests about it.

"You could wear that lovely gown from the stone kin ceremony," she suggested.

I blushed, wondering if there was a protocol about wearing one's gifted wedding gown to a ball at your former employer's manor. But the more I thought about putting it on again, the way it had made me feel to wear it, the more it seemed as though something like a ball was the exact reason they'd sent the dress home with me.

"That's a good idea."

"And I'm sure the girls would love to help with your hair and cosmetics." She examined my curls as she took hold of my arm, walking with me into the dining room. "Care for a cup of tea? I feel like we haven't had much of a chance to have a quiet word the last little while. Unless you're in the middle of things?"

I thought of the elixir on the table, but there was nothing further I needed to do with it. "Sure."

Instead of leading me into the dining room, she kept walking straight into the kitchen. "I want you to be comfortable coming in to get what you need. This is your home too." She reached up to the top of a cabinet next to the sink and pulled down a fist-sized parcel. "In case of emergency." She grinned, opening the wrapping. Inside was a brick of pure chocolate, cut into a bunch of bite-sized pieces. I took one as she offered, and she gave a slow smile as she let hers melt on her tongue. "Sinful. And one of my few secrets from the rest of the house. Well, yourself and Calla excepted."

I glowed, feeling special that I'd been allowed in on her special treat. "Thank you."

"You're welcome, Greta. And I mean that. You're welcome in here to talk, if you need, or to take snacks. Just make a note here if you finish something off so I know to get more."

"I will."

She nodded and turned to pull a whistling kettle off the flame. "This is a new special brew. I talked to Lovette while we were at the conclave, and she recommended a few things. Hopefully along with the stone sleep, we can get you set to rights as far as your energy goes."

I accepted the steaming cup from her, breathing in the crisp citrus smell of the new tea. "I appreciate that you keep trying, Grace, but I don't know that—"

She stilled me with a hand on my arm. "I know. But I'm going to try anyhow. Are you feeling better since our little retreat?"

"I think so. The stone sleep helped, but I need to do it again, I'm sure. My wings are working more smoothly."

"Magnus is so proud of you and thrilled with your progress. He's told you so, I know, but it bears repeating. I'm happy you're here, Greta. In case I've forgotten to say so lately."

"I'm happy to be here," I said, smile wide as the truth of it settled in.

"Good. Go on back to your project. I have a feeling it's important."

I shrugged. "I don't know about that. I'm just practicing so I can keep making more complicated elixirs."

"Sounds pretty special if you ask me. Back to it then." Grace winked at me and sent me on my way.

When I got back to the classroom, the elixir had settled even further and was so dark green it was almost black. The smell of burnt metal was lingering again, a strange side effect of only some recipes it seemed.

I separated the elixir into three smaller vials and stored it in a special case that would prevent any damage to the glass even if it was tossed around. My energy was still good, perhaps thanks in part to Grace's tea, so I went ahead and flipped to some of the pages I hadn't yet had time to catalog.

There was one that allegedly allowed you to take on a temporary glamour. Hair color or eye color change, even a different face and body shape. I would need some ingredients, so I marked it with one of Vassago's silver ribbons and moved on. It was the next one that had me sucking in a breath.

I read the whole thing over twice, not understanding exactly how it would work, but that was secondary to actually crafting it successfully.

For the rest of the afternoon, it got my entire focus, and by the time I was done, my eyes heavy and arms were leaden.

The crimson elixir swirled with flakes of black and gray, and I'd used up the last of Vassago's bloodstone flake stores.

As I gathered up empty vials, my skin prickled like someone was watching me.

"Hello?" I said into the silent room, spinning around and searching the room as I tried to shake off the sensation. There was nothing and nobody there, but I could have sworn I had seen the shadows move out of the corner of my eye.

I turned back to my finished elixir and smiled, watching it swirl in the light. If it worked as reported, Vassago would have his cure.

MAGNUS AND VASSAGO returned just as Grace came to retrieve me for dinner. After storing the flask of elixir in my room, I'd sat on my sofa and fallen into stone sleep, which surprised both Grace and me.

I wasn't sure what drew my attention, but when she knocked on my apartment door, I came slowly back to myself, the feeling not unlike when your foot falls asleep, just throughout my whole body.

Magnus ranted out his frustrations over Grace's delectable roast, and I pitied him the frequent council meetings that seemed only to serve to upset him. "Can you imagine? Gaius being discharged by the council like that because of his injuries? From a battle he was in because he was doing a duty *they* assigned? It's ludicrous!" His fist pounded the table, making the dishes jump.

"Horrible," Grace agreed, putting her hand on his arm to still any further outbursts.

Vassago's features were pensive. "The more I hear about your council, the more I find them to be illogical, at best."

"That's being very kind." Magnus bit the words out. "If I wasn't required to attend, I'd have quit ages ago."

"Can you?" Grace asked, hope in her eyes.

"Can I what?"

"Quit."

Magnus shook his head, but the movement become slower at the same rate his eyebrows drew together. "No. I'm ... required."

"Perhaps the council needs some reorganization," Grace suggested, clearly disappointed that he couldn't just walk away.

"They do. The people in power have been that way a long time. And none of them have ever been out in the field, or if they have, it was so long ago that experience is no longer valid. As a matter of fact ..." Magnus began to describe the history of several members and my mind started to wander.

It was bad form, but I couldn't help it. I pictured the crimson elixir next to my bed, the look Vassago would wear when I presented it to him. I was pulled back at the mention of my name.

" ... had a visitor from the manor today. Didn't you, Greta?"

"Is that so?" Vassago's attention was intense as he turned it on me.

"A messenger with our invitation," I clarified.

"The ball?" Vassago asked, a grin spreading slowly over his mouth.

"Yes."

"And what was your response?"

"The same as yours, I assume."

"Wonderful. I can't wait to see you all made up again, Dragonfly. It was quite the sight. Though I'm certain those people don't deserve to witness it." I blushed, flattered as always by his compliments.

"What did Henrik want to talk with you about?" I asked.

Vassago shook his head, eyes flashing red. "Nothing important. Though we may get to meet this Feiser soon." I squirmed in my seat, the ring on my finger suddenly ten times heavier. "You've had a busy day, Dragonfly."

Grace took that as her cue and shooed us away, clearing the plates with brutal efficiency, Magnus at her side. Vassago led me from the room, hand braced between my shoulder blades.

"I did accomplish several things today. I even took a little stone sleep nap."

His eyebrows went up. "You did? I'm proud of you. Do you feel all the better for it?"

"Yes, it was very restorative." My stomach churned with nervousness as we grew closer to the apartments. When we crested the third-floor landing, I forced myself to keep hold of his hand so I wouldn't lose my nerve.

He chuckled as I drew him into my room. "Is there something I should prepare myself for, Dragonfly?"

I blushed, realizing what this might look like. "I made something for you," I explained.

"Ah. I will receive whatever it is happily, no need for such worry."

He lingered near the door as I grabbed the flask from near my bed. He examined it closely when I handed it off. "What's this?"

"What you've been looking for. At least, I hope so."

His face went still, his golden eyes drifting from my face to the flask and back again. He swallowed, more nervous than I'd ever seen him.

"You mean …"

"The recipe certainly made it seem so."

"What, ah … what is the process?"

"You drink it, much like the cleansing elixir I drank. It sounded as though the results could be as simple as some indigestion but as serious as one final bout of lust, more potent than any you've seen before. I wish you could just take it and be done, but this one is not so simple."

He sat down heavily on my sofa, reverently putting the elixir on the table. "Sit with me, Greta?"

I sat, the butterflies in my stomach compounding. "I'm sorry if I overstepped, I just thought—"

Vassago reached over and hauled me onto his lap, his arms banded so tightly around me I could scarcely move. "You are a wonder, and I will take my last breath positive I don't deserve you." He tucked his face into the curve of my shoulder and held me. His gratitude was profound, with an edge of apprehension. I was sure I'd feel the same if someone offered the one thing I'd searched for much of my conscious life. "As much as I'd like to take it this very moment, I should make preparations first. I want to be sure everyone is safe from me in the event my reaction is poor."

As the night grew heavy, he simply carried us to my bed, hands never straying far from me except to assist with the removal of our clothes. Without breaking the quiet bubble we'd wrapped around ourselves once again, he worshipped me from head toe, my harsh breaths and his throaty moans the only noise. I tired long before him, but he kept me awake with his careful, loving ministrations.

It was far and away one of the best thank yous I'd ever gotten, and he hadn't even tried it yet.

CHAPTER 39
VASSAGO

GRETA AND I lost several days to further translating the entries in Lilith's book and creating at least one of any elixir we had the right ingredients for. I'd taken her into the markets again as well, making a day of it so we could restock and restore ourselves beyond the walls of d'Arcan.

She bounced happily from shop to shop and table to table, warming to the idea of purchasing things with gold she'd earned rather than coins from my pocket. It was all the same, truth be told, but if the small thought shift changed her attitude about spending, I was all for it. I carried her new items as we wandered through town, looking for a moment like a terrifyingly normal couple out for the day.

Mostly, anyhow. My eyes roved the streets constantly for the red-haired man, but he was nowhere to be found. I had gotten a description of the illusive Lord Feiser out of Henrik during our talk as well, so I had two men I was now hunting for.

As for Henrik, we'd come to a tense understanding. He had been thoroughly chastised by Feiser for allowing Greta to leave his house and watchful eye, though I believed Henrik had been less than clear with him about the truth of Greta's situation and residence at d'Arcan. I would be all too happy to straighten things out with him directly, but he remained unavailable.

I held out hope that the upcoming ball would present an opportunity for me to correct any misunderstandings. It was probably not a good thing that I spent half my time fantasizing about doing just that.

Greta requested that Magnus join us in the classroom one afternoon, clearly excited about something. She slowly paced the room as she expressed to us both what she'd been working on.

"If Light blades exist, then that implies that Dark blades could also. Perhaps they already do." She set Lilith's book on the low table that sat between the sofa and the chaise, the book open to a set of pages scrawled over with fae writing and symbols I didn't recognize.

I exchanged a look with Magnus. "Nobody has ever mentioned such a thing, nor have we seen it," I argued. Her eyebrow lifted as she stared at me. The expression made me feel significantly less intelligent than I knew myself to be.

"And you are the keeper of all knowledge at all times about all things?"

Magnus coughed to cover his laugh. "Now, little niece, let's not bait your demon too hard."

"I only mean that there's no way one person can know everything. There are thousands and thousands of books in the world, full of information and knowledge, and much of it in disagreement with the rest about one thing or another. Besides, at this point we all know that the councils can and probably do literally make things—people, knowledge, wealth—vanish. Who's to say that they aren't preventing the knowledge of such a thing from being widely known?"

"To what end though? If it would help us keep the demon hordes in check, why would it not be allowed?" I argued once again.

Her head tilted to the side as she moved back and forth in front of the unlit fireplace. "If a Light blade is specifically for use with demons, then it would only make sense that a Dark blade could be used against angels, stone kin, perhaps even fae. Especially if iron was used. I can think of several reasons why angels in particular would want to keep any knowledge of that kind of weapon a secret."

I blinked, stunned. It wasn't that we'd never had a thought along those lines, but for a woman less than half a century old, who had no experience in battle, she certainly understood how such things worked. It made me proud, but also terrified me. People who figured out the things others wanted kept secret were always in danger.

"Mm." The noise rumbled through my throat, and Magnus once again caught my eye, the two of us exchanging raised eyebrows and an understanding that she was on to something we'd potentially been outright ignoring for centuries.

"What is the reason for this questioning, Greta?"

"I think we should make one."

Her words fell between us with a nearly audible thud in the dense silence. There was nothing but matter-of-factness in her tone, clearly nothing but her scientific mind driving her statement.

"*Make* one?" he asked.

"Yes. I think that's going to be my blade request from Imogen. I'd like to ask her to help me forge it."

"I ..." Magnus stopped short, crossing his arms as he stared back at her. "Your blade? You believe that she can make you this Dark blade as your weapon?"

"I hope so. I could do the other parts," Greta continued, "assuming, of course, the recipe in this book is what it appears to be.

But I'm not skilled in metallurgy, nor strong enough physically to actually forge it. And stone kin have specific smithies, right? Stone kin raised up from particular bloodlines that show that talent? That's how Imogen ended up forge mistress at the conclave, as I understand it."

"Yes, that's how we appoint a forge master. It's quite the honor for Imogen to have been chosen," he explained, pride puffing up his chest as he spoke about her.

"Well, I'm obviously not the forge mistress, so I wouldn't have access to the same tools, nor have the right skills. But she is. She does. And she's waiting for my request. This should be it."

"Yes, but—"

"I'm not sure this is a good idea, Greta." I spoke over the top of Magnus, both of us wound tight at her suggestions.

"Why not?" Her forehead wrinkled in confusion.

I glanced at Magnus for backup, but neither of us had a viable explanation, only a gut feeling that there was a reason this wasn't done. On the other hand, I couldn't help but wonder what the harm would be in seeing if it could be accomplished. There was no law against it, no council edict that I knew of. It just simply wasn't ever mentioned.

"We must be careful," I said seriously, to which she scoffed but smiled.

"I'm always careful."

"You are," I muttered. Magnus and I shared our concerns through crossed arms and tight mouths while she moved around us, pleased with herself for having gotten what she accepted as approval.

"Are you offering blood or feathers?" she asked, and just that quickly, she'd rendered me speechless. Mostly because I'd give her anything she wanted, and it terrified me. I nearly brought my wings out in reflex to her request.

"We can discuss the particulars once Imogen has been brought up to speed," Magnus chimed in. "Exchange of Heavenly essence is highly monitored and regulated—"

"We're not using Heavenly components," she argued, settling down in the corner spot of the sofa. "We're using essences from creatures of Hell. Those are not regulated, correct?"

Magnus opened his mouth, then closed it again. "Are you sure you weren't meant to be a negotiator? Perhaps practice law?" he teased.

Greta smiled. "It may be a technicality, but there's no precedent for this. They no longer count you as a Heavenly creature despite your true origins. Your essence is fair game."

I grunted, as it was the only response I could muster. She wasn't wrong, and now she had me curious.

Curious enough to consider using both my talent and my connections to books that might contain historical accounts to see if such things had been done in the past ... and what the outcome was.

"We will have to be sure before starting," I said firmly, but she saw the permission I wasn't even sure I was qualified to give through my stern tone.

"Of course."

"And it will only work if Imogen is one hundred percent in agreement," Magnus added. "It must be her choice, especially considering the danger that's implied."

"Naturally. Will you speak with her? Or can we arrange a trip to the conclave so I can?"

Magnus sighed. "Yes, I'll speak with her."

Greta beamed and clapped her hands together once, the noise echoing around the room.

"We're going to regret this," I muttered, but excitement fizzed through my veins all the same.

"Most likely," Magnus sighed, though pride and amusement were evident on his face in the lopsided grin and crinkles around his eyes. "I'll get in touch with her at first opportunity. And I'll do my own checking into the archives to be sure there's no chance of us all ending up on the wrong side of a dungeon cell for our efforts."

"Thank you!" Greta bounced up on her toes and kissed the gargoyle on his cheek, then repeated the same with me before gliding out of the classroom. She was headed out to the yard no doubt, to visit with Belmont. The bird still checked in frequently but spent more and more time away from the grounds. I wasn't sure what that meant, and mind-speech was not something he and Greta had developed. Everything made me suspicious lately, and I detested it.

"Oh gods, we're in so much trouble with that one," Magnus exhaled, steadying himself with a palm flat on the nearest tabletop.

I grinned, my heart traveling down the hall with her, nerves and joy all tangled up together under my skin. "You have no idea."

I WATCHED THE drops of blood I'd provided mix into the simmering flask of elixir, dread curling in my gut.

"You could have given me a feather, you know," Greta smiled, stirring everything together carefully with a long-handled spoon made of silver.

"I know. This seemed easier."

"And also more dangerous? More permanent?"

"Yes." I couldn't help but smile as well. She had my number, well and true.

She'd wasted no time getting started once she'd come back inside. Belmont had been nowhere to be found, which was odd, but he was unusual at the very least.

The hard work was already done, and she was truly becoming a marvel to watch when she worked. Her confidence had grown a hundred times over, and with some practice, she might even get the flame striker to cooperate soon.

"Hold still, Dragonfly," I sighed, digging a ribbon out of my pocket and working her hair back into a braid. She'd worn some clips earlier, but they were long gone, and her curls kept dropping into her face as she looked between the book and her mixture. When I went to tie it off, I noticed that instead of ending right where her hairline ended on her neck, the tips extended a bit past. "It seems your hair is growing."

She froze, carefully setting down her instruments before spinning to address me, her excitement palpable. "Do you really think so?"

"I do." I couldn't help my impulse to touch her. "The stone sleep perhaps? Magnus thought maybe that would help."

"Maybe." She tucked herself into my embrace instead of pulling away from it, her forehead brushing against my cheek as she rested her head on my shoulder.

"You really are the most wonderful height, Dragonfly." I stroked my hand down the fresh braid. "You fit me perfectly in every single way."

"Mm," she hummed, and I closed my eyes, reveling in the feel of her weight, her warmth against me. "I didn't need the braid after all," she said, pulling back but not letting go. "It's done. Just needs to sit overnight in a west-facing window."

"Why west-facing?" I asked.

She shrugged. "It doesn't explain why, only says to do it."

"Alright. There are windows facing all directions in the observatory, not to mention it will get the moonlight from above. Perhaps we should take it up there? Stay a while?"

"That would be nice. We can lie under the stars."

"Yes." My pulse began to pound in my throat, every part of me on high alert when she dipped her lashes to look over her shoulder, elixir in hand. "I thought perhaps I'd take the other, as well."

She blinked at me, a slow smile spreading across her mouth. "Only if you're sure."

I nodded. "I sent everyone else away for the night. I'm ready to be done with this curse, Little Dragonfly." I grabbed up several of the blankets strewn across the back of the furniture before looping my arm around her shoulders. I let her lead me up and up, until we were bathed in starlight.

She chose the most appropriate window, then we made a suitable nest out of the plush cushions Rylan kept up there for the students to sit on while he gave astronomy lessons.

In our quiet little bubble, we kissed, touched. Our hands traveled and breaths exchanged as we wrapped ourselves in one another under the blankets.

At one point, with the moon bright above us, despite it still being little more than a sliver, she held up her hand, turning her opal this way and that so it would catch the light. The soft look on her face, the way she was enamored with the colors and her gentle sigh nearly had me undone. I could do nothing more than lie there, trying to remember how to breathe as she marveled at the little ring on her finger, breathing over a pinch in my chest like the last missing piece of my soul had finally snapped into place.

"We should know fairly quickly which direction you'll go," she said, the mood dampened as I pulled the flask of elixir down from the nearest table.

I stared at it, nodding slowly. The idea of her in danger, especially from me, made me nauseous. "If things go badly, you shift," I said. "You hit the button to force the roof closed and you jump out a window. Whatever you have to do to get safe."

"It wouldn't matter if I did all those things. You could still get to me. But you wouldn't hurt me, Vassago." There it was again, the unfailing trust in me that I would never stop trying to earn. She'd been practicing every day, strengthening her will as much as her muscles. She straddled me, tilting her head off to one side. "Still, let's hedge our bets."

My cock throbbed despite the release she'd driven me to with her hands not long ago. "Greta."

"Vassago."

"It doesn't work that way."

"You don't know that."

I hesitated, fingertips stroking up and down the slender column of her neck, her breath rapid and pulse a visible beat in her throat. When I couldn't stand it anymore, I dove in, kissing her mouth, pulling her hard against me as I devoured her taste.

"Please," she begged.

I growled, warring with myself. In the end, it was her soft expression, her hands on my face that had me tipping over the edge and plunging my fangs into her throat. The memories I was served were all of our interludes. I watched her receive pleasure, eyes closed and head thrown back both in real time and in the recent past.

I pulled away after several moments, panting just as much as she was, the sweet tang of her still on my lips. She uncorked the flask, and I drank it down, braced for the worst of myself to come forward, threaten her, remind us both that I was not who she believed me to be.

I felt the poisonous curse moved through me like a tangible, separate entity. It was dark and slimy as it slipped through my veins, failing to grip onto anything as it was pushed out. A sheen of sweat dotted my face as the cure worked on the curse, burning it out.

I fidgeted and swore. I got to my feet and paced, then roared as the prickles and stings of the potion started to drive me mad. My fangs descended, and I felt myself slipping away, the red haze taking control. "Go. *Now*."

"You won't hurt me." Her tone was stern, but I saw the flash of apprehension in her face.

"Greta. Please."

"No. I'm not leaving you alone for this." She shook her head, and I pushed my wings out, feeling like every nerve in my body was exposed to the air.

"You must!" I growled and paced, the curse throbbing under my skin. I heard her pulse, louder and louder as the potion worked and the need to spill blood, *any* blood, became overwhelming. I lunged at her, my wife, my mate. She was wide-eyed but stoic as I grabbed her and sank my fangs deep.

Her faint moan registered as I gathered her to my chest, but I was not myself. I drank and drank, the tiniest part of my brain screaming that I needed to stop. That it was too much. But I couldn't pull away.

"Vassago."

She sounded far away, like she was underwater. There was nothing but the rage, the need, the sound of her heartbeat faster and louder in my ears. Her life flashed through me as I drank, memory upon memory.

"Take what you need," she said, voice breathy. "I know I am safe with you. My mate would not bring me harm."

My chest began to ache then, a hot stab under my ribs. The pain shocked me back from the red haze just enough for me to pull away. Greta was weakened but still alive when I pushed her away from me and forced my wings to take me straight up into the clouds. I beat them hard against the wind until there was hardly any icy air left to breathe.

It felt like my body was tearing itself apart molecule by molecule, everything hot and itchy, my mind battling for control as the bloodlust tried to take over one last time. My vision was fogged with red, the need for destruction riding hard down my spine.

I would let this thing shred me from the inside out, if I had to. If I had hurt her, it would be a kinder death than I deserved.

Time was irrelevant as I hovered in the cold sky, the observatory a faint pinpoint of illumination beneath me. Slowly, I realized that the lust wasn't winning, and I was more in control than I had thought. I drifted lower and lower, lungs working easier, skin far less sensitive than it had been.

Relief pounded in as the slithery feeling started to fade as well, and I coasted back to earth feeling unusual but no longer a mindless beast. I crashed to the marble floor of the observatory, a tangle of feathers and limbs and crawled to her, dread curled in my gut. She was pale, but smiling as her eyes met mine.

"Dragonfly."

I pulled myself on hands and knees to her and laid my head in her lap, feverish and shaking. Time became elastic again as I shook through the last of the terrible curse fighting the elixir within my veins. Apologies spilled from my lips, tears dampening her clothing as she soothed me, her hands petting along my wings. As though I deserved any of that after what I'd done.

Eventually, all that was left was her.

"Is it gone?" she asked quietly. I nodded tightly, trying to relax my fingers. They'd gripped her thighs so hard I worried she'd have marks. "Leave them," she said, combing through my hair with her fingers, pushing it slowly away from my face and working through any knots that had formed in the long strands. "I'm fine. You didn't hurt me."

"But I did. I saw it. Greta, I'm sorry. So sorry." I shook my head, burying it again in shame.

"You didn't. Look at me, Vassago. *Look*," she insisted, holding my face in her palm, pressing light, soft kisses to my cheeks, my lips, my forehead.

I forced my eyes to scan her beautiful face, her throat. There were a few droplets of blood on the collar of her shirt, clear marks from my bite. I cringed, fingertips brushing along the skin. She reached up and took my hand into hers.

"Look closer."

Her cheeks were flushed with color and the bruising around the bite marks disappearing as I watched. I met her eye, relief rushing through me even though I didn't fully understand. In her eyes I found no reproach, no fear. Only what I believed to be … love.

I hugged her tightly against me, tears in my eyes as I breathed her in. "I don't understand, Dragonfly, but I am grateful. I adore you beyond measure and could never have forgiven myself if—"

Her lips met mine again, and I felt her hands slip up my shirt. She pushed it up until it was off completely, before removing her own. She maneuvered us both until she could get to what she craved. Her need was evident in the easy glide, but I required more than the gentle sway she was giving me.

I tipped her backwards, keeping her knees pressed against my chest. The angle pushed me deep, and she moaned my name as her fingernails scraped down my back. I resisted the urge to call out my mist, wanting this moment just for us.

"Vassago."

"You're mine, Dragonfly. No matter what."

"Yes," she whined as I increased my tempo, then her back arched as her climax took control. I pushed her all the way through it before allowing myself to let go, and we both lay there in a puddle of limbs, panting into the cool night air.

We cleaned up as best we could before climbing back into our peaceful nest, her body curled into mine and my soul at peace for the first time in eons. As she slipped into sleep, head pillowed on my chest, I rested my fingertips over her pulse. I smiled, feeling humbled yet again. I had something rare and beautiful in my arms, and I vowed silently to care for it as best I could. Our heartbeats were matched, the same thumping rhythm both in her and in me. Which made sense, after all, since my heart and soul, my everything, belonged to her.

CHAPTER 40
VASSAGO

"**H**AVE YOU SEEN Belmont?" Greta asked, a frown pinching her eyebrows together as she checked her reflection one last time in one of my mirrors.

"No, not in several days, I think."

"I wonder what he's doing," she muttered, concern heavy on her voice. Her fingers fiddled with the chain around her neck, adjusting it so the clasp was at the back, the opal pendant on the inside of her dress. "It's not like him to not hang around."

"Perhaps he's been tasked with something," I suggested, having no real idea what duties a stone kin's familiar was responsible for. I'd done my part and sent off the paperwork Ophelia had provided to my brother Tap, but beyond that, I had no clue where the bird had come from, where he often disappeared to, or even what his function was aside from being quite demanding about his treats and making Greta smile. Though that last one was important, appreciated, and worth the extra snacks lying about both of our apartments.

"Maybe." She ran her hands down the bodice of her dress, straightening out some creases. "How do I look?"

Seeing Greta all made up in her finery again left me feeling regretful that we had to leave the house.

"Perfectly edible, Dragonfly." She blushed and tilted her head, as though requesting a different response. "The Belettes will be shamed to stand in the presence of your beauty." I bowed, one hand extended. She placed her fingers in mine and I raised them to my mouth.

"You're ridiculous," she said through a laugh, shaking her head as we made our way toward the stairs.

"I would never lie about such a thing." She turned pink in the cheeks again, which always made me smile. "Do you have your blade?"

She patted her right thigh. "Yes, and thanks to Calla's instruction and Grace's help, my dress has a false pocket so I can get to it easily. Though my skill in wielding it leaves much to be desired."

"As long as you use the sharp part on the other person, you're doing just fine." I patted my vest pocket where vials of elixirs were stored as an extra precaution.

Imogen had been all too happy to take on Greta's unusual project. Magnus had flown her the flask with the Dark essence as soon as it had sat in the window long enough and had returned with a completed blade less than two days later. I worried for Imogen's state after rushing quite so much, but knew better than to question her method.

The carriage ride to the Belettes' was unusually quiet, and when we arrived, Greta stiffened in her seat, looking positively nauseated. I knew going back might be an odd experience for her, but I'd hoped she'd be able to enjoy her sister's evening.

"I will be with you the whole time," I reassured her, linking my arm through hers as we ascended the stairs to the front door. She said nothing but patted my arm as confirmation she'd heard me.

It didn't take long for me to be proven a liar, however, as when we were greeted by a collection of women lingering in the entry, Greta was swept to the side by Caroline. She and another woman pulled Greta in for hearty hugs, beaming. I never took my eyes off her as they moved her closer to the ballroom, likely so it looked like they were still doing their jobs while having a quick catch-up. I accepted a drink for us both from a man carrying a tray of champagne flutes and followed at a respectful distance as she talked to them.

I took the opportunity to watch her as the helpful household staff passed her off to her sister on the inside of the ballroom. It was honestly a concern how easily I'd take the opportunity to observe her going about her life, but I didn't care.

The way she held herself now was a complete turnaround from the way she had when I'd first met her. I was proud of the confidence she'd found, even in the face of her former employers.

Bea dashed off, latching her hand around the elbow of a young man who had been talking to some older gentlemen across the room. I chuffed, watching his face transform from half-asleep with boredom from the conversation he was having, to bright happiness as he took her in. He clearly saw stars when she smiled at him. Before Greta, I would have marveled at such a thing or scoffed depending on the situation. Now I knew better. I even hoped they had a fair shot at happiness together.

Before they were halfway back to where she'd left Greta standing along the wall, raised voices filtered over from one of the tables. I stood straighter in response to the way Greta's face went blank. Resignation and sadness filled her eyes and one of her hands rose to the waist of her gown. She brushed away imaginary wrinkles, frowning.

I turned my attention to just beyond where she stood, moving forward a few steps to see if I could hear what was being said.

"Who on earth let her wear that gown? She looks like an overstuffed sausage!"

I ground my teeth together at Lara's shrill words, her volume clearly intentionally pitched so that Greta would hear.

"I don't know, it's a bit outdated, but it's not that bad." Henrik shrugged, shifty eyes scanning the crowd for someone.

"Not that bad? She's about to burst the seams! I can't tell you how many times I told her not to eat the day of an event, but that girl never did listen to a *thing* I had to say."

Greta flinched and time ground to a halt as the words landed exactly like the weapons they were intended to be. I watched my magnificent mate subtly fold into herself. Her shoulders dipped, her chin angled toward her chest, eyes on the floor. As her arms crossed over her middle, I clenched my fists and walked toward her.

As I got close, Greta looked up, and the defeat battling with pride in her eyes and the downward curve to her mouth as she saw me only fueled my rage. She put on a brave mask as I approached, but I saw the hurt underneath. These people did not deserve—nor had they ever deserved—this woman.

Bea and the young man stopped a few steps from her, both frowning back at her parents.

I handed her one of the champagne flutes and used my thumb and forefinger to grip her chin. "You're stunning, Dragonfly. That dress was quite literally made for you. Her opinion is worthless, besides. You shouldn't give any of the things she's said to or about you a second thought. They are not worth your incredibly valuable time or energy." It was all true, but I said it slowly and with intention, so my words would erase the ugliness she'd had to hear from her patrons about it. I'd be her strength if she needed me to be, though I had no doubt once she realized her own power, she could easily put her patrons in their place.

"I hardly recognized you, Greta," Bea said, a wide smile on her face. "You're so beautiful. Full of joy!" Her gaze turned to me, and I gave a brief dip, appreciating that she gave me any credit for Greta's happiness.

"Absolutely. I haven't seen you in some time, but you look wonderful." The young man seemed genuine and kind. I noted his features and hoped to be able to keep an eye on him as he took his place among far lesser men in this city. Kindness was unfortunately not a trait many in power liked to foster.

Her smile solidified at that, some steel returning to her backbone as she raised back up to her full height. It was with an unreasonable amount of pride that I noticed she was taller even than him.

"Thank you. You look lovely, Bea. Ellis, it's very nice to see you again. I'm so happy we were able to come."

"Bea has been over the moon that you were able to take the … internship?" Ellis glanced between us. "I'm sorry, I'm not sure what to call it."

"That's as good a title as any, though she'll remain a permanent resident at d'Arcan," I said.

The young man's eyes widened, and he nodded enthusiastically. "How wonderful."

"You should come visit," Greta told her sister.

"I'd love that." Bea pulled her in for another hug. "I've missed you so much. I can't believe you didn't stop to say goodbye the day you left."

Greta made a face. "I'm sorry. You were with your mother, I didn't want to interrupt."

Bea nodded. "I understand. In any case, I'm glad you're here now and that you're where you belong." She looked at me again, a soft smile on your face. "Being away from here has treated you well." I heard the undercurrent, that *I* was treating her well, and once again inclined my head her direction.

I started toward Henrik's table, people moving out of my way in a hurry, though I wasn't doing anything aside from walking a normal pace. I leaned in close to Greta's ear as we went and whispered, "Do you trust me?" She smiled, her eyes showing me everything I needed to know as far as her faith in me. "That's my girl." The endearment made her shiver, and her reaction made me smile.

"What's this?" Henrik frowned. "Mr. Feland? Greta? Let's not be rude."

A slight man had taken a seat at Henrik's table and watched Greta with far too much interest for my liking. I narrowed my focus to him, heart giving an excited thump. I was fairly certain I'd finally been put in the same room as the mysterious Lord Feiser.

"Rude?" I asked, forcing my tone to remain neutral. "How ironic you use that word after your wife just insulted mine."

"Your—" Henrik's eyes widened as he finally took all of her in, his gaze settling on her hand. "Surely you don't mean ... You can't! Otto, this is not what I agreed to—"

"Calm yourself, Henrik," Lord Feiser said, getting to his feet. He had beady eyes and stringy long hair. I worried that he'd blow away in a stiff wind. It made no sense how he'd managed to get himself into such a powerful position by the look of him.

"And you are?" I asked, tone intentionally accusatory.

"Otto Feiser. And I'm fairly certain that's my intended bride you have on your arm."

Greta stiffened. I laughed, the sound painfully loud as the crowd around us hushed in response. "I beg to differ. My wife is exactly where she belongs."

Feiser's smile made my demon stand at attention. Suddenly, Greta scrabbled at her finger, the damnable ring he'd put there hurting her enough to elicit a scream.

"Burns," she gasped, desperate to pull it off. "It's burrowing into my skin."

"Is that so?" he said smugly. "Seems I have first rights being that it's *my* ring that was placed first."

Heart pounding at the sight of her in discomfort, I pulled my sword in the blink of an eye, blade tip aimed directly at Feiser's throat. "She's not an object to be sold. I don't know what they promised you, but the agreement is null. She is my wife, my mate. By her *choice*. And you will remove your ring, or I will remove your appendages one at a time until it is done."

He laughed, and my blood ran cold. "Oh, I've missed you, haughty demon." His hand wrapped around the blade as I pushed the tip into the hollow of his throat, drawing a tiny rivulet of blood, but not piercing it. The force I'd put behind the blow should have nearly taken his head off.

His laughter became an eerie sound, people gasping as they hurried to shuffle away from us. "I tasked Henrik with three things. Just three. Little. Things. Keep the book safe, the girl within sight, and find the necklace. Somehow, despite all the motivation I've supplied, he could only seem to do one of those." He turned his gaze to Henrik, who was huddled with Lara at the table, pale and trembling.

"I'm sorry," Henrik apologized but to whom was anyone's guess.

"Father." Bea's sadness was profound, her beau's body blocking much of her behind it.

"No matter. I know exactly where to find the book, you have delivered the girl to me, and this"—he charged forward, plucking at the chain hanging around Bea's neck, breaking it with a firm tug—"is right where I can take it."

Feiser's gaze turned from beady black to bright green, his willowy form shredding into nothingness as a fit one took its place. It was the appearance of long auburn hair that forced every nerve in my body into awareness, the surprise allowing him the moment of advantage that he needed. He pushed my blade with force back toward me, shame and fear rushing through my body as my grip faltered.

He snatched at Greta's hand and charged through the crush of bodies in the ballroom, delaying me, but only for a moment. She dug in her heels and shifted her weight, refusing to run with him, protesting loudly the whole way. Nobody moved to help her, however, to our mutual dismay. Surprise and frustration contorted his face, and he hauled her over his shoulder as I blinked over to them with my mist.

"Let her go!" I demanded, slicing at him carefully with my blade, unwilling to risk her getting injured.

"No," he answered, smiling over his shoulder as he did a trick similar to what I could with the mist, disappearing only to re-appear somewhere else in the room. "Been a pleasure this time as much as every time before, Vassago. I look forward to having Lilith's book in my hands again. How's that curse treating you?"

I roared, letting out my demon no matter who could see. I knew it wasn't the right response, knew that doing so risked us all, but I couldn't stop it. Naturally, my aggressive reaction only amused him further.

He surely thought I'd become the mindless, curse-driven beast he'd created. But that version of me was gone. All that was left was a demon who had absolute control over his actions. Full intent over what death and destruction I caused. And I intended to destroy him in the most painful way possible.

Wings extended and fangs aching, I followed him out into the yard, my heart pounding over my rage as I struggled to keep up with him. He was fast when he ran, but even faster when he employed his unpredictable vanishing act.

I growled with frustration as he led me into Greta's maze. I couldn't see him through the hedges, and he was getting more and more of a lead on me because I didn't know the pattern of it. The path suddenly spit me out in the center, and I blinked over to the far side as he stepped backwards directly into the wall, Greta clasped against him, her back to his front, his arms around her middle.

The last thing I saw as they vanished into the doorway in the hedge were Greta's wide eyes, her panic and my failure reflected in their depths.

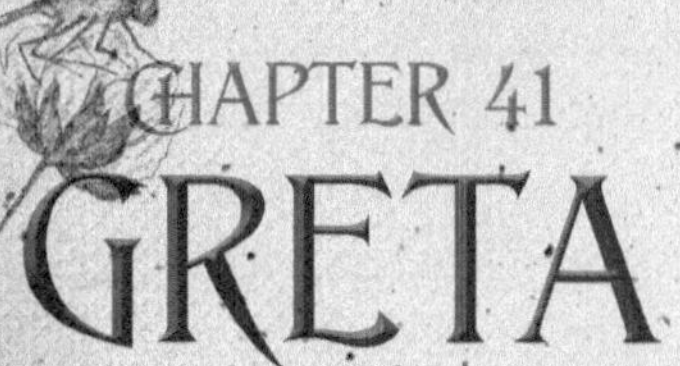

CHAPTER 41
GRETA

I HAD NEVER TRAVELED by portal before, but I couldn't say I'd recommend it. In addition to being fully out of sorts from his rapid teleportation all over the backyard of the manor, our landing had been rough. My body slipped out of his grip as we arrived in a heavily wooded area, and I hit the dirt with such force my breath was knocked from my lungs. My hip dug into the earth as my head snapped hard against my outstretched arm. Thankfully, the ring had stopped feeling like it was sinking through my flesh and into my bone, but that finger still ached.

"Don't even think about running," the man growled at me.

As stars danced in my vision and my stomach was one minor lurch away from turning itself inside out, I had no intention of doing any such thing. I focused on getting myself vertical as he staggered to his feet.

"Where are we? Who are you?" I asked, the color of the darkness in this part of the forest appropriate of the time of evening it was, but somehow ... still not right. I heard the distant sound of heavy wings, and the way they echoed made it sound as though the wood was swaddled in heavy cotton.

This place was much like Earth but was also not like it at all.

I patted my thigh as discreetly as I could, happy to find my new weapon still with me. It was a thing of beauty, my Dark blade. It would leave a terrible wound behind if it were ever turned on me, but that meant it was exactly what I'd hoped it would be. The little nick I'd given myself while Vassago gave me a crash course in using it had required attention wildly disproportionate to the size of the cut. He'd applied a drop of the healing elixir, just to be safe, and I'd been scared enough by the red streaks quickly leaching across my skin from the cut to let him.

The blade itself was black, with tiny veins of red and gold remaining as evidence of the essence I'd made for it. The handle was inset with the same type of opal as my jewelry, and I had no doubt that Imogen had done that on purpose, not just for aesthetic reasons. Calla's items all matched, too, and I knew there was surely some important reason for it, even if neither of us were aware of what that was.

"This?" He gestured widely with his arms. "This is *my* kingdom," he spat, grabbing me by the arm again to pull me along behind him as he started to tromp through the underbrush. "After all my careful planning. After all I did to ensure everything lined up just so." He shook his head, clearly upset. "The timing isn't right, but I suppose it will have to do, won't it, Libelle?"

I flinched at the sound of that name on his lips. "Who *are* you?"

"Who am I?" He stopped walking and laughed in my face, the sound a terrifying shriek that made my blood run cold. He was very clearly unhinged, as well as dangerous. "I'm the rightful heir of this place. And you? You're going to help me claim it once and for all."

I kept my mouth shut as he dragged me along at his side, carefully stepping over downed limbs and rocks while counting my steps. If I could get back to the right section of forest, I might be able to find the doorway again. I rubbed at my opal with my thumb, hoping it would help communicate to Vassago where I was, even from another realm.

The trees began to thin until they opened into a wide meadow. Off to one side, there was an impressive manse—not large enough to be a palace, but still an impressive structure of wood and stone, reaching into the sky with tall windows and wide balconies.

Instead of going in the front doors, he pulled me around to the back and down a damp, concrete stairwell into a cellar. We passed through no fewer than three iron gates on our way, and I was sure I'd seen a mouse skitter past my feet in the low torchlight.

"Your accommodations, *princess*," he sneered, that eerie smile back on his mouth as he flung me into a cell and slammed the door shut. I stepped forward and grabbed the bars, then hissing, I yanked my hands back as they began to burn. He laughed. "Enjoy your stay. When I return, you'll earn your place as my queen and help me finally claim my throne."

With that, he was gone, and I was left in the dank cellar of a mansion, in a realm I was a stranger to, all by myself.

ONCE I WAS sure he was truly gone, I'd called out, but there'd been no response. I heard the rhythmic dripping of water from somewhere nearby, the sound reminding me that I was impossibly thirsty after my travels, but nothing else.

I approached the bars but didn't touch them again. The dungeon was one big circular room with cells lining the perimeter. There was a gated hallway that led to the stairs and outside off to one end, but no other passages that I could see.

Frustration set in that I'd allowed myself to be taken like this. That I had frozen instead of fought back, instead of ... anything.

I tried to clear my head, to think through things so I could get myself home as quickly as possible. Vassago, no doubt, was furious on the other side off the doorway, so at least I had faith that someone was coming for me, provided they could figure out how to open the portal.

I took a deep breath and called on my gargoyle form. I was still unpracticed at moving between my skins, but iron and injury bothered me far less outside of my human body. It took several long minutes of effort, but my body finally transitioned to the greenish-gray stone version of itself. With the increase in size, I heard a few threads pop and grimaced.

It seemed truly unfair that I was wearing my gifted bridal dress in this situation. Any other day I would have been in my utilitarian trousers and shirt, much more capable of movement and far less afraid to damage my clothing. I mentally prepared an apology to the aunts for any damage done.

Thankfully, the access to my thigh sheath hadn't been the only modification Grace had helped me to make. She'd also installed little pockets in the pleats where the skirt met the bodice so I could carry vials of elixir around with me.

I tested a finger against the bars of my cell, getting a faint ache after a moment, but no further burn. Squatting down, I looked into the locking mechanism, but I had no idea what I was seeing. I had no skills as a lockpick. Carefully, I slid my new dagger out of my hidden sheath and pressed the tip into the raised piece inside keyhole. I was disappointed but not surprised when nothing happened.

The sound of someone passing through the locked gates echoed down the hallway. Flustered, I focused on shifting back to my human skin again, I couldn't get my dagger back in the sheath. I sat on the dirty floor, carefully disguising it between the folds of my skirt.

A new man, a guard by the looks of his clothing and how many weapons he wore, appeared inside the circular room. He carried a tray with only a small cup of water and some bread on it. He did a double-take seeing me in the cell.

"I see he's brought me another guest," he said on a sigh, shaking his head. The guard went to one of the cells across from me, the one right next to where the hallway gate was. "Hey! You! Feeding time."

After a pause, there was the sound of something dragging across the floor, then a pair of hands snaked shakily through the bars and took the bread and water.

The guard turned to leave and was already back to the gate before I found my voice.

"Excuse me?"

"What?" The guard sauntered to my cell, arms crossed.

"Could I please have some water?" The cough that followed was only partially for dramatic effect.

He raised an eyebrow, looking me up and down. I didn't at all care for the way he seemed to be trying to see through my clothing but maintained my polite smile. Without saying a word, he walked off and went back down the gated hallway. My hopes sank, the need for a drink only compounding on itself now that I had been so effectively denied.

I took the moments of his absence to put my dagger back into the sheath and examined my cell. To my surprise, the gate clanged once again, and he held a wooden cup through my bars.

"Thank you." I took the cup gratefully, noting that his keyring was not only attached to his belt, but the keys themselves were tucked into his pocket. Any chance I had of grabbing them would be at risk of injury at the very least.

The guard gave a simple nod before going back out, locking up on his way. The scrape of his key in the locks and the heavy sounds of the gates closing settled in my chest with a sense of dread.

I sipped at the water, knowing if I gulped, I would regret it. The flavor was crisp, almost too clean, but it was cool and refreshing. I forced myself to stop halfway, not knowing when I'd be given more or if it was truly just water.

"I'm Greta," I said to the shadows in the cell across from me. There was the sound of something shifting across the floor in response, which spurred me on. "I'm not sure exactly where we are, but I live in the city of Revalia, within the realm of Cyntere. Do you know where that is? I'd like to get back there as quickly as I can. There are people who will be looking for me." I was met only by the sound of a gentle sniff. "How often does the guard come?" Silence. "I was attending my sister's ball just a little while ago. I never even got to dance." The words sounded so silly, so meaningless even as they came out of my mouth, but the layers of my reality were not fitting together, leaving me totally off balance. "I'm not ... I'm not supposed to be here." Emotion swamped me as my eyes filled with useless tears.

I breathed through the sadness, scolding myself. I needed to find some way out of the cell, out of the dungeon. I was too tired to shift back to stone, but I started to work at the lock again, pulling one of the two-pronged pins loose that Sara had used to style my hair. It fit well around the little knob that protruded out, but I needed more leverage. Pulling out another, I started talking again, deciding that even if the other prisoner didn't want to answer, they were probably listening.

"Have you been here long?" The lock made a noise, and hope rose in a warm wave over me. I pressed against the door with my hip, but whatever I'd done wasn't enough. "If I do manage to get out of this cell, is there a way I can open the gates?"

"Not without the keys." The low voice was rusty, gravelly. "They each take a different one."

I stopped what I was doing, peering as hard as I could across the room. He was still shrouded in shadows, but I could see what looked like a shoulder in the low light, covered in a tattered, dirty shirt.

"Could the guard be bribed?" I asked, swallowing hard. I didn't have anything to trade except myself, and my weapons, none of which I was willing to part with. I would, however, be willing to offer either if it would make him open the door. After that, I could only hope I'd gotten good enough with my blade to be the one to make it out of here with his keys in my hand and his hands and sword kept to himself. The thought of killing a man left my stomach rolling, but it had become a very real possibility.

"Yes, but he won't remain loyal. To you or his master."

"And you?" I asked, suddenly worried that I'd said too much. What if the prisoner wasn't really a prisoner? What if he was another fae, planted to see what I might do?

"I am loyal only to one woman. And you are not her."

"That's not what I was asking, actually, I—"

He shifted closer to the bars, his whole upper body illuminated. His long hair was dirty, clumped in heavy strings. The way he had it tucked back revealed pointed ears and a pair of blue eyes that were startling in intensity but deeply shadowed in his gaunt face. His mouth opened as though he were going to speak again, but he made no sound, those bright eyes widening to the point of horror.

My hair pins fell to the floor, one bouncing several steps away on the outside of the bars.

"Saints," I swore, struggling to catch my breath.

While he looked awful by all accounts, there was one feature that left my heart lodged firmly in my throat. He had a scar. One that ran across his face, from one temple, to just below the opposite ear.

CHAPTER 42
GRETA

THE SOUND HE made could only be described as a croak. He blinked, rubbing his eyes with the backs of his hands, getting so close to the bars of his cell that he hissed and pulled back, a mark appearing on his forehead.

My hands trembled, and I found myself sinking to the floor again, my knees unwilling to support me fully.

"You …" Anger suddenly darkened his features, and he hit the bars with his palm. "Another trick!" Desperation rode a hard edge on his voice, anger and sadness swirled together. Betrayal. "I've done nothing to deserve such cruelty! I've given you everything you wanted, haven't I? To put on a face so much like hers? It's too far!"

I held a hand up, trying to calm him as my own emotions swirled in a hasty frenzy through my veins.

"No tricks, I promise," I said.

"You know where she lived. You could be any one of them pretending to be her." He started to scoot out of the light.

"Wait! Please. Rowan is my mother. I mostly go by Greta, but she called me Libelle."

"No." He gasped the word. "It's too far, cousin. Too far."

"I swear I'm telling you the truth. That man, the one who brought me here, I knew him in my world as Otto Feiser. He disguised himself, paid off my employers and put this horrible ring on my finger." I pulled at it again, the tendrils that had sunk deep into my flesh protested, a flash of white-hot pain momentarily blinded me. "I believe he cursed my mate and has caused plenty of trouble for other people I care about. He said he brought me here to help him claim his place as the rightful heir. I don't even know where 'here' *is*." I knew I was babbling, but the urgency I felt in getting him to listen to me made the words pour out.

"He's been working on that delusional plan since he brought me here. But if you are ..." He swallowed, pain in his eyes. "He can actually complete the ritual." He cleared his throat, the sound gritty. "Libelle." He rolled the word around, scanning me over and over again.

"Yes. What is your name?"

He shook his head. "It's better if you don't know."

"Please." I begged, needing one thread to tie him to me, one tiny piece to carry around. He was so close to me and yet untouchable, still verging on unreal. "She never told me anything. But I saw you, with her. A sorceress—" I stopped, unsure how to explain what Ophelia had shown me, his portrait in the smoke.

"Prove you are who you say," he demanded, falling into a hacking cough that racked his whole body.

"How?" I asked, unsure what could convince him.

He shook his head, defeat dropping his chin to his chest. "I saw Libelle a handful of times when she was small. I visited Rowan in secret, someplace far from where anyone would recognize either of us. We agreed it was safer ..." He shook his head. "Libelle had a unique feature. If you are an impostor, you won't know what it was." He grimaced, like he'd tasted something bad.

His words made me pause, but there wasn't time to waste on it now. I listened for a moment, making sure nobody was coming down the hall or lingering nearby. I loosened the bodice of my dress and shrugged it away from my shoulders before commanding my wings to flare out wide.

The man gasped. "It can't be. We did everything we could to keep you safe."

I put my wings away and tightened my dress back up. My necklace was still in place, but I worried for when Feiser realized the one he'd taken from Bea was a replica and unclasped it, securing it in one of the elixir pouches.

"I haven't seen my mother since I was a child. I don't know whether she's alive or dead, though I desperately hope she's alive. I spent most of my life as a household employee for a duke and his wife. Something happened to me ... someone bound my ability to shift. I have only been free to learn how to be myself for a number of weeks."

His attention snapped back to me, and he scrubbed at his face, removing the tears. "I'm sorry, Libelle. We did everything we could. But it wasn't enough."

"It's not your fault," I said. It was reflex, but I believed the words. He shook his head as though he disagreed. "What should I call you?"

He inhaled, his skinny chest lifting. "My name is Ris."

"You loved my mother?" I asked, though the words came out more statement than question.

"With all that I am. I will never stop."

"Is she here? In this realm?"

His eyebrows drew together. "It's possible that she's been trapped, the same as me. But I don't know for certain. She was in your world, with you, last I knew."

I nodded, mulling over how we'd find her if Magnus's guess that she'd come here were true. I'd believed her gone for so long, I wasn't sure how invested I could get in hoping we'd find her.

"Are you …?"

"Your father, yes." The words wheezed from him, the admission leaving us both speechless for a time, though he looked at me with longing and regret in his eyes. "I'm so sorry. For everything."

"Why did he call me *princess*?" I asked, heart throbbing painfully in my chest. I felt I already knew the answer, it was a strange hollow thud behind my ribs. I needed to hear it out loud.

"This kingdom is mine. Yours, if I'm no longer here. His weak tie to our family—the Sylvanus family—is the only reason he's been able to get as far as he has. He couldn't kill me outright, and I hoped … I hoped you and your mother were still out there, somewhere. As long as you were safe, so were we. But he knew far more than we gave him credit for, it seems." He sagged into himself, half disappearing into the shadows again.

"Have you been here all this time?" The notion that he'd been in that small cage for my whole life made my heart squeeze.

"Time moves differently here than it does in Cyntere. For every day that passes there, around three do here." I gasped. Nearly a century in that cage. It was beyond horrifying to even think about. "But yes. I've been here since my cousin decided he wanted my throne. He's been obsessed with it since we were children, but I never thought him capable of going to the lengths he has." He shook his head. "We have to get you out of here. If he manages to complete the ceremony, he will get his wish. With you, the true heir as his queen, he can do anything he wishes as king regent."

"Nobody has questioned your absence?" I asked, horrified.

"They have. But he's not shy about making dissenters disappear. It's a convoluted, ancient enchantment that follows the ruling family, but he can't kill me and then take my throne. Old magic would be invoked and if he survived it, he would be exiled.

Succession must be peaceful. Though he's clearly found several ways to work around some of the finer points."

"*This* is peaceful?" I asked. "You've been locked in a dungeon for how long?"

He slid back into the light, a chagrined expression giving way to another frown. "It's dangerous for you to be here, to be bound to him in any way. He has no moral compass—for good or bad. He's motivated only by his own desires. His power is still limited until he locates The Alchemist." He sighed again. "But desperation is a great motivator. One can only rule in someone's place for a hundred years. He's running out of time."

I swallowed, fear settling in my gut as a cold, hard knot. "That's why he needed me now."

"Yes."

There was a long silence as my ears rang, all the information I was getting battled for space in my mind. "Ris?" I asked, voice hushed.

"Yes?"

"He's already found The Alchemist."

He straightened, panic in his bright eyes. "How do you know?"

"Because it's me."

Chapter 43
VASSAGO

My initial anger had given way to muted emotion, a cold, white space where nothing existed but my rage as I plunged my hand into the sharp hedge looking for any remnants of the portal. I snarled when all I managed to do was get several cuts from sharp twigs that had dug into my skin.

I focused on Rylan, tried to communicate the urgency I needed him with on our weak mind link. It had worked before, so I had some hope it would work again.

Most of the guests had already fled the manor by the time I returned from the maze. I burst through the doors of the ballroom in a fury, finding only a few lingering gossips. I blinked over to Henrik's office, where I found both he and Lara hastily gathering easily sellable items from his safe.

"Leaving so soon?" I said, slamming the door and barring it behind me. Henrik spun with an amusing amount of speed.

"Mr. Feland! I—We—" Gold chains and assorted pieces of silver tableware slipped out of his greedy grasp.

"Sit, Henrik. There is no time, and I have no patience. You will explain, immediately." He hesitated, and all I saw was my mate, in that trickster's grasp. "*Now!*"

"Of course, of course." Henrik dropped into the nearest chair, still clutching his worthless treasure to his chest. I glanced over to find Lara standing in front of Bea, who had her beau's hand clutched in hers.

"I'm sorry you're involved in this, Bea. You and Ellis need not stay. Unless of course, you had any knowledge of this scheme?"

"No, I had no idea!"

"You are free to go, though I would appreciate you not leave the premises."

"If it's all the same to you, sir, I'd like to stay. I want to hear the explanation. If you don't mind."

Through the haze, I found myself smiling. This young woman had an admirable backbone. I nodded her direction, and she pulled away from her mother, pulling her man all the way across the room to a sofa slightly behind me. Her intentional positioning did not go unnoticed nor unappreciated.

"As you please. Henrik? You're wasting my increasingly valuable time."

I was holding my mist, the tendrils cool as they brushed along my face. My demon was also out, eyes red and fangs in violent view.

"It's nothing personal—"

I roared, banging a fist on the table. "That detestable man has stolen the most precious thing in the world from me, it absolutely is *personal.*"

Henrik began to babble, his cheeks red and eyes wild. "He came to us when she was a child. Said we had some mutual ancestry from way back. Distant cousins, he said. He had money, land, titles. It would all be ours, all we had to do was keep her for him. Let her practice her science. I don't know why. He entrusted that book to me, I was to hide it. And we were instructed to find the necklace."

"*Why?*"

He shook his head. "He never said exactly, only that it was important. That we'd have anything we needed, be granted unimaginable wealth beyond the houses, the titles, everything, we just had to know where Greta, the book, and the necklace were when he returned to claim them."

I let all that information sink in. I was betting that they had gotten lax over the years, decided to make extra money when they needed it off these sacred items, then he'd shown back up, intending to claim her as his bride, and they'd panicked.

"How did he appear to you? Always as Feiser?"

"Yes," Henrik nodded enthusiastically. "Only ever like that. What happened today, I ..." He frowned and shook his head as though still unable to comprehend what he'd seen.

"Beatrice?"

"Mr. Feland?"

"In a moment, I'll be taking your parents to d'Arcan. They will be locked in the cellar. I cannot risk them leaving town until I get Greta back. Do you understand?"

"Yes."

I looked over my shoulder and saw the fleeting regret in her eyes quickly replaced by disappointment. Ellis was concerned only with making sure she was okay. I liked them both and understood Greta's fondness for them much better now.

"I would also like you and your friend to join us. The pair of you, on the other hand, would be guests, but I'm sure you can understand my desire to have someone keep an eye on you. Just for now. Is there any of the staff here that I should be concerned about?"

"No, I don't think so. None of them have any particular reason to remain loyal to my parents." Her voice became slightly detached. "I've always wanted to visit d'Arcan. May I collect some things first?"

I might be a demon, but I wasn't a monster.

Mostly.

I got the distinct impression that Beatrice was on my side. More importantly, she seemed to be on Greta's side.

"Yes, as quickly as you can, please."

They hurried from the room, leaving Henrik and Lara huddled together, speechless for the time being. At least he'd figured out his useless excuses were unwelcome.

I made use of several items Henrik had out for decoration as well as his treasure, lashing each their hands together at the wrist with an assortment of chains and then their bodies with my mist before leading them out to the main hall.

A butler lingered near the door, nervous when he saw me approach with his master and mistress in my grasp.

"Please summon my carriage."

"Sir." He bowed and ducked out the door.

"Colman!" Henrik barked. "I am the master of this house, not him. You will listen to me!"

"They are not loyal to you, Henrik. Not a one. You have failed at every single endeavor you have committed to."

He made a noise of offense in his throat. "They are just afraid of you! Have you seen yourself? Evil incarnate. I can't believe I ever had dealings with the likes of—"

My fist snapped out, the large opal ring connecting with his temple. He sagged, hitting the floor like a massive sack of rotted potatoes. Lara squeaked but remained silent otherwise. She didn't bother checking on him either, just preserved herself.

The butler came back in, eyes widening as he took in Henrik's body on the floor. "Your carriage, sir."

"Thank you, Colman." I dragged Lara to the front stoop. Clem stood post at the door of the carriage and rushed forward to accept her when I gestured. I returned for Henrik, and as I got him settled, Bea and Ellis walked out the front door with a small case of luggage. They joined her parents, and I set Clem toward the collegium, taking flight so I could follow.

RYLAN BURST THROUGH the main doors shortly after I'd gotten the very vocal Henrik and Lara installed in the primitive, secure accommodations in the depths below d'Arcan.

Grace showed Bea and Ellis to Greta's apartment for the time being, and Calla trailed her husband with an apologetic but worried expression.

"What's happening?" he asked, stalking down the hall toward me. "Your message came through urgent but unclear. We came as fast as we could."

"Greta has been taken to the fae realm. My trickster was her betrothed in disguise."

"*What?*" Red flashed in his widened eyes. Calla gasped.

I felt my failure as a sharp stab beneath my ribs. "It's a long, convoluted story. I'm not even sure I understand it all myself. You made record time. And I appreciate that mind link working more than you know." He clapped me on the shoulder as we headed down the hall. "I don't even know where to start," I admitted. We went into the classroom, and I retrieved the few elixirs left, unsure what we'd need but ready to employ any and all tools we had.

"We should reach out to Tap," Rylan said. "Where is Greta's raven?" he asked, glancing around.

"The bird? He never comes inside, but he's been absent for several days."

Rylan shook his head. "They do choose the most inopportune moments to go on a journey. Archimedes has been off since we visited the conclave."

"Morticia has been away more than she's been with us as well," Calla frowned.

We stared at one another for a long moment.

"Perhaps the things are related?" I suggested.

He nodded, thoughtful. "Maybe. What's all this?"

"Everything alchemical she's made so far. At least, the scraps she's not already carrying. I don't have any idea what we're truly facing. The man who took her right out from under my nose has evaded me for decades. Stolen from me. Cursed me. He has done so for the last time. His death will be mine, I swear it."

"I'll help you," he assured me. "As will Magnus, I'd wager. But we must think this through."

Rylan examined labels, his calm settling me the slightest bit. His determination had not wavered when Calla had been taken, and neither had mine. Lucky for us all, hers had been the strongest of all. We had known we would get her back, and I felt the same now, we just had to figure out the right tactic.

Magnus stalked through the door, Grace on his heels. "Where is my niece?"

"We're working on that," Rylan said, still looking at labels.

Magnus swallowed, jaw twitching. "Who?"

"The mysterious Lord Feiser," I said, words coated in venom. "Turns out he was my trickster in a glamour."

Magnus swore. "How will we get to them?"

I shook my head and approached the largest of my mirrors. "Here's hoping our brother can help with that part." I began the process of connecting with Tap. He existed at the crossroads, and that complicated things. Still, I was hopeful I could get through to him. "How did you reach him for the wedding?"

"Archimedes," Rylan sighed.

"Damn. Where are those birds when we need them?" I jammed as many vials as I could safely carry in my pockets while I stepped to my mirror, the image clouding up and then clearing again, but never quite finding the target I'd tasked it with. "How quickly can we get to him?"

Rylan shook his head. "A day, at least, hard flying."

"We don't have that time to waste. I'll keep trying."

"Calla and I could talk to that nice couple some more," Grace offered. "I was going to take them a few things anyway. The young woman seems concerned for Greta."

I nodded. "Beatrice may have overheard something important and not realized it."

"Shall we go to the cellar then?" Rylan's eyebrow raised and Magnus cracked a smile.

"I could use a good interrogation," Magnus was already moving toward the door.

"I don't want to was—"

"Waste time," Rylan interrupted. "I know. But we need to have a plan before we do anything, yes?"

I clenched my jaw. "Yes."

"Where was the portal?" Magnus asked, stopping just before he entered the hall, Rylan and I following him while Grace and Greta headed upstairs.

"In the hedge maze at the Belettes' manor." I frowned, thinking of how lovingly she'd spoken of it. Had he opened the portal at will to spy on her? Stalked her while she practiced her experiments, touched her things when she wasn't around? Tampered with them so she'd fail? I saw red again, and my brother dodged as my mist flared outward from my body.

"That's at least nearby. Could have been deep in the woods somewhere we'd never have found," Magnus muttered thoughtfully.

We made our way down the stairs, the sound of Lara berating her husband reaching us from the top of the stairs. "If you'd only done what I said, if only we'd left like we planned—"

"It wouldn't have made any difference! He would have found us no matter where we went. And with what money would we have traveled anyway? You spent your way through all our savings like we were royalty. You and your need for new wineglasses, new dresses for Bea, new décor. You bled us *dry*—"

"I wasn't the only one! What about your fancy liquor, your rings? I should have left—"

"I'm so sorry, are we interrupting?" I said loudly, garnering their attention.

"Mr. Feland!" Henrik immediately turned away from his wife, gripping the rough bars of their cell. "I implore you, please. We are of no risk to you, this is wholly unnecessary."

I glanced at the two men beside me. "Magnus?"

He stepped forward, and Henrik was so startled by the stone kin's size, even in his human form, that he stepped back abruptly and fell directly on his ample ass.

"I do love the chance to ask the important questions unhindered." His slow smile made Henrik pale even further.

"Sirs! Please. We're all men, here, I'm sure we can come to an arrangement."

"There are two demons here, Henrik. And neither will make any kind of deal with you. That alone should tell you the depth of shit you've managed to put yourself in." He hushed, turning the same pale shade as his wife as we advanced on the cell. "Now. We don't have much time, but we're going to start at the beginning."

Rylan's energy was wild as it swirled around him, and I had my mist. Magnus was intimidating by size alone but decided to tease the poor captives further by shifting into his stone form. They both cried out, the stench of their fear filling up the enclosed space.

My ring sent a current of energy through my skin. Hope flared bright, and for the first time since Greta had left my side, I felt peace. I could find her. I just had to find the right way to access the portal. I had my brother and my friend at my side. We would not fail.

My next thoughts surely made me a bad man, but I didn't care. Her rescue lay on the other side of their discomfort, and I was going to enjoy every moment of seeing them thrash while I took all the information I needed from them.

CHAPTER 44
GRETA

R IS SHOVED HIS hands into his hair, eyes scrunched shut. "She said the prophecy would be changed. Put on someone else. As long as we did exactly what she said, you would be safe and someone else would end up The Alchemist! She swore!" His volume had gotten progressively louder as he ranted, and he'd even climbed to his feet, legs shaky but holding his weight.

"She who?"

He made a sound of disgust. "Your mother had found an old wise woman, she lived in the hills outside of Vincara. She's likely long dead now, especially if her methods were the same with all her other customers. When we get out of this, I'll be looking for her, in any case." He gritted his teeth together. "I never met her. Your mother handled it all. Before you returned from your visit, I was locked in here. But I'd hoped ... always hoped ... it had gone the way we dreamed. I'm so sorry."

"I appreciate the sentiment," I said, feeling slightly detached from reality as things I thought I knew reorganized themselves yet again. "But I don't think there was any wise woman."

He huddled close to the bars again. "Why not?"

I told him about the memory I had of a man with red hair hovering over me, how I'd been bound by the magical seal both in body and mind. And when I told him about my wing ways being sealed, he made a sound like a wounded animal before apologizing again.

I shifted my shoulders, remembering all too clearly how it had felt while Lovette and Calla worked on freeing me from the iron thread. I shook my head, unwilling to fall down into the trap of feeling sorry for myself. There was too much we needed to accomplish and not much time.

"We need a plan," I said, removing one of the vials from its pouch and lowering my volume, just on the off chance we were being listened to. "He didn't bother searching me. I have a weapon. Elixirs. When will the guard come back?"

Hope brightened his eyes. "Truly? What an arrogant— In a couple of hours, probably. He likes to make a round, check that I'm still miserable every evening. After that, not until morning."

"Alright. If I can get the keys …"

He shook his head. "I've tried. He's got them secured. He'll hurt you if you make a grab at them." He massaged the knuckles of his right hand, as though they pained him remembering an attempt at just such a thing.

My heart pounded as I considered having to hurt the man who had done nothing more than undress me with his eyes and bring me a cup of water. I knew it was likely inevitable that I would have to hurt *someone*, perhaps even kill, but I'd never done anything like that before.

"How does he treat you?"

Ris smiled, but there was no humor in it. "There is no end to the cruelty he's shown me. I was genuinely surprised he brought you water."

"He's probably been instructed to treat me well."

"Perhaps."

"How do I get back home?"

"A portal. If I were stronger, I could probably make one, given we were outside, away from all this iron."

That was promising. If I could get us out of the dungeon, we might have a chance.

"I have an elixir," I showed him the vial. "I think perhaps it can restore your health."

He nodded slowly, looking down at his emaciated frame. "Quite the task, to be sure."

I squatted down, carefully threading my arm between the bars. If I rolled it just right, it could make it across to him without breaking. "None of these have been tested," I explained, suddenly overwhelmingly nervous.

"I trust you, Libelle."

The unease crept up again, worry that perhaps I was the one being tricked. That maybe he was another fae in a glamour meant to gain my trust. I pulled my hand back in.

"What's the matter?"

"I just ... How do I know for sure you are who you say? I don't know anything about the rules of this place, but I did see that man change bodies right in front of my eyes before he brought me here."

He chuckled, a raspy sound that led to another bout of coughing. "Fair enough. Ask me anything."

I didn't know the first thing to ask him though. Any questions about my mother, he would probably know whether he was really who he said or not. I'd shown him my wings, so that was out too. "My mother, does she have any siblings?" I asked, unsure if I even knew the full correct answer myself.

He chuffed. "A great lumbering brother. We never met, but I saw him from a distance several times. Rowan called him Magnus. At the time, he had several children I'd never met either, but she spoke lovingly of them all, particularly one of the daughters." His eyebrows pulled together in thought. "Imogen, I think. It's been a very long time since those days."

I wanted to believe that it was proof enough. I'd given too much away earlier, trying to entice him into conversation, which was my own fault. I was already stuck here, and I hoped more than I wanted to admit that he really was who he said.

"Okay." I reached out as far as I could and flung the vial low to the ground. It skipped over the rough dirt, making a sharp sound that had my heart stopping for a moment as it hit a piece of rock mixed in. The roll wasn't nearly as good as I hoped though, and he was left to press his whole upper body against the bars, getting several stripes burned into him as he struggled to get a fingertip on the glass.

I held my breath as the sound of the first gate unlocking echoed down the hall.

"Shit," he swore, and grunted as he pressed himself even tighter against the bars, finally getting purchase on the vial. "He's early." Once he brought it close enough, he snatched it up and slunk to the back of his cell. "What do I do?" he asked in a harsh whisper.

"Drink it," I whispered back.

He hissed after a moment, the sound of the keys clanking indicated the guard was coming through the second gate. "Burns. Does that mean it's working?"

"I don't know."

I backed away from the bars, sitting against the one solid stone wall. I took a sip of my water, hopeful he was bringing more but doubtful that was the case.

"You're getting promoted," the guard said sarcastically, approaching my cell with a smug smile on his face. "Shame, I'd have liked a bit more time with you." His eyes roved over my form again, and my stomach pitched.

I got to my feet, heart beating so fast I thought I might be sick as he freed the key ring from his pocket and began to sort through them. I wished I had time to shift into my stone form again and felt for the distant cool tingle that I'd identified as my trigger for it, reaching for it, hopeful that this was the time I could grab it and change skins quickly. I also put my hand inside my pocket, preparing to pull my dagger.

Before I could carry through with any of my plans, the cell door opened, and the guard tossed a delicate powder into my face. I was paralyzed, arms stuck to my sides. Even my head was frozen, my knees painfully locked.

The guard came into my cell and picked me up, throwing me over his shoulder like a sack of grain, much like the other man had to take me away from the ball and through the portal.

"Leave her be!" Ris yelled, a cough interrupting his complaints.

The guard just laughed as he carried me down the hall and out of the cellar. I wanted to struggle, but no part of my body was responding. I started to wonder if I'd gotten stuck somehow, halfway to stone form. He unceremoniously tossed me onto the ground once we were out of the cellar.

"I do prefer a woman with spirit," he said, straightening his shirt. "We'd get along just fine, I think, under other circumstances. I wouldn't have minded seeing you put up a bit of a fight. Unfortunately, you're meant for the boss. Stay here, yeah? I need to go lock those gates."

I wanted to thrash, to spit at him, to scream. But I could do none of those things. Shame swamped me, as I watched his back disappear into the cellar again. My elixir had failed. I had been unable to save my father or myself thanks to some kind of magic dust.

I tried to move any part of my body as I stared up at the sky and found that here, there were three moons. As clouds rolled over the white faces, I cataloged the position of the one larger moon and two satellites, in the event it mattered later. As if I had a *later* to worry about. Mentally, I reached for the tingly stone skin trigger, the only thing I could think of that might free me from this terrible frozen state.

My hand twitched, and I found I could move my head a little bit. I closed my eyes, focusing on the feeling that led me to my stone form and grabbed on tight, demanding the shift I usually requested gently.

I gasped as the cool sensation washed over me and my body changed, the paralysis evaporating. "You can do this, Greta," I muttered, ignoring the tremble in my hands as I stood and pulled the blade out of the false pocket before heading back down into the damp cellar.

I heard the guard laughing, but nothing from Ris, as I moved as quietly as I could through the first two gates. When I approached the third, I found him urinating through the bars into Ris's cell. Cringing, I pulled the gate closed behind me, jumping as it latched with a loud *snick* sound.

The guard swore, fixing his pants as he turned my direction. "What the fuck? How did you— What *are* you?"

Somehow, that question removed any hesitation I might have had. Ris's hand reached out and grabbed onto the guard's shirt, holding him so the side of his face was up against the bars. He cried out as his cheek started to burn, struggling to pull away even a tiny bit.

"Give her the keys," he ordered. His voice was deeper. Stronger.

The guard fumbled, hesitating to comply with the order, even as I drew closer. I was not scary like Magnus, with his bone spear points and double set of fangs, but I was still a gargoyle. I held the blade up in front of me, one hand out for the keys.

Ris stepped into the light, and I gasped at the vast change in his appearance. His face was flushed with color, his cheeks filled out and eyes no longer sunken. His frail body had been restored to a strong, hearty one; the one I'd seen in the smoke portrait.

The elixir had worked.

"He'll k-kill me if I do," the guard stuttered, cheek almost smoking it was pressed so hard into the iron bars.

"We'll kill you if you don't," Ris said.

"You can't do anything," the guard spat at him. Ris pulled him closer with both hands, and the guard screamed out with the pain of being burned.

"Maybe not, but she can." He looked at me, giving a nod of reassurance.

I held the point of my blade to his throat and groped around at his belt, searching for the clip I needed to unlatch the ring. The guard struggled, though out of pain or resistance, I wasn't sure. When they were finally freed, I held them up. "Tell me which one will open his cell."

He grunted. "No."

Adrenaline pounded through me, and I pressed the Dark blade against his skin, the small nick immediately causing him to jolt. He began to sob, perhaps realizing for the first time that there was no way out of this for him. My stomach twisted, and my head felt light, but there was no going back from here. He sniffled and shook, but Ris never lightened his grip, and my blade only continued to widen the painful cut at the base of his neck.

"The one with three prongs. There's a scratch in it, on the left side."

I shuffled the keys around until I found the right one, and hastily pushed it into the lock on Ris's cell. My heart leapt when it actually turned and the door creaked open, the guard sagging further against it as both he and the door were pulled into Ris.

"Thank you." Ris shoved the guard away and slipped out, coming to stand at my side. He pulled the key from the lock and put the ring in his pocket.

The guard stumbled, sagging into himself. "He won't fail. Even if I have." He reached forward and grabbed my shoulders, forcing the blade through his own throat.

I gasped and tried to move away, but his grip on my shoulders remained firm until he began to fade, drowning in his own blood. The Dark blade made short work of him, tendrils of black streaking out from anywhere the blade touched almost instantly.

Ris pulled me away, turning my body and taking over the grip on the blade handle. The guard's sputtering stopped, and he drew my dagger from his limp form. Nothing was said as he pulled the tatters that remained of his shirt off his body and wiped down the blade before returning it to me. I stood there, staring at the blank eyes of the guard, wondering how we had gotten here so quickly.

"You didn't do anything wrong," he said, hands on my shoulders as he stared down at me. "He made his choice. Do you understand?"

Numbly, I nodded. "Yes."

"I need his clothes," he said. "I'll meet you outside?"

Feeling as though I might vomit, I left Ris. Inhaling great gasps of air once I reached the expanse of the cool night, I let go of my stone skin, slumping back into human form as I retched into the grass.

A hand on my shoulder startled me, and I looked up to find Ris peering down at me with concern. "I'm sorry. I didn't think he was that desperate. You've never done anything like that before?" I shook my head. "Then I'm doubly sorry that it happened on my behalf." He glanced around, turning his face up into the moonlight. "It's been so long. Everything out here is so ... open. I'd nearly forgotten." A rueful smile spread across his face.

I pulled myself together and got to my feet, the handle of my blade much heavier than it had been even minutes before.

"We cannot just leave," he said sadly.

"I know."

The heavy beat of wings echoed in that strange, muffled way, coming towards us from the front of the house. My emotions swung wildly as I looked up to find a familiar black bird, headed straight toward us, a knocking sound in his throat.

"Belmont?" I asked, rushing over to where he'd landed on the wooden fence surrounding the main floor of the manse. He paced, peering at the both of us, the flapping and noisy sounds communicated urgency.

Ris swung his head my way. "You know Belmont?"

"Yes," I smiled, happy both to have the bird's familiar presence and something in common with him. "He's been my friend since I started visiting d'Arcan. My mate—" Ris's eyebrow raised. "*Husband*, well, he's both, it's complicated, brought me there when he learned I had an affinity for the sciences." I was nervous all of a sudden; Ris was far scarier and more imposing now that he'd been restored to his normal self.

"I see." The lines between his eyebrows argued that he didn't, but I went with it. "That's where you've been then. What news, friend?"

Belmont paced and knocked, waving his beak toward the front of the house. I stepped forward, peering around the corner of the house. In the drive, there was a carriage, the door hanging open but no driver or passengers that I could tell.

Suddenly he squawked and took flight.

The last thing I saw as I turned to see what he was upset by were furious green eyes. Then there was darkness.

CHAPTER 45
VASSAGO

THE BELETTES HAD been as forthcoming as they were likely to ever be during the time we spent with them in the cellar. Magnus had been the one to call it off, disgust in his tone as we left them huddled together on the floor, simpering and afraid but hardly abused. Rylan had barely even used his powers on either of them, and all Magnus or I had to do was growl and they'd turned into puddles, telling us everything they knew about whatever we'd asked. Pathetic, the pair of them.

And no longer useful.

"What will you do with them?" Grace asked me as we assembled in the dining room for a drink. I appreciated that she wasn't the type to sit around and wring her hands. Instead, she was doling out whiskey with a face that communicated she was far more interested in the logistics, not any kind of sentimentality.

"I'm not sure yet. They're fine where they are for new. Bea may wish to speak with them, besides."

She nodded. "She said she might. Apologized on their behalf.

Nothing much useful was ever said in her presence though, they were at least clever enough for that."

"We should do a thorough search of their country manor when there's time. It may be where they kept other important items and documents."

Rylan nodded, kissing his wife's cheek as she sat down next to him. My chest burned, their affection reminding me that my mate was not nearby. The bond was aching, but every so often the ring reminded me that she was still trying to show me exactly where to find her. The blood bond was unusually hazy, showing me only that she was alive; a vague, distant dot in the expanse of the universe. It was better than nothing, but I needed more help than either were offering.

My ears suddenly clogged, and as I moved my jaw to clear the sensation, Calla got to her feet and rushed toward the door.

"Calla?" Rylan called, following her.

Magnus, Grace, and I glanced at one another, joining them.

"Do you smell that?" Calla asked.

"I don't smell anything, but my ears just got painfully full for some reason," Grace commented, trying wiggle her jaw to clear the pressure.

My stomach sank. The closer we got to my classroom, the heavier the air got.

"Magic," Rylan said, drawing his Light blade.

Magnus shifted as we walked, the sound of his stone feet against the floor a grating noise that made me clench my teeth together.

I noticed the dust motes immediately when we walked into the room—too many, too clustered, pointing me toward Greta's worktable ... and the empty space atop it.

"No!" I swore, crossing the room in a blink with my mist, palms slapping the bare wood. "Lilith's book!" I roared, the anger I had just moved beyond back with a vengeance. "That thief portaled in here and *took. My. Book.*" The insult of that happening right under our noses incensed me.

"How did he get past the wards?" Rylan asked, pacing.

"Fae magic works a little differently, but it smells like earth magic." Calla frowned as she looked around the room. I felt her discomfort as well as Grace's, the feeling that their home had been violated shared by all of us. If he could come and go as he pleased, even here, he was far more powerful than we'd already given him credit for being.

"He may have bound himself to the book. The fae pages ... I've never seen it done, but it's possible."

"I've never felt him," I said. "There are memories in the pages, echoes of the previous caretakers, but he's not there."

"Are you?" Rylan asked. "You've spent plenty of time with it in the past."

I frowned. "No." I'd never recognized myself there, nor Lilith, who should be the first to show. I said as much, and Rylan tilted his head.

"That's illogical. Notably so. I don't even know how one would remove the traces of several people like that."

He wasn't wrong, but that was a problem for another time.

I stepped over to the locking cases, checking for any missing items, but we'd already pilfered so much it was hard to tell. The safe was next, to be sure that the extra containers of the elixirs were still where they should be. Relieved that nothing else had been touched, I turned to my mirror and started another desperate attempt to reach Tap. I also tried to reach my other brothers telepathically, but the links were weak at best and Rylan had been the only one I'd ever had a decent connection to. But I was not ashamed to ask for any help I could get. We needed a portal to the fae realm, and we needed it now.

"I cannot sit around waiting. I'm not even sure what we'd be waiting *for.*" I felt ready to climb out of my skin from having no immediate goal to accomplish. Tap still couldn't be reached, and we were losing valuable time. I rubbed the stone of my ring with my thumb, sending Greta the same message she'd been trying to give me in the hours since she'd been taken.

"Magnus, could some soldiers fly to the crossroads perhaps? We could continue to scour the manor, try to reactivate the original in the maze in the meantime?"

He shrugged. "I'm sure I have some enthusiastic youth who could make the trip, but that still leaves us two days out."

"I'm going back to the manor. You can join me or not, makes no little difference. But I want to be sure I wasn't hasty when I first tried to access the portal."

There was a quick discussion about who would join and who would not. Grace opted to stay behind since we had guests, and Calla won an argument about whether or not she should be allowed to join. Magnus and I kept our amusement to ourselves—mostly—as she got directly in my brother's face, going so far as to poke him in the sternum with her finger as she made several relevant points about her magic not only being powerful, but also the best match for that of the fae realm out of any of us.

"I will not be coddled, Rylan Stolas, not when it comes to things like this. You need me to—"

"I *need* you to be safe!"

"You *need* me to not murder you in your sleep, but I'm not making any promises about that if you forbid me from helping with this, or any *other* situation in which I'm perfectly capable of holding my own. I can fight, I have my own powers—ones that have been well proven, I might add—and I am *not* going to be left behind because you think that's the safer option."

Magnus cleared his throat and shifted next to me, the corners of his mouth twitching as we lingered in the entryway of d'Arcan. My heart cheered for her. I loved her boldness, and she wasn't wrong, though I did understand my brother's stance. I predicted similar arguments in my future.

Grace, bless her, began to applaud. "Well said, my lady! Get out of here, the lot of you." She shooed us out the doors with her hands. "Go find a way to get Greta back and leave the fighting for the damned fae who took her, if you please."

Rylan sighed, his hand at the base of her spine as we gathered in the courtyard. "Have I mentioned today how much you infuriate me, Little Owl?"

"Only once or twice," she replied, wrapping her arms around his neck. He gave her a boost, his arm under her rear and she locked her legs around his middle. He snapped out his wings and took flight in the same moment he dove in for a kiss. They were disgustingly in love and a perfect match for one another.

I shook my head and leapt into the sky after them, absolutely refusing to give up any similar interactions my future might hold with Greta.

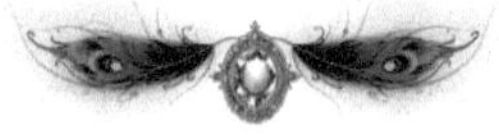

THE REMAINING STAFF were all in bed by the time we got to the manor, though a butler dutifully responded when he heard the doors open, a large umbrella in his hands. I apologized for the late interruption, and he scurried back off to his quarters, only too pleased to give us the run of the house.

We separated, efficiently searching the easily accessible rooms for any trace of magic, but there was none to be found inside.

"The maze is where the portal was," I instructed, leading us all through the backyard. We divided, half taking one entrance and half the other. The moon was bright enough to help light the way, along with some lanterns we'd taken from the kitchen. Footprints in the grass were easy enough to follow the center.

"Nothing unusual," Rylan reported, both of us taking in the statue and the fountain. "That's ... certainly something."

I couldn't help but smile, remembering Greta's face when she'd told me about this place. "He's handsome enough ... for an angel anyhow."

"Says the demon who looks like one," Rylan teased. "Is that her old work area?"

"Likely," I said, taking in the worn wooden table that was less than half the size of the one she had at d'Arcan, and the clever storage boxes she'd used underneath. I pulled the boxes out, sorting through the useless contents quickly. They'd certainly not provided her with anything worthwhile during her time here, not that I was surprised.

"Where was the wormhole?" Magnus asked.

"Here," I said, approaching the section of hedge where I'd last seen them.

Rylan and Calla set to examining it, but they had just as little luck as I'd had.

"I can smell the magic," Calla said, "but it's ... I don't know how to describe it. Flat. Like the energy has all disappeared from it. It was here and left a trace, but it's not active any longer." She frowned, her dark braid slipping over her shoulder as she bent down to look closer at the foliage.

The beat of wings drew our attention, and Rylan straightened as Archimedes flew in from overhead. As he flapped down to land on the shoulder of the angel statue, a man walked into the maze.

"Seir?" I blurted, immediately recognizing the familiar features of my brother. "What are you doing here?"

"Have you missed me?" He sighed, a grin on his face despite the harsh words he was offering. He opened his arms and stepped forward, wrapping me in a quick embrace, then Rylan. He appraised Magnus, who looked down at him with a raised eyebrow and a face that dared him to try the same thing with him. Magnus only grunted as Seir wrapped his arms around his ribs but started to chuckle.

"You're all mad," he grumbled.

"Definitely," Seir confirmed. His golden eyes glowed, and his smile revealed several additional pointed teeth.

The stone kin cat that usually followed Calla around trotted in after him.

"There you are, Morticia," Calla greeted the cat, who rubbed around her ankles. "Where have you both been? Has Belmont been with you?"

Seir watched their interaction with interest. "She's quite the creature. Found me and sent me on my way with efficiency. Though I'm betting she's still cross with me for being able to move as quickly as I do. Being able to appear just about anywhere I like within a few moments definitely has its advantages. At least coming here, I was able to bring them with me."

Calla glanced up, acknowledging his commentary, but she was clearly focusing on whatever the cat was trying to communicate to her.

"How did you know to go there?" she asked the cat, then turned to Archimedes who seemed unusually tired. He had already tucked his head under his wing as if to catch a nap. He hooted a series of soft sounds, making Rylan frown.

"The demon hordes that popped up within the city walls came through portals, not rifts between the worlds," Rylan said. "Someone let them through intentionally."

Magnus swore. "I knew there was something suspicious about all that. Gaius should never have been injured so badly, either. There's a troublemaker on the inside, just as we suspected. The more I learn about the council the angrier I get."

"Why did they come to you?" I asked my brother.

He splayed his hands wide. "They stopped off to see Tap first, naturally. He's the one who guides familiars, after all. And manages all the doors."

"Where is Belmont?" I asked.

"In the fae realm," Seir confirmed. "Tap sent him directly."

She had some help already, then. My chest loosened a fraction.

The tip of Seir's prehensile tail reached over to give Morticia an affectionate pat on the head. It had a tufted end, and she leaned into it, her eyes closing. That was one of the only features I'd been sad to lose when I'd made the full transition from Hell to Earth.

"Not that we're not glad to see you, brother, but why did Tap send you?" Rylan asked.

Seir smiled. "You know he can't leave his post. Things get all twisted up when he steps away from the gates. He's *still* cleaning up the shitstorm that was waiting for him when he got back from your wedding," he gestured at Rylan. "So he sent a portal with me so you can get where you need to go."

I exhaled at his assertion, my relief palpable. "What are we waiting for then? My mate is in danger."

Seir grinned. "I thought it hilarious that Rylan ended up mated—no offense Calla, you're lovely, and I pity that you have to deal with his broody self for the rest of your life—but you too, Vassago?"

"Yes. She is my mate as well as my wife, and I want her back. *Now.*"

He chuckled, humor as light as ever no matter the circumstances. "Yes, of course. Alright then. Is everyone armed? Do we have everything we need? Once I deploy the portal, we will only have so much time to come back through."

"How much time?" Calla asked, patting herself as she checked for her weapon.

"Two days."

"That's plenty," I said confidently, ready to leap through and face whatever might await us.

"Time moves differently in other realms, Vassago," Seir chided, hair falling into his face as he shook his head. He'd cut his hair short since last we'd seen him and had a hard time keeping it out of his eyes. "You know that as well as I do. Luckily, we get more time there than here, but we still need to be watchful."

"Of course," I nodded, anxious to get moving.

"Does anyone know anything about where we're headed?" Seir asked, pulling a vial out of his pocket.

"No," I frowned, realizing that for all we'd discussed it, my knowledge of the fae realm was extremely limited.

He shook his head again and put his arms down. "Are you serious? How have none of you visited yet?"

"You have?" Rylan queried, curiosity at the fore, like always.

"Of course I have!" Seir tossed up his hands as though we were the ridiculous ones. "It's how I'm going to be able to direct this portal. I befriended an old man there forever ago. Haven't seen him in ages, but we spent many a night at the tavern, drinking and gambling and working out all the problems of the world."

"You don't have to go to another realm to do that," Magnus sighed.

"True, but the reason I went in the first place is—"

"Later, Seir. Tell us what we need to know and let's *go*." I wouldn't mind hearing about my brother's exploits sometime ... but not now.

He smiled again, vial in hand. "Everything moves differently there. The air, the water, time ... *everything*. For the most part they're like us, but many are shifty assholes who can dress up in any body they like. They call it a glamour."

"Yes, the one we're after did that. He's got green eyes and auburn hair. Eerie smile."

Seir nodded. "These two tried to show Tap what they could, and he told me. Iron is the enemy—do we have that?"

I looked to Magnus, who rattled a heavy chain looped over his shoulders and chest in an X.

"Good. And in your blades?"

"Light but not iron," Rylan confirmed. "At least, not much."

"Better than nothing. Alright." He tossed the contents of the vial at the hedge in nearly the same spot as the original had been. A sticky black liquid spread out into a vaguely oval shape. "We have two days to get back or Tap will be absolutely *furious* if he has to leave the gates and come look for us. Landings can be rough, try to stay relaxed."

Calla and Rylan went through the strange black void together, then Magnus. I glanced at Seir, who was far too happy for my liking.

"Thank you," I said, not wanting to miss my chance to say so.

"Nice to see you, brother. Safe travels."

Then he put his hand in the center of my back and pushed.

CHAPTER 46
GRETA

MY HEAD THROBBED when I opened my eyes. A strange yellow light streaming into them from several large candles made me feel nauseous. I'd been propped up in an uncomfortable chair with my hands tied to the arms, my head left to loll at an awkward angle. I blinked and tried to work out the kink in my neck, finding that I was in a room far different than the dungeon I'd barely escaped from, but my situation was sadly not much improved.

"Good, you're not dead." The green-eyed man sat on a nearby sofa, slouched forward with his elbows on his knees, watching me.

"Where am I?" I asked, more reflex than anything.

"Your palace, my queen." That eerie smile spread across his mouth, but the endearment felt like a curse. "That ring I gave you, how does it feel? Are you ready for it to become permanent? I'm sure it's burrowed nice and deep by now. It doesn't like other magic, does it?" His laugh echoed through me as I cringed at the thought, turning the opal around so the stone was on the inside of my finger. I couldn't bear it if he tried to take it from me.

"And you're to be my king?" I asked, the words leaving a slimy taste in my mouth.

"Quite." He looked me up and down, and I felt like scrubbing myself with steel wool.

"What is your name?"

He chuckled, shifting his features to that of the willowy man I'd met at the Belette manor. "Otto Feiser, at your service."

I wanted to know how such a transformation was done. It was similar to how we took stone form, but not the same. I shook my head. "Feiser doesn't exist."

"No," he said, getting to his feet and shedding the false features. "I suppose he doesn't."

"So, who are you, really? If we're to be wed, I think I should know."

"Has nobody ever told you names are important? That they hold the essence of who we are, that they have meaning? That they shouldn't be given away so casually?"

I shook my head, and he tutted his tongue at me, pulling Lilith's grimoire out of a bag and slamming it on the nearby table. My head pounded in response.

"I suppose I can't hold it against you, since your parents were absent and neglectful in every way. Thanks only in part to me." He laughed, the sound chilling my blood. "My mother also had limited usefulness, so I understand." He opened the book, turning to where all the fae recipes were written. "Everything in here has a purpose, a function. Serves a need." He flipped pages, stopping at a recipe near the back of the book. "You're going to make me this one. Then we will be wed, and I will finally be able to claim the throne that is rightfully mine."

I said nothing, just watched as he gathered supplies. There were several recipes at the back that had been too complex or required too many ingredients I didn't know how to source for me to attempt. Even some of the names had been so off-putting I hadn't dared try them without some guidance from Ophelia. It felt like a safe bet it was going to be one of those he wanted me to work.

"Broc was a loyal man," he glared over at me, eyes holding mine. "Those are increasingly rare to find."

I didn't know if he was seeking an apology for the guard's death or simply trying to tell me he was displeased with what had happened. I shivered, feeling unnaturally warm when he finally looked away. I hated the feeling of being tied down. It spiked my heart rate in the worst way. I shifted my leg, finding the sheath was still securely in place. Had he *still* not searched me?

"Could I please have some water?" I asked.

"Is that how you got him to open your cell? That sweet little voice?" He frowned as he walked over to a table near the door and poured water into a small horn cup from a metal pitcher. "Tell me, how is it that my cousin, who has been on death's doorstep for decades now, suddenly seems so revived?" I shook my head, worry setting in for Ris. "He got away from me," he hissed, face so close to mine I could smell the onions on his breath. "A man I've had under my thumb for a century, and he got. Away. From. Me. That's *your* fault."

He grabbed the hair on the back of my head and yanked. The contents of the cup were dumped into my open mouth, causing me to sputter and choke. By the time I managed to swallow, my throat burned worse than it had when I asked, and the cold, paralyzing fear I had for this unhinged man had increased exponentially.

He laughed again, the sound so unnatural it felt like nails scratching into my brain. "Sorry for the dramatics, but it's necessary you see. I need you to make that elixir." He started to untie my hands, my confusion reaching an all-time peak. "It would be so much easier if this kind of thing worked on your father. Seems there's at least one benefit to you only being half fae." He grinned again, making me shiver. "For me, anyway. Stand." My body did what he commanded of it, without my input or control.

I gasped, trying to understand how he was controlling my movements. "What's happening?"

"Go to the table." I walked stiffly toward the table, my brain unable to comprehend why I was doing something I hadn't decided to do. "Make the Elixir of Naming. Don't stop until it is done. *Correctly.*" He punctuated the last with a pointed finger. "Marrying you isn't enough for a full transfer of power. I need that for the ancient magic to recognize me as king."

"Please, this is unnatural, I can't guarantee what will happen if I don't have control over my hands." It was horrible, as though I were watching from somewhere beyond myself as my body did what he'd ordered it to. "I'll do what you ask but let me do it of my own free will."

He sat in his chair again, watching as I worked, toying with the necklace he'd taken from Bea. I hadn't noticed until now, but he was wearing it around his own neck. I wondered what exactly he needed it for. It was a stone kin heirloom, not a fae one.

"Do you think me a fool? Absolutely not."

"Aren't you already the ruler of this place?" I asked softly, glancing over at him.

"Of course I am."

"Then why do you need me? Need this?"

He huffed. "Because the rules of succession are unavoidable and mixed with ancient magic. It's to my great fortune that you are The Alchemist and the heir all in one tidy package. Your inheritance was a boon I never expected to get. And your foolish parents"—he shook his head—"they tried to send it away."

"They were trying to protect me."

"Protect you?!" he shouted. I flinched, but my hands kept right on working. "*I* protected you. *I* kept you safe. They prevented you from spreading your wings, both literally and figuratively. They sought out a sorceress for a snake oil potion. They hurt you more than they helped. *They left you.*"

Knowing that there was no sorceress, that it had been him all along, I wanted to throw back an accusation, but held my tongue. "Do you know where my mother is? Is she dead?"

He laughed again. "Oh, poor little orphaned princess. I have no idea. Your father left you with her, and she just"—he gestured widely with his arms, a broad smile still on his mouth—"poof! Disappeared one day." His dark laugh and my memories showed that's not at all what had happened. The man in the suit, whoever he was, knew something. "Don't get me wrong, I'm grateful. That allowed me to work my own little magic." He wiggled his fingers my direction. "I was able to keep you as hidden as I wanted until the time was right." He shoved to his feet, glancing over my shoulder on his way to the door. "I'll be back in a while. This process bores me, and it's not like you're going anywhere." His laugh followed him all the way out the door, which he bolted with a heavy lock, and down the hall.

I was no closer to truly understanding what was happening, but at least he'd talked to me. My body would continue making this elixir no matter what. I could only hope that making it would take enough time for me to find my stone form and shake off whatever this compulsion was or for someone to find me.

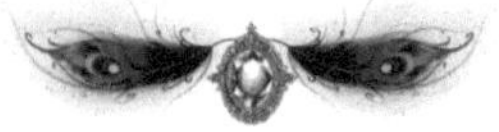

WHEN THE FIRST phase was done several hours later, I was allowed to sit, to eat a bland meal of porridge, and to use the bathroom only to relieve myself. I looked longingly at the tub while I was in there, the lingering layer of dirt and sweat from my travels and the dungeon making me itch. But I was still an automaton running under compulsory motion.

I had no doubt that more of the potion he'd given me had been mixed in with my food, and it was, unfortunately, a losing situation. If I was made to eat and drink while already under the influence of the spell and it was mixed in with those things, there was no way for me to avoid taking more of it. The spark of my stone skin was also out of my reach, a dim twinkle in the vast expanse of space.

The red-haired man returned and left several more times while I finished up the elixir. With the way he kept his name secret, it was no surprise that Vassago had never heard it.

Hours escaped me, the lack of true daylight leaving me unsure how long I'd been in the fae realm. The windows were shuttered, the massive candles providing light never seeming to melt much at all. I was allowed to sleep at one point and woke up hopeful I'd be free of the compulsion, but to no avail.

I called out when I finished, but he hadn't been lingering in the hall waiting on me. It didn't even sound like there was a guard stationed outside. The elixir was charging in the east-facing window above the worktable, and I was exhausted, dozing as I stood there. The hateful ring started to burn, startling me awake, but the opal flared right after, sending a rush of comfort through me, balancing the hopelessness.

The elixir in the window had gone still, the threads of glittery gold that had been swirling in the orange liquid gone.

Time had run out.

CHAPTER 47
VASSAGO

"WHERE ARE YOU taking us, Seir?" I complained, more edge to my tone than I intended.

After the uncomfortable journey through the portal—using one always felt like my insides were trying to become my outsides—and an even rougher landing where we all piled up together in the dirt, I was perhaps not as charitable as I should have been with him.

"The tavern where I used to meet with Van. Maybe he's still rotting there with his bucket of ale. Wouldn't that be something? He was positively ancient then, he'd be petrified now. Pickled, more like, after all the drinking." He grinned widely, tromping through the leaves at the front of the group with enthusiasm.

I glanced at Rylan, who frowned as though he might be moments from scooping Calla up and carrying her as she trotted along beside him. Magnus was hyperaware of everything around him, gaze sweeping the trees and sky.

"How long did you say it had been since you were here?" I asked.

"Fifty Earth years, give or take. Which means ..." He squinted and looked skyward. "Around a hundred and fifty here."

"She's been here for *days*?" I seethed, fangs rushing to the surface. Even as quickly as we'd arrived, Greta had been subjected to triple the amount of time passing.

"I told you, everything moves differently here."

I fumed silently to myself, following him as the trees thinned and a narrow dirt path appeared, leading to a road. The road opened up fairly quickly, and a large village came into view.

"The Empty Cask is right over there," Seir pointed. "I'll just pop in? If we all go, we might be a little bit obvious."

"I'll go with you," I insisted.

He sighed, and I was sure he was rolling his eyes even though I could only see the back of his head. "If you insist."

"I do."

"We'll wait over there," Rylan gestured to a circle of stumps near the far edge of town.

The tavern was doing a steady business, but nobody gave either of us more than a cursory glance. No one except the barman. He glanced up from his work polishing the bar, did a double take, and smiled.

"I'll be damned. Where the devil've you been?" He came around the bar and clapped my brother hard on the back as he drew him into a hug.

"Sorry to vanish like that, Pol. I had to get back to work, you know."

"Excuses," he grumbled, but he was laughing. "Your friend doesn't come to see me anymore either," he shook his head. "But unfortunately, not because he went back to work." His smile slipped. "Get you fellas something?"

"We can't stay, I'm afraid. But we were hoping you could help us." Seir produced a gold coin I didn't recognize.

The man accepted it with a gleam in his eye. "If I can, you know I will." He waved us over to the far end of the bar, hushing his tone so we could have as much privacy as possible.

"This is my brother. His lady was brought through a portal earlier, we need to find her."

"I'm sorry to hear that. A portal you say?"

"I came through the pines to the south, but I'm not sure where they landed."

"She was taken by a man with red hair and green eyes. He's got a laugh like dull knives," I said.

The barman stilled, his face going through several subtle shifts until he finally said, "Then she'll likely be at the palace. There's a bit of a to-do going on there, you should know. People been passing through all day on the main road. *His* people. There aren't many, mind, but plenty with some power behind them." He looked around shiftily, being sure nobody was paying us any attention. "We all comply with the false king because we prefer to be breathing, but that doesn't mean we agree with him."

"I understand. And I thank you, friend. Can you tell us how to get there? I never visited, myself."

The barman directed us down the road, but not before getting a promise out of Seir to come visit again someday soon. We collected the rest of our party and took to wing, the sense of urgency driving against my nerves as we flew through the strangely thick air, our destination appearing through the trees as a massive wood-and-stone palace.

The closer we came to the structure, the more violently my heart pounded within my chest. "She's here," I said, gripping at my vest with my hand, nearly doubled over in the dying grass. We'd landed at the back of the palace where the edge of the forest met sadly neglected gardens.

"There's good news," Seir muttered. "Awfully quiet for somewhere holding an event today. I don't even hear any horses."

"Do we just ... sneak in through the kitchen?" Calla asked.

"There's no telling what's in there, though," Rylan argued, rubbing at his chin.

I rubbed at my ring, hoping that Greta's close proximity would give a more precise location. It flared warmly but provided no direction.

As we examined the building, discussing our best tactics, a man rushed out of the trees at the opposite end of the building. Each of us took our fight stance out of reflex, swords drawn and magic at the ready. He slowed, hands dropping to the blades at his belt before rising in a defensive motion as he closed the distance between us.

It took me the barest moment to recognize him as he got closer, thanks to the scar across his face. "You." His head turned a fraction my direction, his focus pulled from Magnus.

"Me?" he queried.

"We need to get into this place. Are you here to stop us?"

He shook his head slowly. "No, my goal is the same." His stance softened, and he dropped his hands to his sides.

At that moment, a familiar raven flapped around the corner, a knocking sound in his throat. "Bird," I said, unreasonably pleased to see the feathery menace.

He croaked, pacing along a set of windows, turning his good eye into the frosty glass. He tapped at the sill, looking back at us to see if we were getting his message.

"She's in there?" I inquired.

Belmont took off, landing on Ris's shoulder. "Can you get inside on your own, Belmont?" The bird knocked, head swiveling. "Alright, if the way is blocked, you can always follow us." He gave the raven a quick stroke down the beak, and he took off again disappearing around the corner of the palace.

Magnus stepped forward, a scowl on his face. "What is your name?"

The man straightened, a brief look of happiness on his face before he stuck one of his hands out. "Hello, Magnus. I regret meeting you for the first time this way. Rowan—" He shook his head, realizing that might not be the right tack. "I'm Ris Sylvanus. I am king of this place. Though"—his brows pinched—"I've been away for a long time." He frowned at Seir. "You?"

Seir slapped his hands against his thighs, startling us all. "I thought I recognized you! Though that dashing scar is a new addition, yes? Not to mention about a hundred-and-fifty-years' worth of aging. You were maybe a little smaller, the last time I was here?" He strode forward, arms out and pulled the stunned Ris into a hug, complete with enthusiastic back pats. "Good to see you. How's your dad? Pol says Van never visits anymore."

"Pol?"

"Yes, Pol!" Seir nodded enthusiastically. "The barman at the Empty Cask?"

"Of course. Father's been gone some time now. He chose to go into the Tombs of the Elders after I took the crown. Said it was time he joined my mother."

Seir's joyful expression dropped. "Oh. I didn't realize. I'm so sorry." Seir patted his shoulder again, then stepped back.

"Don't be. He was happy with his choice. Though circumstances being what they are, I think perhaps he maybe would have lingered a bit longer had he known what my cousin was truly up to. Have you all come to take Libelle home?"

"She's my wife," I asserted. "My mate."

"I see." Ris's gaze drifted over me again. I was certain he was measuring my worthiness.

Seir gestured at us both, proudly proclaiming, "Ris, these are my brothers. Vassago and Rylan. That lovely lady is Rylan's wife, Calla. And you know Magnus, it seems."

His smile was genuine as he stepped forward to shake my hand.

"Pleased to meet you. I'm truly sorry about all this, my cousin has wrought trouble across many realms it seems."

"Is Rowan here?" Magnus asked.

"I don't know. I told Libelle the same. As much as it pains me, I don't think so." His eyes grazed us all again, our wings, the magic that flowed around Rylan, my mist. "What are you?"

Seir grinned wide and pointed, starting with me and ending with himself. "Demon, demon, witch, gargoyle, demon."

Ris's eyebrow raised. "I see." He turned toward the palace. "My cousin has always maintained a small but strong force of private soldiers. But I have no idea how he might have things organized given he's had the run of the place for nearly a hundred years."

Seir rubbed his hands together. "We're not afraid of a good fight, are we brothers?"

"What is his name?" I asked. "He's wronged me for the last time, though we've had several altercations. I want to know who I'm going to kill."

Ris smiled. "I'm afraid there's a line forming for that honor. His name is Vos Quille." Ris pulled a blade from his belt. "This belongs to Libelle." He turned it over in the moonlight. "It's a lovely blade. Worked terribly well on our guard in the dungeon. But she dropped it when Vos snatched her up. I only just managed to get away ... I failed her again." He frowned and looked my way. My heart clenched, realizing what he was saying.

Her hands had been bloodied.

I felt an odd disappointment that I'd missed it; regret that I hadn't been there to comfort her through the range of emotions that inevitably had come after. Rage bubbled under my skin, and I fought to channel it where it truly belonged, thankful my curse was gone so I could direct it properly. While Ris might carry some responsibility for whatever happened in and after they were out of the dungeon, this was all the red-haired man's fault, and I finally had a name to direct my anger to.

Seir was the first one to smile and head boldly across the yard. My brother was nothing if not enthusiastic. "Shall we go give it back to her then?"

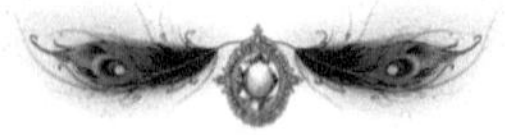

RIS LED US into the palace through a stone door hidden behind a trellis and years of overgrown vines. I felt like my heart was lodged in my throat, the insistent beat showed me I was getting ever closer to Greta. My only wish was that it was more of a comfort and less of a distraction.

The passage he took us through between the walls emptied out into a wide corridor. Ris insisted on leading the way as we navigated toward the ballroom Belmont had indicated. We had yet to see the bird on the inside of the building, but he was clever. Just having seen him was a hopeful sign.

Applause echoed down the hall, and we increased our pace. There was only one guard outside the ballroom doors, and once he regained his composure, he bowed to Ris.

"Majesty," he muttered.

"Where are Vos's soldiers?" Ris asked.

The guard shook his head. "Inside. Most are ... gone. Any suspected disloyalty is managed with ruthless efficiency."

"How many?" Rylan asked.

"Eight. Plus, the people his guests brought. But there are only six families representing today. The wedding was put together rather in haste."

"Wedding." I heard the word and my body moved automatically toward the doors. Magnus's firm grip stalled my motion, but a growl snarled out of my throat. "She is my *wife*."

"Then his claim will not stand," Rylan reminded me calmly.

"Any mages?" Ris asked.

"No, not except for His Majes—I mean, the false king, my lord."

"Thank you, Deni." Ris bowed his head.

"Sire," he inhaled. "You have my sword as well."

Ris shook his head. "No, you are better served alerting the kingdom that their king has returned."

"Yes, of course." He spun on his heel, leaving us in the hall.

"So, melee style then?" Seir queried, pulling his sword, a broad grin on his mouth.

"Seems so," I agreed.

"Calla, perhaps you should—"

"In. Your. Sleep," she replied, not meeting his eye. Puffs of dark-green magic came out of her mouth when she spoke, and I remembered what I'd seen the night we came to her aid all too well. She alone could level this palace given proper motivation.

"We need her, Rylan. She's more than capable of defending herself."

He glared holes through my skull, his mouth a firm line before softening, mostly because he looked over at her and couldn't help himself. "I know. But I don't have to like seeing her in harm's way." He turned to Ris. "Anything we should know about fighting him?"

"He can move quickly. Like my mist, but not. Unpredictable," I jumped in.

Ris nodded. "He's clever to the point of unhinged. Has the ability to space jump as a diversion technique. He's skilled with blades and hand-to-hand; we're all raised with it. He's not shy about being brutal if you're in the way of something he wants." His jaw clenched, and I thought I had a decent idea about where his scar originated. "If she already made the elixir, he can complete the ritual that will make my power his. We must stop him from doing that, at all costs."

"Right," Magnus growled.

Seir suddenly walked toward the double doors, clearly tired of waiting. "Three demons, a gargoyle, a witch, and a fae king walk into a ballroom." He turned around, a laugh bubbling out of his chest. "Sounds like the start of a good joke."

There was a broad smile on his mouth yet no humor in his ruby eyes as he watched me stride forward and kick out, forcing the doors to swing wide open.

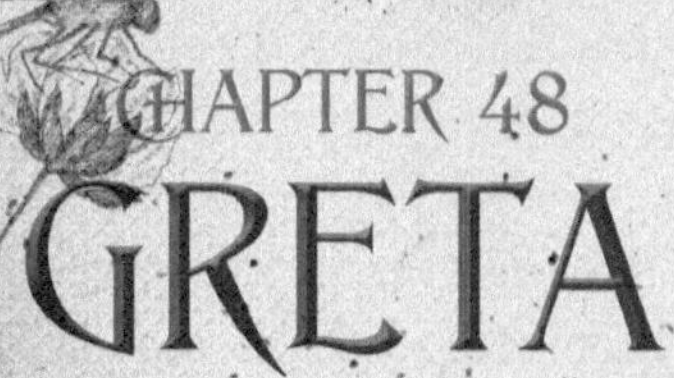

CHAPTER 48
GRETA

I CLENCHED MY JAW, refusing to agree to the vows I'd been prompted to recite.

"Speak the words," my captor threatened, "or I will ensure this, and every other night of your miserable life, leaves you wishing you had." My body trembled under the threat, not to mention the weakness his compulsion had left me with, but I said nothing. "You are guaranteeing yourself nothing but pain," he spat, eyes flashing, but I held my silence. "You could be a perfectly satisfied partner in this. Happy even." His eyes narrowed as I stared back defiantly. "*Fine*. As you wish, little princess. Don't say I didn't warn you. Continue," he ordered the clergyman.

The ring bore into my skin with every word he uttered in a version of old fae that resonated deep in my bones. I was still under compulsion as far as my body went, but he couldn't force me to speak the words.

A saw a shadow move out of the corner of my eye, and I nearly smiled in relief. There was a suspicious raven-shaped figure moving at the edge of one of the heavy curtains.

I jumped as the doors of the ballroom crashed open, stalling the clergyman's hasty recital of vows. The two guards that were stationed near us drew their weapons, tightening in next to the priest.

"Will you take him as your husband? In times of illness and those of health, in—"

"Who dares interrupt the sacred vows?" my captor asked, letting my hands drop. He growled, teeth bared, as Vassago walked into the room, followed by Ris, Magnus, Rylan and another man. "*You.*" I turned my head and inhaled, tears making my eyes burn as hope flooded in. My captor snatched the vial of elixir from the altar, tipped it into his mouth, and consumed the contents before flinging it to the floor, breaking it. "Finish the ceremony!"

The clergyman stuttered and tripped over his words but continued.

Gasps rang out, and several of the noble families slid closer together on the benches they were seated on, the remaining handful of guards at the ready. It seemed they were awaiting his order to abandon their posts next to the rows of seats so they could engage the intruders, as none had moved.

The ballroom doors were closed again, a chair noisily scraping across the floor the only relief in the clergyman's recitation.

"Shall we kill them all?"

I didn't recognize the brunet demon grinning ear to ear, asking such a question, but he was clearly part of Vassago's family.

"I expected so much better of you," Ris accused, the nobles cowering under his voice.

Magnus took a step back toward the doors, extending his wings with a wicked smile on his face. He looked especially menacing in his stone form, but the chains he had draped over him added a whole other dimension.

"Going somewhere?" Vassago asked one of the nobles who'd slid from his seat, sword pointed at his throat. Suddenly, nobody seemed very interested in leaving.

I turned to the clergyman. "Please. I am not here of my own will. Don't do this."

He frowned, finishing his section before saying, "I am sorry, my lady."

I bit off a curse, the vibration in my bones from his words getting worse.

"You're not leaving here, Vos." Ris approached him slowly, like he was trying to keep him from spooking.

"And you're already too late to win this, cousin." My captor turned to me, one arm out. "Your spawn is truly lovely, Ris. To think you nearly squandered her gift." He inhaled as an orange glow started to creep around him. He turned, locating Vassago, who had murder in his eyes. "I'm sure she'll make a wonderfully docile wife."

My mate snarled but moved with purpose. His mist curled around his body, and I could feel him coiled tightly, ready to leap.

"Guards, kill them all!" Vos ordered, then vanished, only to reappear near the back of the room.

Everything turned to chaos. Swords clanged and the screaming of the noble families became louder than the clergyman, though he did his best to keep up.

Vassago and Rylan paired up to fight the six guards that had been stationed with the families. The two of them stood back-to-back, somehow fending off attacks from all six at the same time. I watched in awe as they struck and dodged, moving so fluidly it was like a well-choreographed dance. The guards who had been holding their own stood no chance at all.

The new brunet demon wasted no time running through two noblemen who tried to make a break for the doors, pulling one of them to the floor with what looked like a tail wrapped around their ankle. Magnus was right there with him, dispatching two more who offered their wives or children up as shields.

One by one, they began to fall, nothing more than wasted talent and misplaced loyalty bleeding on the floor. Vassago turned his focus to my captor, whose laugh rang out every time anyone got close to him, only to blink across the room. I could barely keep track, his movement so fast and unpredictable it was like he never stopped moving.

The two men instructed to guard the clergyman hadn't done more than blink as they watched their comrades fall. They only shifted their weight, ensuring that the clergyman kept talking with their blades directed at his chest.

Calla had somehow skirted around the room unnoticed and approached me from behind. A rope of green magic extended from her hand and wrapped around the clergyman's throat, choking his words off into nothing more than a soft wheeze.

The guards turned to engage her, and Belmont flapped up, cawing loudly directly in their faces. Both waved their arms ineffectively as the massive bird dipped and dove for their eyes, fiercely determined to cause as much damage as possible.

She reached down through her pocket with her right hand, pulling out her blade. One of the guards abandoned his fight with Belmont and aimed his sword at her chest, but she was faster. She ducked under his arm and lodged her dagger in his ribs, yelling out as she did so.

Rylan's head snapped over to her, his eyes wide. His expression softened when he found his mate not only whole but the victor, and he returned to his own quarry, driving his sword through the chest of the final remaining guard.

Belmont had fully gained the upper hand with only one target to manage and was flapping madly as he continued his assault. The man was bloodied, screaming as he stumbled toward the windows and fell to his knees, his hands waving uselessly around his head. Somewhere along the way, he'd dropped his sword.

Familiar mist curled around my face, and Vassago appeared, kneeling next to me. His hand caressed my face. "Are you injured,

Dragonfly? He's dead, either way, I just need to know how much to make it hurt."

"I'm alright. I can't move though. He's given me a compulsion. I can't do anything unless he gives me direction." Shame flooded me, even though I knew it wasn't my fault. The rest of the men were still fighting, the noble families reduced to the matriarchs and children while my captor darted around the room, avoiding them all, an orange haze growing around him. Calla stood in front of the clergyman, both hands extended as her magic tightened around him like large snakes.

He went straight for his pockets, pulling out vials as he went. "Restoration, life, unmaking, fortification, cleansing." He glanced at me. "Cleansing it is." Vassago popped the cork and fed me the vial, the liquid cool as it ran over my tongue and down my throat. As I swallowed, I hoped for a far less eventful time of it than I'd had before.

The clergyman's wheeze was beginning to taper. He was nearly purple but kept speaking. Likewise, the guard Belmont was managing had gone quiet.

"Are you also under a compulsion?" Calla asked him. He gave a vague head shake. "Then why do you not stop?"

"He'll kill me if I don't complete the ritual."

"You're dead either way," she said sadly, shaking her head.

"Are you going to kill me, my lady?" he asked, something like pleading in his eyes.

A blade burst through the center of his chest, his eyes wide as he looked down in surprise, his hands groping at the foreign protrusion.

"Her hands will always remain as clean as possible, though clearly, she knows how to use them. But mine?" Vassago's face, surrounded by wisps of mist, appeared next to the clergyman's ear as he shifted the blade upward, causing the man to rise to his toes. "Mine have been filthy since the moment I fell, and I have no compunction about killing anyone who threatens my family."

The clergyman made a gurgling noise as Vassago leaned in and tore out his throat before pulling his blade out. As Vassago rinsed his mouth with whatever was in the chalice at the center of the altar, the priest fell, wide-eyed and lifeless, to the floor.

"No!" the false king shouted in rage, his green eyes flashing before disappearing behind another jump.

White smoke appeared around me. Unlike before, no magical seal appeared at my center, thank goodness, though the smoke still went through several colors before I was free to move again under my own direction. I felt slightly fuzzy-headed as the remnants of whatever potion he'd given me finally wore off. "Thank the saints." I tested my hands, marveling at the feeling of being in control again.

Vassago helped me to my feet, his hands traveling over me warmly, checking for any injuries. His mouth descended on mine, his arms wrapping around me fiercely.

"I'm sorry," he swore, breath warm against my ear. "You'll never know how sorry I am, Greta."

"I'm okay," I assured him. "I'm okay." The second time may have been for me, but I think it helped us both. I reached down through my pocket, disheartened to find my blade missing from its sheath.

Ris's voice boomed around the room. "If you are *ever* found to be disloyal to the Sylvanus crown, you will meet the same ends as your husbands."

"You heard him. Now leave!" Magnus boomed, opening the door enough that the remaining women and children could hustle through.

"You are *my* subjects! You will remain until the ritual is complete!" the false king demanded, desperation edging his voice. They all ignored him and fled. "I have not waited this long and come this far to lose to *you*, Ris Sylvanus. I have made too many preparations! The kingdom is mine!"

The door closed again, and without human witnesses, the whole feel of the room changed.

"Now that there is no risk of collateral damage ..." The brunet demon advanced almost playfully, his sword swinging around in circles as the green-eyed man flashed around the room several times. He walked forward at a sedate pace, eyes on Ris. "Your father did always laud you for your dedication to strategy," he grinned.

"Father was not the strategist," Ris corrected. "Mother was."

"I know. I think that's perhaps why he admired your inheritance of the trait. He was dedicated to her like nothing I've ever seen. Drank buckets of ale just to survive another night without her." The brunet demon clenched a fist over his heart in a gesture of respect.

"I'm clearly rusty, but I appreciate the compliment."

"Shut up! Nobody cares about his dead parents. This is my realm! My throne!" the usurper shouted, standing with his feet wide, arms extended. "And I can already feel the transformation happening. You're. Too. *Late*." His laugh was even more unhinged than usual, the sound scraping across my bones. Wings exploded from his back, willowy bones under a thin membrane of brown scaly flesh. He flapped them, rising several inches off the ground. "I can't jump." His face fell, but only briefly. "It's working! I have wings! Surrender, cousin, and we can end this."

"Never," Ris snarled. "This belongs to you," he said, handing me the Dark blade. "Something seems wrong. Those are not what royal wings normally look like. We need to hurry." He made eye contact with Vassago, who released me and gave a short nod.

Rylan joined Magnus, and Calla lingered behind the false king with me. She cautiously extended her magic, trying to do the same kind of thing to him she'd done to the clergyman. He must have sensed it, because he spun, blade singing as it cut through the air above our heads.

Seir grabbed out with his tail, lashing it around one ankle, pulling him off balance. Vos roared, and spun, swinging out ineffectively with his sword. Seir and Rylan circled him, Magnus rising enough with his own wings that he was able to loop a length of chain around Vos's throat. As he screamed from the iron searing his flesh, the two demons both leapt. Each grabbed a wing with one hand while swiping their swords across the backs of his knees with the other, rendering him immobile.

"How dare you!" he roared, stumbling.

Magnus grunted, yanking at the chain to pull Vos close enough to also circle his chest, leaving him without use of his arms as well. He hung there, legs useless, Magnus keeping him upright.

"Belmont? Do you know where my book is?" Vassago asked. The raven knocked, swiveling his head in a nod. "Would you please show Seir where to find it?"

Seir grinned and followed the bird from the room. Rylan shifted so he would be able to back Magnus up if needed.

"Kneel, Vos," Ris ordered.

Vos had no choice, thanks to his injuries and the force Magnus put behind pushing him down, but he let loose that terrible laugh again. His ring burned what felt like into the bone of my finger, and I couldn't understand how his enchantment was still working. Calla stepped over to her husband's side, her green earth magic adding to the bonds along with a slight electrical current from Rylan.

"I am king here," he insisted, voice shaking with an edge of defeat.

"If you were, you would not be on your knees." Ris crossed his arms, examining Vos closely as he walked a circuit around him.

"You can't kill me! If you do, you'll die or be exiled," he argued.

Ris tutted with his tongue. "You think you know the ancient magic well enough to correct me, Vos? You don't even understand all of it."

"Of course I do! Everything I've done was to get to this point. My whole life dedicated to taking what is mine!"

Ris leaned down into his cousin's face, expression tight with anger. "And yet you still don't understand! Those wings were certainly not royal. Your crown never formed either."

"What's your point?"

"You were never going to be king. No elixir could make you worthy of the throne, Vos."

"Worthy! There is nobody more worthy than me. I trained beside you, I learned everything I needed to know, I kept quiet despite all the insipid *talking* your father loved to do. I was patient! There was no part of the enchantments I didn't learn. The throne should have belonged to me! It would have been mine ages ago if not for *her*." He sneered at me. "You were going to run away with your little stone kin lover, and I would ascend in your place. That was the *plan*. Then she was born and ruined everything!"

Ris frowned deeply, shaking his head. "I would never have abandoned my responsibilities here, Vos."

"But you would! You did! You have no idea how many nights your father prepared me to be the one to take the crown."

"You're wrong. I know. I always knew. My father and I spoke at length about it, many times. But none of that makes you *worthy*." Ris looked almost sad. "You hurt people to take what you thought you were owed. We have ruled here peacefully for thousands of years. What you did ... it's unspeakable. You've tainted everything the Everwood people stand for."

Vos descended into mindless rage, babbling incoherently about what he thought he deserved.

I dug around in my skirt and pulled out a vial. It was one of the rarest I'd made. The ingredients had been so unique, I'd only been able to produce the one little vial, but I finally understood what it was for.

"What's this?" Vos chuckled as I removed the cork. "A gift from my new bride?"

"We never married," I told him.

"Of course we did, I was there, remember?" Madness flashed in his green eyes.

"No, we didn't. The vows were never finished, and I never said the words. The only man I am now or ever will be wed to is him." I nodded at Vassago, who gave me a soft smile. I allowed myself to feel all the anger that had become buried by fear and snatched at Vos's hair like he'd done to me, pouring the elixir down his throat. "My gift to you. For your hospitality."

He tried to thrash but had no range as he sputtered and choked on the liquid. Magnus held his jaw shut so he had to swallow it.

"What was that! What have you given me?"

"Nothing so terrible as the compulsion potion you gave me," I told him, Vassago's eyes tracking me as I stepped back. "What's made can be unmade."

Ris's head tilted, a question in his face. Seir and Rylan were positively joyful, the meaning having already become clear to them. Magnus and Vassago figured it out moments later when Vos began to scream. Rylan and Seir moved away and Magnus turned his head as the false king's new wings began to turn to ash. The bones charred and the scaly flesh peeled up as it burned. The orange haze around him turned black, then disappeared altogether.

Whatever power had been leant to him from the Elixir of Naming was rapidly burned away. The process was efficient but clearly painful.

"No. No." He chanted the word several times, still trying to thrash despite the way the iron chains bit into his skin.

Vassago straightened his vest and approached him again. "That curse stole more than a hundred years away from me. My will. You stole hers as well, and that is unforgivable."

"You should be thanking me! I made you better. Without that bloodlust you're just another demon."

Vassago clenched his jaw, his fist. Then he smiled. A terrible grin, one that set a chill in my spine and sent the whole room into an unnatural quiet. His fangs had descended and his eyes shone a violent ruby. "You will never steal from me again, Vos Quille. Not Lilith's grimoire, not my wife, not even my time." I flinched as Vassago's blade moved with stunning speed, severing one finger at a time and then his hand. He repeated the process on the other side as Vos hollered, the sound choked. Magnus grunted and tightened his grip on the chains. "My curse is gone, for the record. I do this of my own free will, and with great joy."

Vassago moved so quickly I barely saw the shift. His mouth latched viciously onto Vos's throat. He bit down hard, dragging in deep mouthfuls of blood as the false king tried in vain to scream. Vassago paused for several long moments, then pulled back and spat all the blood and gore out in the false king's face. "Disgusting," he swore, wiping his mouth with the pocket square from his vest as he crossed back over to my side.

With no hands to staunch the gaping wound in his throat, blood pumped idly down the man's chest.

Seir looked positively joyful as he approached the weakened Vos. "King Van would *never* have let you take the throne." He reared back and hit Vos in the face as hard as possible with the book.

Vassago made a motion to snatch the grimoire from him, but Seir just laughed as he stepped off to the side with the book, completely unrepentant.

"Where is my sister?" Magnus rumbled, leaning down right next to Vos's ear. Magnus tightened the chains, spinning Vos so he was facing him. "Where. Is. Rowan?" Ris shifted his weight, anxiously listening for the response.

"Gone!" Vos gagged on the word, pain evident in his face.

"Gone where?" Magnus demanded, giving him a shake.

Vos's teeth clacked together and his whole body swayed like a rag doll. He could only gurgle over the blood on his vocal cords, the sound scraping along my bones in a way that made me want to scream. "You'll never find her."

As I sat there, numbly staring at Vos, who Magnus had tossed to the floor in disgust, Belmont called out loudly. I turned to see what he was upset about and found the guard we'd assumed was dead had crawled close and reared up, raising his sword high above my head. Vassago called my name, his mist caressing my face just as I thrust my dagger out and up like he and Magnus had taught me, making my body as small as possible. The guard fell on my blade as he swung down, his sword tip catching on the floor. It fell from his hand and clattered to the side as my dagger drove into his middle and then up, courtesy of his weight and gravity. The way the blade vibrated in my hand, cutting through flesh and catching on bone made my stomach roll.

His one bloodied remaining eye stared down at me in condemnation and surprise as he slumped over, and I pulled the blade free of him again. I pulled hard enough it swung to the opposite side of my body, nicking Vos in the shoulder. He'd wriggled closer to me in an attempt to get away from the men, though how he was still breathing was a mystery. Realizing he was that close, I pressed the blade in, making him jerk away.

The guard tried to prop himself up on one elbow, all of us watching in horror as the effects of the Dark blade worked rapidly on his body.

"What … is … this?" he asked, hands useless as he groped at the bloody wound, black streaks working their way across his skin with every beat of his heart. They reached his face before ten beats had passed, and the veins of his eyes before twelve. His whole body writhed, and then he went still, the black streaks covering more than half of his skin.

It was equal parts fascinating and horrifying to watch, and I worried that I'd done something terrible having this blade forged.

Vassago materialized fully next to me, his hand reaching out to squeeze mine before dropping away.

Vos had started to hiss and pant in earnest, black tendrils already spreading across his chest, crawling up his face.

Ris rose to his full height above his cousin. "You'll never cause another moment of havoc on my kingdom, Vos Quille. May your name forever be shamed."

Vassago reached out, and I gave him my blade. "Look away, Dragonfly."

I didn't.

I watched as my husband removed my captor's head from his body with the Dark blade. It rolled off to the side, a silent scream frozen upon it as the rest of his body was dismembered efficiently, the pieces scattered across the room.

The hateful ring Vos had given me as Otto Feiser finally withdrew from my skin and fell off, nothing more than a useless piece of metal as it rolled along the floor of the ballroom to fall over at his side. I rubbed the reddened skin where it had been, relieved that it was finally gone.

Vassago came back to my side and ran his hands along my shoulders, his face leaned into my hair. "I'm sorry," he apologized again. "You did so well, Little Dragonfly. But you should not have had to do any of this. Forgive me."

The new demon came over, one hand out in introduction. It was such an odd gesture given the circumstances, but he was so genuine it was hard not to go along.

"Hello. I'm Seir."

"Hello. Greta. Or Libelle. Either is fine."

"Pleasure to meet you." He grinned and loped off again, helping to pile up the bodies of the fallen nobles who had been loyal to Vos.

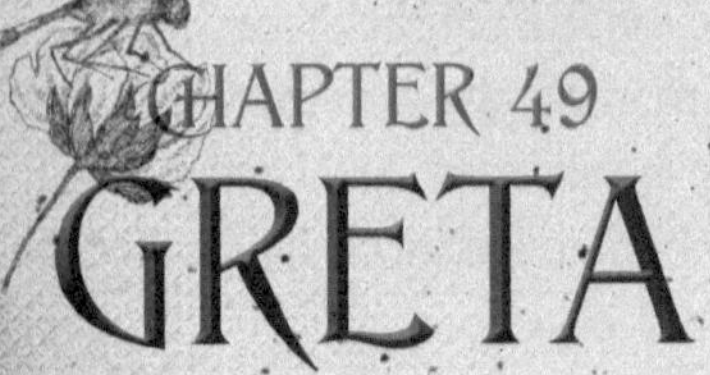

CHAPTER 49
GRETA

RYLAN HELPED DISPOSE of all the bodies in a shockingly efficient manner, his high intensity electrical magic making short work of everything it touched. Calla and I opened the windows to let in some fresh air, and Belmont flew out, cawing and knocking, but returned to pace on a sill.

"Thank you, friend. You did very well," Ris said, offering a small bow of thanks. Belmont examined us both with concern, chatting the whole time.

"Was he the one that took your eye?" I asked, gesturing to where the final guard had fallen by my own hand. Belmont cawed, the sound brutal, and he did that strange nod again. "I'm glad you had a chance to return the favor," I said, feeling strangely empty.

I glanced over at where scorch marks were all that remained of Vos. "Did you find the necklace?" I asked. "Bea's version," I clarified.

Vassago frowned. "There was no necklace."

"He was wearing it earlier." I had no idea how long ago that might have been. "When he first brought me here. But he left me alone in that room for a long time, there's no telling where he went."

"Where's yours, Dragonfly?"

I pulled it from the little pocket where I'd kept it hidden and re-clasped it around my neck. "It got warm when I was making the elixir. It's done that several times."

"Something to discuss with Ophelia, perhaps?" He took my hand and led me across the room.

"I could use a drink," Magnus sighed, stretching out his wings one final time before shifting back into his human form.

"Come, friends," Ris said, looking over the mess the fight had left behind. "The kitchens have always been well stocked. Hopefully some of my father's favorite vintage has been spared."

We followed Ris through the palace toward the kitchens, several members of staff gasping and pressing themselves against walls with their heads bowed as we passed.

The kitchen operated as usual, the staff fawning over Ris as he strode directly into the pantries, searching for what he wanted.

"Please, go sit! We'll bring you something, your majesty! It's so wonderful to see you again!" The head chef was a portly man with a wild mustache, well-trained enough not to mention that all of us were covered in blood and gore. "Is he ...?"

"Dead," Seir supplied helpfully. "Vos Quille is very, very dead."

The relief from the staff was palpable, though nobody said a single word.

Ris emerged from the pantry with several bottles clutched to his chest. "Glasses?" he asked.

"Of course, of course." A woman scuttled to a cabinet and re-trieved them, rushing past us through a door that connected the kitchen to a broad dining room.

She set the glasses out on the table, helping him set bottles down one at a time so they wouldn't break.

"We'll bring you all something in just a moment," she was wide-eyed as she took in the size of Magnus, the rejuvenated king, and three demons. Even Calla and I were tall compared to most.

"This was a brew my father made specifically for my mother. She loved apricots, so he added them to the mash. He hated it." Ris smiled as he poured. "But she loved it. So naturally, he insisted every barrel from that year be her recipe. She preferred wine, so we were left with a cellar full of her special ale that nobody else was allowed to drink."

"This is miles better than the swill we drank at the Empty Cask. Tasty!" Seir exclaimed, eyes bright as he proceeded to drink half his glass in one go.

"One of the best I've ever had," Magnus said, glass raised high.

In truth, it was something I could happily enjoy, and I didn't even like most ale. "It's delicious."

"I don't know how to properly thank you," Ris said, eyes drifting to the table. "Any of you."

"You would have done the same," Vassago said.

"Yes. I would have." Ris nodded. "You are all welcome to stay as long as you like. Clean up, eat, sleep. I have much to sort out here. A hundred years of Vos's deceit, lies, and tyranny."

Seir had already made a quick trip to the tavern to tell Pol and the lingering townspeople that King Ris Sylvanus himself had been restored to the throne.

My energy flagged as we ate the rich stew the kitchen staff served, drank ale, and Ris told us some of the many transgressions Vos had committed while he was wasting away in the cellar under the manse.

"That'll be my first stop. That house needs cleansed."

"I'll stay," Seir said happily. "Assuming you can get me back home when we're done."

"Appreciated," Ris smiled. "If your doorway has closed, we'll find you another."

A lull fell over us all as the food settled, the ale creating a comforting warmth. Vassago's hand ran through my hair as my eyes became unbearably heavy.

"Sleep, Dragonfly. You're safe."

AFTER EVERYONE GOT some rest, a little more food, and a thorough cleaning up, we flew to the woods where Seir's portal awaited. The people of Everwood had arrived in droves to the palace, demanding an audience with their king. Ris was needed by others, and we had to get home ourselves.

"So, are you going to stay? Or will you go? The door is always open, either way." Ris asked Belmont, the bird perched on his shoulder, plucking through Ris's hair. "I do always miss you when you're gone, but I appreciate you keeping an eye on her more than you know, old friend." Belmont blinked several times and made a low keening noise before flying back out into the night.

"What does that mean?"

"I'm not sure. I think he's undecided about where he wants to be."

"Well, if he's at my window demanding treats in the morning, I suppose we'll have our answer."

Ris laughed. "It's Mother's fault he does that. She spoiled him rotten." Vassago grunted in response to that, his frustrated amusement where Belmont was concerned endearing. Ris hugged me tightly. "I have much to repair here. I hate to leave you again, Libelle, but I must stay, and you must go. I'll visit when I can, though. And you're always welcome here. This is your kingdom, too, such as it is right now. I have much to share with you, to teach you."

"I'd like to come back, one day soon. That may be safer for you."

He nodded slowly, regret in his face. "Yes, you're probably right. But once everything is stable again, and I'm sure I can trust someone in my absence, I'll be searching for Rowan. I need to know what happened to her."

I could only nod. The prospect of having a father I could visit was such an unexpected development, I couldn't even conceptualize also finding my mother.

"Our resources are open to you, King Ris," Magnus offered, the honorific leaving Ris to clutch at his chest in a gesture of gratitude. "Vos's response leaves me with hope that Rowan can be found, and I want nothing more."

"The doors to Everwood are always open to you all, and I will share all that I'm able."

We hugged again, the tears in my eyes a mixture of gratitude and sadness.

Rylan and Calla went through the portal first. Magnus lingered a few moments as though trying to decide whether or not to say something further, then he went through and back to our world. Vassago loosened his grip on my hand so I could have one final, lingering embrace with the man I'd first glimpsed only a few short weeks before in a portrait of smoke.

"I'm so sorry for how you got here, Libelle, but I'm endlessly happy you came."

"Me too."

Ris finally broke the hug and pushed me back toward Vassago, his eyes just as moist as mine. "I'll see you soon."

I nodded, then closed my eyes as we stepped into the black hole that would take us home, my insides upside down for a prolonged moment, then we somehow almost simultaneously stepped out of the hedges in the maze.

I looked around, feeling like it had been far longer than we had actually been gone.

"Where is everyone else?"

"Rylan and Calla likely went directly to his manor. Magnus went ahead to d'Arcan to see Grace."

I sagged. "I was hoping to get to speak with them to. Thank them."

Vassago's arm came around my shoulders, his mouth pressing into my temple. "They know, Dragonfly. This is what family does. Well, *this* family. You'll see them soon enough, besides." He smiled.

I couldn't help but smile too. It was all too bizarre, but he wasn't wrong. He scooped me up again, white feathered wings carrying us toward the collegium. I couldn't wait for the day that I could fly under my own power.

As we came through the front doors at d'Arcan, Grace rushed out of the dining room with Magnus.

Bea and Ellis came out next, and my sister launched herself at me. "You're okay!"

"I'm fine," I answered, though I wasn't sure how true that was as everything started to catch up with me.

"I'm so glad." She squeezed me tighter, and I couldn't help but relax into it, her affection aggressive but appreciated.

"Hello, Ellis."

He smiled, lifting his hand in a little wave. "Greta."

"There's one more matter to settle, Dragonfly," Vassago said, glancing over at Bea. "Henrik and Lara are downstairs. Their punishment is yet to be decided."

"Oh."

"That'll wait," Grace argued. "You need some rest after all this!"

"That's alright," I answered, getting to my feet. "I'd rather have it all done so I can sleep for a week."

"You should stone sleep, niece." Magnus nodded sagely.

"I think Bea should come with us," I suggested.

"As you wish."

Vassago led the two of us down into the cellar, a space I hadn't known existed until now. Henrik and Lara instantly kicked up a fuss, begging both Bea and myself for pity. Even Bea seemed exhausted by them, and I wondered how many times she'd been down here in our absence.

"Silence!" Vassago said, mouth set in a feral smile that was all razorblades and ice.

Gone was the warm man who shared my bed and braided my hair so lovingly. Still, I knew he was nearly feral on my behalf—I had nothing to fear from him no matter how terrifying the shift in his appearance might be.

"What is the fate of these two, my heart? What price shall they pay for their part in all the things Vos had planned? The years of outright lies they told?" My former employers tensed against one another as he advanced closer. Lara tried to squeeze herself behind Henrik, but his grip kept her at his side. "What cost do they owe for the theft of not only your father's money—*your* money, while you made do with scraps and castoffs—but your freedom to grow and learn as a young stone kin should?"

"We stole nothing! It was all given in trade, a business agreement—"

"The money Vos bribed you with wasn't his to give." Vassago advanced one final step toward the bars of the cell, drawing his sword, the length of it pressed to the side of Henrik's throat. "How shall they repay each and every moment you suffered mistreatment or neglect at their hands?" His voice had gone low and cold, his body strung tight. "Shall we count the scars left on your flesh? Every hour you spent sleeping instead of being able to live your life? The way they watched your power diminish after he intentionally crushed it within you instead of finding you the help you needed from your kin?"

They both looked from him to me, horror that their fate was in my hands passing over their faces. I placed a hand on Vassago's shoulder, the subtle shift of his weight telling me he would stand down if I asked, no matter how much he longed to end them right there.

"I don't want to smell any more blood today," I muttered, feeling oddly disembodied as I weighed the situation. Bea was at my side, silent, but the squeeze of her fingers against mine told me she would stand with me.

Vassago's ruby eyes turned my way but no other part of him. It was moments like this I remembered how many years he'd been a warrior, how well he'd honed his endless patience. I was also reminded that neither of us were human … but they were. Bea was. And the time left for any of them was much more limited than it was for us.

Lara's eyes teared up, and I could feel her about to beg. My thoughts were only of Bea then, how if I made the simple choice, one that made them disappear from my life forever, I was also robbing my sister of the same thing that had been taken from me. No matter how much I thought she'd understand, I couldn't do that to her. She deserved to make her own decisions where her parents were concerned.

The long breath that seeped from my lungs communicated more to my mate than I could have guessed.

"You are undeservedly blessed," he bit the words off as Henrik and Lara flinched from them. Then he stepped back and lowered his sword.

"Thank you, we'll do anyth—" Henrik rushed to say, hands palm to palm in gratitude.

"Yes, you will," I cut him off. "Anything I ask, you will do it. Any fate I assign to you, you will accept gratefully, as I'm allowing you to live."

"Beatrice, certainly you're not going to leave our fate in her hands?" Lara said. I think it was the tone that made Bea tense. It was the same cruel one she always chose to use with me.

She shrugged her shoulders back. "You never did right by Greta," she said. "Whatever she decides, I will agree with."

"What?" Lara shrieked. Both Belettes began a frantic argument then, vacillating from begging to condemnation to accusing her of being brainwashed.

Vassago settled his shoulders, a much more relaxed grin on his mouth. Despite his eagerness to make short work of them, he was pleased both by my display of confidence and Bea's trust in my choice.

"Tell me, Henrik, before we find out what it is my beloved wife has in store for you, what was the necklace you hired me to find required for?"

Henrik fidgeted. "I don't know the particulars, only that he was going to use it to trade with the stone kin council."

"The stone kin council?" I asked.

He shrugged, pacing in the small cell. "He had business with them, I don't know. Something about it belonging to a founding family. They wanted it back."

Vassago's eyes narrowed. "Keep talking."

"He needed Greta for chemistry or whatever—"

"Alchemy," I corrected.

"Sure, sure. We made sure she had things to practice with. He had me keep that book safe because it had something inside that was needed for his plan, but he didn't trust it being in his realm. And he needed the necklace to trade with the council. That's all I know!"

"But you gave the book to me. Greta as well," Vassago accused.

"We needed more money! And his terms were that I know where those things were, not necessarily that I keep them in my home."

"You're cleverer than I gave you credit for," Vassago sighed. "But also have the intelligence of an overbaked pie."

Bea looked horrified after a stifled laugh came out of her mouth. "I'm so sorry. I hate that I was part of any of this. All I can think of is my ridiculous bedroom and all those dresses. Everything I had that should never have been mine."

"It's not your fault, Bea," I assured her. I frowned, a thought prodding at me. I turned to Lara. "What does a good gown cost? Like the ones you had made for Bea?"

"A gown?" Lara stumbled over her words, throwing hesitant glances at Henrik. "Most around a hundred gold coins, I suppose. Why is that relevant now?"

I shifted my attention. "What did you accept for me, Henrik? What was my price?"

"To be fair, this man bartered with me—"

"To show what an absolute piece of filth you are. Do not get things confused, sir. My intention was to see just how little you really thought of her so I'd be prepared to punish you for it later. I'm not afraid of telling her the truth nor of facing her wrath should it upset her. And it *should*. You know all too well how unforgivably you underbid her worth. Answer her question."

"Feiser offered everything we could ever dream of. The houses, my title ... everything."

That was somewhat reassuring, but he'd made that agreement for himself, not for me. I'd seen no luxury during my time with them, despite having been the reason they flourished. "And to him?" I gestured at Vassago.

"Seventy," he muttered.

"Oh," I said, all the breath rushing from my lungs.

"You can't be serious," Bea gasped.

"I started at a hundred!" Henrik argued, as if that made it better.

"It doesn't matter," I said, stopping the bickering that had begun. "I appreciate that he gave you anything at all to get me out of that house when by rights I should have just walked out the front door when I came of age. I never belonged there, and he was guaranteeing I never had to return. It doesn't matter what he paid or what you asked. No amount could make up for what I lost all those years."

"Forgive me, Dragonfly." Vassago's mouth pulled into a sincere frown.

"It's alright." I wasn't sure if it was; my insides had gone still and cold. "I think," I said, pulling myself together and turning back to my former employers. "That you could perhaps both do with some time earning your way instead of taking and enjoying what others worked for." Vassago looked over at me, his eyes a glowing ruby. Lust pulsed from him, and I knew he'd gone from restraining himself from killing my patrons to keeping still to prevent himself from prematurely whisking me away to somewhere with a bed. "Some time at the stone kin labor encampment should give you ample time to reflect on all the choices you've made that led us all here."

"Camp?" Lara asked, eyebrows pinched together.

"Yes, I think that suits just fine," Vassago all but purred. "I'll let Magnus know they can be collected at his convenience."

Either they were too shocked to respond or they were simply considering their protests, but both of my patrons were unusually quiet about their situation.

Once we were out of the cellar, exhaustion set in like a ton of bricks, despite the rest I'd had in the fae realm. I hugged Bea, wished her good night, and allowed Vassago to carry me up to his apartment.

I gave him a lingering kiss, then did what I could to get comfortable before calling stone sleep to take me over.

CHAPTER 50
VASSAGO

WE SPENT SEVERAL days following our return from the fae realm in my apartment.

The first whole day Greta was locked in stone sleep, reviving herself the best way she could. I used that time to record in ink what I had learned from Vos's hate-tainted blood. After Greta had fallen asleep at Ris's table, I had shared with everyone what I'd seen.

Magnus had plenty of new information to sort through in regard to his council. Vos had been the one to tell them of the relationship between Ris and Rowan. Any pairing between such powerful stone kin blood and a fae prince had been rapidly and vehemently forbidden. Much like Calla's parents, Rowan disappeared not long after the decree. For the first time in a long while, Magnus had a solid lead for several missing stone kin, and he was following it with enthusiasm.

I was not keen on letting Greta out of my sight, and fortunately she was content enough to allow me to be overbearing as she recovered from her ordeal. She never once commented that she could tell my guilt was eating me alive. Pampering her was the only way I could keep from blaming myself utterly for everything that had happened, but I could see the softness in her eyes when I suggested another bath or new braids. She understood and was going to let me do what I needed in order to ease my conscience.

Belmont had yet to tap on the window; it seemed he had stayed to keep Ris company a while longer.

Our young guests returned to the Belette manor, as Bea was eager to put things her parents had ruined to rights and Ellis was happy to be at her side offering whatever support he could. Naturally, we offered our help if she needed it. Ellis had a good job with his merchant father, and I wouldn't be surprised if wedding invitations arrived in short order.

Magnus shared bits of news with us while delivering baskets of supplies sent by Grace. One evening, he shared several extra bits of news.

He'd seen the commissioned necklace installed in the stone kin archives on his last visit to the council building, and mentioned that things felt even less stable there than they had before. Gaius was not recovering as he should be, either, and was all the crankier for it. It sounded like he'd met his absolute match in Lovette, and she wasn't letting him boss anyone, especially her, around, no matter how upset he was about things.

"There's something he's not telling anyone," Magnus sighed one evening. "It's important. Hopefully he shares his troubles with someone soon. I can tell it's eating him up. I've never seen him so full of misplaced anger."

Greta empathized, her heart so much larger than any of us deserved. "You haven't been friends, not for a while," she surmised.

Magnus ran his fingers through his hair, chagrined. "No. We had a falling out many years ago. A battle ... it took too much from us both. Blame was put where it should not have been. Then another instance recently ..." He shook his head.

Greta shrugged, pulling the basket inside the room. "So, make it right."

"How do I do that?" he asked.

"I don't know, uncle," she said, reaching out for a hug. "But I'm sure you'll figure something out."

He nodded, looking far more lost than I ever expected the massive man to as he wandered down the hall.

She closed the door and turned to me, a blush slowly rising from her neck to her cheeks. "Why are you looking at me like that?"

"How am I looking at you, Dragonfly?"

"Like you want to eat me."

My blood warmed, and I blinked across the short distance between us, hands in her hair as she gasped and sagged against me. The mist curled around us both, a safety net and binding rope. "Perhaps I do."

"Again?" she teased, reaching up and snagging my bottom lip with her teeth. "Haven't you tired of me yet?"

My Dragonfly had gotten plenty bold in the hours we'd spent tangled up together since our return from Everwood. She too had claws and teeth, and we'd both figured out plenty of enjoyable ways for her to use them.

"Never," I assured her, grasping her face as I leaned in to kiss her.

Her arms banded around my waist as I stood there with her, our heartbeats pounding in time through our skin, her breath hot little puffs on my cheek as I ravaged her mouth.

"We—" She pulled away, but I brought her back for more. "Should eat—" She smiled, but I just kept kissing her. "Oh saints," she sighed as I kissed down her jaw and then her throat, licking along the spot she'd told me belonged to me. "I can't say no to you, Vassago. It's dangerous."

"I find it perfectly wonderful," I joked back. "Give me your words, Greta."

"Yes," she breathed. "Take what you need. It's all yours."

I pushed my body up against her, my cock straining against my trousers. My fangs ached as I opened my mouth, teasing the scars of my previous bites with my tongue. She made a little noise in her throat, one that I never could resist, and plunged my fangs down, reveling in the burst of bright essence that bubbled up on my tongue, the flashes of her life that brought me closer to her. As I sipped at her throat, her hands worked at our buttons and ties, freeing us from the bonds of our clothing.

Without letting go, I filled my hands with her backside and walked us over to the bed, her legs locking around my waist once I'd laid her on the edge of the mattress. There was no waiting for either of us, the bite intensifying everything until we were nothing more than sensation and need. I notched myself at her entrance and plunged deep, her moan echoing through my ears as I finally pulled free of her neck. I gave the marks one more lick, the lingering droplets giving me one final flash of her world.

"Eyes on me, beautiful wife," I said, loving the glossy quality of them as I rocked deep. I adored the way her body bounced with every motion, how her mouth parted as she panted through the pleasure. I leaned down on my forearms so I could kiss her mouth again, never able to get enough of the way she tasted no matter what part of her I was enjoying.

"Vassago," she groaned, arching against me but finding nowhere to go.

"Yes, Dragonfly?"

"I need …" She turned her head, gripping my wrists with her hands as I drove into her harder, deeper, relentless.

"Words, Greta. Give me your words."

"I …"

She tried, I'll give her that. But it was too late. Her body clenched around mine, her mouth opened, and a soft moan came out but nothing more as her eyes fluttered closed. "There's my girl." I kept going, but there was no denying myself when she looked like that, her body clamped around mine, and her love a soft glow in her face. My release shook me from the base of my spine to my toes, and I slumped over her, sweat mingling between us.

She smiled up at me, and I felt unworthy for the hundredth time that day. Then I swept her up and carried her to the bath so I could clean her up, get her fed, and start all over again.

OUR HONEYMOON OF sorts ended after a week when Rylan and Calla returned home. We emerged from my apartment rested, peacefully unaware of much that was happening in the city around us, and fortified for whatever came next.

It was odd to think that classes would be starting again, that everything was settling back into some kind of normal pattern when we still had so much to figure out. It was equally strange to think that no more than several weeks before, Greta hadn't even come into my life yet. There was no separating her from it now, short of death.

"One day out of my cave, and I'm already tired of the world," I teased. "There's too much intrigue here, how do you stand it? I may have to see if Greta would relocate to one of the monasteries with me."

"It's always like this. At least, it is now," Rylan teased, the pair of us looking over a contract in my classroom. "There were many years that were much more peaceful." A smile spread across his mouth, the laughter of our mates echoing down the hall. "But I would not go back."

"I'd like very much to go back to the way *some* things were not all that long ago. I can't keep up with all the excitement," Magnus complained, eyebrows raising as he joined us to have a look at the paperwork. "All of it? From here to Thorne Street?"

"All of it," Rylan smiled. "I've been waiting ages for Old Man Parsimon to accept my offer to buy. I think now that he's retired, the option is much more attractive. That or the fact that I won't stop making a bid every few months has worn him down."

"That's the total price?" I asked, the number significant, but not shocking. "He's undervaluing the land."

"I'm not going to tell him, are you?" Rylan asked.

"Certainly not."

"Then we agree?" Rylan prepared one of the quills and ink pots so we could all sign. "All of us, equal shares?"

"Yes."

"Agreed."

Magnus signed his name first, followed my myself and then my brother.

"Good. We can start the expansion then."

"A house," Magnus grinned. "I think Grace will be pleased."

"I do enjoy our cozy apartment," I mused, rubbing my chin.

"You don't have to build, Vago."

"I'll see what Greta wants to do. She's had enough upheaval lately. I want her to decide."

"I think that's a fine idea," Magnus said, clapping me on the shoulder as we made our way out of the classroom and down the hall to where our mates were gathered, laughing over tea and Grace's honey cakes.

The bond in my chest gave a tug, my ring flaring to life. I caught Greta's eye when I came through the door, her smile wide.

Anything, I was reminded. I would give her anything she wanted.

And I was eternally grateful she wanted me.

EPILOGUE
GRETA

"**W**E DON'T HAVE to push today, Dragonfly, I'm proud of you either way," Vassago said sweetly, fingers scraping through my hair as he braided the strands. "Your progress has been tremendous in such a short time." He brought one of his silver ribbons out of his pocket, tying off my hair, which had grown another fraction of an inch in a few weeks' time.

"I know." I stood on my tiptoes and gave him a kiss on the cheek before heading further out into the grassy yard.

Calla and Rylan sat on one of the new benches he'd had commissioned from a local artisan who used the same marble the observatory was made from, cataloging what was planted in the garden beds. Grace and the girls were turning over the soil, getting ready to plant again, and Clem had the horses trimming the weeds in the pasture. I hadn't planned on a full audience, just Vassago and maybe Magnus, but I wasn't about to back out now.

Just as I was starting to prepare, Magnus landed with a stirring of dust, pulling me into a strong hug.

"I thought you were on patrol?"

"I am," he winked at me, stepping back so that I had some space. "What good is being in charge if you can't bend the rules a bit when your niece has something she wants to show you?"

Nerves took up residence in my stomach in the form of butterflies, but I tried to make good use of them instead of letting them hold me back. Turning my back on my audience, I embraced my stone form and released my wings. The process had become much faster and more fluid, my stone skin as easy to put on as clothing now that I was familiar with how to grab ahold of it. My wings themselves were much denser than they had been at first, the bones had all healed up perfectly and the colors within the opalescent white intensified the stronger I became.

Heart thudding behind my ribs, I concentrated with all my might, having found in my practices that a fast flutter was far more effective for me than a wide slow flap. I had embraced my overall dragonfly-ness slowly but it was working.

Vassago inhaled as I lifted off the ground more than several inches, and Magnus gave a whoop and clapped as I rose a little higher and turned. I pushed the air under my wings, asking it to direct me over to the garden beds. Grace gave me a broad smile, and the girls all cheered. I made my way back to the opposite end of the yard, pushing my endurance before going back where I had started from and slowly lowering myself to the ground.

"Excellent work, little niece!"

My muscles were still getting stronger, burning and sore, especially since I had spent so much time recently practicing, but I could *fly*. I blinked back tears in my eyes as I landed, and Vassago immediately swept me up and swung me around. "You're a marvel, Little Dragonfly. I adore you endlessly." I dipped in for a kiss, breaking away at the sound of fresh applause.

"Look at those incredible wings!" Seir trotted across the yard, pure joy on his face.

"Thank you," I said, unsure if we'd been expecting a visitor or not.

"Seir," Rylan said, getting to his feet. "What a nice surprise."

"Indeed," Vassago said, the three of them exchanging quick embraces in greeting. "To what do we owe this visit?"

Seir grinned. "I come bearing gifts," he said, bringing several vials out of his pockets. "Tap sends his regards, as does Ris."

"Oh?" I perked up at my father's name.

Seir's smile broadened, if possible. "Besides, I had such a marvelous time the last time we were all together, I wanted to see you all again. But mostly the gifts."

"Go on," Rylan said.

"Permanent doorways," he said. "Portals built in collaboration between Lilith, the Fae King, and the Demon Prince of the Crossroads, He Who is in Charge of All the Doorways, the Manager of All Things—"

"Seir." Rylan sighed, an amused grin on his face, nonetheless. I could tell that this brother was well known for his dramatics.

"Sorry, anyway. Portals, like I said. Permanent. Warded, secure, simple to use." The idea was enticing, but I couldn't help the tiny little dagger of cold worry that slipped through. "I know," he said, bowing much like Vassago did, the vials still in his hands. There were seven in total, though it wasn't clear if they were all for us. "It sounds risky, but I promise, we've examined all the angles. They're safe. And very handy, if I do say so myself, and that's from the person who can travel anywhere in a moment's time."

"Come inside," Grace interrupted. "You lot can discuss this all over some lunch."

"It's nice to see you again, Grace," Seir said. "I appreciate the offer, but I'm afraid I can't stay. I'm just delivering these." He handed one to Rylan and one to Vassago. "We all get one. That's the way it works."

"You saw Lilith?" Vassago asked.

He nodded enthusiastically. "She was incredibly helpful with this little project, but never hangs around long. She's ... a little ... well, whatever crazy she's got, she's earned." Seir asserted, jamming the rest of the vials back in his pockets. "How's your demon problem?"

"The hordes?" Rylan asked. "No outbreaks since before we went to Everwood. Why?"

Seir grinned. "That's good news. I got myself assigned to that investigation, but there's not much happening with it. I'll be sure to keep you informed if anything comes up."

"Promoted, then?" Vassago asked. "Well done."

Seir laughed. "Not really. I'm still just a glorified messenger boy, but I don't complain, and nobody else can move as fast, so I sometimes get to ask questions."

"More than we ever got," Rylan chuckled.

"What do we have to do?" I asked. "For the portal?"

"Just pick a spot you want it to be, pour the vial and speak the words. They're on the label. But make sure it's somewhere you *really* want it. There's no moving it once it's in place."

The brothers shared a conversation about things Hell-related while Calla, Grace, and I discussed where the doorway might be best suited.

"I almost forgot," Seir said, pulling a sword from his belt. "Ris said you might want to have your forge mistress look at this." He handed the blade to Magnus.

"That's Vos's sword," I said.

"He said that whatever your blade did, this one is similar. Said you'd probably know what that means. Do you?"

I nodded a chill running down my spine. "Yes. Did nobody get cut by it?"

"No, he was evading more than he was fighting," Rylan said. "I can't even remember him having it out."

"If this was the sword used on Gaius, that might explain several things," Magnus frowned. "Thank you, demon."

"You're welcome, statue man. Remember, place your portal with care. You just have to know your destination, and it will take you."

"Like visualize where you want to go?"

"Yes. Or a person. It's guided by both. See you soon?"

"You sure you can't stay for a drink or—" Grace couldn't help herself, but Seir wasn't kidding when he said he could move fast. I blinked, and he was gone.

"I could use a drink." Magnus smiled down at Grace, throwing an arm around her shoulders as he guided her back toward the main building. "Maybe some lunch."

"You ate before you left! No more than a couple of hours ago," she scolded, but she laughed as well. There was little to no chance she'd withhold food, no matter how much trouble she gave him about it.

Rylan and Calla still discussed where the best place for the portal was when Vassago approached me, a salacious grin on his mouth. "How about you show me a new trick, Dragonfly?"

"Trick?" I asked.

"The one where you move those glorious wings and race me to the observatory."

"If I lose?"

"Either way, you win, Greta. You should know that by now."

I saw all his plans for us reflected in his eyes and just shook my head. "You're trouble."

"The best kind. What do you say, wife? Do you have the energy for one more flight?" He grinned as his lovely white feathered wings stretched out wide.

I braced myself, narrowed my eyes, and fluttered for all I was worth. My beautiful mate's laughter chased me as I ascended straight up into the air, the feel of it around me something I hoped never to take for granted. His wings moved the wind in a way that pushed me closer to my goal, as well as him. I glanced over my shoulder, his smile clear into his eyes and joy heady.

I'd already won.

Want to visit the Vincara monastery with Vassago and Greta?
Get the bonus scene by visiting:

https://BookHip.com/XFBVSXX

What's next?
Book 2 of The Gargoyle Knights Series,
The Gargoyle's Gift, for Gaius and Lovette's story!
AND
Book 3 of The Demon Princes Series,
The Demon's Delight for Seir's story!

Want to be the first to hear breaking news and
other info from L.? Sign up for her newsletter!

http://bit.ly/ALANewsletter

You can also join her reader group to chat
with her and other readers!

https://bit.ly/LilysReaderLounge

Did you like *The Demon's Discovery*? Leave a
review on Amazon, Goodreads or Bookbub to
share your thoughts with other readers

ACKNOWLEDGEMENTS

This book fought me EVERY. STEP. OF. THE. WAY. Seriously, this book and I fought for nearly a *year*. Even though it gave me the hardest time ever, I'm so proud of how it turned out and I hope you love it as much as I do!

My husband for always being my first reader, the one to help me talk through the same issue seventeen times and make suggestions that sometimes seem wild but nearly always help me get back on track. For holding down the fort when I sneak off to the she-shed and making sure I eat. I love you.

My Write or Die friends, Shain & Dannie, you guys get so much credit for talking me through things, holding my hand and making my writing so much better, always. I heart you immeasurably.

Krista, Jessica & Stephanie you always make my stuff so PRETTY! I couldn't do it without your help and I mean that.

Beta & ARC readers! Do you even know how vital you are to authors like me? I hope you do. You're the cat's freaking pajamas and I cannot express how grateful I am to you! Seeing any post with my stuff on it is a humbling, thrilling experience. I couldn't do this without you. <3

I can't wait for you all to see what's coming next! There are more demons to make fall in love, and some stone kin I can't wait to help find their mates.

Note: This world is planned to be seven books, one for each brother PLUS a novella for our stone kin friends in-between. I hope you stick with us!

For sneak peeks, discussion and other fun tidbits, make sure you're signed up for my newsletter, & join my reader group.

ABOUT THE AUTHOR

L. Alexander writes Paranormal and Fantasy romance with sweet & spicy cinnamon roll heroes, fated mates, monsters, magic and more. She guarantees a happily ever after no matter what and has a soft spot for broody anime characters.

www.authorlilyalexander.com

@lilyalexanderwrites on Instagram

Lily Alexander on Facebook, TikTok,
BookBub and Goodreads

L. also writes Contemporary Romance
under the name Lily Alexander.